"Don't y[...]d. "We've solid[...]other. We think alike, we feel alike. There's so much about us being together that can't even be put into words. Don't you see?"

Tess raised her hand and held Noel's cheek. "I see, Noel. I see so many things. You've always known, though, that there was a prior commitment. I've been kept from Royal too long and I won't have it anymore. Yes, I agree a lot has happened. I never would have believed that I could love someone the way I love you."

"Tess . . ." Noel whispered.

"But it's wrong. We found each other at a time when we shouldn't have. Now that I've finally found Royal, no one is going to keep me from his side." She began to leave the room, but Noel's voice stopped her.

"Not even me, Tess?"

Tess didn't know how to answer—she didn't have an answer. Because suddenly all she wanted to do was lose herself in Noel Montgomery's arms.

VANITIES

REBECCA·FORSTER

PINNACLE BOOKS
WINDSOR PUBLISHING CORP.

PINNACLE BOOKS are published by

Windsor Publishing Corp.
475 Park Avenue South
New York, NY 10016

First Printing: July, 1993

Printed in the United States of America

Part One
1985

One

The wheat spread in a golden wash toward the horizon where it meshed with a multicolored sky before falling off the face of the earth. A man stood silhouetted, surveying the incredible field and the magnificent Kansas sky.

Behind him by a hundred yards, he could hear the sounds of his wife's evening work. Faint smells of roasting chicken and baking bread reached him, mingling with the smell of the earth and the sweat of his body. In his left hand he held a head of wheat. Methodically he ground the heel of his right hand into it, feeling it was dry. In his practiced hands the kernel separated from the chaff as easily as lovers parted to lay side by side in silent celebration of their ripening emotions.

Usually he smiled, proud of his efforts when the wheat was ready. This evening, though, the man simply lowered his hand, letting the kernels and chaff fall to the ground. There was a sadness in this crop. A sadness in the knowledge that everything ripened and was sent on to become something else: wheat, corn—even people.

At first glance, to a casual observer, his face would have seemed hard and unforgiving, chiseled handsomely aloof by time and labor and worry and pain. His eyes were shielded by his frayed straw hat. They appeared as nothing more than two sparks of light in his motionless face. A closer look, though, would show that the man was watching. Watching for the first sign that she was out there, coming back to him once more before leaving the final time.

He heard something clatter in the house behind him. A dropped dish, a hot pan. He didn't flinch, though it was unlike the woman in the house to make a mistake of any kind. The woman in the wheat, though, she made mistakes — earthly ones.

She couldn't cook well, she wasn't cut out to drive a tractor or slaughter a chicken. But the other qualities she possessed, the sublime ones, those were beyond reproach. She could sketch a tree so that the farmer could feel the weight of its branches; paint a pond so that he was refreshed by the coolness of the water. She could talk about the wheat, and make him believe it was a gift from heaven instead of the result of his hard work. Her soul, her heart, her mind and talent were of a world so different from the one she had been brought into the man sometimes wondered if the good Lord hadn't made a little mistake in sending her to them.

Then he saw the wheat ripple, parting as a path was cut slowly, dreamlike, through the sea of undulating grain. Without realizing it the farmer straightened himself, pulling his worn body taller and tauter as he waited, anticipating the first sight of her.

He heard a rustle in the field. She was close. The farmhouse and the noise of the evening meal preparations faded from his consciousness. Only the woman in the wheat was real.

Finally she was visible, breaking through the grain

gently, materializing as though part of the landscape, a petal blown from a flower into the working fields. In her hands she carried a stalk of wheat, holding it gently against her cheek: complexion and grain the same color—golden; hair a shade lighter, like the August sun at noon over a flat plain.

Her mind was elsewhere. She didn't see him at first and so the man had a chance to simply look at her, marveling at what he had wrought; time to wonder where the months and years had gone since she was a babe until the time she became a woman. His heart clutched. His rigid jaw trembled with emotion. Thankfully the light had faded now, and she couldn't see the tears welling in eyes hidden by the brim of an age-old hat.

"Pa?" she breathed, tossing the wheat stalk gently away, finally catching sight of him. She laughed then, running to him, arms open.

"Tess," he murmured. "It's late."

His right arm rose to engulf her. He thought of the dirt on his hand and the whiteness of her blouse, then thought no more of it as he clasped his wide flat hand around her shoulder and felt her melt into him. They were two of a kind. Dreamers. He would miss her.

"Sorry, Pa," she whispered, turning her shining blue eyes toward him. Then more seriously, "Is Ma mad at me?"

He shrugged. What could he say? Her ma had been mad since the day she found out she'd given birth to a daughter who lived in the clouds.

Tess laughingly answered her own question. "She's mad." The sound of laughter both pleased and hurt her father. He could hear her disappointment, her desire not to anger her mother on this day of all days.

11

"I'm really sorry. I'll get in right now and help with supper."

She started to leave, but he held her fast, his hand tightening around her shoulder. "You can wait on that. Walk with me."

"Gladly," she whispered.

They walked away from the house, toward the barn. Inside they heard the milk cows moving. In a pen on the right the pigs nuzzled their troughs. Tess's father led her to a pile of hay. She sat without thinking, leaning back as though it was an easy chair. He joined her, but sat straight, squinting out toward the land, trying to remember when was the last time he was disappointed that he had no son to carry on after him. He couldn't remember. Tess was too perfect for him ever to feel the slightest twinge of regret that she was his only child.

"Tomorrow's the big day," he said gruffly, wishing he could say more.

"I know. I'm trying not to be too excited. I don't want Ma to think I'm anxious to leave you both."

Tess's father nodded knowing that, indeed, she was anxious to go, but too clear of heart to admit it.

"You've been waiting a long time for this," he noted. "You should be excited. Not every day a girl like you gets to go to college. I only wish . . ."

"You only wish me the best," Tess said softly.

She would not, could not, allow him to feel as though he had failed her because he couldn't afford to send her off to college in a manner finer than they had kept her all these years.

"Yes, I wish you the best," he reiterated.

They let a long silence lie between them as they listened to the sounds of the farm settling in for the night. A tiny flying creature spun around her father's head. He reached to the ground and found a pebble. He held it gently in his fingers.

"If I haven't already told you, Tess, I'm proud of you. I haven't told you that I think it's wonderful about your scholarship. I want you to know now I could never have asked for a better child. In all my dreams I couldn't. You never disappointed me once. I know you'll make me proud there in that college. Just remember, even if you ain't got the finest clothes, you got something more than them that do. You got a gladness of heart that will see you through fine. You got talent and drive. You're going to be all right."

He sighed then, exhausted from such a long speech, worried that if he said everything he felt she would think less of him. It was good that a woman feel the man of the house was the strongest. He had always taught her that. Poor Tess probably had a hard time believing it, though, since it was the woman of this house who sometimes seemed to crack the whip.

His wife was a good woman, just set in her ways. A black-and-white woman. Tess laid her hand on his arm. He saw her long delicate fingers, and felt a pride that they were also full of strength.

"I love you, too, Pa," Tess said, so quietly he wondered if it wasn't only the breeze playing through the wheat.

Then she kissed his cheek, and he knew that she had said those words to him. He let his eyes slide toward her. When she moved the hay came with her, sticking to her hair and clothes as though it, too, would hold her on the farm.

"You ready to go then? California's a long way

13

away."

"I'm ready," Tess answered. "I've been ready for a long time. Not to go away from you, but to be on my own so that I can make you proud of me."

"You will, Tess. You'll come back to me a lady, an artist, and I'll be bustin' my buttons. Just don't wait too long to visit. Don't ever mistake waitin' for not doin'. Then you'll be fine."

"All right, Pa. I won't. I'll do, and I'll do well. I promise."

He nodded his head. Knowing it was time to go, he hesitated nonetheless, not wanting this moment to end. The house, the fields, they would be so empty come morning.

"Tess! Harv! Supper's on."

Her voice came cutting through the night, and Harv Canfield knew he could wait no longer. He rose, putting out his hand for his daughter. Tess took it, releasing it as they came close to the light that shone on the porch and bathed her mother's tall sturdy figure in a harsh incandescence.

For a moment Tess thought she heard her mother sigh; imagined she saw her mother's eyes soften. Then she realized she must have been mistaken. Her mother had turned away and was through the screen door before Tess could speak.

"She's gonna miss you, too," her father said. "Maybe more than me. You know she always wanted to be closer to you, Tess."

"She will. Someday," Tess answered confidently, hiding the pain in her heart. "We just haven't reached our time yet. It'll come."

"I hope you're right. A mother and daughter need

14

that."

"Just like a father and daughter," she teased. "We had our time from the minute I was born. Some people just take a little longer to warm up. Not to worry, Pa. The time's coming."

With that she went up the steps and into the kitchen. Harv Canfield heard the clipped conversation of two women moving about in the same kitchen. It warmed him, made him feel as though there was a rightness in the world. Tess's life was changing. His would, too.

Just before he went in to say grace over their meal, and to eat with his daughter before she left for a place he could not follow, he wondered if it would be the best for all of them.

Two

"Come on! Don't be an idiot. Nobody's going to see us!"

Carol waited at the mouth of the alley, hands on hips encased in an expensive skirt that showed them off to their worst advantage. Davina Montgomery hesitated, looking behind her and seeing no one, but scared nonetheless of the dark place Carol called her into. She was supposed to be going home. Her mother needed help. Then again, her mother always needed help. Well, Davina needed something, too, and now that Carol Sweeney had offered her friendship, Davina knew exactly what it was that she wanted. Davina wanted to belong to the real world and forget the fantasy world her mother lived in.

Quickly she made her decision and skittered toward Carol. Together they ducked into the alley and joined two other girls who were already settled on boxes behind a makeshift wall of plywood and trash. Davina hung back while Carol plopped herself in the middle of the group.

"Well?" Carol glared at Davina, who thought this was a rather odd way to treat a new friend. "Sit down before someone sees you."

Davina sat in the first spot she saw. Unfortunately, the box she chose was wet. The back of her skirt now felt cold and clammy. Not daring to move, or admit her mistake for fear Carol would send her packing, Davina remained quiet, her black eyes earnest in her round, serious face. Hands in her lap Davina looked at the little group, resisting the urge to twirl her fingers through her raven curls.

Mary Jane Parker, Leslie Spencer, and Victoria Ray all waited expectantly for Carol to speak. Only Leslie seemed perfectly at ease. The others were in various stages of discomfort, though they were trying hard to hide it behind masks of affected boredom.

"Okay." Carol sighed heavily, as though the mere task of speaking was too mundane for her. "The meeting of the Sisters of Sin is called to order. First order of business is to vote on a new member."

Davina blushed as the girls scrutinized her, their faces betraying nothing. They actually seemed to be taking Davina apart piece by piece. Unfortunately, their attention didn't linger long enough to put her back together. Slowly they swiveled their heads back toward Carol, their leader.

"The new member is Davina Montgomery. I've been watching her, and I think she's got what it takes. Old lady Baron got on her case in English a week ago, and Davina stood right up to her. Not only that, but I found her scratching her name into a stall in the john. I talked to her, and I think she thinks the way we do. We're sick of people telling us what to do, and so is Davina. What do you say?"

For a while everyone was silent. Then Mary Jane spoke up tentatively.

"I think it's okay."

"Why?" Carol demanded, her snakelike eyes running the other girl through.

17

"Well, we could use someone else if we really want to make this a bitchin' club. There's only been four of us for a real long time and well . . ."

Her voice trailed off. She didn't have a good reason why Davina should be allowed into the club. Rather, Mary Jane hoped that she was saying the right thing and it would please Carol. Instead she had bumbled the whole thing. Now Carol would think she was stupid and Mary Jane would be up all night trying to figure a way to get back into Carol's good graces.

"I guess it would be okay," Leslie commented tentatively. Mary Jane breathed a sigh of relief. Carol's attention was now focused on her very best friend. "If you think she can contribute something it'll be okay. We've all been in trouble at school and for a lot more than talking back to Mrs. Baron. So I say we let her in if she proves she's worthy."

"Good idea," Carol purred, eyes narrowing.

The original group had evolved under Carol's mastery so nobody questioned the membership. At first it had been a lark, a way for them to feel as though they were as good as or better than the cute little in-crowd types that roamed around their high school. Slowly Carol and her little band had striven to set themselves apart not only by word, but by deed. Davina was the first to enter the Sisters of Sin from the outside. She would be their test case.

"What do I have to do?"

Davina ventured her question in the smallest of voices. She hated the thought of doing something really horrible. After all, there were enough bad things to do at home, why would she want to do really bad things away from home? Still, these girls could be her new family. The idea was much more enticing than thinking of her mother as her only family.

Davina chanced a look around the group. Only Carol and Leslie were staring at her. The others were looking down at their feet.

"I think you'll have to get something the entire group will be able to use." Carol spoke slowly, forming her thoughts as she went along, like they were hard things she had to pick out of her mind. Leslie warmed to the idea.

"Yeah, something that will kind of benefit us all . . ."

"Something that we've always wanted . . ." Mary Jane quipped.

"Something we couldn't get for ourselves in a million years . . ." Victoria finished gleefully.

They all laughed cruelly, feverishly excited by the challenge they were conjuring up, delighting in Davina's stricken face. They made it sound so awful. So treacherous.

"I-I-I don't know what I could get you," Davina stuttered. "I don't have much money. I don't know anyone who does."

"Who said you needed money?" Carol snapped. "In fact, you don't need money at all. If you want to be a Sister of Sin all you have to do is go into Groman's department store and get each of us a new scarf—silk—in the color of our choice."

Davina blanched. They wanted her to steal. Every fiber in her body told her to get up that instant and run home. No matter how horrible home was, it couldn't be worse than getting caught for stealing and being thrown in jail. She was just about to bolt, just about to leave Carol and her band of sinful sisters, when Leslie spoke again.

"Of course I think part of the deal should be that you get two for yourself. After all, I haven't seen you wear anything new in ages. It's only fair if you take two for yourself."

Davina's heart skipped a beat. Leslie had noticed how old her clothes were. How humiliating. But Leslie was also holding out the hand of friendship by insisting that Davina not only take the greatest risk but the greatest prize. For that kindness Davina would have walked on coals for the other girl. Slowly, without reservation, Davina smiled at each girl in turn. The girls were all smiling back, silently offering their admiration on the condition Davina would do this one little thing.

"When do you want them?" she asked, her voice full of confidence.

"Tomorrow," Carol answered. "Same time, same place."

Davina nodded. Without another word she slipped out of the alley and walked the six blocks to Groman's department store.

It was a busy day at Groman's, much to Davina's chagrin. She stood just inside the door of the bustling emporium, her book bag clutched to her chest, knowing she could never steal anything in a million years and knowing dismally that the Sisters of Sin would never give her another chance to prove herself if she didn't.

"Is everything all right? Miss?"

Davina jumped, a small yelp escaping her lips.

"W-W-What? I-I-I didn't do anything!" Davina stuttered, the blood draining from her face.

"Of course not. I didn't say you did," the prettily dressed woman beside her said, laughing.

Davina eyed her carefully, knowing the laugh was directed at her. A salesgirl. That's all she was. Hardly older than herself but dressed like a rich girl. And she smelled so good. Davina's heart hardened. Life was so unfair. Davina didn't have a nice dark dress nor did she have perfume to put on. How dare this woman laugh at her because she didn't have those things. How dare this woman even talk to her.

"Well?" Davina asked imperiously. "What do you want?"

"I just want to know if you're okay. You looked kind of sick standing over here." The girl was still grinning, making Davina angrier by the second.

"I'm fine. I just want to get something for my mother. My mother," Davina hesitated before she continued. Everyone knew it was better to use a little bit of the truth if you were going to lie. "My mother is sick. I want to bring her something to cheer her up."

"Oh, well, we've got lots of great things. I'll bet you'll find something nice. Just make sure you don't come down with whatever your mother has. You do look awfully pale."

"I won't," Davina assured her. "I won't."

She watched the young woman walk away on her high heels, her skirt swaying against shapely legs. Suddenly Davina was aware of everything around her. The mindless people who spent money like water; people so less deserving than her. The smiling clerks handling the beautiful merchandise as though it were their own. The bright lights, the clean floor, the high, open ceilings, the noise and laughter and sheer abandon of shoppers who hadn't a worry in the world.

Davina laughed, one harsh, short note. She shook her head, her fear gone and replaced with a heady feeling of purpose. No, she wouldn't catch what her mother had, though she worried that she might. She was going to be well; she was going to have all the things her mother had never had and she was going to start getting them right now.

Minutes later Davina found the accessories department. Without regard for the danger she was putting herself in, she stuffed six scarves into her book bag before turning on her heel and marching out of Groman's with her head held high, her book bag swinging casually in her hand.

Once out the door, though, Davina's resolve disappeared and dread was her companion again.

Her heart beat a wild tune as she traversed the two blocks to the bus bench. She forced herself not to look behind her to see if someone from the store was coming after her. Even after boarding the bus for the long ride home, Davina could not seem to calm herself. Under her sweater her blouse was soaked with perspiration, her right eye twitched at regular intervals while she stared at the back of the bus driver's head and a headache was forming at the base of her skull.

By the time she stepped off the bus, though, and walked up the six flights of stairs to the dump she and her mother called home, Davina was no longer afraid. Davina was angry: angry that she hadn't figured out before that she could take what she deserved. She had been a good girl for so long, and what had she gotten for it? Nothing. Now, with encouragement from her friends, she would finally have what was rightfully hers. At last, she would have a place in the world, nice things to wear, respect.

Inside the apartment she went immediately to the bathroom and took the scarves out of her book bag.

Locking the door, Davina smoothed them out. To-gether they looked like a riotous rainbow. It occurred to her that she had forgotten to ask what the girls' fa-vorite colors were. Looking at her booty, though, Davina knew that it wouldn't matter. All six were beau-tiful. They were the most beautiful scarves she had ever seen in her life.

Just as she was carefully folding the last of them the bathroom door began to shake, rattling and booming as angry fists banged on the outside. Davina jumped, mad that she had been so startled. Why on earth should she be surprised? Her mother came home at the same time everyday.

"Are you in there, you little bitch?" her mother screamed.

Davina sat back on her heels. Slowly she gathered all the scarves to her, holding them against her chest, burying her cheek in their silky softness but unable to step through the rainbow into her fleeting world of sat-isfaction.

"Davina! Davina! Come out right this minute. I've been slaving away all day so you can have enough to eat and a roof over your head, and all I ask is that I come home to a clean house every now and again. Do you hear me? This is the last straw. If you can't do any-thing to help out, then I don't want anything to do with you! Do you hear me? I don't want you! I wish you'd never been born!"

Davina buried her face in the scarves, throwing them over her head, hiding herself as she tried desper-ately to block out her mother's words. Tears sprung to her eyes, but she held them back, not daring to let even one teardrop fall on her hard-won fortune.

Outside the door, on the carpetless floor, Davina

heard her mother's quick, hard steps going toward the kitchen. Angelica Montgomery continued to curse her daughter, muttering as she went to get what she needed. Davina's skin went cold. She willed her ears to close so she wouldn't hear what was to come. Nothing short of death could keep the noise out, though. Her mother was back, screaming obscenities at the top of her lungs, then whispering them through the door just before she raised the butcher knife and brought it crashing down into the wood. The wood splintered against her mother's madness — madness that grew worse every year.

Suddenly, as though the scarves had magical powers, Davina rose from her place on the cold tile floor and went to the door. Enough was enough. Things had to change or she, too, would certainly go mad. Thinking of her new friends, thinking of the power she had possessed inside Groman's as she took the scarves, Davina threw open the door and faced the knife.

"Go ahead, Mother, if that's what you really want to do. Kill me."

Angelica Montgomery was so stunned she let the knife fall from her hands and clatter to the floor.

Davina looked at the fallen knife, then back into her mother's tortured eyes, a scornful look on her face. Davina raised her chin and held it high, her eyes glittering with triumph.

"Excuse me, Mother," she murmured, walking past Angelica, heading toward her bedroom. Never once did she look back.

Three

Bonnie Barber was by far the prettiest girl in the room. She stood out without even trying. Her auburn-haired beauty was beyond compare: parchment pale skin, aquiline nose, emerald eyes under dark lashes. She had the incredible ability to appear both sensual and innocent, depending on how she parted her full lips and hooded her eyes when she smiled in response to a question.

Usually she didn't speak. Her father preferred to answer the questions put to his daughter. Almost from birth Bonnie had been trained to react properly during these interviews, first by her mother and now, since her mother's death, by her father. In fact, Carl Barber had forced her to master her technique. That, at least, was worthy of her gratitude. She was aware this morning that she had reached the pinnacle of her talent. The casting agent sitting across from her was duly impressed. Bonnie relaxed inside while she adjusted her outside in a manner that would illicit the best response. Her face, her body, still radiated for the benefit of the man in the leather chair. Her father continued to speak, less quickly than he had initially. Obviously he felt their triumph too.

"Bonnie's quite a little trouper. Never been late for a call. Can you believe it? Only fifteen . . ."

Mentally Bonnie smirked. How long was he going to keep shaving three years off her age? It wasn't just her tightly bound chest that would eventually give her away or her swelling hips and tiny waist. It was the settling of her face into planes of perfection, the worldly knowledge behind her green eyes, that would finally either do them in as a team or shoot her to independent stardom.

Despite her amusement Bonnie dipped her head demurely, listening to Carl sing her praises.

"Yep, fifteen, and hasn't missed a call yet. She's a professional, my little girl. And this part in Daniel Ryder's sitcom sounds just perfect for her. She hasn't had much experience with comedy as you can see from her résumé, but she's a pro. And once you've learned the basics you can use them anywhere. Am I right? Am I right?"

Carl beamed, his hand falling heavily on his daughter's thigh, giving it a squeeze. Bonnie tensed. His fond pats had taken to lingering a bit too long lately and his hands found themselves in the oddest places as he offered his encouragement and affection.

She flicked her eyes toward the man in the chair. He was smiling, too. Both men, in fact, looked as though they had just made the best deal of their life. What did she care? She was going to work on a series, and that was all that mattered. Bonnie could feel it in her bones. This was the break she was looking for.

If she worked her interviews right, if she made the right kind of impression on the small screen, her future was secure. There was no doubt in her mind that she could parlay this into a glorious future that didn't include her father. She was, after all, eighteen, and well able to take care of herself.

As her eyes caught those of the casting executive she allowed her gaze to deepen. She saw him start, saw his smile falter then broaden as he understood the full meaning of her expression. With incredible effort he broke the connection.

"I think," he said to Carl, "we won't be looking any further. In fact, I believe Bonnie is just perfect for what I have in mind. Just perfect, indeed."

"Well, now," Carl bellowed happily, "isn't that just fine? You just get me a contract, and I'll have it signed and back here in a jiffy. Of course, there are a few concessions we're going to have to ask for. But you understand that, don't you? Business is business."

Bonnie's heart sank. He was going too far again. Urgently, she whispered a prayer that this time he wouldn't push their luck. She missed out on a movie-of-the-week because he had asked for more than they were willing to give, and he hadn't given them an out in case of their refusal. She had been fired from a commercial contract because he insisted they move the location once it had been established. He was doing it again, and Bonnie was breaking out in a cold sweat. She lay her hand tentatively over his, then dug her nails into his flesh as he continued to speak.

"We'll want to make sure that she has top billing and, of course, all expenses will have to be paid for our travel to and from Sacramento."

Carl pulled his hand away. Bonnie's nails had left deep gouge marks. But Carl was a pretty darn good actor himself. He hadn't yelped or whimpered. He simply rubbed the marks without looking at her. Silence greeted his demands. Bonnie closed her eyes, praying as she had never prayed in her entire life. When the man in the chair spoke, Bonnie realized there must be a God, or else the casting director's libido was stronger than his business judgment.

"I'll make sure that she appears prominently in the credits. Unfortunately, I don't think we can pay expenses to commute to the set. You understand, don't you, that we shoot every day. It would be ludicrous to try to get her here and back five days a week. But I do have an idea. We can get her into a supervised living arrangement during the week and then send her home on the weekends to be with you. How would that be?"

"Well," Carl answered, not liking the way this conversation was going, "I'll tell you, I'm usually on the set to take care of my little girl. Know what I mean?"

"Of course, I understand. In the kinds of situations she's worked on in the past I'm sure this was quite acceptable. But we work on closed sets. I doubt if I could swing a special pass for you on a daily basis." The casting director smiled benignly, his hands up in a gesture of empathy. "Certainly, on the special occasions, I don't see why not. What I had in mind was this: Bonnie could stay at my house. We have a lovely maid's apartment above the garage, and my wife would love to act as Bonnie's guardian, I'm sure. We have no children, you see, so Bonnie would be a delight. Now this would solve two problems. Bonnie would go into the studio with me every day, so you wouldn't worry about her, and you wouldn't have to spend a penny of her rather generous salary on housing. I think it sounds quite wonderful." He turned and looked directly at Bonnie. "What do you think, my dear? Does this sound like something you might enjoy?"

Bonnie's lashes fluttered, thankful her prayer had been answered so easily. Beside her Carl began to stutter objections, but Bonnie played her hand, knowing

28

that if push came to shove there was nothing Carl could do about it. It was time she flew the coop anyway. The only thing her father did for her was perpetuate the myth that she was fifteen. That was one thing Bonnie would be happy to shed.

"I'd love it. Just imagine, Daddy, being part of Mister Carlton's family during the week, then coming home to see you on the weekends? There wouldn't be any distractions so I would have plenty of time to learn my lines, and I'd be fresh for shooting every day. Oh, I think it sounds marvelous. Oh, please, Daddy, say yes. An offer like Mister Carlton's just doesn't come along every day." Slowly she slid her eyes toward the man in the chair.

"It doesn't, does it, Mister Carlton?" Bonnie asked throatily. "I mean, you don't offer this kind of thing to just anyone, do you?"

The first few words croaked out of Carlton's throat when he answered. "Certainly not, young lady. I can truthfully say I've been waiting a long time to find just the right girl to take on as my protégé."

"And I've been waiting just as long for someone in the industry who can guide me. Not that my father hasn't done a great job, but I think he deserves a rest, don't you, Mister Carlton?"

The man in the chair nodded happily, almost salivating while Bonnie grinned beatifically. Carl Barber witnessed the beginning of the end of his life on easy street.

Damned if he probably wasn't going to have to get himself a job. No counting on Bonnie to take him along for the ride. In a way he was kind of proud that she'd leave him flat. He always told her waiting did no good—you had to seize the moment. Now she had, and he could see from the look in her eye that she was going to hold on to it, even if it meant leaving him in the dust.

Carl smiled weakly. Bonnie was moving on. He was being left behind and Carlton was going to get a whole lot more for his money than he bargained for. Everyone in that room knew it — only Carl Barber wasn't happy about it.

Part Two
1988

Four

"Hit her! Hit her hard! Come on, Canfield! This isn't a game anymore. It's the finals. We've got to beat Marymount if it's the last thing we do."

Tess heard Jimmy Peyton call and made the mistake of looking over her shoulder toward the coach of UCLA's powder puff football team. Instantly, just as she was reaching for Kelly, trying desperately to grab the flag out of her back pocket, Tess slipped on the lush grass and fell. Behind her three other girls lost their momentum and fell, crushing the breath out of Tess even as she began to laugh.

When everyone finally uncoiled, Tess rolled onto her back, her bright blue eyes dancing with amusement even as she took deep gasps of air. Jimmy Peyton loomed over her, legs spread and arms akimbo. He looked huge from Tess's vantage point, despite the fact he was shorter than she. His lips were set in a grimace; his eyes, behind horned-rimmed glasses, were angry little spots of brown.

"Don't ever look over your shoulder like that! Powder puff football is just a name. Those girls on the Marymount team are not going to be playing like ladies. Keep your mind on the game."

With a great heave of her chest Tess finally caught

her breath well enough to speak. She pushed herself up on her elbows, surveying the playing field. Her teammates had scattered. Some were laughing, but most were wiping the sweat from their brows, exhausted.

"You know, Jimmy, you've just hit the nail on the head. This is a game. I didn't join this team because I wanted to win the state championships. I just wanted to have some fun. Doesn't look to me like too many people are having fun here."

"Of course it's fun," Jimmy sputtered. "And winning is even more fun. Now get up and let's try it again."

"I don't think so, Jimmy. I've got to study for finals. I can't be out here practicing day and night. So either I'll play in the game on Saturday without practicing, or you can get one of the other girls to take my place."

Tess was sitting up now, picking grass out of her long blond hair. In one fluid motion she was on her feet, walking to the sidelines where she collected her things. Jimmy followed like a puppy.

"Aw come on, Canfield, don't be a quitter. I'm sorry. I've been pushing a little hard, maybe, but I need you. You run faster than anyone I've ever seen and you're taller. It's all that wheat you ate when you were a kid. Tell me you'll be at the game on Saturday. Promise? I won't push it anymore. I'll act like this is fun and not serious if it makes you feel better. Look, Canfield, I'm smiling. I can even laugh."

Only someone with a vivid imagination would have construed his harsh bray for a chuckle. He was too serious to know how to laugh right, but Tess joined in anyway. She had never seen so many people in one place forget that life was meant to be enjoyed. Maybe it was college that brought out the aggressiveness in them, but Tess had a funny feeling it was a character trait built into these people from the time they were born. She shook her head.

"That's a good try, Jimmy. I'll do my best on Saturday, but you can count me out for any more practice. The only thing I want to do is get my tests over with and head on home for the summer. I haven't seen my parents all year, even at Christmas, and I have no intention of sticking around here any longer than I have to."

"You know," Jimmy said, less urgently now that they were finally standing still, "most of us would rather never see our parents again. I can't believe that you're actually anxious to be going home."

"That's the secret of my sparkling personality. I enjoy my parents, and if you could see our farm, you'd never want to leave it." Tess pulled a sweatshirt over her head, knowing she didn't exactly enjoy her mother, but she did love her. "Besides, if you didn't have all the money in the world you'd know that absence does make the heart grow fonder. When you can't see someone because you can't afford the airfare it makes seeing them that much more special."

"Yeah, I suppose. Listen, I have enough of this kind of talk in philosophy with Professor Stadler. So just promise me that you're going to be here Saturday, on this field, at exactly ten in the morning. If you promise that I'll get off your case and buy you a pizza."

"You mean you'd cut practice short?" Tess let her hand flutter to her chest in mock amazement. "Just for lil' ole me?"

"Canfield, you make me want to scream."

"Yeah, I hear that all the time from guys like you. Listen, I'll pass on the pizza, but I'm going to take a rain check. My allowance is running out, so by the end of the week I'll need a square meal."

"You got it. See you Saturday."

Jimmy jogged off, calling to the scattered team as he went. Tess shook her head, wondering if she should remind him that a moment ago he had been ready to call off practice for the day for the sake of a pizza and her company.

The June breeze teased her hair as she headed toward the dorm. The campus trees were bursting with color. Tess felt wonderfully free, as though the world had conspired to make her life simply perfect.

UCLA had exceeded her expectations, both professionally and socially. Though the campus was as large as a small town, Tess never felt intimidated. The people were nice. Professors were actually interested in her progress, and her fellow students included her in their social plans. So, though she never felt as if she was an intimate part of the school, Tess was made to feel a welcomed guest.

From the beginning it was clear she would appreciate this experience in California, but she also understood her real life lay elsewhere. She wasn't exactly sure where that was, but the somewhere else was a little gentler than the frantic pace of southern California. That somewhere else was smaller than this sprawling city. That somewhere was filled with greater contrast, with people of greater depth of emotion and sensitivity. The constant sunshine was as depressing to her as the winter would be to a Californian in Kansas. As an artist she knew her ambition, inspiration and the place she chose to settle were inexorably linked. When she found that place Tess would also find dear friends and the ultimate love she dreamed of.

All this was only a delightful stopping place, and the friends she made, fond acquaintances. The university was just an experience not to be taken too lightly nor too seriously. Every day of the last three years had been filed neatly away to be pulled out and shared with someone dear to her at a later date.

Tess didn't believe that her inability to feel at one with the university and its people was a failing. Instead she considered herself rather adult. Too many young women in the dorm treated these years as though there would never be any more. For Tess, these were the first steps in her life. She took each day tentatively, enjoying it while she tried her wings.

Tess managed the half mile across campus without noticing time had passed. Taking the dorm steps two at a time, she dug in her pocket for her keys and let herself into the almost deserted building. The day was so beautiful practically everyone was outside enjoying it. This pleased her to no end. There wouldn't be any interruptions while she hit the books. No friends popping in to tell her about their latest love affair or their difficulties with classes.

Twenty minutes later Tess had showered, put out her study materials and splurged on a Coke and candy bar from the vending machine at the end of the hall. As was her habit, she straightened the picture of her parents so they would be staring directly at her while she studied. Their images reminded her of the sacrifices they made so she could live properly in Los Angeles while she took advantage of the scholarship that paid her tuition.

"One more year," she whispered mischievously to the picture. "Then you'll be out here to see me graduate. One more year."

Three hours later Tess was engrossed in her books when suddenly she felt a tug in her stomach, a wrenching so sudden and odd she sat back and closed her eyes as she waited for the spasm to pass. When it did, Tess checked her watch. It was almost five, and she'd had nothing all day but a candy bar. She closed her books and threw on a pair of jeans. Hunger. That's all it was. Just hunger. She headed toward the cafeteria hoping a bit of food and a break from her studies would calm this unexpected feeling of dread.

Mildred Canfield was so engrossed in mending the chicken coop, she thought she imagined the high-pitched scream before silence descended over the sprawling acres of the Canfield farm once more.

Laying down her hammer, she turned and held a hand over her eyes, squinting into the red ball of sun that hung low where sky met land.

Mildred's ears strained, trying to identify farm sounds in that scarlet afternoon as she scanned the horizon: a crow called triumphantly before sweeping down to claim forgotten wheat kernels, chickens scratched the dry earth, the motor of the combine churned. Mildred's heart pounded faster when she realized the motor sound was even, the combine wasn't moving ahead and the scream she had heard had not been repeated.

Slowly at first she walked west, parallel to the tall wheat, perspiration dotting her forehead. The motor should have been rising and falling in the natural cadence of a laboring machine. Faster her feet moved. Sensible feet shod in shoes that could traverse the rutted road and cut through the wheat, expertly delivering her to the flat, stubbled land where she could see more clearly; where she could put her fears to rest because Harv would be happily sitting in the cab of his prized machine.

Mildred broke through the line of wheat breathing

hard. The huge combine was stationary and she couldn't see Harv in the cab. To her right Bobby, the hand, sat in his truck waiting to be called for the haul. His truck and the combine were equal distance from her.

Mildred ran frantically now, waving her hands above her head. Bobby saw her when she was a hundred yards from the combine. The truck roared to life and its wheels sped over the naked earth.

"Harv!" she called, keeping hysteria from her voice as best she could. "Harv Canfield, answer me!"

Bobby pulled the truck up beside her and she flung herself into the cab of the truck, letting him drive her around to the side of the idling machine.

"Oh my God!" Bobby screamed as he reined in the truck and cut the engine. Both he and Mildred were out of the cab at the same time, doing what had to be done for the injured man.

"His arm, Bobby! It's in the puller belt. We've got to get it free. He's going to bleed to death if we don't."

"Won't be much left of that arm, Missus," Bobby cried as he jumped into the cab and turned off the motor to the belt.

"Better to save the man than the arm," Mildred hollered up at him, taking time enough only to feel for her husband's pulse and draw her hand over his deathly white cheek. There would be time enough for love and worry when they had him free. "Get down here now. Let's get him out."

"Yes, ma'am."

Bobby shot out of the cab. Together they struggled, trying to do as little damage as possible to Harv Canfield's arm when they pulled at the belt. Pushing and pulling, using all their strength they were finally able to draw Harv away from the machine and lay him gently on the ground, hard as a bed of nails because of the wheat stubble. His arm was destroyed and Mildred felt her heart break even as she talked.

"Bobby, get on that damn CB and call the doc. Tell him we need the Aeroambulance fast as he can get it here."

Bobby flew toward his truck as Mildred pulled her husband's big red kerchief from the pocket of his overalls and expertly tied a tourniquet just below his shoulder.

As she worked Mildred was aware of every inch of her body. She felt her lips, as tight and parched and linear as the stream dried up in August. She felt her hands, old and worn and not worthy to stroke her husband's face even in comfort. A wisp of hair, gray and dry, flew into her eyes and she knew it wasn't beautiful any longer. How she wished she could be beautiful just once more, the moment Harv opened his eyes. She wished she could be beautiful like Tess.

"They're on their way, Missus."

Bobby was back beside her, kneeling in the stubble, his hands moving now and again as though they wanted to help, do anything to ease the suffering his boss must be feeling. Mildred didn't move, only kept looking into her husband's face until the sound of the helicopter forced her to look hopefully heavenward.

Moments later the paramedics were loading Harv Canfield into the helicopter. Mildred moved forward. One of the paramedics held out his hand, stopping her from entering.

Mildred clasped her own strong hand over his and moved it off her shoulder. She would not be stopped. Harv was hers to protect. No one would keep her from it. She stepped into the helicopter, leaving no room for one of the paramedics. The last thing she saw was the

40

man's face and Bobby's turned up to watch them fly off toward Wichita and help.

The call came at nine o'clock from a man Tess would never meet. He was a sheriff's deputy. His voice was nice: cool, hesitant, with just the right inflection of grief for people he would never meet.

"Miss Canfield?"

"Yes?"

"This is Sheriff's Deputy Johnson . . ."

"Yes?" Tess asked, curious to hear what he wanted.

". . . From Wichita?"

Tess was silent. A deputy from home. Not from Los Angeles. She steeled herself. Contrary to popular belief bad thoughts didn't run through her head at the first inkling of bad news. Instead her mind went blank. A piece of paper waiting to be written on. She knew she wouldn't want to read the message. She also knew she would have no choice.

"Miss Canfield, I'm sorry to inform you that your father had a combine accident this afternoon . . ." Tess felt her body relax. Pa was careful. If it was an accident she knew he was hurt, but not dead. ". . . He was being airlifted for treatment to Wichita along with your mother. Miss Canfield, I'm sorry to inform you that the Aeroambulance went down, killing all persons on board as they approached the hospital landing pad. Of course, there will be an investigation . . ."

Tess heard no more, only felt the horrendous tear inside her where her heart used to be. And, in the vacuum created as her heart was ripped out of her, every emotion she ever knew deserted her. She would no longer see beauty in the sky, long for the open fields of the farm or look into a face and know love the way she had known it before. In that instant Tess Canfield knew that there was nothing left for her to live for. Nothing in the entire world.

The phone dangled, banging against the wall as she crumpled to the floor and pulled her legs against her chest. A girl from the third floor found her ten minutes later. The deputy was still calling her name over the phone.

Five

"It's bad, Doctor. I don't know how much longer I can take it. There's got to be something you can do for her. I don't have any kind of life, and neither does she. Half the time I'm afraid she's going to kill herself, and the other half the time she looks like she wants to kill me. I'm twenty years old, and I've been working night and day just to keep body and soul together for the last two years. You've either got to cure her or you've got to tell me how I can get her the kind of help she needs."

Davina sat straight in her vinyl chair and tried to keep the resentment out of her voice while she spoke to the doctor who treated her mother's depression. Or was it schizophrenia or possibly paranoid delusions? Davina had been to so many doctors with Angelica she'd lost track of the diagnosis. The only thing she was sure of was the prognosis: her mother would never be well mentally, but was in superb physical condition.

Now, after years and years of hearing that prognosis from a hundred different lips, Davina was bound and determined that she was not going to live her life with a crazy person. She deserved more and she was going to have it . . . no matter what it took.

"I understand your frustration, Miss Montgomery, and I applaud the care you've taken with your mother all these years. Unfortunately, as I see it, your options are quite limited. Let's see, I've been treating your mother for . . ."

He stopped, put on his reading glasses and opened a file that lay by his right hand. Davina wanted to scream. Six months! What kind of doctor couldn't remember a woman he'd seen three times a week for six months? She bit her lip, suppressing her rage and praying that he, by some miracle, would come up with an answer to her problem.

"Ah, I see. I've been treating her for six months now and, to be truthful, I've seen very little to give me hope. You're mother is hopelessly committed to her delusion that your father, through his wealth and influence, is torturing her by blacklisting her. She feels her inability to get and hold a job is his doing. She also feels that you have been secretly indoctrinated by him to make her life miserable."

"I know that," Davina snapped. "I've heard it a hundred times before from other doctors and from her. What do you think we do at night? Play tiddleywinks? I'm constantly listening to her ranting and raving about this nonexistent man. I'm telling you it's a fantasy. When she was better, when I was younger, she told me she got knocked up by some guy in the army. I don't know anything more about him. Now why haven't you been able to convince her that the only one causing her problems is her?"

"It's not as easy as that. Though we've been treating her with medication and psychotherapy, I'm afraid that not every case is easily curable or containable."

"So, what do I do?" she asked sullenly.

"Well, you have a few choices. You can get someone in to watch your mother during the day, or I could recommend a number of fine institutions which would make her comfortable. She's a young woman though, only"—he referred to his file again—"only forty-two, so she could be in an institution of that sort for many, many years. Have you insurance that could properly pay for such an extended stay?"

"No. My benefits wouldn't cover something like that. I'm only a secretary at an insurance company. What about a state institution?"

"Waiting lists as long as your arm, I'm afraid." He raised his hands in a refined gesture of hopelessness and smiled. He was thinking, Davina was sure, that with such a bleak picture he would be assured Mrs. Montgomery would be paying him a good long time, or rather Davina would. "So you see, your choices are limited. Have you no family that could help?"

Davina shook her head. This was all such a waste of time. She was already an hour late getting back to work, more than likely she would be docked those wages. Damn her mother. Damn these doctors. Well, she wasn't going to take it anymore. Her mother had been right about one thing—this was a conspiracy. Not a conspiracy wrought by a nonexistent husband; it was a conspiracy brought on by her own mother. Davina was absolutely positive that a firm hand with her mother would put an end to all this nonsense and her own financial suffering.

"I think I've heard all I need to hear," Davina said curtly.

She rose and smoothed the skirt of her cheap suit. She hated the feel of cheap cloth. For some reason not only her mind, but her very body was repelled by the borderline poverty she had experienced all her life. Once she had tried to do something about it. She had joined the Sisters of Sin and stolen fine things, worn them and known that she had been born to better than

45

she had. But one day she had been caught, the sisters deserting her like the proverbial rats on a sinking ship and her mother had worsened. Life was a bitch with a capital B.

"I hope I've been some help."

The doctor rose, too, saddened that this interview should be coming to an end. Had he known Mrs. Montgomery had such a lovely, young daughter he would have requested family conferences long before this.

"Not much, Doctor," Davina answered.

"I'm so sorry. Perhaps we could continue to discuss this — over dinner?" he asked hopefully.

He'd been divorced long enough to feel that familiar stirring again — the need for female companionship of Miss Montgomery's sort was becoming most insistent.

Davina eyed him coldly. "Perhaps not. In fact, I don't think you'll be seeing my mother, much less me again."

Davina left the doctor blinking rapidly behind his glasses, chagrined that he should be dismissed so lightly as not only a psychiatrist, but as a suitor. Many women would give their eye teeth to be seen with him. Miss Montgomery obviously needed as much help as her mother.

It was dark and hot by the time Davina made it home.

Home was a three-floor walk-up in one of the worse neighborhoods Sacramento had to offer, and she and her mother had been living there ever since they got kicked out of their old six-floor walk-up for not paying the rent on time.

Someday she'd get out of this hellhole. Someday,

but not today. Today there were other more pressing matters on her mind and she was going to make her plans crystal clear to Angelica. She unlocked the door, went in and tossed her purse on the chest in the hall. Davina was silent, listening for the telltale scurrying that would lead her to her mother. She heard it a moment later and headed toward the kitchen.

"You haven't even dressed yourself," Davina railed the moment she saw her mother. Nothing irked her more than this idiotic notion her mother had that she was an invalid. "How long can you stay in that stinking robe? And your hair! It's matted. Would it kill you to take a brush to it now and again? I've provided you with everything you need to get yourself up and looking human."

She advanced on her mother, who cowered in the corner, a coffeepot in one hand, a soup ladle in the other.

"I was just fixing dinner. I didn't have time. I'm sorry. I'm sorry. You startled me. Aren't you home early?"

Davina eyed the kitchen. There were no pots bubbling and boiling with the promised dinner. There wasn't even a crumb of food to be found on the countertop.

"Don't give me that crap, Mother. You were hiding in here."

Davina moved quickly, snatching at the ladle, but her mother was faster still, snatching it back. Her sick mind clicked into gear, shoving her into the fury that had so frightened Davina as a child and even now put her on the defensive.

"Don't you touch this! Don't you dare come near me like that again! I'm still your mother, and I can do what I want with you. I can kill you if I want and nobody would care. Nobody would even know. If they found out I could tell them how you abuse me. Abuse me!"

She was screaming now, holding the ladle above her head as though it were a weapon. For the first time in her life Davina didn't even flinch. Her mother couldn't do her any harm. She was a sick, frail, stupid woman. Davina had the strength of youth and the fury of deprivation. That would defeat her mother no matter what.

"Don't be absurd. You couldn't kill me. You don't have the guts. You've never had the guts to tell the truth in your whole life. The truth is, without me you'd die. You'd just crawl into a corner and die."

Davina turned her back on her mother and stormed into the bedroom. There she ripped the offending suit from her body and grabbed the one good thing she owned, a robe of real satin. Putting it on she felt for the first time that day as though she might, after all, be human. Behind her Davina heard Angelica come into the room. Without looking she knew exactly what was happening.

Her mother was slithering along the wall, her eyes darting about looking for creatures — or perhaps Davina's father — in all the little nooks and crannies of the room. Davina whirled, gratified when her mother shrank back against the wall as though threatened.

"See," Davina teased cruelly, "you don't even sneak well. You can't do anything for yourself. Everything you try, you give up. If you really wanted to, you could make yourself well. If you really wanted to you could be a normal human being again and contribute something instead of always taking, taking, taking. I'm sick of your taking. I'm sick of your stupid face and this hovel we live in and my job. You're the mother. You're supposed to take care of me!"

"I would have," her mother answered in a small voice, her eyes closing as though to ward off her daughter's hatred. "I would have really. But he left me without a cent. He makes money hand over fist. He lives like royalty and leaves us to rot here. It's not my fault. It's his."

"*Whose,* Mother? Whose fault?" Davina glided toward her mother, her anger quiet and cold now. She put her hands on the wall, caging the woman, leaning her face close as she whispered, "Whose fault is it that we're like this? My father's? That nameless, faceless sailor you picked up and screwed? The guy who shipped out? If he really is what you say, tell me who he is. Tell me, and I'll go to him and make him understand. He'll give us money for everything. For doctors. For clothes. For a place to live. If he's real, Mother, tell me now. If he isn't, shut up."

For a long while the two women stood together feeling each other's breath on their own skin, their eyes linking them in fear and anger. Angelica turned her eyes away first, knowing she couldn't tell her daughter what she wanted to know. He would kill her if she ever told. He'd told her that. Hadn't he? Or had she imagined it? No, no, he told her. He must have. He made his money in bad ways. He was rich and he was powerful and he used women badly to make his money. He would be ashamed and his shame would be dangerous. Angelica was so sure of that. But she had to end this thing with her daughter. She had to think of some way to end it. Maybe she should tell. Maybe she should . . .

Davina pushed away from the wall in disgust. She hated being that close to her mother. In a way she thought that Angelica's madness might be catching.

49

Davina turned away and reached for her hairbrush.

"I thought not. You can't tell me because he doesn't exist, does he, Mother?"

This was said so sweetly the woman against the wall felt herself shrinking under the meanness of it. Shrinking, shrinking until soon there would be nothing left of her. Davina must stop now. No more talking or certainly Angelica would simply fade away until she was nothing more than a pinpoint of darkness on the wall. One more word and she would—be gone.

Slowly she turned and left the room, shuffling back to her own bedroom to lay down and stare at the ceiling. She must figure everything out.

Angelica settled herself and lay motionless on the bed for hours, listening to Davina make her dinner, watching the television, moving about doing any number of unknown tasks. Then the night became very black, filled with the ominous quiet that the hours after ten took on.

She was going to be safe, from her own anger and that of her daughter and the man who, she was sure, thought of nothing other than her destruction. Frantically her mind raced, filing away all these thoughts and feelings so that she would remember to tell the doctor. He would know what to do. He always said words to make her feel better, safer, normal.

But the night was no escape. The door to her room opened. A shaft of light cut through the blackness; her eyes flickered toward it. Davina was silhouetted there. For a moment Davina didn't speak. Then slowly the words came.

"You won't be going to any more doctors, Mother. I've just terminated your contract. It's sink-or-swim time, Mom. Sink or swim."

The door closed. Davina was gone. In the hall, with

the peeling paper that some other tenant had put up in a vain attempt to make the apartment cheery, Davina leaned back and let the wall support her. Her entire body vibrated with shame and sorrow and outrage. Angelica drove her to be so cruel even when she didn't want to be. With a bit more money, only a bit, Davina could have cared for her mother the right way. But without that, without the funds to live like a proper human being, Davina was left only with the strength that anger brings and that was the way life would just have to be.

Hardening her heart against the little-girl love that still lingered for her mother, Davina pushed away from the wall and cleared her mind of any thoughts of Angelica while she hunted for a bottle. A good stiff drink would drive away the last of those unnerving feelings of remorse.

And in the small bedroom, Angelica's tortured mind thought of nothing but Davina and how like her father she was. Deserters both of them; heartless the two of them. The night closed in, bringing with it despair. Despair turned to desperation and desperation personified itself in a bottle of pills she had hidden away in the medicine chest. Angelica had always known the moment would come when she could no longer live in this world. The time had come. She was too tired to go on trying to make things different and right.

Slowly she unscrewed the cap on the bottle of pills. Carefully Angelica counted them, as though precision had something to do with her objective. For a while she cradled the pills in her hand, admiring the workmanship it took to produce such lovely little things. Who, she wondered, thought to make half the capsule yellow, half the capsule red? Who was it that figured out how to stop the pain so effectively? Did they know

51

that their handsome little pills would be used to stop the pain completely?

From the living room came the sound of a glass breaking. Davina was still angry. She was throwing things. Angelica reached for the water glass by her bed, tightened her grip around the handful of pills then lifted them to her lips and dropped them down her throat one by one before laying back on her threadbare linens and closing her eyes.

Angelica Montgomery was dead by morning.

Six

"Hey Bonnie, how's it goin'?"

Bonnie didn't bother to open her eyes. She knew that incredibly bright, cheery voice belonged to the woman voted most likely not to succeed—Lulu the fool. Lulu with the great body and superbly dyed platinum hair and the brains of a potato. Bonnie sighed, wondering why she always managed to choose pool time at the same instant Lulu was looking for company.

"Hello, Lulu," Bonnie murmured laconically, hoping the minimal effort put into her greeting would be enough of a hint for Lulu.

Bonnie wanted to just soak up the sun for a little while in peace before her appointment. True to form, Lulu missed the point. Bonnie felt the blonde fluttering about, adjusting her towel over the webbed lounge chair properly so she wouldn't have crisscrosses on her thighs, fussing with her suntan lotion, arranging her all too perfect coif.

"Well, I do declare we really seem to be on the same schedule these days don't we, Bon-Bon? Just every time I'm out here to work on my pitiful little tan I find you doing the same thing. I'm amazed that you don't just burn to a crisp, you know. Redheads are that way,

53

aren't they? For the most part? Isn't that true, Bonnie?"

Slowly Bonnie lifted her torso off the lounge chair and balanced on her elbow, forcing herself to look directly at Lulu. The other woman's eyes were saucer wide as she waited for an answer to one, or all, of her questions. Her lips were so highly glossed they looked like they might slide right off her face, but she still managed to smile with them. Bonnie smirked, liking the image of a lipless Lulu unable to speak because all she had was a huge expanse of skin where her mouth should be. Unfortunately, kindness reared its ugly head and Bonnie patiently explained her situation to the dim-witted blonde.

"I use a special lotion, Lulu. I come out here for the warmth and the quiet. Know what I mean?"

Bonnie offered a hard, gem-green stare that only made Lulu grin wider.

"Oh, don't I know it! Sometimes I get so tired of all the partying and auditioning and such that I think I'll just die if I don't get a little peace and quiet."

She leaned back on her lounge and began to slaver creamy lotion over her already perfect tan. The lotion smelled like coconuts, the sun felt hotter and Lulu was totally oblivious to the chill emanating from the woman beside her.

"Nothing like it, peace and quiet. I went to the mountains once with a friend of mine. Well, he really wasn't a friend if you know what I mean. He was like a business associate and, after that weekend, he put me in a bunch of commercials that paid the rent for at least a year. Anyway, we went to this really cute little cabin way up in the mountains—Arrowhead—like five thousand feet up, and I walked in the woods, and it was just dandy. But you know, right after lunch I kind of got the itch to come back to the city. After all, too much quiet is a bad thing, too. That guy made us stay two whole days in those mountains. Imagine that. . . ."

Bonnie didn't hear the rest of Lulu's enthralling story. Her towel bundled under her arm, she was halfway up the stairs to her apartment before Lulu even noticed she was gone. Bonnie didn't bother to stop when Lulu called to her.

Inside, behind her locked door, Bonnie tried to keep her anger in check. She could feel her back teeth grinding. Closing her eyes she made a concerted effort to relax. Wouldn't do to ruin her perfect face because she was unable to control a little annoyance now and again.

Stripping was a quick matter. One hook kept her tiny little top together. A flick of the wrist released her heavy breasts. Another liberated her from the confines of her itsy-bitsy bottoms. Bonnie was in the shower a second later washing off the lotion and her Lulu-inspired irritation.

While she toweled in her exquisitely appointed bathroom, while she dried her long, luxuriously waved hair, her fury returned, directed this time at the men in her life. Ben had been noticeably absent of late, calling at the last minute to beg off their dates. It had been over a month since he had brought her even the littlest bauble. If he'd been paying her way she would have starved. As it was, Bonnie Barber relied on him only for the extravagances in her life, as well as most of her business contacts.

The other gentleman who found himself on Bonnie's blacklist was Sy, her agent. Unfortunately, he called almost every day, and every day there was nothing for her except maybes, ifs, and possibilities. Since that damned sitcom went off the air a year earlier Bonnie had been reduced to a handful of guest spots and a few commercials.

Those gigs were hardly what she'd come to Los Angeles for. If she wanted mundane she'd still be living at home with her lush of a father in Sacramento or married to the boy next door pushing out babies every two years. The one thing Bonnie knew was that she was star material. She just couldn't figure out why everyone else didn't see it, too. After all, there was no one more accommodating in all of Hollywood than Bonnie Barber. And, to top it off, she had a good bit of talent, too.

Angrily Bonnie swathed on her makeup. The end result was flawless, but she used her pencils and brushes as though they were weapons. By the time Ben rang the bell she was dressed in her best: a see-through chiffon blouse, pockets strategically placed over her nipples, and finely tailored white slacks. She ignored her shoes as she went to answer the bell. At home Ben didn't like to feel as though she towered over him.

She opened the door ready to do battle. Yet instead of seeing his quickly failing middle-aged face, Bonnie was staring at a beautifully wrapped box held in a liver-spotted hand. Ben appeared a minute later, smiling sheepishly at her.

"Oh, Benny." Bonnie sighed, clutching his wrist as she pulled him into her apartment.

She offered him a dazzling smile and a quick peck on his cheek, her anger hardly forgotten only the corners blurred as she wrapped her long-nailed fingers around the box.

"For you, baby," he said.

Bonnie didn't notice the slight catch in his voice. She was already seated, tearing daintily at the silver blue wrapping.

"You shouldn't have, you sweetie," Bonnie purred before giving him a petulant look. "Of course you should. You've been so bad lately, you know that? I was beginning to think you didn't like me anymore. But oh, I was so wrong wasn't I? Oh . . . oh . . . Benny!"

Bonnie was honestly speechless now, holding up an exquisite necklace of gold and tourmaline. It wasn't the most expensive gift he had ever given her, but it certainly was the loveliest.

Anxiously she fumbled with the clasp, unable to get it open fast enough. Benny was there instantly, taking it from her hand and fixing it around her long neck. She waited for him to bend his head for a nuzzle, which she would turn into a terribly effortless seduction as a thank you. But he just stood behind her, his hands on her neck.

"I'm glad you like it," he said solemnly. "It's a going-away present. I can't see you anymore, Bonnie."

Deadly silence dropped over the room like an avalanche. Bonnie was aware of everything: the hard contour of her designer sofa, the gentle hum of the central air-conditioning and the pasty feel of Ben's hands on her skin. She pushed herself away from the sofa with great deliberation, turned and faced him. She was appalled to find he couldn't look her in the eye, but rather fixed his gaze on her huge, half-exposed breasts. What a worm he was! And she had slept with him! Still, if the situation could be salvaged she would have to do it.

"Why not, Benny?"

Bonnie's voice was peaches and cream. She was a great actress when she wanted to be. The only thing that betrayed her were her eyes. They seemed to flatten with her ire, deepening in color until they appeared to be great pools in which poor Benny might be swallowed whole.

"It's Suzanne." He shrugged his shoulders helplessly. "She saw the receipts for your coat and, well, I guess there were a couple of other things that made her suspicious. Aw, Bonnie, my wife means a lot to me. She's the mother of my children for God's sake, and I've got Samuel's Bar Mitzvah coming up. I sure don't want to make any waves before that. You know how it is, baby. Maybe we can just lay low for a while. I've got my family to think about and, well, you're young."

His voice brightened as he realized he might have hit upon an argument that would make sense to Bonnie. Of course he knew he didn't love her, but she had been one hell of a lay. The fact that he was also just a little bit scared of her had made the relationship just that much better. She was so tall. She was an Amazon. He would miss her. The thought of fondling his middle-aged wife for the next couple of months until things cooled down made him cringe. But Bonnie's eyes continued to flatten and deepen and he knew this line of reasoning was probably moot. Still, he went ahead with it.

"You don't want to be hanging around with an old fart like me for the next few years. There's a lot of great-looking studs out there, Bonnie. Bonnie?"

"I see, Benjamin. So to you this has been nothing more than a fling. You never had any intention of marrying me, or turning me into a star with your network. That's finally the truth, isn't it, Benjamin?"

Cold. Her voice was so cold. There was no reason to make any pretense of how she felt now. Ben was getting frantic, though. Having convinced himself that his gift would defray her anger, he was unprepared for the onslaught when she let loose.

"Well, no, in the beginning — that's not the truth. And besides, when the right project comes along you know you'll be first in line, baby."

"First in line? I wanted to be first, *period,* Benny. I've paid my dues. I gave you the best year of my life and for what? Baubles? I thought we had something here, Ben. I thought I meant something to you."

Methodically Bonnie spoke and moved at the same time, inching toward him around the sofa. Ben moved back. Bonnie saw beads of perspiration dotting his ever receding hair line. He blinked behind his glasses. His pants were cut so slim over his scrawny legs he didn't have pockets in which to shove his hands and hide their nervous tics. So he held them out toward her as though it would stop her progress.

"Don't be ridiculous," he objected, attempting to sound controlled. "You knew this didn't mean anything from the beginning. You used me the same way I used you."

"Is that so?" Bonnie laughed ruefully. "Well, I would say that you got the better end of the deal. I haven't exactly seen my career take off because of your extraordinary efforts on my behalf, have I, Benny? No." She was growling now, her voice coming from the very pit of her stomach. "In fact, I haven't seen much of anything from you except these half-assed gifts. And what have I given you? *Everything!* I waited here for you to come to me. I hung on your arm at every party we went to and made you look like a stud. I . . ." Bonnie turned her head away in disgust and lowered her voice. "I slept with you, Benjamin." Her head snapped toward him again. "I would say I've given you quite a lot, Benny, and I think a lawyer might just be able to do something with our little story. Maybe we could get a palimony suit going? How wonderful! I could have you served at your son's Bar Mitzvah. What do you say, Benny? Huh, how does that sound?"

Bonnie had backed the sorry little man into the door and he frantically grasped for the knob behind him. His face was pale with fury and horror. He had no idea whether she was joking or not. That, more than anything else, terrified him.

"You wouldn't dare. I'd make you look like the whore you are in court. I'd pull out all the stops. I've got the money. I've got the power."

"You've got shit, Benjamin, and without me you won't even have a good lay. Now get out of here. Now! Get out!"

Ben turned, grappling with the knob until finally the door flung open and he threw himself into the hallway. Behind him, as he hurried to the elevator, Bonnie ranted and raved. A few people poked their heads out their doors. Ben escaped into the elevator to the sound of applause from two of Bonnie's neighbors.

Prettily, Bonnie curtsied to her starlet neighbors, held up the necklace for them to see and went back into her apartment to begin planning her next step.

Half an hour later Sy called with news that lifted her spirits. She was scheduled for an interview at three o'clock.

Masters and King were looking for a hostess for

their new game show. It wasn't exactly the break of a lifetime, but it could offer the exposure she so desperately needed. Funny how Bonnie had done better in this town when everyone thought she was fifteen. Now that she was a ripe twenty-one she was actually having to work for a living.

Bonnie started to dress at one and was sitting in the lush lobby of Masters and King at exactly five minutes to three. When she was ushered into the inner sanctum it was Giles Masters, producer and host of the new show, who greeted her.

"Lovely. Simply lovely," he purred. "My mother had hair the exact shade of yours."

Bonnie looked directly at him, a glorious smile plastered on her face. "There are few people who truly appreciate red hair. I'm so glad you do."

The next few hours went very well, indeed. In fact, Giles Masters thought they should continue their discussions over dinner. Luckily, Bonnie was free.

Seven

Tess rented a car in Wichita and made the long drive to Andale alone, though any number of acquaintances would have picked her up at the airport. Andale was a small, intimate town, nestled cozily on the otherwise flat, forbidding land of Kansas. Many residents would have deemed it an honor to drive Tess to the farm, assist her with the funeral arrangements, talk to her long into the night so she didn't feel alone. But alone was exactly how Tess Canfield felt and she reveled in it. She wanted to feel the desolation, understand how much she had lost, and the only way to do that was in silence.

Miserably, though, the miles rolled under the wheels of the car without her remembering driving them. Tess found her thoughts moving to the past rather than focusing on the present. She remembered her mother's last letter, so warm and hopeful for the year ahead. Her mother always found it easier to be close through the written word rather than the spoken one. She thought of her father as they sat at the kitchen table last summer discussing her hopes for the future, laughing at his vain attempt to grow azaleas when he was so adept at growing wheat.

She forced herself to concentrate as she pulled the car off the road when she finally reached the house. For a few moments, as dust settled around her, Tess considered her home.

The huge house stood empty, the white clapboard appearing to be newly painted. The curtains were drawn as though her mother hadn't managed to get out of bed that day and open them. The barn was closed. In their pen, the pigs moved about slowly. To the north Tess saw the silos standing guard over all the farms in the area. Her father's wheat was stored there every year awaiting sale. His beautiful, beautiful wheat.

Without thinking Tess flipped the door handle and slid out of the car. Kansas was pleasant that day. A soft late June sun warmed the land and made everything look ochre. But even in the gentle day Tess felt something was wrong. Something was just a little out of place.

Slowly she walked away from the car, passing the house, the barn and the pens until she stood in front of the field. Stretching in front of her were the acres and acres of land her father had so lovingly tended year after year. So many acres, added to with care until Tess no longer knew how much land belonged to the Canfields.

It was then, as she contemplated the horizon, Tess knew what was wrong. It was June and the wheat was completely harvested. She was looking at miles and miles of stubble. Pa wouldn't have finished until the first part of July if he had lived to harvest the full crop.

Tears burned the back of her eyes, then fell silently over her cheeks. There was no reason to stop them, no one to see. Her hair felt heavy against her neck. Inside her skin, her soul was ripping, cut in two as cleanly as the wheat had been taken from the field.

In one fluid movement Tess collapsed, falling to her knees at the edge of the field. Forlornly her hands reached out, trembling just above the earth, then falling to the hard stubble. She caressed it, feeling the daggerlike shafts bite into the soft skin of her hands. Frantically they moved over the ground as though she could wash away the reminder of how her father had been hurt, why her parents had been in that helicopter. It was the wheat that killed them. The wheat they slaved for had taken their lives.

From somewhere far away she heard a terrible cry, like the squawking of a hundred blackbirds shattering the warm sky into a million shards of blue and white. It wasn't until she felt two strong hands lifting her from the dust, felt two strong arms about her gathering her into the safety of a man's tall, barrel-chested frame that she realized the cries were her own keening—the sounds those of her deepest grief.

"It's okay, Tess, it's okay. Come on inside now. We've got some talkin' to do."

"Thanks."

Tess smiled weakly, accepting the steaming cup of tea that was offered. Still, she couldn't look at the huge man who so graciously cared for her in the kitchen of her own home. She was ashamed he had found her like that, rutting in the earth like a starving animal. Her father wouldn't have wanted her to grieve so desperately; certainly her mother wouldn't have appreciated her emotional display. But Tess

64

could no more have helped crying out in pain than she could now help feeling shell-empty. So empty in fact that she hadn't the strength to lift the cup to her lips.

"Drink it, Tess. It will do you a world of good. Haven't known a farm girl yet who couldn't get her head together with a little hot tea."

Tess raised her sad eyes and finally smiled weakly. "You're a good friend, Charlie. Always have been. Pa would have been grateful. How'd you know I'd be here?"

"Didn't."

He pulled out a chair, turned it around and straddled it. His thighs were huge and strained against the worn denim of his jeans. Tess never could figure out how a man who worked as hard as Charlie did could retain such a bulk. He pulled a little at his full, dark beard, then tipped his hat back on his head.

"You know I've always been a persistent cuss. I just kept comin' by to check. Knew you'd show up sooner than later. Wish'd you'd called. Me or Carrie would have come to get you at the airport."

Tess shook her head. "I wanted to come alone. It was important to me."

"Yep. Well, there's something to be said for that. Did you have a nice flight?"

Tess sought refuge in her tea now. She had no desire to share what had happened on the plane with anyone, sure that it was only a temporary aberration. How could she tell this man that from the moment she reached the airport a deathly fear held her heart in a vise? The instant the plane's wheels left the ground she wanted to scream, sure that she would be the next Canfield to die as her airborne vehicle

65

crashed to the earth. Tess closed her eyes, trying to shut out the horror she had felt and the guilt she still felt for surviving.

"It was fine, Charlie. How's Carrie?"

"Just fine. Saddened by what happened to your ma and pa. Everybody is. We was all right fond of 'em, you know."

"I know, Charlie," Tess said softly, letting her eyes wander toward the window. She considered the field for a bit. "You've been busy. I guess it was you who brought the farmers together to finish cutting the crop. I remember when we did that for old man Hanson's wife after he died. Nothing finer than the farmers giving their time to help someone in need. Is everything stored now?"

"Yep. Good crop this year. Harv knew that. He was counting on it."

Charlie let his voice slide away since he couldn't look at Tess anymore without telling her everything. They, all the farmers around, had drawn straws and he had lost. He was the one who had to give her the news. He wished it had fallen to someone else. He wished he could think of something else to talk about so he could put off the other.

"Tess . . ."

"Are they . . ."

They both spoke together. Charlie nodded her way, relieved that this wasn't going to be the moment to have his heart to heart with her.

"Sorry. I just wanted to know where they are? Still in Wichita?"

"Yeah. Got 'em there till you tell us what you want done. I told the priest. Figured you'd want him kind of standin' by. He says anytime. He can have the rosary anytime. The burial, too. Do you know if they got plots?"

Tess shook her head. "No, they don't. They wanted to be buried right here. I don't know if that will be okay since I don't plan on working the farm. Thought I'd rent it out. But they really wanted to be right here . . ."

Tess's voice broke, her hand rose to cradle her head. She sobbed gently into it. Charlie reached out, and touched the top of her silvery head wishing he had brought Carrie with him. He felt like a damned fool when a woman cried. Tess shook her head and raised dry eyes to him, forcing herself to calm.

"Sorry."

"No, hey, it's okay. But, Tess, there's things you got to know. I hate to be the one. Hate to tell you now. But you can't bury your parents here."

"I didn't think so. I mean, I knew there had to be some kind of law about it. It was just a thought. You know how Pa would have loved that."

"It's not that, honey. It ain't that it's illegal. It's just that the farm ain't goin' to belong to you no more. You understand?"

"What?" Tess breathed. "No, I don't understand at all."

"Didn't think you would." Charlie slid off his chair and moved around the kitchen, touching a thing or two now and again. He didn't look at Tess. How could he? "Your pa, Tess, he was in about the same boat most farmers were back a few years ago when they lost their farms. Carter did us in, ya know. Harv took out some high-interest loans to buy those hundred acres from Jessica Dalton and another two hundred from old man Miller. Wheat prices were high then. Everything was going great so we figured no problem paying back them loans. Then wheat prices fell, and we was stuck with twenty percent interest on our land. It was no good. Most everybody who had them loans went under. Your pa, though, he was a pretty smart cookie. He managed to make his payments. Oh, he'd have a really tough year now and again but he'd make up for it. You never knew, did you?"

Tess shook her head vehemently, thinking how hard it must have been for her parents to send her the small allowance every month for books. And how did they pay her board? Why hadn't they said anything?

"Now don't go blamin' yourself for goin' off to school. Your ma and pa was so proud of you they would have worked three lifetimes to make sure you got the best education. That's how much they loved you. But, Tess, you can't make the payments. Even if you could work the farm by yourself I don't see how'd you'd carry on with the book work . . ."

"I'll give it up. Give up my studies," she protested.

"Don't be an idiot, Tess. You think your pa would want you to do that? Besides, you're no farmer. I know'd that the minute you was born. Just look at you. You even lost the callouses on your hands."

Tess turned her palms up. He was right. In three years her body had softened, rounding itself to the hours sitting behind easels, painting her fantasies. She hadn't been in a field working under the glaring sun for so long. She couldn't do it. Nor, if she were honest, did she want to.

"You're right Charlie. So I guess I'll just have to sell. I'll put the money to good use, though, I promise. I won't fritter it away. I'll use it just as my parents would want."

"Tess," Charlie broke in angrily, "haven't you been listening to what I've been tellin' you?"

Softening when he saw her face fall at his reprimand, Charlie was immediately ashamed. He came close to the table, using it to balance himself as he hunched down next to her. "I'm sorry, baby, but there just won't be nothin' left. You're gonna have to auction this place fast as you can to keep 'em from takin' it from you. Maybe even the stuff in the house. You gotta settle those loans if you want to have anything at all for yourself."

After a long while she said, "I see. When will all this happen?"

"Can you stay for the summer?"

Tess thought about her tests, time lost, money even tighter than before, of the painting she had left half finished in the campus studio.

"Of course I can stay," she answered without remorse.

She was, after all, her father's daughter—and her mother's.

Mostly there were serious buyers milling around the Canfield farm as the auctioneer went about his business. There were also some curiosity seekers, a couple of kids who were resting after their bike ride brought them to this point. There were also two people from the Federal Land Bank auditing the sale, making sure dissolution of the farm would result in full repayment of the loans and cover the interest. They were both women. Somehow that made Tess feel worse. It was okay when men had to be hard and calculating. Women should be sympathetic. Neither of these ladies seemed to understand that.

Tess sat on the tractor watching the proceedings. The tractor had been auctioned first thing so she didn't have to worry about people coming up to look it over. In the house she packed four boxes of mementos: her mother's favorite quilt, family photo albums, the dishes, her father's fishing rod. There wasn't much else of sentimental value. Her mother never kept things around that weren't useful. Now, though, Tess realized her parents had never been able to afford anything other than useful items.

There was also the suitcase Tess found hidden away in the attic. Opening it she found her mother's wedding dress. A simple dress of white cotton that had been lovingly embroidered about the hem and the edge of the veil. Inside the case was also a wedding picture. Her mother had actually been lovely before the years of hard farm work wore away her innocence and her preoccupation with looking attractive for her husband who was often too tired to notice her appearance.

Tess cried over that dress, shamed she should have thought her mother devoid of feminine feeling. For the dress was beautifully preserved, the tissue paper wrapping obviously new. She wondered how often her mother had climbed the attic stairs to hold that dress in her roughened hands, to think about her wedding day. Now she would never know the answer. So much was left unsaid.

Tess put it aside and would take it with her. One day, perhaps, she would be married in it. One day she would love someone enough to live with them and die with them. She only hoped she was as lucky as her

70

mother had been.

"How's it going?" Charlie was beside her, his voice pulling her back to the present. She blinked.

"Fine. I think I'm doing a lot better, Charlie. I see that there was nothing to be done here. This was the only choice. I've let go. No more guilt."

"Good girl. Listen, I didn't tell you how pretty that service was you had for your parents. Right nice. Everybody said so."

"Thanks. I think it was how they would have wanted things," Tess answered. "Did I thank Carrie for all the help afterward? I think we fed the entire town that day."

"We did. But you gotta remember we still only got a hundred twenty in Andale. Ain't much of a place for anybody 'cept those who love it."

"I know. I always thought it was sad the whole world didn't get a chance to live in a place like this just once in their lives."

"If they did there wouldn't be places like this no more. We'd be just like Los Angeles," Charlie remarked, chuckling.

"Guess you're right. I'm lucky I've had both."

"Which one you gonna keep, Tess? You gonna stay here with us?"

Tess shook her head, her hand touching Charlie's broad shoulder. "No. I've been gone too long. You've been awful kind, Charlie, a good friend. But I don't have a future here."

"You got such fine friends in California?"

"No," she answered thoughtfully. "Actually I don't. I never got too close to anyone. In my head I always saw myself somewhere else. This was home, but I would live — somewhere else. Guess I should have paid more attention to the people I went to school with. I just didn't think I'd need them. Still, I've got to go back. My scholarship will last me another year. It's important. I've got to have that degree."

"That's wise. Just remember. You ever need us, we're all here for you. Won't be the same, you know, without the Canfields around."

"It better not be." Tess chuckled sadly. "Besides, I'll be back. I'm sure of it. I can't imagine that my life would change so much I'd forget my home. I'll be back, Charlie."

Beside her he nodded. They both let their eyes fasten on the auctioneer. They listened to the fast talk and watched the furious bidding for the fine land Harv and Mildred Canfield had tended. But Charlie and Tess both heard her promise again and again in their minds and they both believed it. She would be back. Someday.

Eight

"Christ almighty," Davina muttered under her breath. "I never knew she had so much junk."

It was July and hotter than Hades in the small apartment on K Street. Davina had laid her mother to rest over a month ago in an inexpensive plot graced with a small, cheap cross that bore her name and the date of her death. There had been no ceremony.

Davina hadn't the foggiest idea if her mother harbored any religious convictions since she couldn't remember being taken to church or discussing the spiritual mysteries of the world. She also didn't want to have to pay a minister. Davina had been paying for her mother's crutches for so long she wasn't about to lay out for one more. Angelica had given her nothing but grief in life—the hell if Davina was going to go into debt just because she died.

Of course those feelings weren't Davina's initial ones when she found her mother, bloated from her overdose, contorted in death on her bed. Shock. That was the first. She was so shocked that her mother had the guts to do something like that, that Davina stood in the doorway looking at the body for what seemed like hours.

Anger. That was next. How could she have done that

in their apartment? If the woman had any common decency she would have gone away from home, let someone else find her and clean up the mess. Davina knew it was the last slap in the face her mother could offer her.

Pain. Surprisingly, she felt pain at her mother's passing. That emotion, the sadness, surprised her. They had been at odds from the moment Davina had been born. Mother and daughter had tormented one another to the point of psychological destruction, yet there was Davina feeling sorrowful, actually crying over her mother's body.

As much as she hated to admit it, there had been good times before she learned to despise her mother. Like the time they went shopping, ignoring the rent that was overdue, splurging on matching gingham dresses. They had lunch at a real restaurant. Not a cafeteria. Davina remembered that day.

She remembered a night, too. How old had she been? Ten? Twelve? Her mother came into her room. Davina pretended to be asleep. She didn't want to hear any more bad words. She didn't want to be hit. She had closed her eyes tight and felt her mother come toward her bed, standing beside it for what seemed an eternity. She had even felt her mother's hand move, so she steeled herself for the blow. Instead, Angelica stroked her hair, whispered something soft. Davina remembered that, wished for a moment like that again, wondered if anyone would ever touch her with love once more.

But she dismissed it all: pain, anger, and shock were gone because Davina made it that way. She, after all, had to go on. There was no one to help her now. Allway Insurance had even threatened to dock her if she took off the whole day for the funeral. In spite Davina had stayed away. They didn't cut her pay. People could be made to feel responsible if you pushed them to the limit.

Now, though, everything was back to normal. She went to work. She sweated in the oppressive summer heat. Davina went to a movie every once in a while and paid the bills and did her wash. Her mother's memory faded faster than Davina could destroy it. Unfortunately, it wasn't completely gone and wouldn't be until Angelica's room was cleaned out, her things given away.

This was the Saturday Davina had chosen to take on the task. Normally she could have simply tossed everything into a box and set it out for the Salvation Army. On the off chance that her mother had hidden something of value all these years, though, Davina decided to go through her belongings piece by piece.

Settling herself on the floor in front of the dresser she put her Scotch and water beside her on the right. On the left was an empty box.

The first drawer yielded nothing but yellowing underwear. In the second were a few sweaters, a box of costume jewelry and a ticket to the theater. Davina wondered when her mother had found time to sit through a three-hour live performance. Then she wondered where she found the money for the ticket.

In the last drawer there were stockings, scarves, and even a diaphragm. Davina laughed. Her mother had been attractive once, she knew, but the thought that she would ever need a diaphragm was actually comical. Everything was dumped into the box. Let the Salvation Army have a giggle, too, she decided.

The bedside table yielded only trash: a paperback novel, half-consumed prescription drugs used to try and make her mother's mind healthy. None of them worked. These were dumped in a trash bag. The closet

75

looked almost bare; Angelica's wardrobe had been no better off than Davina's. Davina felt a twinge of regret. Had she really neglected the woman or was it that they simply didn't have the money for extravagances like clothes? She checked in all the pockets, found nothing, then folded the clothes into the box. Shoes were the next to go. Funny how her mother kept her shoes so neat, all stacked in the original boxes. One by one Davina tossed the shoe boxes toward the bigger one, giving a little yelp every time she made a basket. One, two, three boxes.

The fourth was almost airborne when Davina checked herself. This one was weighted wrong. Shoes didn't feel like this. Grasping it with both hands Davina sat on her heels and pulled it into her lap. Briefly she closed her eyes, said a quick prayer that she was about to uncover a secret money stash, then pulled off the lid.

At first glance Davina's heart fell. It was a second before her curiosity took over. She settled herself more comfortably, taking things out of the box one by one and laying them in a neat row.

Photos. There were so many photos. The woman, of course, was her mother. Gorgeous in her short-skirted dress. Even her funny wide-brimmed hat did nothing to take away from her flawless beauty.

She was smiling, not at the camera, but at the man whose arm was wrapped about her waist. He was so handsome even though he didn't smile. A beret was cocked on his head, he wore a uniform and, most terribly, he looked familiar, as if Davina should know who he was. She had the creepy feeling she'd seen him often, his face peeking out at her from somewhere.

She piled the photographs, all taken at the same place, her mother wearing the same dress, and put them aside. Davina could just hear her mother insisting that the photographer keep snapping away. Her mother had been crazy even then, she was sure.

There were other things, too. A cheap heart and chain, the gold leaf flaking off. Davina turned it in her fingers. There was no inscription. A plain gold band. A wedding ring? Davina tossed it onto the rug. Letters came next. Not many, but enough. They had all been written by Angelica—written, but never sent. Thoughtfully Davina read them, her mother's sickness evident in every word.

Dear Noel, they all began, *I know you probably don't care if you ever hear from me again.*
. . . I know you won't want to hear this. . . . I'm pregnant.
. . . How dare you not write . . .
. . . I'm taking the baby . . .
. . . This is the last letter. If you don't respond you'll never see your daughter . . .

Then there were no more letters. Quickly, Davina went back to the envelopes. There were no postmarks, no stamps. Each one was addressed to the same man, in care of the army. The same man. Her father.

Frantically, now, she dug through the box. There wasn't much left. Letters from him declaring his love for her, each signed in a bold hand. Then the unbelievable—a marriage license. Her mother had married her father. She was not a bastard as she had been told. Now Davina wondered if, indeed, she had been abandoned? Had her father really left, not caring what became of them?

Of course he had. Her mother had become too sick for him to deal with any longer, so he left her. It must

77

have been easy for him. He was in the army, moving around, probably in Vietnam. Of course he abandoned them. After all, there must have been letters her mother sent, letters he received and ignored, so she took to writing letters she never mailed. Angelica saved herself from more rejection, more hurt and vented her anger at the same time.

Amazed, Davina picked up the last two pieces of yellowing paper. A marriage license. A birth certificate. Divorce papers. The same names on each one. The names of her mother and her father. "Damn," Davina muttered. "Damn, damn, damn."

Without thinking she picked up the glass and threw it across the room. The cheap glass shattered, spraying shards everywhere, making the room stink of liquor. She felt hot tears springing to her eyes, but fought them back. After all, this time he wasn't worth the effort of crying. She was a woman on her own, after all. Davina had cared for her mother when he didn't. How dare she even think of weeping for the bastard. No wonder her mother's frail mind had snapped, left alone with a baby daughter, abandoned by the man she loved.

Suddenly Davina's mental railing stopped. It was as though an explosion ignited her brain, stopping every thought with its intensity. Then, as the fireball of realization cleared and she saw through the haze, Davina rose slowly and carefully. She stood in the center of the room, looking down at the picture of her mother and father for an instant. The name on the marriage license, the birth certificate . . . the magazine.

She rushed from the room to the table just beside the couch where she kept all her magazines. Frantically, she leafed through them, tossing them aside one by one until she found what she wanted. When she did, her amazement was so complete Davina sat down heavily on the couch and stared for hours at the photograph. Her mother had not been lying. The man was rich, living like a king. Davina stared at the picture. It was him, only older and better looking. It was him. Her father.

There wasn't much to do before she left. The apartment was furnished so Davina simply gave her notice. Her job was of little consequence — especially now — so Davina left the same day she told Allway she didn't need their stupid job anymore. Her savings account was minimal. She transferred it into her checking account knowing that soon she would have little need for such a paltry sum. Davina went shopping and bought a far too expensive outfit, packing it neatly away in her one suitcase until it was needed.

Now it was the end of July, and Davina was pulling her sorry-looking car up to the curb on Beverly Glen, parking it in front of a gated home that was one of the most beautiful she had ever seen.

She had been to his office and was turned away three times with the excuse he never saw anyone without an appointment. She left a note with the number of her hotel on it, then waited by the phone for a call that never came. Davina didn't know his well-meaning secretary read the note and discarded it.

Money running out, Davina decided on desperate measures. She waited in the lobby of the building that bore his name. She watched. She counted the minutes and then she saw him. He walked past her. She smelled his after-shave, saw his beautifully cut clothes and his hair as black as hers with just a hint of wave that had translated into her halo of curls through the genetic process. She had followed his chauffeur-driven limousine to this house not once, but twice.

Now, as the day faded and a light breeze blew through this rarified neighborhood, she waited again. Today she would not be stopped.

His car pulled up to the electronic gate at exactly seven o'clock. She was out of hers before the gate pulled back far enough to allow his car to slip in.

The driver had seen Davina coming, but wasn't fast enough to stop her. He was only half out of the car when she reached the passenger door and yanked it open. The black-eyed man inside turned toward her looking neither astonished nor angered, but Davina's matching eyes glared at him. She opened her full lips and the words, so long practiced and perfected in their sophistication, fell from them in a furious torrent.

"You bastard. You left my mother, and she killed herself. You're my father, and damned if you're not going to pay for leaving her and me!"

Nine

"Oh, Giles, I don't think we should do this. Giles . . ."

Bonnie's head fell back with studied perfection: just far enough so her suitor could nestle his lips in the curve of her throat, far enough so her thick hair fell almost to her waist yet not far enough to force her lovely breasts into his chest. That would make Giles think she was ready to do the dirty deed without a bit more incentive. Coyly, Bonnie laid her hands on his chest as though to push him away, making absolutely sure there seemed to be no strength in them.

She had led Giles Masters on for a month now, carefully choreographing her seduction, rousing him to a state where the only thing he could think about was her. Naturally there was a method to Bonnie's madness. After all, he was a rather attractive older man, and hopping in the sack with him would be as pleasurable for her as it would be for him, she was sure. But she wanted his infatuation to last. Landing the job as hostess on the new game show had taken little effort since Giles's lust was instantly evident.

But, for the first time in her life, Bonnie knew restraint would buy her more than immediate surrender.

There was, of course, the off chance Giles Masters already knew about her less than sterling reputation. The television industry, after all, was an intimate little trade and people talked. Bonnie, though, was willing to take the chance that her modest act wouldn't be detected. That was the kind of attitude a class act like Giles would understand and appreciate. Not to mention the way the poor guy wore his emotions on his face the way other people lit up a smile on cue.

If Bonnie could keep him enamored, millions of viewers would see his adoration of her every day of the week; if Giles Masters was in love with her they would be, too. The camera was such a valuable friend when one knew how to use it.

Bonnie felt Giles's hand shoot from her waist, landing square on her rear end as he pulled her anxiously to him, effectively curtailing her planning. The size of his erection not only impressed her, but threw her into gear. Though her mind was still working clearly enough to murmur a lifeless "wait," her body refused to be denied.

There, in Giles's gorgeous mint green and white office, Bonnie succumbed. A month was a very long time, to say the least. With delightful abandon she relinquished herself to him. Giles, to his credit, was quick both on the uptake and with his hands. He stripped Bonnie's clothes off with little regard for the fine workmanship, gave her milky skin a quick once over with his hands, then pushed her away and looked at her—inch by delicious inch.

On cue Bonnie let a ripple of desire course

through her body, her eyes latching on to his, her lips parting with a quiver.

"I know it's not right. We're colleagues. We'll be working together," she whispered, "but God help me, I want you Giles."

"That's all I needed to hear, my dear," he whispered back.

Bonnie almost laughed. She loved this part of the game: the heartfelt confessions, the ruddiness of flesh in the ready, muscles tensing for what really was a most ludicrous act. Trouble was, no one appreciated her finesse when it came to the subtleties.

Giles's hands still on her waist, Bonnie slowly raised her arms, pulling her fingertips up over her taut stomach as she caressed her body. She hesitated when her fingertips reached her breasts, a girlishly shy gesture. Then, just before Bonnie unhooked her bra, she sighed.

"For you, Giles, only for you."

The timing was perfect. As the last syllable faded away, the phone rang and her lush breasts fell from the wisp of peach silk that held them in abeyance. Giles groaned, almost falling forward into her ivory orbs, his lips searching for her nipples as hungrily as a newborn babe.

They collapsed onto the lush carpeting in a tangle of clothes and arms and legs until finally, with a cry of triumph from Giles and a squeal of joy from Bonnie, the act was complete, their partnership sealed—at least for the duration of the show. Thankfully the phone had stopped ringing.

"Bonnie, Bonnie, such a perfect name for you. You are a joy," Giles muttered as he lay sprawled across her.

Bonnie's physical automatic pilot took over as programmed. Her long-nailed fingers on one hand entwined themselves in his damp hair; the other five fingertips raked over his bare back. He was not as tight sans clothing as he appeared when impeccably dressed. That was okay with her. After all, the guy was probably forty-five, maybe even fifty-five, if he was a day. All her energy was now being concentrated on mental gymnastics. She thought of the pros and cons, gauged the possibility of success, then jumped right in.

"It was a wonderful experience, Giles," she said softly, just a hint of a smile in her voice. Bonnie never let her voice grin, otherwise her conquest of the moment might become too content with his prowess. "I can't believe how good we are together. I mean, I think we've found more than physical compatibility here, don't you?"

Giles nodded against her rib cage, then used his index finger to wind little circles around her belly button. Bonnie hated that. She wasn't crazy about the quality of his office carpeting, either, but she would put up with both.

"I knew you'd agree. I think we've realized that we have the perfect chemistry to make *Table Top* one of the hottest game shows around. Not that the concept isn't enough to shoot it right to the top, of course," Bonnie added hurriedly, "but you and I, together, I think we'll be giving viewers something they've been looking for for a long time. Chemistry, Giles. Such incredible feeling between us. I think we could be, you know, like the next Burns and Allen. Oh, Giles, it's almost too fascinating to consider."

Bonnie let her voice rise to a triumphant call, then trail off, allowing Giles to take time to consider what she'd said. Of course, if he showed the slightest indication that he didn't like the idea, Bonnie was prepared with a quick and self-effacing retraction. Luckily, though Giles's ego was big, he was also a good businessman.

"You may have something there, Bonnie. People like us come along maybe two, three times in a lifetime. We could parlay this into something really unusual in the game-show business."

Giles sat up. Bonnie noticed his back was hairier than she had at first realized. Not much she could do about that except not look at it. She sat up, too, nuzzling her bare body into his. He still had his socks on. She closed her eyes and listened to his voice.

"Yeah, we'd kind of be the Johnny Carson of game shows. It's different. Really unique. And I know you can carry it off." He tweeked her bottom, giving her a vote of confidence. "Not only are you gorgeous and intelligent, you've got a great voice. It will work."

"What exactly, Giles?" Bonnie purred. "What do you have in that fantastic mind of yours?"

"Well, let's see." His arm came over her shoulder and his hand fondled one of her breasts as though that would help gel his idea. "I think we should model it on the Carson thing, you know. You could be my Ed McMahon."

"How silly." Bonnie giggled, masking her feeling of victory. "I don't look a thing like him. Tell me more."

"We could start each show with a little monologue. Let the people really get a feel for our personalities. I'll have Jack, the head writer, do us up some scripts so that we really are identifiable. I don't want either of us to just be a pretty face on this one. So we'll do this little monologue thing, then we'll do some camera stuff. You know, let the camera linger on you, on us, so that the viewers get the feeling that we're kind of a family. Jesus, Bonnie, I think it will work. Our first time screwing and already my mind is like crystal clear. I can see it. It's a winner."

"Oh, Giles, you are a genius," Bonnie purred as she wrapped her arms about his chest, her legs about his hips and rolled herself on top of him.

This, she decided, was going to be a piece of cake.

*Part Three
December 1989*

Ten

Tess sat on a low stool, bent into a pretzel position that would have pained her if she realized how long she'd been like that. As it was, she was oblivious both to the time and the physical discomfort, too intent on her work to care about anything other than meticulously cleaning the lips of the angel that had been painted on the wall so many centuries ago.

"You're doing a fine job."

A soft yet deeply masculine voice startled her. The brush slipped, creating a hairline smudge on the angel's full cheek. Angrily, Tess turned toward the voice, blue eyes blazing, a reprimand at the ready.

"How could you do something like that! This is difficult, you know. I was told no one was going to be allowed in here while I'm working. So I would suggest, if you don't want me to report you to the lady of the house, you get back to your work and let me do mine." Tess flipped her head back to the wall and straightened her back as she muttered to herself, "Never disturb an artist at work. It's the worst thing you could do, interrupting my concentration that way."

Carefully, she dipped her fine brush into the clear cleaning solution, then leaned forward again, hoping to rectify the damage that had been done before the smudge on the cherub's cheek dried. Just as Tess was about to apply the brush again she caught sight of movement from the corner of her eye and saw the man's feet clad in scuffed loafers plant themselves beside her chair.

"I thought I told you that I would report you to Mrs. Cudahy," she threatened angrily, "so get out of here. My work has to be complete in time for the Christmas party, and I assume yours does, too. So if you don't want her to come down on you, not only for disturbing me, but for neglecting your own work, I suggest you take off."

"I'm finished with my work," the man said merrily.

Tess sighed with great patience and flicked her eyes toward him. He was terribly handsome despite his unkempt appearance. His fawn-colored hair fell over an exquisitely broad forehead. In fact, in an artist's eye, he was chiseled beyond perfection. Quite like the Greek statues she had studied. Tess felt the tips of her lips rising as she realized her schooling made her tend to view people through the eyes of someone who would recreate them. Instead, she scowled.

"Well, isn't that just dandy you're all done," she quipped sarcastically. "So leave me to finish mine. It's late, and I've still got a lot to do. If you're finished go home and relax there."

"Well," he said thoughtfully as he crossed his legs and sat on the cold marble floor, "that is exactly what I'd hoped to do. Relax at home, I mean. But I am home and my castle is filled with people like you renovating it from top to bottom so my wife can show it off at the incredible Christmas party she's planned. So you see," he shrugged disarmingly, "I haven't anywhere else to go. Except the club." Tess saw his eyes cloud with what she thought was pain. "And I spend too much time there as it is. My children are away. My wife is busy with one charity or another and the cook is off. Now, perhaps you could suggest a room that isn't occupied by any number of artists plying their trade? If you could, I'll gladly go there. I'm always being told what to do when I'm home, so why should today be any different?"

While he spoke Tess felt her head hang lower and lower. How could she have spoken so horribly? This was Royal Cudahy. Hadn't she seen enough pictures of him strewn about this huge estate to recognize him? But he looked so different in those pictures: forbidding, aloof, cold.

The man sitting beside her, actually beneath her since she was on her folding stool, looked more like an absentminded master of an English boys' school.

"I'm so sorry. I apologize. I-I-I had no idea," she stuttered.

"Don't be silly." He waved his hand about as though her ill humor was of so little consequence as to be unworthy of notice. "I think it's wonderful that you take your work so seriously. I like to believe that when I spend enormous amounts of money I'm actually getting something for it."

"Oh, you are, I promise. I've been working on this frieze for four months now. It's exquisite. I wouldn't do anything other than my finest work," Tess assured him, still unable to look him in the eye. He seemed to sense her chagrin, offering her the moment she needed to recover herself.

"I haven't been here for as many months. Business."

Tess wondered why he thought that clarification was necessary. She didn't ask.

He was smiling now. "What exactly are you doing?"

"I'm ashamed to admit it after all my talk of disturbing an artist, but all I'm really doing is cleaning. I'm carefully taking away all the dirt and grime that collected on these walls over the years. More than likely, when you purchased this estate the frieze looked perfectly fine. To the uneducated eye it would look quite lovely. But, as you can see, if I work very carefully, I can pull away the years and beneath what once was a sky that appeared to be almost gray in color we find that the artist actually meant to have a bright blue sky. The cherubs' lips are a stunning red, and their hair a bright yellow, not a dull gold. You see?"

Tess warmed to her subject so fully she forgot her earlier embarrassment and turned her dancing eyes toward Royal Cudahy. He smiled back at her, but his expression said that he was more than simply pleased with her work. Tess, looking only for his appreciation of the project, didn't see the depth of his interest in her.

"Yes, I do see. I see that blue eyes can be extremely bright," he whispered, then grinned. "On the cherubs, I mean."

Royal looked toward the wall.

"They're cute little things, aren't they? You know, I hate to admit it, but I didn't even know this room existed when we bought this house. In fact, I didn't really see the house until the day we moved in. My wife fell in love with it. I thought it was a bit much."

"It certainly is large," Tess agreed, "and if you can afford to give it the care it deserves you're really living in a piece of history. Think of how marvelous that is, to be the custodian of history. Pasadena has some of the most marvelous old homes and this is the best I've seen. A true Tuscany villa right here in the middle of southern California. I understand it was brought over stone by stone. How marvelous."

"Yes, actually, I suppose it is incredible. I never really thought about it. Actually, the thought that struck me at the time we bought the place was I had just spent a good deal of money for a home that seemed cold, and so large you'd never be able to find your family. But then my family isn't around long enough to find anyway. This seems like an odd sort of room to me. Do you know what it is?"

"Certainly. It's an atelier. Originally meant for an artist's studio. I suppose whatever great man had this home built probably had an artist in residence. You have so many fine murals that there would have to be an artist not only to paint them but to keep them up. It would be wonderful if those days still existed," she added wistfully.

"Sounds like I'm talking to someone with the soul of a true artist?"

Tess didn't hear the teasing note in his voice, she only heard the truth of what he said.

"And the heart and the mind," she murmured before brightening. "But not the financing. I'm afraid these days it's tough to make it in the art world unless you have enough to eat and a place to sleep. Nobody's going to be your patron unless you've already got a good start."

"Art patron? Now there's an interesting career. I must look into it — sometime. Right now it's after seven, and I haven't had a thing to eat. I'll bet you haven't, either. How about some dinner? You can get right back to this. I'd hate to have you pass out in my atelier. In this place you wouldn't be found for years. Wouldn't it be a shame to die for your art?"

Tess laughed. "But I couldn't intrude on your family time."

"You must be joking. I already told you, everyone is out for the evening. Even the cook. I think one of the gardeners might still be here, but he can't cook worth beans. I, on the other hand, remember my salad days quite well. In fact, I believe I could whip up something that would give you the sustenance you need. What do you say?"

Tess cocked her head and really looked at him. He seemed so young and gentle. It was hard to imagine him as the uncompromising attorney she had heard he was. He seemed to actually be pleading with her to stay with him a while. Royal Cudahy appeared, well, lonely. It was the one human frailty Tess could succumb to with ease. She was as lonely as any human being could be.

"I'd like that. But I also think I better take care of this little guy's face." She pointed her brush to the smudged cherub. "After that I'll join you. About forty-five minutes?"

"I can hardly wait. I want to hear all about the world of art. Who knows, there might be a tax deduction in it all and I sure could use it these days."

Royal unwound his tall frame and stood up, towering over Tess. For an instant she had the sensation he was more powerful than she could ever imagine. Here, she determined, was a man who got exactly what he wanted out of life. Then he smiled in that disarming, almost childish, way and was gone. She returned to her work with a smile on her lips and a perplexing, surprising wrinkle on her brow.

By the time Tess made it to the kitchen it was well past eight-thirty. She flew into the imposing room with an apology ready.

"I'm so sorry, I hadn't realized how fast the time was going. I hope I haven't ruined your dinner."

"Not at all. Sit. I've kept everything warm."

Royal was at the stove, a huge white towel wrapped

94

charmingly about his waist. Tess couldn't take her eyes off him as she slid into a high-backed wooden chair.

"You should have called me. I would have stopped," she insisted.

"First, I don't walk any further than I have to in this house, and secondly I didn't want to disturb you again. I could see how important the work was to you."

"I suppose," Tess answered, snapping her napkin open as he brought two plates to the table. "How lovely. A peasant feast!"

"Didn't I tell you I could do magic in the kitchen? Chicken in tomatoes—quick and easy—a hunk of bread with real butter, and a tall glass of milk. That'll keep you going."

"I should say! I haven't eaten a real meal like this in ages."

"You should stop paying so much attention to your work."

"Oh, it's not really that," Tess answered, picking up her fork, letting it hover over her plate.

In the warmth of the kitchen with the quiet all around, Tess forgot she was speaking to a very wealthy man. Instead, she remembered her mother's kitchen, her father anxious to hear all about her day. The Christmas right after her parents died had been hell for Tess. This Christmas promised to be no better. She appreciated this man's effort to make her feel comfortable in his home. Royal Cudahy's was probably the only cheer she would receive during this season that used to be so special to her.

"You sound as if you don't enjoy your work very much," Royal said, picking up his fork. It had been quite a while since he had dinner in the kitchen. It was novel and wonderful. He must remember to tell Astra how nice it was. Then he realized Astra had no desire to even know the kitchen existed. Royal decided to enjoy this foray into what he assumed was normalcy.

"Oh, I'm very grateful for my work. Mister Jamison is an expert at restoration, and I'm learning so much. I'm very grateful for the job. I need it so badly. But there's also school. I'm trying to finish my degree. I've fallen behind about a year, and it seems there's never enough time for everything."

"That's quite a schedule. Can't your parents help so you don't have to work?"

"My parents are dead," Tess said flatly, knowing that any further explanation would bring tears to her eyes. She was determined to keep those tears private.

"I'm sorry. Did they die recently?"

Tess nodded. The tears were coming, welling up from the pit of her stomach, trying to spill over her eyes. She heard the sound of a fork on a plate. Royal Cudahy was eating and chatting.

"Don't you have any brothers? Sisters? Other family who could . . ."

A sob broke through. Tess buried her face in her hands. He was the first one to really ask her about her parents. Her friends at school were afraid to talk about it. She had moved out of the dorm to an inexpensive room off campus, effectively isolating herself. Letters from home were private; there were no people to watch her as she cried. Mr. Jamison only cared if she did her work. Now Royal Cudahy was getting the end result of a year and a half of pent-up pain.

"Hey, I'm sorry. I'm really sorry."

Royal was around the table in an instant, his arms surrounding her as he pulled her close. Tess's body shuddered with the intensity of her grief. She was better than this, her mind screamed, as another part of her begged for Royal Cudahy to comfort her. She felt him stroke her hair. Thankfully, he didn't say any of the ridiculous things he could have. He simply let her be. When he finally spoke it was to ask her the perfect question.

"I don't even know your name. If you're going to cry on my shoulder don't you think I should find out?"

Her sobs, though muffled against him, were broken by a hiccuping laugh. She felt better. Much, much better.

"Tess. Tess Canfield."

"Thank you. Now, I think you need more than dinner. Stay there."

He left her only to return with a beautiful crystal glass filled to the brim with wine the color of fine leather. He set it in front of her.

"Now," he said gently, "let's get to know one another."

Tess smiled. She would like nothing more.

They spoke for hours. Tess telling him about the farm, her happy memories, the love she had for her father, how she never felt close to her mother but loved her nonetheless.

Royal spoke of his own life. His humble beginnings. Marrying the boss's daughter. He spoke of how much he respected his wife. How proud he was of her for keeping such a fine home, how grateful he was that she had the social graces that allowed him to make not only a professional name for himself but create a place for them in the community. But the compliments paid to his spouse seemed hollow, almost as though they were memorized.

They spoke for hours on end. The wine was filled and refilled. Tess forgot the atelier and the cherubs. Instead, she allowed Royal Cudahy to weave a web of warmth and caring about her with fine silk strands that she would find impossible to break in days to come. In fact, it wouldn't be until a long time in the future, when she thought back to this very night, that Tess Canfield would remember Royal Cudahy never said he loved his wife. In fact, she would remember that he never admitted loving anything or anyone.

Eleven

Three people were in the foyer with the tree: two young men and a young woman. All of them pissed the hell out of Davina because of the way they looked—so comfortable and chic in their jeans and work shirts; the way they laughed—carefree as though not a problem in the world could affect them; the way they created a fairyland yule tree out of a hulking pine—like they really knew what they were doing. She hated their kind of merriment. Most people would consider it unfettered, naturally casual and heartfelt, but Davina knew better. The professional tree decorators were nothing more than mindless simps. They put on a good show but, basically, people like that were good for nothing other than hanging lights and bulbs on other people's trees. She would no more wish herself to be a part of that little group than she would wish herself back with her mother. The problem was, Davina didn't exactly know where she wished herself.

Turning away from the landing above the foyer, Davina went back to her room and slammed the door. On the exquisite little table by the window stood the remnant of her late-afternoon snack. The bed was rumpled still from her tossing and turning as she had tried to nap the afternoon away. Her closet was close to bursting with all the gorgeous clothes that she had frantically snatched up during the last year and a half as though she were a starving child let loose in a supermarket. In short, Davina had gorged herself on the things her long-lost father could afford to give her.

She had taken every advantage of his wealth and position—she had taken it gleefully, remorselessly. If Davina could have run him into the ground, sent him to financial ruin, she would gladly have done so. Of course, that was her subconscious thinking.

Consciously, Davina would never want to carry out such an idiotic plan because everything Noel had worked for, everything he had built, would be hers one day. That day just wasn't coming fast enough. The sad fact was, Davina hadn't exacted her pound of flesh yet, and she wasn't sure she ever could. Noel had so much to take and she had so much frustration to vent. Davina hated everything about him, including his unequivocal acceptance of her so long ago. He hadn't even had the courtesy to fight her allegations, deny paternity. At least that reaction would have given her something to sink her teeth into.

Plopping herself in a silk upholstered chair Davina looked out onto the gardens and the bleak December day, remembering the car's open door and the handsome man who was her father as she confronted him.

"So, Mister Montgomery," she spat, "you're my father."

Noel Montgomery's driver was behind Davina, his hand on her shoulder as he waited for instructions from his employer. Noel still looked at her with a blank expression. He was neither surprised nor afraid nor ashamed. If anything could be said about the way he looked, it would have been that Noel Montgomery looked curious. He lifted his hand. The driver backed away.

"Your name is?" His voice had a rough quality that was not displeasing.

"Davina Montgomery."

"Your mother?"

"Angelica Montgomery. I have the marriage certificate and the birth certificate and the divorce papers. Right here." Davina dug in her purse, pawing at the contents, becoming more furious as her efforts proved clumsy and ineffectual.

"It's all right. I believe you. Get in."

Get in. That was all he said. It was so easy, his acceptance so natural, that Davina had wanted to scream. Instead, she eased into the car. He moved over, looked at her carefully, then spoke to the driver who had reclaimed his seat.

"Go ahead, George. It seems that I won't be having a quiet evening to myself after all. Drop us at the front door."

"Yes, sir."

The car began to move. Davina fought with herself, refusing to give in to her feeling of awe. It wasn't only that this handsome man was her father, or that the wealth he enjoyed was beyond compare; it was that he opened the door so welcomingly and let her in.

For years Davina had fought with her mother, tried to force an ounce of affection from that woman. Now Noel Montgomery seemed to offer her hope, if not affection. That made Davina mad. Mad that so many years had been wasted. And, since she couldn't blame a mother unable to fight back, she would blame him. She interpreted his calm acceptance of her as apathy; his generosity as payment for some deeply hidden guilt. Davina would cut him no slack.

As he instructed, they were dropped in front of the house that sat so far off the road Davina had not been truly aware of its enormity. Fabulous old willows caressed the porticoes. The huge white columns she had seen from across the street weren't just a façade for the anterior, but wound around the perimeter holding the second-story over a beautifully broad porch.

"Go in there, Davina."

Noel lifted his hand, indicating a darkly paneled room. Davina hesitated. He had said her name as though he had been saying it for a hundred years. He smiled then, beautifully and gently. She turned on the heel of her new, expensive shoes that now seemed less elegant than they had in the store, and went where he indicated. He joined her a minute later.

"Well," Noel said, taking the seat next to her on the couch. "You're my daughter, and I honestly don't know what to say. There are so many questions. I'm sure you have one or two yourself. Why don't we start with you?"

"Don't you want to see my proof?" Davina drawled. Couldn't he see she didn't want it to be this easy?

"There will be plenty of time for that, but if it will make you feel better, then yes, I'd like to see it." Noel still smiled, his eyes warm and inviting. He looked at her as though trying to see something that wasn't there: a moment of her childhood, an instant of her infancy.

Davina had taken the envelope from her purse when she was alone in the room. Now she handed it to him, her eyes sparking in defiance as he looked from the documents to her and back again. Finally Noel took them only to lay the papers aside, all his attention riveted on Davina.

"It's been a long time since I've thought about those days. I guess I managed to lock them away quite effectively." There was a note of wistful sadness in his voice. He picked up the papers and handed them back to her. "You should keep these. Your mother's dead? How did it happen?"

"She killed herself. Took an overdose of pills. She couldn't take it anymore. The doctors couldn't help her. I couldn't afford to keep paying for them."

Davina threw her explanation at him as though it was a gauntlet. Whatever she had hoped, that he would get on his knees and beg forgiveness, that he would shed a tear for her poor life, wasn't to be. Instead, he hung his head; she could see the shots of silver laced among the black waves. She waited for him to speak.

"I'm sorry. I wish I'd known. I would have helped."

"Why didn't you know?" Davina demanded. "She was your wife. You weren't some lay she had for a night the way she used to tell me. She told me you were rich, but I didn't believe her. She never told me your name. Then I found the letters. Letters she wrote to you but never mailed. Probably because she was too scared of being rejected again. Too sick to think straight. And you, you stopped writing. Left her with a baby."

"Whoa, wait just a minute," he objected gently. "I didn't leave her with a baby. I didn't even know she *had* one. Your mother was always on her own agenda. I fell in love with her because I thought she was a free spirit. I realized soon after we were married that there were some problems inside her, but I had no idea that she was mentally ill. I wouldn't have abandoned her, whether she was sick or not. She's the one who left me. I received the divorce papers almost as

103

soon as I landed in Vietnam. Never a word of explanation. Angelica never even told me about the pregnancy. I know you don't want to believe me. I'm sure you loved your mother very much as I once did . . ."

"Don't be absurd," Davina snorted.

"Oh," Noel said sadly. "I see. I'm sure it was a terrible burden. I'm sorry."

"Like hell you are," she snapped.

"I'm not going to argue the point with you. I haven't seen or heard from Angelica in over twenty years. My hurt was dealt with years ago and I went on with my life. I respected her wishes when I found she had divorced me, and I didn't try to contact her after the first couple of times. I'd seen it happen too often to my buddies. Men would ship out. Some could go home to a family, some would be forgotten so that their women could get on with their lives. It would be impossible to try and explain it to you so you'd understand how we simply accepted things like that. At the time I was devastated. But I came back from war lucky to be alive and I was going to live again—the way your mother had chosen, too."

"But she didn't live, don't you understand that? She couldn't even hold a job the last few years. I had to quit school, support the both of us when all this time you had . . ."

"Wealth? Money? Is that what you want?"

"You had everything," Davina answered, ignoring his pointed question.

"Not everything. Drink?" Noel went to a corner of the room. He pushed a button. A panel slid back, revealing a bar glistening with crystal and silver. Davina watched him closely. He moved as though he didn't have a care in the world. Actually, he didn't realize how many cares he was soon to have and all were personified in the young woman who sat on his sofa.

"Scotch." Davina informed him. "Straight up with a splash."

"Heavy drink for a young lady." He wasn't impressed the way she thought he would be.

"I've lived long enough to know what I want," Davina said offhandedly.

"And what you want is to blame me for your misery." He came back to her, gliding over the lush carpeting. She took her drink, loving the feel of the heavy crystal in her hands. "Perhaps we should get something straight. I think it's rather amazing that I have a daughter. I'll be delighted to make you a part of my household. I would hope that we might eventually become a family. But that's as far as I'm willing to go. I'd like to tell you that news of your mother's death devastates me. It doesn't. We weren't married long enough. We didn't share the things we should have shared to make us a family. I'm saddened by it, of course. And I know you want to hear that I am willing to take all the abuse and anger you want to heap on me. But I'm not going to do either of those things.

"I will open my home to you. In time, perhaps, we'll each open our hearts to one another. I've never had children, yet I always thought I'd make a good father. But we don't know one another. Perhaps we won't like one another. Perhaps we will. Maybe even come to love one another. I'm used to an equitable working relationship and that means everyone pulls their own weight. You make the effort and I'll match it. Vice versa also applies.

"We've got a lot of catching up to do, Davina Montgomery. I want to know it all. I want to feel everything you've gone through and then I want to

105

start making memories for the two of us. If you don't want to accept that, then you'll be back out on the street. Make up your mind. Stay here and think about it while I go and change. We'll have dinner at seven. I hope you'll be here to share it with me."

He walked out of the room, but not before coming to her and putting out his hand to touch her curly black hair. He touched her so gently, with such awe that Davina felt the stirrings of a softer emotion—not love, but certainly forgiveness for her misunderstandings. Then, as he left her, she thought back to all the years of abuse and deprivation. She wouldn't let him do this to her. Not yet. Not before he paid.

So they had passed that first year, wary of each other, sometimes making an inroad or two. Noel had been more than generous offering her an education, a job, time to adjust to her new surroundings. But Davina ignored all this, peevishly pushing him to his limit as often as possible with her contrary ways instead. She tried to go back to college and ended up getting kicked out her second semester. She didn't even bother with a job. She'd worked hard enough for so many years. The one thing she did take and use with a relish was his name.

Noel Montgomery, whiz-kid publisher who took an idea and then parlayed it into one of the slickest male magazines around, was a name to be reckoned with. *High Life* magazine was an exquisite cross between *Playboy* and *Esquire* and everyone knew Noel Montgomery had the touch. From the very beginning the magazine was classy and titillating, its pages filled with only the top-notch advertisers who could afford to spend $100,000 a color page. And there were *High Life* television specials produced, of course, by Noel.

106

There were *High Life* cosmetics for men and women. *High Life* feature films.

In short, Noël Montgomery had everything a man could want: money, power, fame. Luckily, that was exactly the package his daughter wanted, too. Unfortunately, Davina was smart enough to know that using what he had was far different from it belonging to her. Now she had forced the issue. Their second Christmas together and she had informed him that she would sue him for what was rightfully hers if he didn't take steps to turn over a substantial stock offering to her.

She hadn't really meant her demand to come out the way it did. But he was sitting there, at dinner, so calm and collected, telling her about the latest acquisition he was making — a radio station in Denver — and he was talking to her as though she was a part of the whole thing. That was when Davina exploded.

She wasn't part of anything! She was just a hanger-on who happened to have his genes. So Davina made her move, threatening a lawsuit. Noël had carefully put his napkin on the table, pushed his chair back and left the house. That had been two days ago. Davina wondered when he would respond, or if he would. Perhaps he would just have someone come and throw her out. She felt tears coming to her eyes. She was so tired of all this: of being on the outside looking in, of her own anger and loneliness. There had to be a time when all that would stop. There had to be, because despite her hard exterior Davina Montgomery really wanted nothing more than to belong somewhere. Anywhere. In fact, anywhere was better than here, alone, in this silent huge house. She had to get out.

An hour later Davina was swathed in a brocade motorcycle jacket and pants by Calvin Klein, a pearl-encrusted bra compliments of Donna Karan and was on her way out the door. Dancing always helped.

The house was dark when she got home. Dark except for a small desk lamp burning in Noel's study. Davina stumbled toward it without thinking. She was drunk and the pills she had taken for her outrageous headache hadn't helped any. She'd been had in the back seat of a car by a man she'd never laid eyes on before. She hadn't eaten, only managed to bum two lines of coke that made her feel worse, rather than better. Now Noel was there, waiting for her, and Davina knew she was in no shape to face him. But maybe, just maybe, he might say something, do something to show her the way and help her find what she wanted.

He looked up as she fell against the door jamb. Davina thought she pulled herself up rather well, but Noel looked away in disgust. He wasn't going to help her. Not this way. Catering to her, coddling her would make it worse and, he knew, this relationship could do nothing more than become worse. He was ready to make it better.

"Did you have a good time?"

His voice floated to Davina as though from far away. Her head lolled, then snapped up as she tried to focus on him.

"Yeah. I had a great time. You should try it. Dancing, drinks. Might lighten you up a bit."

"I don't think that's what's needed, Davina. I think we ought to bring you down to earth a bit," he answered.

"Yeah, and just how do you propose to do that, Papa?" she drawled.

"Well, for starters, you're going on an allowance. I suppose I was so grateful to find I actually had a child I wanted to spoil you the way one does an infant. But you're not an infant, Davina. You're a grown woman who has known and accepted responsibility. It's time you did it again."

"How about that? And what if I don't want it?"

Davina pushed herself away from the door and staggered into the study. She had meant to go directly to his desk, lean over it, and face him down. Instead, she made it as far as a high-backed leather wing chair. There she collapsed, her legs opened in an unbecoming manner.

Noel's eyes flickered slightly and a sadness ripped at his gut. She was a beautiful young woman, but after the drinking and God knew what else, Davina looked tired and bloated. Had he brought this on or, perhaps, did she possess some of her mother's uncertainty of mind? Immediately Noel denied that possibility. He was a good judge of character. Deep down Davina was worth a lot more than she gave herself credit for.

"Then you're out of here with a settlement, and I promise you it won't be generous," he said quietly.

"I'll take you to court," she insisted.

"I'll fight back. Remember, I have better resources. I have the money, and I have the experience. You'd be lucky to get anything. Now, do we deal?"

Davina glared at him. Her eyes hurt, but she held his calm stare. Forcing her mind to work quickly, despite the liquor, she weighed the pros and cons. He was right. She had zilch. When she was in a better position, then she would lower the boom. Now she would listen to him, learn from him. Then she would turn those lessons back and destroy him.

109

"Sure, why not? A deal. What do I have to do?"

"That's better."

Noel controlled himself, keeping his relief hidden. Davina would misconstrue a smile. Strength was the only thing his daughter understood and respected. Noel couldn't help feel a glimmer of hope. They might just make it after all. It was funny how much he wanted that, and strange how this one challenge he had never asked for now became his overriding quest. He wanted to win Davina's love. He wanted to keep her from destroying herself, and maybe him, in the process.

"Monday morning you will report to the offices of *High Life*. You will begin work in the mail room. You will be paid an intern's salary and you will use that money for your expenses. The balance on your credit cards will be paid, but any expense incurred after today will be your responsibility. You will work in every department of *High Life,* learning the business from the bottom up. You will do this for a year. In a year's time, if you prove yourself, you will be given a permanent assignment in the division in which you seem most suited. After two years we will discuss the possibility of you heading a department. If, at anytime, you screw up or try to pull rank you are out of the company and out of my life. That's the deal. Take it or leave it."

"Have I got a choice?"

"Of course. That's all life is, a series of choices. You make a good one or a bad one. No matter which one you go on with your life."

"I deserve more. I'm your daughter," Davina grumbled.

"You deserve one thing, and only one, because you're my daughter. You deserve a second chance, and that's what I'm giving you. I will not accept the guilt you attempt to bury me with. I will not accept your anger. I will accept one thing, though, and that is responsibility for you—to a point. If you accept your own, our life together will be a wonderful one. But it boils down to your decision. I made my decisions years ago, and I'm happy with the rewards. I want you to be happy with yours. Good night, Davina. Give me your answer in the morning."

In the dimly lit room, Davina struggled to her feet. She stood looking at Noel, her father, for a very long time, then turned as graciously as she could and left the room.

Upstairs she stripped and fell onto her bed, throwing one arm over her pounding eyes. Something had to change. Something. She wasn't going to give it all up. She wouldn't give him the satisfaction. Then she remembered something, that ridiculous saying about flies and honey. It seemed reasonable. Maybe it was time to change tact. Davina passed out, smiling to herself sweetly as though she was practicing for her new role in life.

Twelve

"Hey, ladies, hope everything is just dandy back here. Yes?" With a rush of frenetic energy common to backstage men in the television industry, and in the wake of Aramis applied with a heavy hand, one of Bob Loehmann's lackies rushed into the blue room. As he talked he preened for the two women, turning his small hips this way and that, grinning to show his perfectly capped teeth. Neither of them was impressed. "Nobody with a case of nerves? Hah, hah!"

Bonnie rolled her eyes heavenward. The man with the too tight jeans and too big hair didn't wait for an answer. Casually, he put his hand on Bonnie's shoulder. She shrugged it off. He went to the other woman who seemed perfectly pleased with the jerk's attention. "Of course not. No reason for anyone to be nervous, is there ladies? Just because Bob Loehmann's *Real Story* is the hottest talk show around, and six million people will be hanging on your every word, not to mention the live audience that will be out there, is no reason to feel your stomach churn. We're all professionals. Now, just remember, when Bob asks you something really personal, it's nothing personal. Get it? Hah, hah!"

He looked at the woman whose shoulder was still encased in his hand. She appeared to have blanched. He was laughing gleefully, fully convinced that his reverse psychology was the proper way to put people at their ease. Bonnie shook her head. It was a shame that lack of intelligence was a requirement for working on a television show.

"But what on earth could he have to ask me that's personal?" she asked, her voice quavering. "I just wrote a book."

The man leaned down and chucked her under the chin, his inspid smile never wavering. He added a wide wink to the show. "We do our jobs around here, you know. We've researched you better than the FBI could. Don't worry. Bob will find something interesting — and personal — to talk about."

Straightening, he adjusted the gold chains at his neck, aimed a cocked finger at the woman in the chair, then clapped his hands and rubbed them together with a sigh.

"Well, if there isn't anything else I can get for you ladies I'll be on my way. Lots to do, you know. This show doesn't just happen. Bonnie, you're up next," he said as he sailed through the door. "Try to keep your boobs in your dress. This is prime time."

Bonnie glared after him. What she wouldn't give for a good film. Even a documentary. Anything to get away from television and the twerps who felt your body and soul was fair game for pot shots. Crass, overfamiliar idiot! That's what that guy was. But what could she expect? His boss, Bob Loehmann, the esteemed host of *Real Story,* wasn't any better.

She turned away from the door and began to pace the blue room. Fresh coffee, cheese and crackers, soft drinks, and Perrier were set out on a round, laminated table. She ignored all of it, even though she could have eaten a horse. But her makeup was done and her call was coming soon. Her companion, the author of *How To Cope With Widowhood,* now sat in the corner of the

113

room, terrified, worried about the intimate details of her life which would soon be offered to millions of people for their prime-time pleasure. Bonnie glanced at her, sniffed, and paced. Even with expert makeup the author still looked like a frump who probably didn't have even one secret worth revealing on *Real Story.*

Ignoring her completely, though the woman continued to eye Bonnie with an expectancy common to those put in close quarters with a real celebrity, Bonnie knit her brow. If the author had been anyone worth knowing she wouldn't have been so impressed with Bonnie. That was Bonnie's yardstick: the less impressed people were, the more she wanted to get into their good graces. Besides, Bonnie had other things on her mind. Things that were more pressing.

The *People* interview was just one. She thought the interview had gone so well; she'd been very impressed with her professionalism. Obviously, the reporter had preconceived ideas about her, and hadn't listened to a word she said. So her glorious picture (the best she had ever taken) on the cover of *People* had been diminished by the headline: BONNIE BARBER — FAMOUS FOR BEING FAMOUS. Inside it got worse. The reporter implied that Bonnie's only talent was for leaning over just the proper degree to show off her ample tits during the family hour. He totally ignored her part in the witty repartee she and Giles engaged in each evening. He ignored the fact she had a fine track record as an actress — of course, that *had* been a few years ago with that series, but it was still nothing to sneeze at.

Then, of course, there was also Giles. She had thought it was the real thing — love. Bonnie imagined Giles was as ambitious as she. Therefore, she overlooked his aging body and his insatiable appetite for sex. Six months into the relationship she had realized, to her horror, that Giles Masters was losing steam. He was perfectly happy to make *Table Top* a success, but he had no desire to stretch, reach for the brass ring. He was at the end of his career; she still had so much to accomplish. No, that wasn't it. She *deserved* so much more. Instead of a canoe ride, Bonnie was primed for a high-speed chase.

Engrossed in her thoughts and plans, Bonnie snapped at the production assistant when he hailed her.

"What!" She twirled on him, catching a glimpse of the middle-aged author who jumped as though she'd done something wrong.

"They want you on the set, Miss Barber," the young man said lazily. He'd seen enough of these top-heavy broads to know that not a one of them was going to last. Bonnie Barber's attitude was not impressive.

"Oh, I see," Bonnie muttered, pulling herself up straighter. She would be damned if she would apologize to a nobody kid. "I'm coming."

"Good luck," the author ventured as Bonnie passed.

Bonnie let her heavily lashed eyes flicker the woman's way, offered her a lukewarm smile, then left the room, plastering her best star-quality smile on her face for the benefit of the host and the cameras. The host was between wives and dreadfully powerful in the industry. If she made a good impression he might be her ticket off *Table Top* and out of Gile's bed. One never knew, Bonnie reminded herself.

The applause was thunderous as she sauntered out on stage. Bonnie didn't miss a beat. Putting her fingertips to her lips, she threw kisses to the audience.

Gracefully, Bonnie moved toward the host, who half rose. She offered her cheek, never turning from the camera. They bussed lightly before Bonnie took her seat. The host clapped, encouraging the audience to keep it up. He loved this kind of reception for his guests as long as he was the one to indicate when enough was enough. He did so a moment later.

"Oh, my," Bonnie breathed, letting her fingertips trail along her décolletage. "What a wonderful audience!"

"They're smart, all right. They know a good thing when they see it. Isn't that right?"

Again he lifted his eyes toward the audience and they broke into another round of applause. Bonnie soaked it up, glimmering as bright as any star. Again, they quieted. The applause signs had been turned off.

"So, Bonnie, what's new in your life? I've heard rumors that you might be getting into a little bit more than turning over big cards on a game show?"

"I don't know where you could have heard that, Bob," Bonnie breathed, her look saying that, indeed, her life was filled with exciting options. "Of course, as an actress, I'm always on the lookout for the right vehicle. There has been some talk about doing a movie, but nothing is settled yet."

"Hey, now," he enthused, "that would be dandy. But I suppose it is difficult to find just the right thing for someone like you."

Bonnie shot him a look. In an instant she saw that she had not been high on his list of guests. He was bored. He was not into this at all. Not only that, he didn't seem at all impressed by her obvious physical beauty.

"It's difficult for anyone in Hollywood these days. In the old days options were limited and so was competition. I mean, when you started out, Bob, I think programming stopped at ten at night, so the choices just weren't there."

Bob Loehmann grinned in a horizontal manner that indicated he was ready for a fight if she was. The audience was totally oblivious to the undercurrent on the stage.

116

"In those days there was so much talent that only the best of the best made it. Now there seems to be a spot for just about anyone," he responded as he raised his hands. "But hey, these people don't want to hear about the old days. They want to hear about Bonnie Barber, game-show hostess extraordinaire! Tell us, truthfully, just between us"—his eyebrows shot up suggestively—"what's going on with you and Giles Masters? Is it true that his tricks are more interesting off camera? And I don't mean cards, either."

The audience roared. Bonnie wouldn't give in. She put on her innocent, ladylike face.

"Oh, I'll tell you, Giles is the most wonderful man. You know, when my father was sick he was kind enough to help me find just the right doctors. We were afraid that Daddy didn't have long to live, but with Giles's help the doctors are hoping for a full recovery. Of course, I've had him brought here so that after a full day of taping I can rush right over to the home and be with him as much as possible. And Giles sends a car every Sunday so Daddy and I can get to church comfortably."

Bonnie smiled sweetly while the lies fell from her lips. Her father was sick all right, but she hadn't seen hide nor hair of him in over two years. That was the way she wanted it. She also wanted to control this interview.

"That a way, Bonnie," a man called from the audience.

"Bless you, Bonnie," a woman's voice said.

Bob Loehmann fidgeted. This was not what the pre-interview notes indicated would happen. He made a mental note to put Bonnie Barber on his blacklist. Before he banished her forever, though, he gave it one more try.

"Come on, Bonnie, we want to know the truth. What's going on between you and Giles Masters? I could see what he might want with a girl like you, your talents are obvious, but what would a girl like you want with him? What is it, Bonnie, the *real* story?"

"What Giles and I have," Bonnie breathed, "is a warm and wonderful friendship. Giles believes in my talent as an actress, and has been a supportive friend over the last few years. I'll be forever grateful, I'll love him always, for giving me the chance to be a part of America's favorite game show. I think we really offer the viewer a chance to see that television isn't all make-believe. Can't you just tell when we talk that Giles and I actually like each other?"

Bonnie turned toward the audience she couldn't see because of the lights and asked their opinion. The audience answered with spontaneous applause. Bonnie sat back, satisfied. Bob Loehmann drummed his fingers on his tacky little table.

"So there's no truth to the rumor that you landed the job because of your talents offstage?"

"Bob!" she trilled. "I know you. You're always looking for the dirt. That's what makes your show so interesting. But if you want to know something like that, I guess you'll have to find out from Giles. A lady never tells."

With a flick of his finger Bob Loehmann ordered a commercial break. It was way too early. Bonnie hadn't had her entire five minutes. She didn't really care, though, since the impression she had made was one of seriousness, piety. It was a good ploy, an excellent one. She would be more beloved than ever now and none of her viewers would be any the wiser.

An assistant put his hand on her shoulder. Bob Loehmann ignored her as she rose to leave.

"Good night, Bob," she purred. "Thanks for an absolutely wonderful evening."

He didn't say a word as she sidled off the stage. Bonnie passed the author in the hall. The woman moved her lips, silently and furiously. Bonnie assumed she was communing with her dead husband. Maybe she was even thanking him for this opportunity.

Luckily the blue room was empty when she returned. Bonnie grabbed her purse and a bottle of Perrier. Just as she was about to leave the studio, the monitor in the blue room indicated that the Bob Loehmann show was about to begin again. Bonnie thumbed her nose at the monitor and was almost out the door when the voice-over announced the guest for the next week.

"Tune in, ladies and gentleman, when we devote the entire half-hour to Melinda Scarsdale, the *High Life* Woman for the year. You won't want to miss it!"

As Bonnie closed the door on the blue room, a real thought was finally forming in her one-track mind.

"Sy," Bonnie snapped into the phone.

"Bonnie, baby, how'd it go tonight?"

"My own agent wasn't watching?" she asked angrily.

"Of course I was, baby," he said sheepishly as he rearranged himself in bed, trying not to disturb his wife. They'd been asleep since ten. He was too old to stay up and watch Bob Loehmann jerk every hopeful's chain. Beside him his wife pulled a pillow over her head and wondered sleepily why she hadn't married a plumber. "I just wanted to know how you felt it went, kid."

"It sucked," Bonnie complained, "but you'd know that if you watched. Listen, though, Loehmann isn't the reason I called. I got an idea, you know, a strategy for my career. I've been locked into this role of sweet little thing on that damned game show too long. It's going nowhere."

"Honey," Sy said urgently, "it's the number-one show and you helped make it that way. If you play your cards right, no joke intended, you could be working for the next ten years. How many actresses you know can say that?"

"And how many actresses," she drawled, "would have even taken this shit spot?"

"I didn't hear you complaining when you went for the interview. The money's good . . ."

". . . And you collect your ten percent without having to do a thing. Sy, I'm an actress. I want an Academy Award."

"You gotta get into the movies first."

"Maybe I gotta get me a new agent who can see as far as a film," Bonnie retorted.

"Aw, come on, Bonnie," Sy mumbled. "It's not like I haven't been trying. They've got you pigeon-holed so you might as well enjoy it. Why fight it?"

"Because it's what I want, Sy. Now what I realized is exactly that. The powers-that-be can only see me one way. They're one-dimensional thinkers. What I need is a new image. They've got to look at me in a different way, you know."

"Sure I know. But haven't I been telling you to get someone other than those PR guys on the show to work with you? You need to get someone out there fighting just for you. Listen, I can recommend some really good people in public relations . . ."

"What I need, Sy," Bonnie lectured, "is my agent to get me the right booking. I want to be the next *High Life* Woman, Sy. I want you to get me that spot, and I want to get it soon."

On the other end of the phone Sy couldn't repress his groan of dismay. Why did these women always want the impossible? Why? He was about to reason with her when he realized he was listening to a dial tone. Bonnie had hung up.

Part Four
1990

Thirteen

March was cold and bleak, promising much needed rain but never delivering. So California grew more depressed, thoroughly anxious. Nothing could amuse the residents who were short tempered on the freeways, with their children and their lovers, with themselves. Everything seemed to come to a standstill. Workers pushed papers laconically across desks, made repairs with less thought and enthusiasm and generally didn't give a shit what anyone else thought about their performance. Tess Canfield was not immune to the general lethargy that settled over Los Angeles.

That Wednesday, looking around her home, she saw that nothing she started had been completed. Books lay strewn over the dining-room table, a half-finished painting was easled by the bay window, breakfast dishes still sat unwashed in the sink despite the late afternoon hour.

Knowing she had to pull herself out of her dismal mood, Tess stepped into the shower at five minutes after three. The hot water and scent of her shampoo revived her. For a long while she stood motionless, letting the water course over her body, trying not to think of the situation she had gotten herself into, trying not to imagine what her mother and father would have said. Reaching for the faucets she turned off the water. It was too soothing, allowing too much time for a relaxed mind to look at itself clearly.

Stepping out of the shower Tess dried herself, wrapping first her hair in a fluffy white towel, then her body. Humming in a desperate attempt to regain a mood confident enough to tackle her painting again, Tess walked down the short hallway toward the kitchen. Just as she turned the corner into the living room she was grabbed. A hand shot out from behind the door and clasped her still damp shoulder, twirling her into her assailant. A scream froze on her lips as they were covered by the man's insistent ones. Shocked for a moment, she regained her senses and pushed him away.

"Royal! How could you? You scared me half to death."

Her towel had come loose and slipped over her breasts. Royal's eyes raked over her tawny skin. Quickly, she pulled the towel up, embarrassed still that he should feel so free with her. But then, why shouldn't he? She turned away, ashamed as she always was when she realized how much she owed him — was owned by him.

"Don't," he said softly, reaching out this time with love.

Tess stood still, her hands clutching the towel around her tighter, tears slipping through her lashes. She couldn't look at him.

"Tess, honey, please don't cry. What's the matter?"

She shook her head. "I don't want to make love."

"We don't have to," Royal responded, his voice softening in the way that told Tess exactly how much he cared for her. But she didn't want to hear that tone. She didn't want to fool herself any longer. "Tess?"

"It's no good, Royal. I don't think it ever has been. It's wrong."

"No, no," he whispered, gathering her to him despite her weak protest. "It's good between us. You must never say that. I was wrong to sneak in here like this. I'm sorry. I'll give you back the key . . ."

"Why?" Her head snapped up as she raised her wet, angry eyes to his soft hazel ones. "This isn't really my house."

"Of course it is. I bought it for you. It's your home. I've never thought of it in any other way." Royal's hazel eyes widened, astonished that Tess should be upset by his silly little surprise.

"No? You don't think of this place as the house you keep your mistress in?" Tess demanded.

Hurt filled Royal's face as his full lips drew together to keep from quivering. Again Tess was struck at the wonder of this man. She read about him in the paper, saw him on television talking as though he would steamroll over anyone who tried to stand in his way when it came to his legal dealings. Yet with her he was vulnerable, gentle, so ready to please.

"No, I don't think of this house that way. Nor do I think of you that way. I think of it as the place that keeps the woman I love safe and warm. I think of it as the only place in the world that I can go and feel that same safety and warmth and caring. God knows I don't get it at home."

"Then do something about it, Royal. Please, do something . . ." Tess's voice broke and she turned away from him. It was so hard to feel his hands on her, look into the face she loved and still resent him. "Do something about the way we live. I'm lost, Royal. I don't know where I belong anymore and I don't know how this happened. When did I give up my dreams and began to live for you? When did I throw away my principles?"

"The moment we fell in love, Tess. It's as simple as that. Sometimes there are no reasons for the way things happen, only emotions that drive us on. Sometimes it's best not to look for facts, but simply accept things as they are."

Royal ran a hand through his hair and turned away from her as if he was waiting for the jury to agree with his arguments. He sighed heavily.

"And, as to the second part of your question, you know I can't tell Astra yet. It's not the right time. We've been over and over that."

"I know," she said, her voice small, pleading. "I know what you said but I can't believe that she doesn't know about us already. I've met your friends, we're seen out, you're hardly ever home. Doesn't that tell her something?"

"That doesn't mean much to a woman like Astra. You see, she was raised to accept whatever her husband does. It's that old, rich-world mentality. Astra gets exactly what she wants from our marriage: money, prestige, a position in society.

"I *am* going to divorce her. I simply want to make sure that she has something else to replace me. I want her to have some focus, some direction. Her position in the world must be protected, and that will be difficult when she's without a husband. And, of course, there are the boys to consider. They'll both be in high school soon. Let them make that transition with their family intact. Please, Tess, for me. Wait just a little longer."

"I *can't,* Royal. I never wanted this to happen in the first place. You're a married man. Our affair wasn't right. But now that it has happened, now that we've gone on so long, don't you think you have a responsibility to me, too? While you're waiting for Astra to focus her life, mine is falling apart. I haven't been able to paint. I don't have to work. You take care of everything I could ever need or want. I don't fit in at school, either. I've been playing at being a student. I don't fit in anywhere."

"You fit in here, with me, in my arms."

Royal moved toward her again, but Tess held out a hand, stopping him.

"Let me get dressed. Let me be alone for five minutes. I'm sorry. I don't mean to sound demanding. I guess it's the weather. I'm sorry."

She moved out of the living room and closed the door behind her in the bedroom. Tess dressed quickly, unable to look at her naked body. Days like this were so awful; days when she questioned what was happening with her life. Tess Canfield, mistress, was not how she envisioned her role in life. It was certainly not the calling her father had seen for her. Dear Pa and all his dreams. He had told her he was proud of her. How would he feel if he could see her now?

But she had been so lonely. No family, no close friends. And she had been scared. Bills, school, work, work, and more work. Those situations were no excuse for sleeping with another woman's husband. But then, that wasn't how it seemed in the beginning.

Royal had been lonely, too. They had simply come together, reveling in the warmth they provided each other. Tess had loved him for the emotional care he lavished on her. She couldn't remember when he began to keep her. How she hated that phrase!

He *wasn't* keeping her. She came and went as she pleased, thought as she had always thought and behaved as she always behaved. The only difference was she didn't sit down every month and pay the bills — and she didn't think of herself with respect any longer.

The one factor in the equation that didn't add up was her almost immediate love for Royal Cudahy. Her heart had opened with such gratitude for the time he spent with her that the rest had followed naturally, without shame and, perhaps, without the proper amount of thought. Now she was what she was: a mistress kept by a powerful man. Loved by him. And damn it, she loved him, too. That was the true problem. Tess knew she may hate the packaging, but she couldn't deny that her heart had been given to the man waiting for her in the living room.

Combing through her damp hair, Tess watched herself in the mirror, looking for a sign that she had become a terrible person because of her love for a man who was already committed. She couldn't see it. Her hair, though wet, was still golden, her skin was burnished, her eyes were blue as the heavens. They, she and Royal, would have such beautiful children. If only Astra were stronger. If only Royal could ease himself out of his loveless marriage more quickly. *If.* That was the biggest word in the world.

Slowly, she put down the brush. Soon a decision would have to be made. If Royal chose to stay with his wife and sons, Tess knew she would be hurt dreadfully. If he chose her, she would be the happiest woman alive. But if he didn't choose, then she would be nothing more than a lady-in-waiting, forever lost in that nebulous realm where nothing was permanent — not things, not love — and the passing of time brought neither joy nor sorrow, just moments of pleasure and age. Tess would have to make him decide. And she would have to do it soon.

Tess found him in the kitchen pouring two large

glasses of orange juice. He grinned when she came in, his eyes lighting up as though he had just received the best present under the tree. How could she not love him when he looked at her like that?

"Here, I thought you might need this."

"Thanks." She took the glass from him and leaned back against the counter. "You know you're going to have to do something soon, don't you, Royal?"

The smile faded. He looked older without it. She saw the lawyer in him, the determination that made him a holy terror in the courtroom. She wasn't frightened, only amazed that part of him existed.

"Tess, listen to me. I know all the pitfalls of this relationship. I'm a lot older than you are. You deserve to have the kind of life every young woman dreams of. I'd like to be the man to give it to you. But I have a twenty-year commitment to my wife. We were very young when we were married. Eighteen." He laughed without mirth, his eyes floating up to the ceiling as though he could see the beginning. "I was so young. I worked so hard. And I changed. The thing is she never did. I can't throw her away until I help her begin to adapt to the ways of life without me. If I simply left Astra, I have a funny feeling you'd respect me less if I could be that cold toward her. I know these arguments don't excuse my behavior toward you, but I want you to know one thing. I love you. Love you with all my heart. You make me feel needed, as though nothing in the world can hurt me. I'm asking you to let me do this my way. I'm asking you to wait, if you can, because no one will love you the way I do — ever."

For a long while neither of them moved. They stood apart, yet felt closer than they had in a long while. Tess had asked him to make a decision. In her heart, as she felt her love swelling for Royal, she didn't realize that he had simply turned the decision back to her. Nor did she really look at his eyes when he said the word "love." Had she, Tess would not have seen the deepening of emotion. She would have seen that love was a word he used like so many others.

She went to him and slid her arms around his waist, her head laying against his chest. She felt him sigh, felt his body flutter with joy as she took him in her arms. His came around her in the gentlest of embraces, his lips kissed her hair.

"I'll wait, Royal. I'll wait and love you, but don't make it too long."

"I won't, my love. I want to be with you more than anything in the world. You take care of me so well. You make me feel like I belong."

Tess closed her eyes and listened to his words. Funny, but that was how he made her feel. She'd never considered that Royal needed someone to take care of him, too. Suddenly, his mood changed, as though with her acquiescence all their problems had been solved. He held her at arm's length, the boyish grin back on his face.

"Listen, I know just what we need. A break from this dismal place. We need to go away together and I have just the perfect thing. I'm going to take you to Athens. Actually, not to Athens, but to the most incredible yacht you've ever seen!

"Dimitri Argyroupolis and I have to meet to iron out some problems he's having, and he suggested we do business on the yacht. I haven't been there in ages, and I know you'll love it. How about it? You'll have plenty of time to relax in the sun and in the evening we'll sit under the stars and be waited on like a king and queen. And I know you'll love Dimitri. He's quite the ladies' man, though, so I'm warning you, no flirting. I'd hate to be bested by a man twenty-five years my senior. Tell me you'll go, Tess. Please."

Tess grinned at his excitement, but her smile faded as he outlined his plan. Athens. Greece. The home of classical art. What she wouldn't give to see it all. But . . .

"I can't, Royal," she answered, shaking her head sadly.

"Don't be silly, of course you can. I won't take no for an answer."

"No, Royal, I haven't been on a plane since I left Los Angeles for Kansas to bury my parents. I didn't even come back on a plane. I got all the way to the airport only to find I couldn't get on. I'm afraid. I really am. Don't make me do it," she pleaded.

"Of course I wouldn't make you do it, darling. But you know you're being silly. Your parents were killed in a helicopter, not on a commercial airline. Flying is safer than driving."

"I know all those statistics," Tess objected, angry that he should take her reservations so lightly.

"Honey, I'm not making fun of you, but you must realize you can't go your entire life being afraid of flying," he soothed.

"Why not?" she rallied. "There are lots of people who never fly."

"Not the future wife of Royal Cudahy. The future wife of Royal Cudahy will have to be fearless since he intends to show her the world and the world her. Please, Tess, try for me. If you find you can't get on the plane I'll send you right home. But for now, at least, say you'll try."

Tess stood rigid in his arms, feeling the fear deep in her stomach. She closed her eyes and conjured up the plane, thought of sitting in it, the doors closing, being

131

locked in up in the sky where no one could save her if anything happened. Then another thought came to wash away the fear. He had said she would be his wife. Suddenly, that was the only thing she could think about. Her eyes opened, she tiptoed up and kissed him lightly.

"I wouldn't dream of disappointing the world," she said softly. "I'll go if it means that much to you."

"Thank you, darling. Thank you."

Tess sank into him, taking strength from his excitement and reassurance. Later that night, though, as they lay together in the darkness, the fear returned. She saw the faces of her parents swim before her eyes and saw the pain in them. She thought, perhaps, they were trying to warn her. Or were they just sorrowing that their daughter loved a man who could never really be hers?

The sky was a jewel, sapphire like the ocean that met it on the horizon. Together sky and sea melded, creating a bubble of clear blue through which the skiff jutted, dancing over the ocean as though it was a pocket of rarified air. A man in a pristine uniform piloted the small craft, guiding it surely toward the ship that waited five miles off the coast of the smallest of the Greek Islands.

In the back of the skiff Royal sat with his arm around Tess, thinking he'd never seen her look lovelier. Though she had tied her long blond hair carefully under a pink silk scarf, strands of it escaped to blow about her face. Her face was pointed expectantly forward as though she was straining to reach their destination. This time her desire to reach her goal was not born of fear, but of excitement. She was so lovely. No man could have been prouder than he to have her on

132

his arm.

For hours on the plane, Royal worried that Tess would never regain her blush, that her eyes would never again wear any look other than anxiety. Royal had felt guilty that only his insistence forced her onto the plane, but, as with most of his feelings of contrition, this one had disappeared as he settled back to enjoy the flight. Her hand firmly in his, he had slipped into sleep, oblivious to her hours of agony as the plane flew on and on and on. Though the flight seemed endless to Tess, thankfully it was without incident. Now they were in Greece together, and she wondered how she could have ever considered staying behind.

Tess's hand gripped his now with enthusiasm as she pointed toward something of interest on the shore since the motor was too loud for them to speak. Dutifully, Royal looked in the general direction, pretended to have seen what caught her eye and kissed her as though telling her he appreciated the scene. That slight effort was all she needed. Royal adored the fact that Tess was so easily pleased. She never demanded, only shared. She was such a pleasure. No wonder he cared so much for her.

In what seemed like moments the skiff's motor was cut and the man guided it easily alongside the sparkling white yacht. Carefully, another crew member tied it down, reached a hand to help Tess climb onto a small dock, then handed her up the stairs.

"Here we are," Royal enthused when he joined her.

"Exactly where are we?" She laughed, her pink dress catching the breeze as she twirled toward him.

"On the *Adriana,* ma'am," came a voice from behind her. Tess turned toward a hard-faced man who stood quietly waiting for them to acknowledge him. When he saw he had their attention he spoke again without smiling. "Welcome aboard, Mister Cudahy, Ms. Canfield. We've been anticipating your arrival. I hope your flight was enjoyable."

"Yes, thank you, Captain," Royal said easily, obviously no stranger to this ship. Tess moved a little closer to him. This was all so overwhelming. Kansas seemed a universe away. "Is Mister Argyroupolis aboard?"

"Yes, sir. He left word that you were to get settled and have something to eat. He'll join you for dinner."

"Fine then. Shall we, Tess?"

His hand on her back, Royal guided Tess across the gleaming deck, following the steward who had been summoned silently. She looked over her shoulder now and again to give Royal a secret, delighted smile that made her face light up like the sun. She was glad she had come with him to see the world. She hoped soon she would see more of it with him as his wife. Royal grinned back but Tess had turned away and didn't see the empty points in his eyes that should have made her wonder if he was as happy as she that they were together.

As they were guided serenely over the decks and down the wide halls that led to their staterooms, neither of them was aware that Dimitri Argyroupolis watched their every move from his penthouse suite, gauging the quality of Royal's mistress.

She was indeed of finer lineage than the others he had brought over the years. Dinner would be quite enjoyable. That hour seemed very far away to him. But then half the pleasure of satisfying one's curiosity was in the wait. If there was one thing Dimitri understood it was how to play his hand.

He turned back to his immense desk littered with papers and telephones, the trappings of a man in command. Slipping on a pair of half glasses he at-

134

tended to business. Pleasure always could wait. It was never as satisfying as one imagined in the long run.

"Royal, this is incredible!" Tess breathed the moment the steward had left them. "I feel like a princess. I had no idea such things really existed. Look at the woodwork." She ran to the headboard of the bed and ran her hand over the carved mahogany. "And the chairs! I swear they're covered in silk."

Royal laughed as he slid out of his jacket and turned to view himself in the wall of mirrors. "Of course they are. Dimitri came from nothing. Now that he has all the money in the world he only wants the best of everything. He'll never sit on a donkey again as long as he lives—I hope."

"I imagine he won't," Tess murmured, continuing with her exploration. Royal heard her exclamation of delight from the bathroom and followed her as she went to the adjoining suite on the other side.

Leaning casually against the door, he watched her, so childlike in her delight, so generous in her praise of Dimitri's taste in art. He was lucky to have the love of such a woman. Tess was so young, so exquisitely beautiful that it made his heart ache. She deserved so much more than what she had. He closed his eyes, knowing his failings kept her from having it all.

"Royal? Royal, are you all right?"

She was at his side now, her fine, delicate hands reaching toward him, touching his face. Hers was a charming map of concern. He leaned down and kissed her lightly, taking her into his arms.

"I'm fine, love," he answered, though his heavy sigh told her differently.

"No, you're not. What on earth were you thinking?"

He shrugged. "About how things change when you

135

least expect them to. Even someone like Dimitri could wake up and find himself back where he started. It happens all the time. He's smart, sometimes not intelligent, but he is one of the smartest men I've ever met. Yet now the authorities are coming down hard on him because some of his ships aren't considered safe. I'm always fighting to keep him on the right side of the law. But another spill like the one off New York and he's going to be in very deep difficulties."

"But certainly he has enough money to overcome those kinds of problems," Tess assured him, leaning her head against his chest.

"Perhaps. He stretches himself thin, leverages himself too dearly. Half the time I don't know what goes on. His empire is too big. I'm only one counsel out of many. It's difficult to know what to advise when I'm unsure of what's happening in other areas of his empire. And, as Dimitri's future goes, so goes mine, my darling. He's my most important client. His business keeps me a wealthy man, far beyond my wildest dreams. His business and Astra's family wealth, of course. . . ."

Tess stiffened in Royal's arms. She hated to be reminded of his family and despised it when Royal mentioned his wife's wealth. Sometimes she wondered if, perhaps, his reluctance to leave his family had more to do with Astra's financial power over him than his concern for her feelings or his sons' peace of mind.

Immediately she banished the thought. Royal wasn't like that. She knew him too well to believe it. Besides, he was a rich man in his own right. He didn't need Astra's money.

Tess raised her hands and placed her fingers on his lips. He took her hand gently away so that he could look deeply into her eyes. He smiled, thinking how her eyes were not quite sky blue but not the blue of the sea, either. Then his face was serious again.

"Would you still love me, Tess, if I were so poor I could only make a modest living writing wills for the masses?"

Tess's lips parted in surprise just before she smiled, allowed the smile to become a grin. "You're teasing me, Royal." She laughed. "I'd love you even if you were a one-armed bandit. You know that. Now stop this nonsense. I hate to be teased. Let's unpack and go exploring. What do you say?"

"I say there are better things to do on your first moments aboard ship," he murmured, pulling her back just as she was about to leave.

"Oh? Is there some ceremony one has to take part in?" Her eyes hooded as their bodies pulled together with the familiar longing that never seemed to wane.

"As a matter of fact," Royal answered quietly, his fingers expertly unlacing the bodice of her shell pink dress, "there is. Everyone knows that on the high seas you make love as often as possible."

Slowly, he pushed the dress from her shoulders. Tess shivered, not from chill, but from desire. Her fingers were tugging on his shirt, carefully freeing it from his belt. The soft cotton of her dress fluttered to her feet and Royal's hands gently cupped her breasts, pulling her bra down so that they were freed. His head bent, she felt his lips teasing her, his teeth nipping at her. Her head fell back, her long hair grazing the small of her back as her eyes closed and she gave herself up to him.

Royal held her, lowering her body to the lushly carpeted floor as she pushed at his clothes until he, too, was naked atop her. They rolled, gently, slowly, until finally, unable to restrain themselves, Royal took her to the gentle sway of the ship beneath them.

When Tess opened her eyes again Royal was cradled next to her like a baby, curled into her slick body. For a moment she could only think of how grateful she was to him for showing her the true way of love. He had eased her loneliness and her fear after her parents died. Suddenly, though, she realized that she was considering her emotions as gratitude and that surprised her, even dismayed her. Why on earth would she think such a thing? What they felt for each other was love, wasn't it?

"See how wonderful these seagoing traditions can be?" Royal murmured contentedly. "After all, you never know when a journey will be your last. Do you, Tess, my beautiful, beautiful girl?"

Tess trembled in his arms until he tightened his hold and loved her again. Visions of her parents' faces had come to dance in front of her again. Their last voyage had ended in death, and they would not have approved of the voyage she was taking now. How on earth could something that felt so right be wrong? She seldom asked herself that question, but when she did she knew the answer.

Tess turned into Royal and banished her guilt in love.

"Dimitri!"

Tess heard the subtle note of surprise in Royal's voice. She turned toward the center of the huge salon, expecting to see their host coming into the room. Instead, he stood in the middle of it, as though he had been there for some time.

His huge body was relaxed, his hands casually stuffed in the pocket of his linen slacks. But his eyes were bright pinpoints of light, small eyes in a craggy face, that pierced Tess. Surprised by both his physical and sudden appearance, Tess remained where she stood while Royal went to greet the man.

"I didn't hear you come in," Royal hailed him. Tess tore her eyes from Dimitri long enough to glance at Royal.

There was a hesitation in his voice she'd never heard before, and his deference frightened her. Beside Dimitri Argyroupolis, the man she loved seemed to shrink a bit, seeming less a golden god than he had been only moments before.

"I walk in my home as though it were a temple, Royal. I revere all the good things that have come to me. I see you've brought something quite exquisite with you."

Dimitri's voice was grainy and cool like the morning tide over white sand. His eyes never left Tess, even as he took Royal's hand in his and shook it perfunctorily. Then he began to move, gracefully for such a large man, toward Tess. Mesmerized, she watched him come, wondering where it would be that he chose to stop and greet her. She lost her mental bet as he moved confidently into the serene space that surrounded her, bringing with him a jolt of energy that seemed almost predatory.

Tess looked to Royal for assistance, threatened by the man's closeness. Royal remained where he was as though the dance had been determined and there was nothing he could do about it. On his lips was an insipid smile, as if he was waiting for the billionaire's approval of Tess. Anger began to boil inside her, then she felt Dimitri take her hand in both of his, covering her fingers — fingers that were too soft for a man.

"Dimitri Argyroupolis, Tess Canfield."

Royal's introduction was dreamy, self-satisfied. Tess

139

felt him fade into the background as she, in turn, became an all too physical focal point of their host's attention.

"Tess, a lovely name," Dimitri said.

Tess's eyes met his defiantly. She wasn't afraid of him, but rather nervous because Royal seemed to be. She rose to this man's unspoken challenge as though protecting Royal from him.

"Thank you. It suits me," Tess answered curtly, though her voice was as sweet as honey.

Her honest eyes met his and, for an instant, Dimitri Argyroupolis seemed hesitant. Then his gaze was bright again and perused her body as if to confirm that she measured up to some unspoken standard. Tess removed her hand from his grasp.

"You have an unusual collection of photographs, Mister Argyroupolis," she commented, turning toward the wall, hoping to bring Royal closer to them.

Luckily, he did move. Standing beside her, though, he neither took her hand nor wound his arm around her. She felt better for his proximity and softened when she looked back at the old man. For indeed, he was old. The tan, the exact cut of his hair, his clothing, made him seem if not young, then at least of something less than advanced in age. Now she saw he must be at least seventy.

"Call me Dimitri, please," he answered, moving to the other side of her as he placed his large hand on her shoulder. He removed it the instant before she was going to ask him to. "And the photographs are indeed fabulous, are they not?"

Tess saw him flick his wrist. Behind them a waiter began to fill a tray with drinks. Dimitri seemed not to notice the man as he offered refreshments. He handed her a delicate crystal glass, never taking his eyes from

140

her as he continued to speak about the photos.

"I've always had an interest in photography. Candid photography, that is. To catch a person in an act, any act, without their knowledge, is to know them. This one, for instance," Dimitri said, holding out his hand toward the photo without touching it, "is one of my favorites. The lady of means caught with the expression of a shop girl; the gentleman who has acquired much in his life looking as though he has lost his soul to boredom. The photographer, obscure except to those who . . ."

"Jacques-Henri Lartigue," Tess said, interrupting him. "I believe the photo was taken in the early nineteen hundreds. I've seen it discussed in many books."

Dimitri's thick dark brows rose only slightly. Tess was sure he seldom was amazed at what other people knew and, if he was, he preferred not to show it.

"Exactly so," he answered. "The photograph is Auteuil, *Friday at the Races*. I believe the year was nineteen eleven to be exact. You know your photography, my dear. Of course, these are not terribly precious, their monetary value is negligible. Still, it does my soul good to see faces such as these, caught for eternity."

"Monetary worth is the least of its value, Mister Argyroupolis. I would imagine that its historical value is extremely precious. You do believe that there is historical value in this type of work?"

He moved away and went to a long, low couch. Slowly, he lowered himself and crossed his legs. Royal went to join him. Tess bristled, wishing that he had at least stayed with her. They weren't trained dogs there for his amusement, after all. She stood her ground.

"Please, Ms. Canfield, sit."

Tess inclined her head, graciously doing as she

141

was asked.

"I'm intrigued by your comment. You would find some photo of a man and woman of class of historical value?"

He was baiting her, teasing her, and Tess knew it. Yet she was powerless to stop herself from trying to put him in his place. Though her respect for Royal was immense because his wealth had been hard won, her respect for Royal's client was nonexistent because he chose to use his wealth for intimidation.

"Absolutely. In its most basic elements it is historically valuable. The clothing, for instance. A textile artist and historian could make much of it. Look at the feathers on the hat. It is of historical value given the conservation difficulties we experience now that no one ever considered in the nineteen hundreds. The way the man and woman relate to each other are historically relevant from a sociological . . ."

"I see," Dimitri cut her off, obviously tiring of her opinion. "Royal, did you look into the matter with the Jamaican registry for me? The docks in Los Angeles and New York are still giving me difficulties on that."

Startled, Tess almost spoke up to reprimand him for his rudeness, but a quick, warning look from Royal hushed her. Her face flushed with anger. She might be young, but she was well versed in etiquette. No matter how rich you were, you didn't treat a guest rudely. What was the matter with Royal?

With great effort Tess controlled her anger as she lifted her glass to her lips, knowing she and Royal would have much to discuss later. There was absolutely no reason Royal should accept this treatment, either. He was a great attorney. He did have other clients, perhaps not as rich as Dimitri Argyroupolis, but money wasn't everything. She was sure he would see that.

Tess excused herself four hours later. It had taken four hours to eat the sumptuous feast that had been laid before them in the gold and crystal dining room. Caviar eggs, lobster bisque, quail, a myriad of sorbets. Tess lost count of the delicacies that had found their way to the table.

Everything was delicious, naturally, and served with impeccable decorum. Yet the two men had talked of nothing but business. Once she had ventured a question and received a pat on the hand from Dimitri, on whose right she had been seated.

"A spirited little girl, Royal," he had said. "But she should learn when a lady speaks."

Tess couldn't believe her ears. She had never considered herself a proponent of women's liberation, feeling that people should be rewarded for their talents, not their sex, but she was about to change her political standing. Yet what she thought and what she did were two very different things.

Not only was this man Royal's client, he was also one from whom power emanated as easily as the sun radiated warmth. For some odd reason Tess felt as though she was physically imprisoned by his every whim. Finally, at ten o'clock, she found she could leave the table, offer a civil good night and flee the dining room.

After taking a wrong turn and becoming so lost a steward had to escort her back, Tess found her stateroom. Now, though, nothing impressed her: not the gorgeous view of the Greek Islands, not the abundance of priceless works of art, not the wealth of their host. She only wanted to be off this ship and home in her little house where the world revolved around Royal. That was a happy world; this was a sham.

Trying not to blame Royal for that evening's fiasco,

Tess drew a bath, hoping to calm her nerves. Every comfort had been considered: bath salts, a thick terry robe, perfumes, hairbrushes, and combs were all laid out by an unseen servant. Though it felt odd to be pampered so, Tess took advantage, hoping to drown her anger in scented steam.

Stripping, she stepped into the tub and sank down until only her shoulders peeked above the bubbles. She closed her eyes, resting her head against the curved back of the onyx tub. Slowly, she relaxed, every tense muscle calming under the hot water and the scented bubbles. When the door to the stateroom opened and closed, Tess barely heard it. Tired from the long flight, exhausted by the assault of Dimitri's wealth and manner, Tess didn't call out. She was miffed with Royal anyway. He had treated her as though she was a concubine and not the woman who would one day share his home and his name.

Aware that Royal was in the room, Tess kept her eyes closed, enjoying her little charade. Let him work to get back into her good graces. After all, she had held her tongue, sitting at dinner like a little child waiting for a parent's praise.

Tess felt him sit on the side of the tub. She remained still, aware of every nuance of her body. She felt soft and ready for love. Tendrils of damp hair escaped the pins and lay against her neck. Her lips were open, wet with steam. Then the water parted; a hand reached under the bubbles and touched her breast, first tentatively, toying with her nipple before capturing the perfectly formed orb and letting his hand slide down her body toward her flat stomach, her . . .

Tess's eyes flew open. She cringed away from the feel of his touch. This wasn't Royal at all. Sitting on the edge of the black tub Dimitri Argyroupolis stared

144

down at her, his eyes glittering with anticipation.

"What in the hell do you think you're doing?" she screamed, her voice catching on fear and tears as she huddled against the corner of the tub. "Where's Royal? Get out of here this instant or I'll make you sorry you were ever born."

To her amazement the old Greek threw back his head and laughed. The sound of it curtailed her tears, but did little to assuage her anger.

"Just what do you think you could do to me on my own ship that would make me sorry?" he asked, obviously delighted by her threat.

"I . . . I don't know," Tess stammered, fully aware now that there was nothing she could do to him. If she screamed no one would hear her. Even if they did, the servants wouldn't dare come to her rescue.

"See? It is so simple when you think things through. And as to Royal?" Dimitri shrugged nonchalantly. "Well, I believe he is still in the dining room. Unfortunately, our wine was a bit too strong for him. He will sleep there tonight, I think."

"So you just decided you would sleep here," Tess drawled, knowing that the only way to deal with someone like Dimitri was to stand up to him. Tears would never sway him; anger would only delight him.

"The thought crossed my mind. You are a lovely young woman, Tess. I am an experienced man. Royal is a boy compared to me," he bragged matter-of-factly.

"Royal could be a cow for all I care, and loving him would be preferable to the thought of laying down with a pig like you."

"Oh, you are a hard one. I shall enjoy this immensely. Royal didn't tell me you had such spirit. In fact, Royal didn't tell me a thing about you."

"Let me tell you, then. I am not for sale, and I am

not above bringing charges against you for sexual harassment in any court in the world. I grew up on a farm, and I have a couple of tricks up my sleeve that we used on the horses. Now if you'd care to give it a whirl I guarantee you that you won't be playing stud the rest of your life. So get out of this room and leave me alone or I will show you the kind of ladies Kansas breeds."

Dimitri watched her carefully while she spoke. He did truly see a beautiful woman lurking inside the girl before him. She needed only a little more time to blossom, a loving hand to bring her to the fruition of that beauty.

The surprising thing was, she wasn't joking with him now. She honestly didn't want him. He had made a mistake, though it was only a small one. Men like him never made big mistakes.

He stood up, towering over the tub. Though Tess protected herself pitifully, her arms thrown over her naked breasts, Dimitri admired her courage. He had no desire to take a woman, any woman, by force. He had only thought, given Royal's last mistress, that this one would be quite the same.

"I'm sure Kansas breeds very fine women who have the ability to tame a stallion. I do not think I should like to be tamed in quite that manner." He walked slowly toward the door. Tess watched him carefully, not trusting that he would leave. Her heart was in a vise as he turned back to her again. "But don't fool yourself. I have chosen not to press this matter. If I did, Kansas or not, you would be mine. Tell me only one thing. Why are you with Royal Cudahy?"

"I love him," Tess said quietly.

Dimitri's laugh sounded all the way through the suite. Even when he closed the door Tess imagined that she could still hear it.

Climbing out of the tub she wrapped herself in the terry robe and lay on the bed, wondering if Royal would come to her that night, wondering if Dimitri knew something she did not. She fell asleep with quiet tears wetting her cheeks. This was not how things were supposed to be. This was not the stuff dreams were made of.

Tess lay under the broiling sun as she had for three days. She read and sketched, her tan deepened from a honey gold to bronze. Royal breakfasted with her in their suite, then went off to do whatever it was he did with Dimitri. He returned in the evening, sometimes to dine in their room and once to take her into a village on the island. For three days she had not seen Dimitri, and was finally beginning to relax. His late-night visit was not forgotten, but she realized it would not be repeated. It seemed Dimitri Argyroupolis had forgotten Tess Canfield existed.

Flipping onto her stomach, Tess pulled at the bottom of her suit and sipped at a lovely punch a steward had placed beside her. With a giggle she realized that she could easily get used to this kind of treatment. Thank goodness she wasn't the type to confuse a moment's pleasure with the idea that it would be with her for a lifetime.

Just as she lay her head on her crossed arms, a shadow fell across her, cutting the Aegean sun in two. She opened her eyes, saw Dimitri standing above her and cringed.

"Not to worry, Tess Canfield. I am only here to talk to you, though I must say that I would still enjoy the opportunity to please you. You are quite exquisite."

Chuckling, he sat in front of her on a deck chair,

splaying his long legs out in front of him as he surveyed the ocean as though it belonged to no one but him.

"I'd rather not discuss that if you don't mind," Tess answered curtly.

"Of course not. You're not the kind of lady to enjoy that type of repartee," he said. "I understand that now. I'm afraid I was a horrible host. You see, it's not often I find someone with firm ideas visiting this ship of mine. Most of those who come here, men or women, come for pleasure or business or money or all three."

"I came for one of those things. I came at the pleasure of Royal who is the man I am committed to," Tess said.

She curled into a sitting position and grabbed her robe. If it was talk Dimitri wanted she would gladly oblige. Tess had to admit that she was intrigued by this man. He had everything, yet he still wanted her. Of course, his desire could have been merely a whim based on his need to control everything he saw. She possessed enough vanity to hope it was the former.

"That is a funny thing. You don't seem like a woman who would enjoy playing second fiddle," Dimitri noted.

"But I don't. Royal treats me like a queen," Tess said proudly.

"I am sure. But I didn't mean in the way he treats you. I was referring to his wife. I understand he has a wife at home?" Dimitri was teasing her now and inadvertently he had told Tess something she hadn't known.

Startled, she flushed with happiness and embarrassment. Royal must truly love her if he had never brought Astra with him. Yet under Dimitri's watchful eye she also felt the shame of her relationship.

"Yes, he does. I'm not proud of the fact that I love

148

him and he is still married, but that will change soon."

"I see. I am sorry."

"Sorry?" Tess's lips parted. What a strange thing for him to say.

"Of course I am sorry," he bellowed, "that you should be wasted on a man who has already made his bed."

"No need to be sorry. Royal and I have no wish to hurt his wife, but we love each other deeply. I find it joyous that he loves me so well."

"Ah, how well he loves you. He hides you away from his friends, I suppose."

"He does not!" she objected. "Everyone knows he's unhappy with his wife. He's only waiting for the right time to tell her he's leaving. I find that admirable that he should care so much, be so responsible."

"And when, if, you are the wife, do you think there will be another Tess Canfield to take your place?" Dimitri postured.

"No," she said simply.

"So sure of yourself. So very sure. I hope you are right. Now, I wish to apologize. I don't do that very often, hardly ever to women. But I made a mistake. You are young and sure of yourself, of your lover. I hope you are right about both."

He slapped his ample thighs and pushed himself off the chair, a huge grin on his face.

"I *am* right."

"So you say, Tess. I think you're a special woman, one who is not bought with power or money. I would like to see you again sometime. I would like to see what you become. It isn't often that I look at people long enough anymore to judge their value. I am much better with things. But I have watched you." He chuckled at the surprised look on her face. "You think I work as

149

hard as Royal? No, when he is poring over contracts I sit and watch my world go on about me. You've been part of it for three days. You are a lady, Tess, who I think has great potential for love. I would like to know if it is ever realized. Will you promise to tell me? I think it should amuse me to hear of your adventures with Royal."

"Then I'll never see you again. I wouldn't dream of telling you the secrets of my heart," Tess answered flippantly.

"No?" He raised one amused eyebrow. "That sounds like a challenge. Nothing I like more than a challenge. Shall we shake on it? I will bet that someday I shall know more about your love than you do."

"Not from my lips." Tess held out her hand.

She smiled, too, liking him more with each moment. Gone was the predatory glint in his eyes, replaced by a delightful glow.

"Perhaps you're right. I usually win, though. Now, it is your last few days with me. Your lover is working. I will take you and show you my treasures. Royal tells me you are an artist. Perhaps I should add one of your works to my collection."

Tess stood up and hung her head for an instant. An artist, she thought wryly. It had been a long time since she'd finished anything she started. Squaring her shoulders, she looked at him.

"I'd have nothing you'd want now, but someday, perhaps."

"Someday I would like to have your friendship. Let us start today. I think I like you better than Royal, anyway. He says 'yes' too often for my taste. I like a good 'no' now and again."

"I suppose I've given you enough to last a while."

"I would say so."

150

He offered his arm. Tess took it. A bond began and grew as they walked the ship, discussing the artworks Dimitri had collected over the years. Their tour didn't end until dusk when Dimitri left her at her stateroom. She showered and dressed carefully for dinner, surprised that she was looking forward to seeing him again.

In many ways he was like her father. A man of action who went about getting what he wanted. He worked hard as a young man, overcoming horrible obstacles. So had her father. The only difference was Harv Canfield had craved the solitude of the farm and Dimitri had created his solitude.

Now Tess felt as though she had broken a barrier with him. He accepted her as a person of worth, and they had made those first tentative steps toward enjoying one another as friends. It had been a long time since someone had extended their hand to Tess in friendship. When she returned home she vowed that she would end this self-exile from the world.

When Royal came in to change she found that she had almost forgotten he was the reason she was on Dimitri's ship. A little bit of her heart was disappointed that he appeared. But that part was so small Tess was unaware of her disappointment, unaware that she had even questioned her commitment to him.

"I wondered how long he would keep you working," she said as she went to him and offered her cheek for a kiss.

His hands felt different as he put them on her bare arms. There was a bit less warmth. Perhaps, though, the lacking wasn't in him. Just maybe it was in her.

Tess forgot that feeling by the time dinner's second course arrived. It would be a very long while before she remembered it again.

* * *

The small boat roared to life. Tess, sitting on a tiny platform on the back of the yacht, tensed the muscles in her arms, waiting for the yank of the ropes. A moment later she was up and skiing through the crystalline waters, forgetting everything but the power boat in front of her.

Though it had been years since she'd water-skied, the talent for it came back immediately. She even took the chance of jumping the white wave that came her way.

From the boat she heard a roar of approval and knew that it was Dimitri enjoying her performance. Had she a little more courage Tess would have lifted a hand to wave at him. As it was, she simply glanced toward the yacht as she spun by it. Dimitri, with his usual zest, was waving frantically to her, a grin on his face. Royal was beside him, smiling benignly as he watched.

Royal didn't care for the outdoors the way Tess did. He especially eschewed the water, believing the surface to be an illusion, the depths filled with terrors. It was the only thing they truly disagreed on. Still, he enjoyed watching her brown body tense with concentration.

In the second her eyes raked over the deck of the yacht, in the moment she thought how fantastic Royal looked in his white pants and shirt with the sleeves rolled up over his strong arms, in that second Tess lost her concentration. She was making a turn, her eyes had left the boat and her ski hit a wave head-on. Instantly, her body was jarred and thrown up and, she thought, away from the powerful speedboat that had held her ropes.

She hit the water hard, not knowing if the roar she

heard just before she went under was the force of her fall against water as hard as concrete, or the dismayed call of Dimitri aboard the yacht.

Then she was falling, falling, feeling so warm, then suddenly cold. She tried to move her arms, in fact felt as though she was moving her arms, climbing toward the surface of the sea, climbing toward the light and air. But the feeling was only a mirage. Instead, she was swimming weakly downward into the cold forever embrace of the sea. Her lungs cried for air. She was beginning to panic. Her head hurt so badly, she couldn't focus.

Tess was losing consciousness, descending deeper and deeper until a hand miraculously took hold of her. It was strong and sure and pulled her away from the depths, dragging her to where the sun glinted off the deadly blue of the ocean. Just as her head broke through the water, just as she felt an arm wrap about her neck, Tess Canfield lost consciousness, only to awaken hours later in her bed on Dimitri Argyroupolis's yacht.

"Thank you," she whispered weakly.

"Shh," Dimitri cautioned. "Hush now. It was a terrible fall. The doctor has seen you. You'll be fine. A bruise on the beautiful skin is all. Just a bruise. But you must rest now."

"No," Tess groaned, fright caving in on her. She remembered it now: the feeling of calm, the sureness of death in a watery grave. She hadn't been ready to die, but was powerless to stop death's coming. He had saved her. "I want to thank you." She held his hand as though it were her lifeline. Without him beside her she was afraid she would fall again.

"I only wish it was me you had to thank," he replied gently as he took her hand and passed it away. Another

153

man grasped it. She could feel his own fear, feel his dread. Her eyelids fluttered as she fought the sleep. The doctor must have given her something. She tried to focus and when she did it was Royal she saw. "It is Royal you have to thank. I think he saw his life sinking with you, dear Tess. It is he who saved you, not I, though I wish I had. It would be worth such gratitude."

Painfully, Tess turned her head to look into Royal's hazel eyes; eyes the color of early fall. The color of fear. She closed hers, tears seeping from the corner. She hadn't the strength to thank him as he deserved. How blessed she was to have him. How very blessed to have someone who cared less for himself than he did for her.

The last thing she remembered was Royal's head lowering onto the bed beside her. What she didn't know was that he was thanking God he wasn't going to have to explain her death to anyone—especially Astra.

"Dimitri, I'm sorry we're leaving early." Tess's arm was linked through his as they waited for Royal to finish a call to the States. "Now that I've come to like you I hate to leave."

"I will take that as a compliment, although it wasn't as prettily said as I would like."

"Too many people say things you want to hear, Dimitri, I only tell you what is in my heart."

"My heart is saddened, too, by your departure. There was so much we needed to find out about one another. Still," he sighed, "I can understand. I think you gave Royal quite a scare. He wants you back on land before anything else happens. You'll feel better among your own things, I'm sure."

154

"I feel fine now," she said happily. "But I suppose you're both right. This has been a bit more exciting than I ever expected. Perhaps when I get home I'll start painting again. I'll paint a portrait of you from memory."

"I will hang it in a place of honor," he said quietly, executing a small bow as Royal came to join them.

"Dimitri," Royal said, winding his arm about Tess's waist. "Everything is taken care of. I've managed to convince Tandy and Johnson that they should not consider a hostile takeover of your tooling holdings . . ."

"Royal, please. We'll talk of that over the phone. Now I only want to kiss Tess and wish you both well. I'll expect you back soon, and I will not take 'no' for an answer. Next time no work, only ouzo and lamb for us."

"Next time no waterskiing." Tess laughed, then softly kissed both his cheeks before she whispered, "Thank you again, Dimitri. I am glad we talked. I'm glad we didn't leave things unsaid."

"Should you need anything," he whispered back, knowing he did not have to finish the thought. Tess nodded into his shoulder, then smiled a glorious smile at Royal before they made their way down the ramp.

As the boat drew away from the yacht, Tess waved. Dimitri looked old and alone standing on the prow of the ship. She hoped she would see him again. As though reading her mind, Royal put a reassuring arm around her and kissed her hair. She leaned into him, happy that she was not as alone as Dimitri.

"Ladies and gentlemen, we'll be landing at Charles de Gaulle International Airport in approximately ten minutes. Please fasten your seatbelts and return your

155

tray tables to their upright position. The weather is overcast with winds coming from the south. The time is eight-ten in the A.M."

Beside her Royal slept. Tess carefully did as she was instructed, leaning over her lover to fasten his belt without waking him. She felt the plane lurch, the engines cut as they began their descent. Over the loudspeaker came the same instructions in French. Tess settled back, her eyes forward as she listened without understanding.

Again she had the unsettled feeling that the man just behind and to the right of where she sat was watching her. Not exactly watching but, rather, contemplating her. Though she didn't find the sensation unnerving, she was curious about his interest in her. Yet when she had risen to freshen up in the first-class ladies' room, he had only nodded to her as she passed. Now she wondered if she should perhaps introduce herself. Just to satisfy her curiosity it would be nice to know why he found her so intriguing.

As she was about to do just that the plane lurched again. This time her fellow passengers sat up straighter in their seats, every nerve aware that this was not the normal sound a plane made on descent.

Tess steeled herself, panic rising from the pit of her stomach. She had boarded this plane in Athens without a thought to her previous apprehensions. After all, they had come all the way from Los Angeles, changing planes in Paris to reach their destination in Athens. Nothing had happened then and nothing would now. Still, she couldn't help the instant, cold terror that gripped her.

A flight attendant walked quickly past her. Tess's hand found Royal's. He slept on. The plane lurched again. Suddenly, she felt someone's hand covering

156

hers. Her frightened eyes turned back, seeking the man, the one who hoped to calm her. It was the same one who displayed such interest in her.

His eyes were dark, but of a hue that didn't hide the kindness in them. Their warmth seemed to radiate across his face from his creaseless brow to his fine-lined lips. A stray beam of light caught his black hair, glittering off the fine strands of silver hidden in the lush waves.

"They're hitting air pockets. It's all right."

He sat back, the protective hand withdrawn. Tess smiled weakly. She felt almost mesmerized, whether by his looks, his words or the calm assurance he had offered, she didn't know. She wanted to look back at him again, but her eyes had snapped forward and she waited for the next hesitation in the plane. It seemed to be dropping faster now at an angle that was far too steep. Carefully, she looked out the window and saw, to her horror, the ground coming closer with an immediate clarity that was frightening.

So many things happened at once then. Royal woke up. Sleepily, he asked "what," then grabbed her hand and groaned. A flight attendant fell in the aisle, clutching at Tess's seat to keep herself from sliding toward the cockpit.

"Head down," she screamed, but Tess was frozen in position. She couldn't move, no sound came from her throat as she tried to scream.

Then her head was shoved down forcefully toward her knees. It had been him, the man in the seat just behind her. She had time to hope that he had fastened his seatbelt again just before the plane hit the ground and she heard the plane ripping apart, saw the floor beneath her disintegrate and the ceiling above her burst into flames.

Her hands fumbled with her seatbelt. She could feel the smoke searing into her lungs. She couldn't breathe. Couldn't breathe! Help, Royal, she wanted to yell. But Royal was no longer in the seat beside her. There was nothing beside her but a gaping hole and part of a wing. Her eyes burned with heat and smoke. Finally, she felt the belt give. She was free. But free to do what?

In front of her a man and a woman still sat in their seats, casual in death, their heads faceless, burned beyond recognition by the initial explosion. From behind her Tess heard panicked screams and desperate moans. People were moving but she couldn't see them, only feel their hands and feet as they crawled over her, their breath as they inhaled when pushed away by someone more frantic.

Desperately, she tried to move but her legs wouldn't work. She put out her hands to pull herself out of her seat. A man landed atop her. She tried to push him away and, as she did so, pain seared through her arms, coursing through her body until it exploded in her brain. Tess saw the flames perfectly now. The explosion, the fire—the fire was coming closer—this was not her imagination.

Her throat. Scorched with heat, constricted. She couldn't scream, couldn't beg for help. Somewhere in her mind Tess realized she was feeling what her parents had felt. Now she was at one with them. Closing her eyes she waited for death, fiery death. It was coming to her now the way it should have come before. She should have been with her parents in the end and she wasn't. God was bringing her along more slowly.

The incredible calm that grasped her was flung away just as quickly as hands clawed their way to her. Someone outside was pulling at her. She pulled away. Ready now to join her family, but the person on the outside would have none of it. That person meant for her to live so he struggled, fighting his foe of fire and smoke, finally triumphing as he dragged Tess's limp body from the plane and forced her to run. When she collapsed he took her in his arms, strong arms that were sure life would continue. She didn't want it to, though, not without her ma and pa—not without Royal. But Tess didn't have the strength to fight back so she didn't try. Instead, she lay in the arms of her rescuer, letting the pain take her to another place, the one where hopefully she would die.

Fourteen

Davina pulled the sheets around her naked body. She was cold, always cold these days. March's bleak days dragged on and on until she thought she would scream, driven mad by the grayness and the sameness. Somewhere she heard a knocking accompanied by a low humming sound that set her teeth on edge. Nobody wanted her to sleep. Nobody wanted her to be rested or happy or content. The world was involved in a conspiracy against her, with Noel leading the treachery.

He had been as good as his word. A year ago Davina was relegated to the mail room, assigned the most trivial, demeaning and menial of tasks. She sorted the mail, pushing her metal cart up and down *High Life*'s halls. She ordered office supplies and brought coffee into the conference room during editorial meetings. She, Davina Montgomery, had brought coffee when she should have been sitting at the head of the table, at the right hand of her father. How horrible those first few months were.

Everyone in the office knew about her and took every opportunity to twist the knife further into her back. Oh, they seemed nice enough on the surface. From secretaries to executives the *High Life* employees played their part, smiling at her and offering their assistance. But Davina was smarter than they were; she knew what was behind the smiles and their offers of help—falseness.

The minute she was out of earshot those smiles turned into laughter and gossip. Noel Montgomery's long-lost daughter was nothing more than a gofer and they loved it. How it delighted them. Well, no more. It was almost over now. Finally, Davina was beginning to take command of her life. Soon she would work her way into a position of power at *High Life* and everyone would know what was what. Thankfully, a small group of loyalists already existed.

Davina smiled lazily, thinking of those farsighted few who had thrown in their lot with her: Stephen, an art director; Eric, in sales; Marsha, a production assistant. Even two or three of the secretaries realized that their bread would soon be buttered by a new hand and all they had to do was wait, work with her, to make sure that butter was thick and creamy.

The knocking became more insistent, the rumbling came closer, vibrating ever more urgently until Davina thought her body would erupt with the resonant sound. Bolting up in her bed, almost awake now despite her hangover, Davina angrily shook her head, trying to clear it completely. Concentrating as best she could, she focused on the sounds.

The rumbling came from outside. Gardeners mowing the lawn. When this house was hers, no work would start before noon. The knocking was another matter. It took her a moment to realize the insistent sound was coming from her bedroom door. She pitched back the cover and, naked, stormed to the door, throwing it open.

161

"What!" she bellowed, her eyes flashing her displeasure.

Benton, her father's longtime servant and the bane of Davina's existence, stood in front of her. He was a spy, Davina knew. She had played the game for a while, sweetly acquiescing to Noel's grand plan for her. She had hidden away all her seething anger, and he seemed quite pleased with her attitude, promoting her to production just before he left for Greece and Europe. He had been taken in hook, line and sinker. Benton, though, was another story. He hadn't cut her any slack. His sickly gray eyes always looked right through her. Standing in front of him in all her glory, Davina dropped the show. After all, Noel was gone and Benton was ripe for a little fun.

"Benton, I'm sorry," Davina said sweetly. "I didn't know it was you. I would have put something on if I realized . . ."

She lowered her eyes, inviting him to look at her lushly rounded body. Davina's fingers tickled her long dark curls, pulling them over her shoulder in a gesture of moot modesty. She glanced up, hoping to see him clutching his heart at the sight of such a treasure. Instead, he continued to look directly at her face, calmly informing her of the hour.

"You asked to be called at nine, Miss Davina. I've been trying to wake you. It is now exactly nine-thirty."

"What a shame you had to waste so much time," Davina murmured, leaning toward him, her breasts enticingly available. "Is there anything I can do to make up for putting you out so?"

"No, thank you, miss," Benton said quietly. He turned and walked evenly down the hall, his shoulders straight, his hands hanging loosely by his side.

Davina slammed the door behind him. Angrily, she stomped into the bathroom. So she'd be a little late for the meeting at ten. It would do those simpletons some good to cool their heels.

Almost everyone at *High Life* acted as though they were working toward the Nobel prize. Meetings, work, decisions—they treated each day as though it was life or death that the magazine get out on time. Well, this meeting couldn't happen without the boss's daughter. She was, after all, the new assistant to the vice-president of production. She'd come a long way in two years, and she was damned if she wasn't going to go a hell of a lot further.

"Let's get this show on the road," Davina called cheerily when she entered the production offices on the third floor of the *High Life* building.

A shower had pushed her spirits as close to happy as they could get. The beautiful clothes Noel still bought her helped. Owning a BMW helped. The little upper she had taken helped, too. A small little pill that seemed to make her life one hundred percent brighter.

Yet as she strode through the outer office she was dismayed to see no one was about. Curiously, she walked slowly toward the small conference room at the end of the hall. Davina heard a short burst of collective laughter, then silence.

They were already there. Talking about her, probably. How dare they? How dare they discuss her when she wasn't there, or even gather as though her presence was of no consequence? She threw the door open so roughly that it banged against the wall. Every eye in the room turned toward her. Their faces were a collage of amazement, triumph, amusement, and concern. At the head of the table sat Meagan Dayler, vice-president of production. She looked at Davina as she would an errant child, her appraisal coolly disapproving.

"Davina, I thought you had called this meeting for ten?" she said casually.

"I did. I was just a little late today. Car trouble," Davina answered, pulling herself up. She hoped that alone would be enough to intimidate Meagan. The older woman only raised an eyebrow.

"I'm sorry to hear that. Perhaps, next time, you could phone, and let us know you're having difficulty."

"I did. But no one answered," Davina said quickly without a trace of embarrassment, though everyone in the room knew her excuse was a lie.

"I see," Meagan answered, staring intently at Davina, her gaze unwavering.

Meagan Dayler had been in the publishing business a long time. She had a lot to share with this young woman who might, very possibly, take over the magazine. Meagan would have liked very much to feel good about that possibility. Instead, thinking about the future made her feel sick. *High Life* was a class act; Noel Montgomery's daughter wasn't.

"Why don't you sit down now and take over?" Meagan directed.

Davina smiled. She had gotten away with it again. Davina moved toward the head of the table.

"You can take a seat next to Blanche," Meagan ordered, not about to give up her seat. "I think I'll sit in so I can see how everything goes now that you're here."

Inside, Davina raged at the older woman, but took

164

the seat in the middle of the table anyway. She flipped open her briefcase, looked around to make sure everyone's eyes were on her and began.

"We will be on press with the July issue on the second of next month. We've had a request from advertising to hold the inside cover for Toyota until the fourth. . . ."

Meagan Dayler sat back in her chair, her tented fingers tapping against her lips as she watched, and listened to, Davina Montgomery. When the meeting drew to a close Meagan found she was shaking her head, slightly and sadly. Davina had potential that would never be realized. There was too much anger in her. Dangerous anger that would thwart everything she tried to do. Davina Montgomery would never be satisfied with simply doing a good job; she would only be satisfied with dominating any job she took.

The meeting ended and people rose, falling naturally into small groups as they went back to their jobs. Meagan put a hand on Davina's arm, holding her silently until everyone left the room. When they were alone Meagan went to the door and shut it. Davina bristled, but had no time to put Meagan on the defensive.

"Davina, it's not going to work," Meagan informed her without a trace of emotion. "Either you shape up, or I'm going to have to ask your father to ship you out the minute he returns from his trip. You've got a real knack for production, there's no doubt about that. But having a talent doesn't mean you're the best person for the job. Do you understand?"

Davina remained silent. Meagan reached out and touched Davina's shoulder, underscoring her point and concern. Davina pulled her arm roughly away from the other woman's maternal touch. Meagan sighed and adjusted her glasses.

"You have a responsibility, Davina, to this magazine and to the people who work for it. If you're going to lead them, as I'm sure you intend to do someday, then you must show them how responsible you are. You have to inspire confidence as a leader and a member of the team."

Davina's lips slowly moved into what could pass for a smile.

"I don't think the question is *if,* Meagan," she drawled. "The only question is *when.*"

"I think we'll have to see about that," Meagan answered shortly. She had been with Noel Montgomery too long not to be infected with a fierce loyalty.

"You can see all you want. I *know.*" Davina tapped the side of her head with a scarlet nail. "I know, Ms. Dayler, that I'm the last person you should fuck with."

"If I didn't know better, Davina, I'd say that was a threat."

"A promise," Davina answered happily. "It's a promise."

"I see."

Meagan walked out first. Davina interpreted this as a triumph. Happily she went about her business, expertly executing every order on her desk and solving a problem or two that seemed insurmountable. Her elation didn't last, though. One of her inner group, a birdlike girl named Mona who didn't want to remain in the typing pool, came to her just before the lunch hour.

"I think there's something you should see, Davina," Mona whispered, nervously handing

Davina a piece of paper. Davina took it without giving the girl a benefit of a look or smile.

"That old bitch," Davina growled as she read the memo a second time.

The message was written in longhand from Meagan Dayler to Noel Montgomery in Paris. In no uncertain terms, Meagan requested that Davina be transferred from production immediately.

"Type it," Davina ordered. Mona's face registered her shock. Davina felt the thrill of superiority. "Don't be an idiot. If you don't type it Meagan will rewrite it and have someone else do it. She's not stupid, you know. Just type it, have her sign the hard copy, then destroy it."

Mona nodded. Her fingers shook as she took back the memo. Head down, she tried to scurry out of the room, wondering now if she'd done the right thing. She didn't get very far.

"Mona, I mean destroy it completely," Davina hissed. "And if you ever breathe a word of this to anyone I'll have your job. On second thought, I'll have your head."

Mona made her escape, sure that Davina Montgomery meant every word she said, and quickly decided it was time to look for a new job.

Davina went to the huge front doors for the fifth time, opened them, peered at the empty drive, slammed them and retraced her steps ending where she began — in front of the wall of mirrors that led to the dining room.

She looked perfect, no doubt about it. Even after a long day in that hellhole called an office she had managed to pull herself together beautifully. Now

167

that her hair was being cut by a true professional, for which Noel paid a hundred dollars a shot, it fell in a glorious halo of blue-black curls and needed little effort to keep it impeccable. Her figure could use a little work, but then whose couldn't? Just an inch off the hips. Her tits looked great, though, especially in the dress she had chosen. Christian Lacroix certainly had a way with plunging necklines.

Davina shook her head, watching her three-tiered rhinestone earrings dance, reflecting the light of the foyer chandelier. She leaned closer to the mirror, practicing her repertoire of expressions.

Peevishness: bottom lip slightly pushed out. Seduction: both lips slightly apart, the tip of her tongue showing through. Anger: lips pulled tightly together. Delight . . . She stopped to eye her reflection curiously. Funny, she didn't have an expression for happiness. She would work on it later. Now she had something important to do.

Davina had spent the last four hours arranging for food and drinks in the dining room. She was expecting her friends, but they hadn't come. Now it was close to ten, and she was alone. The instructions to be at her home had been specific. Nine was the appointed hour. No one had come and no one had called, leaving her angry enough to spit nails. If Meagan Dayler hadn't been enough, this was too much. Davina hated to wait. She took action.

Turning from the mirror she was just about ready to race up the stairs despite her very high heels when she saw Benton watching her with that dead fish look of his. Had he been there long enough to see her making faces at herself like a three-year-old? Davina adjusted her body so that her nipples poked through the thin jersey of her dress.

"I'm going out, Benton," she informed him defiantly, as though combativeness would help her save face.

"Fine, miss. I imagine your father will be calling soon. Is there a message?"

Davina snorted and pushed past the servant. "Tell him I missed him so much I couldn't bear to be in this house alone."

"As you say, miss," he answered evenly.

Davina turned on the stairs and walked deliberately back to the man. She stood close to him, her lips almost touching his ear.

"Benton, I was joking. Get that stick out of your ass."

She was gone five minutes later, her BMW tearing out of the drive like a bat out of hell. Inside, Benton wondered if Mr. Montgomery had really known what he was doing when he took Davina into his home. He hoped the man of the house would be home soon. Otherwise, Benton might be forced to act and he'd hate to lose his temper over the likes of Davina Montgomery.

Davina reached Eric's apartment without any trouble. There hadn't been a cop in sight so the minor transgressions she committed while she drove went unnoticed, except by the motorists she almost took out as she sailed through a red light or two. Unfortunately, parking in Westwood was a bitch so, instead of wasting time, she pulled into a loading zone and walked the two blocks to Eric's security building.

Before she buzzed, Davina walked down the ramp to the iron gate that kept the tenants' cars somewhat safe from vandals and thieves. Satisfied that his car was there she wobbled back up the concrete ramp and buzzed a random apartment. As she suspected, the idiots in that apartment simply let her in without asking who it was.

Once inside she called for the elevator, entered and pushed the button for the tenth floor. Eric was about to get the surprise of his life. She rang his bell and waited, her patience translating into ice-cold fury.

"Davina, hey."

Eric cracked the door only enough for her to see that he was still dressed from work. She smiled, sweetly with her lips, monstrously with her eyes.

"Eric." Her voice was low and husky with warning. Eric blanched before his color came slowly back to his face. He had almost had enough of this. "What are you doing home, Eric?"

Davina put out a hand and pushed at the door. He held fast, then realized he had nothing to fear. This was his place. If she really got out of hand he'd have her thrown out. Damn if he wouldn't. Eric let go of the door. It swung inward, revealing a sight that chilled Davina. Stephen, Marsha, and two of the secretaries from work sat on the floor of Eric's apartment. Three pizza boxes were strewn about, along with beer and soda cans. Music played softly on the stereo.

"My, my, how cozy."

Davina ambled into the room. Everyone looked away, then took a chance they wouldn't turn to stone and looked back at her as she stood in the middle of the haphazard circle. There was courage in numbers. It seemed to infect them all to a degree. Eric had moved into the room and stood behind the sofa.

"Want a piece of pizza, Davina?" he asked, trying casually to play the host. Unfortunately, his voice broke.

"Pizza? No, I don't think so. You see, I sort of went past the point of hungry, despite the fact I have a feast laid out at home. Waiting for friends who never came just kind of killed my appetite. Know what I mean, Marsha?"

Marsha turned away muttering, "Davina . . ."

"What? Speak to me, Marsha. I thought I'd see you all at my place. Didn't I tell you my father's gone again? The whole place would be ours. Didn't I tell you nine o'clock? I waited. I waited to greet all of you at the door. I stood around for almost an hour and a half while you people sat here drinking beer and eating fucking pizza."

Davina's voice rose in perfect octaves until she was screeching her last words and kicking at the nearest greasy box. Cries of surprise and indignation went up from the five young people in the room. Stephen acted first. He was up on his feet and had Davina by the arms, pulling them back and down so they were pinned at her side. She struggled and shook him off.

"Davina, there's no call for that," Stephen said angrily. "Why don't you just leave?"

"No, not until I get some answers from my so-called *friends*. I told you what time to be at my house. I specifically remember telling you."

"That's just the problem." Eric spoke up, his handsome face contorted with worry. Kissing ass was one thing, but Davina had crossed the line. "You *told* us. We're tired of you giving the orders, Davina. It wouldn't hurt you to ask occasionally. We decided, individually, not to go to your place tonight. Then we got to talking, and we ended up here."

"And you couldn't call me?"

Davina was absolutely shocked. Her friends, turning on her for no good reason. What was the difference between telling and asking, for God's sake?

Marsha had found her courage and her voice rose sweetly in a room rife with emotion. Davina's eyes snapped toward her as though she could incinerate the beautiful blonde with one searing look. Marsha raised her chin and kept her eyes steady, though her hands wrung themselves in her lap.

"We just didn't want to, Davina. All you ever do is run people down. It's not fun anymore. Sure, we all have gripes with the job, but with you being mad is a way of life. We're just kind of tired of it."

"Oh, I get it," Davina cooed as if she just figured out how to put the pieces of a puzzle together. "You're just afraid. You're afraid that hanging around with me is going to get you in trouble. What a bunch of cowards," she sniffed. Her body was jerking under her lovely dress, her lips twitching. She shook her head, oddly trying to make herself seem the wounded party.

"Yeah, we're nervous about it." Stephen spoke now. The ball was rolling; they might as well see the play through. "We've all worked hard to get where we are, and we're not going to see our careers go down the tubes because you waltzed into *High Life* and pissed everyone off. Guilt by association and all that. Look at the stupid tricks you've been trying to pull on Meagan. She's a good lady, sharp, she doesn't need your kind of shit."

"What?" Davina's eyes widened, her heavily applied makeup giving her face a gruesome appearance as she exaggerated every expression. "What? You're worried about Meagan Dayler's feelings? If she can't take a little shit from me then she isn't worth her salt. . . ."

"Don't say that, Davina," Marsha cried. "She's

172

worth ten of you and, like it or not, she's our boss. We're not going to do anything that will make us sorry."

"Well, you just did something that will make you all sorrier than hell," Davina railed, "or are you forgetting that someday I'll own *High Life* magazine? Someday I'll be the boss, and I'll see every one of your asses in a sling for what you did tonight. For what you said to me. I'm Davina Montgomery. I own *High Life*. It's rightfully mine. I own it, do you hear me!"

"Not yet you don't," Eric said quietly. "And you probably never will."

Davina pulled back as though slapped. Stunned, she was speechless for just a moment as she and Eric faced off. She almost laughed when she realized he was right. Noel Montgomery was alive and well and young. Of course, her father owned the magazine. But she was well on her way to a powerful position. It wouldn't be long now before she would wield that power over these idiots. In fact, there was something she could do to speed up the process a bit and settle a score at the same time.

Slowly, Davina turned her back away, feeling the tension and apprehension of everyone in the room. Those vibes were like a shot in the arm. Without another word she left Eric's apartment. There was an awful lot to do and not much time to do it.

Dark places had never bothered Davina. She didn't feel threatened or spooked as she walked calmly through the deathly quiet night halls of the *High Life* offices. In fact, she felt an unusual calm as the shadows embraced her. Even when she reached the personnel offices she flipped on only a small light, preferring to struggle to find what she wanted rather than light up the entire room and dispel the darkness. Meagan Dayler's file was easily located. Flipping it open Davina found everything she needed. Her instincts had been correct.

Meagan Dayler lived alone in the Encino Hills. Nice. A neighborhood surrounded by hills and brush. No relatives in the area. Her file indicated a cousin in Oregon should be contacted in case of an emergency. Davina chuckled as she slipped the file in place. This was going to be one hell of an emergency.

Davina put her briefcase on top of the photocopy machine. Carefully, she opened the storage cabinet and took a bottle of toner from inside. She unscrewed the cap. The toner smelled awful, just the way she wanted it to. This was going to work, she was sure of it.

Just before midnight Davina went back down the elevator, her briefcase heavier than when she came in. Luckily, the night guard was away from his desk. Davina thanked her lucky stars for the call of nature. Quickly, she pulled the register toward her and signed herself out. She knew the guy on the desk wasn't the swiftest. She posted her leave as two A.M. He'd never notice and, if questioned, he would swear to anything rather than admit he'd been away from the desk or snoozing on duty. Davina felt quite proud of her little ruse.

In the car again, she drove carefully, thinking of nothing other than completing her plan. There was no reflection on the rightness or wrongness of what she was about to do, only the awareness that it must be done if she was going to save face, if she was going to amount to anything.

She found the street she was looking for with little difficulty. The night air was chilly and a fog had rolled in. The bedroom community in which she stood slept peacefully. No lights in the surrounding houses indicated an insomniac's last-ditch effort for comfort.

Meagan Dayler's home was as dark as the rest and as mundane. A typical ranch house, no more than three bedrooms. Davina walked carefully toward the side of the house, waiting for the barking of a pet. There was none. She smirked. Meagan probably didn't have the capacity to even care for a dog, much less the people who worked for her.

Davina found a side yard that was open for about ten yards. A tall wooden fence cut the grass in two. Davina knew she wouldn't have to climb it. More than likely two of the bedrooms were on this side of the house. All she needed to do was work her magic right here and she'd have a sixty-six percent chance of completing her mission.

Hunching down beside the house she held the bottle of toner as she surveyed the wall. There were lots of windows, all protected with grill work. Davina looked them over carefully. All those years of living in holes with her mother had finally paid off. She could spot grills without releases in an instant.

"Stupid, Meagan," she whispered, taking comfort in the sound of her own confident voice.

To her left, rather high up, curtains blew through a small rectangular bathroom window. Even in the dark Davina could see movement as the curtain moved in and out of the open space like someone breathing.

Standing on tiptoe, Davina splashed the toner up

and through the window. A bit of it trickled down on her. She turned her face, but not fast enough. The chemical bit into her skin. She wiped it away immediately, the sting throwing her anger into another gear. Now she worked quickly. She had the matches, but the window was high. Quickly she snuck back to the front of the house. A hose was rolled neatly by the front flower bed.

Carefully, Davina unhooked it, glanced over her shoulder to assure herself nothing had changed and ran back to the window. Gaining just enough height, Davina balanced on the green rubber hose, struck a match and held it up. It blew out. She took a deep breath, gauged the intermittent breeze and tried again. This time she cupped her free hand around the match and held it to a corner of the curtain that lay on the sill. The fabric took so quickly Davina jumped away, knowing she wouldn't have much time.

Frantically, in the glow of the fast-growing flame, she ran, remembering to take the hose with her. From the front of the house the flame couldn't be seen yet. Even as Davina got back into her car and drove past Meagan Dayler's home it still looked as peaceful as any on the street. Quietly, Davina wound her way through the curving streets of Encino Hills until she reached the crest of an uninhabited foothill. There she pulled off the road, knowing she could simply drive down the other side. No one could place her at Meagan Dayler's home that night.

Throwing the shift into park, Davina adjusted her seat so she was in a semireclining position. In the five minutes it had taken her to reach the summit of the hill the fire had spread. There was an eerie, but hardly unusual glow coming from the ranch house. Because of the dark Davina couldn't see the smoke, but she knew it was there. That was when Davina knew her fortune was changing for the better. She leaned her head back and watched.

Suddenly the roof of Meagan Dayler's home erupted into flames, the shingles feeding the fire like little, defenseless virgins offering themselves up for sacrifice. Davina bolted up in the seat of the car and laced her arms around the steering wheel.

Fire moved more quickly than even Davina would have imagined. In a matter of seconds the house looked like an inferno. Then something happened that was beyond her wildest dreams. Meagan Dayler ran screaming from her house. Of course Davina couldn't be sure the woman was screaming since she was too far away to hear. But she imagined that a woman on fire would make some sort of horrible sound. What a sight. What a night.

Disappointed, but knowing the time had come, Davina turned the ignition on her car and backed out of the dirt turnout. She had seen enough. Lights were coming on in the neighborhood, soon fire engines would be careening up the winding roads and Meagan Dayler would be taken to one of two places: the hospital or the morgue. Davina couldn't wait until morning to find out which one it was.

In the morning she knew she would finally be able to relax and start making some important decisions. After all, if Meagan wouldn't be in for a while it fell to Davina to keep the ball rolling at *High Life*. Now there was only one thing left to do. Make sure that someone saw her far away from this place. Coco's would do. Coco's was a place people went to be seen. Davina drove along Mulhullond, found the freeway and headed toward Hollywood.

* * *

Coco's was incredibly good for a Wednesday night. Crowded, noisy, smoke filled, wild. Davina loved it from the moment she first discovered the place. Unfortunately she never quite felt like she fit in. There was something different about the people who came to play after hours at Coco's.

Davina dressed the way they did, in all the right clothes, but the other women seemed to carry those clothes with just a little more panache — as though they'd been born in them rather than shopped for them. Davina danced like everyone else, but she imagined her arms and legs didn't have the fluidity of movement the other bodies maintained. Davina smoked and drank and laughed but, more often than not, she found she was laughing by herself, always on the edge of some circle, never in the center. Still, she enjoyed being here. Tonight she enjoyed it more than ever.

She ordered a drink and drank it down more quickly than usual. She needed to prowl, needed to make herself known to these people this evening. Instinctively she knew that wouldn't be difficult. Something new was emanating from her; a power that had never been a part of her before.

Boldly, Davina pushed through the crowd toward the dance floor, stopping only once to answer a man's admiring stare with one of her own before flipping her head back in a wordless promise. She wended her way through the writhing bodies and opened herself up to the pumping, pounding music. For a long while she stood motionless in the center of the dance floor. Then, slowly, she began to turn. Turn and turn and turn until her mind left her and only physical sensation remained.

Davina's arms rose above her head only to flutter

178

downward toward her body. She cupped her breasts, her hips writhing to the insistent pressure of the music and her self-inflicted caresses. Her hands moved down over her hips, her thighs, then up again until she was lost in the sheer joy of movement, the thrill of her own finally freed body and mind.

When she opened her eyes she saw that the other dancers had moved away, circling around her, giving her room to move. She was so wonderful, Davina knew, that they couldn't keep their eyes from her. With growing abandon she whirled in the center of that circle, creating a heat within the barrier of the almost silent crowd.

Davina saw the way the men looked at her, desiring her. She would never give in. She saw the way the women looked at her, angry that she should be the center of attention. Davina laughed. She would never relinquish the spotlight.

On and on she whirled, watching the faces: black, white, beautiful, tired, frantic, frustrated. They all stared at her. She made another turn, then hesitated, her dance cut off for only a second, but it was long enough to see the look on a particular woman's face. A look of admiration. From a woman no less.

Davina held out her hands toward the woman, who instantly moved in to join her. Together they began a dance that brought the crowd forward, pushing toward them as though they could possess them. On and on the two women went, never touching, but somehow joined invisibly as though they could never part even if they wanted to.

Faster, more insistently, the band played. Thicker became the smoke surrounding them. Images flashed through Davina's mind: her father and his black eyes; her mother and her dead ones; Meagan Dayler and her bright, bright body melting under the fondling flames.

And the final image. The woman who danced with her. Even behind her closed eyes Davina could see her. Skin whiter than white, hair the color of the heart of fire, eyes as green as emeralds. She loved that woman then. Loved her until the music ended and they stood face-to-face for the first time. In the silence, just before the applause, the other woman's chest heaving as she tried to breathe, Davina looked into the green eyes of that woman and thought she saw something linking them to one another. That frightened Davina. She didn't want to be joined with anyone.

Stumbling now, she left the dance floor and the club, left the woman with the red hair and green eyes and skin the color of frost and forgot her. When Davina pulled into the drive it was four in the morning. She felt drained of all energy. Everything Meagan Dayler had given her, the power and confidence, had been taken away by the woman who danced.

Davina dragged herself into the house, devastated that she should return home no better than she had left. As she closed her eyes and turned toward the curving stairway she saw a shadow in front of her. It moved. Her heart stopped. They had found out what she'd done and come for her. Then the shadow came forward into the soft light that had been left on in the hall.

"Miss Davina," Benton said quietly. "There's been an accident."

The power returned. The hope. The excitement. She prayed he was dead. It had to be him. Who else would Benton worry about? Noel Montgomery had

180

had an accident. Things couldn't be better. Davina leaned back against the door, faint with the thrill of it. Benton came to help her. She leaned against him. He would be hers, too, after all.

Fifteen

"You look awful, darling."

Giles raced up to Bonnie, taking her arm to help her to a chair. She jerked it away, hardly in the mood to play his delicate little love games.

"Just get me a seltzer, will you?" she muttered, one hand to her head.

Giles rushed to do her bidding. He was becoming absolutely obnoxious. If only his adoring public could see him now. Hardly the virile brute they loved to fawn over on that stupid game show.

Bonnie fell into a chair, leaned her head back and massaged her temples.

"Let me do that, my love," Giles murmured.

His square fingers were on her skin before Bonnie could stop him. He had shoved a cold glass of sparkling water into her hands. Bonnie gritted her teeth and tried to relax. She might as well enjoy it. He wasn't going to leave her alone, no matter what.

"Thanks," she said without much sincerity.

"Nothing, it's nothing," Giles commiserated. "Aren't you feeling well? I'd hate to have to tape

182

without you today. But I will, of course, if you're not up to it."

"I'll be fine. That's enough, Giles," she said peevishly.

Bonnie brushed his fingers away. It bothered her that she was bored with him. He was the best thing to come into her life in ages, but everything he did lately rubbed her the wrong way. Perhaps it was because Giles was so damned satisfied with his life. And why shouldn't he be? He had money, respect, a string of hits behind him. His career was over. Giles could afford to coast comfortably.

"What is it, honey? You can tell me." He had managed to slip around in front of her and now knelt at her feet. It was all she could do to keep from kicking him away like an annoying puppy. She closed her eyes again and took a long, cooling drink.

"I was just up late last night," she murmured.

"Coco's again?" Giles clicked. Bonnie detected a hint of irritation in his voice. "I wish you wouldn't go there. If you want to go out, I'll take you. We're a duo, after all, a couple."

"Sometimes, Giles, this part of the couple likes to be on her own, know what I mean?" Bonnie's voice was leaden with patience. Giles didn't appreciate the effort.

"I understand you need to be alone now and again. But I always thought you wanted to be by yourself. Why go out carousing with those kind of people? They aren't your type. Not really. You're so much better than they are. So much more sophisticated." Giles was mewling at her, running his hand up her long silky leg. Bonnie didn't have the energy to shake him off so she just laid there. "You have a reputation to uphold. Our show is number one because it's a family show. How would it look if one of the tabloids caught you dancing at a place like that?"

Bonnie almost laughed. The tabloids would have had a super time last night. A shot of her dancing like a harlot with another woman would have been front-page news. Even now the experience pleased her.

Dancing with that woman had felt wonderful. That woman, whoever she was, though not the most beautiful, had something Bonnie could relate to. Maybe it was the lateness of the hour. Maybe it was the booze. But maybe, just maybe, it was the woman herself. A kindred spirit, waiting to burst free, waiting to be recognized for the glorious creature she was. Yes, Bonnie was sure that's what had happened.

But the woman had disappeared and Bonnie had gone home with the first man to wrap an arm about her waist. She and the woman had been parted as easily as they had come together and Bonnie could hardly remember her face. Maybe, sometime, they would see each other again. Now, though, she had to deal with Giles. He was, after all, her meal ticket and the fare had been great despite her slight stomach upset everytime she thought of bedding him.

"Oh, Giles," she purred, pulling herself upright with some effort. "You'll forgive me, won't you? I don't know what gets into me. Sometimes I just need something different in my life. I know you can understand that? I feel . . ."

Bonnie's green eyes disappeared under her lowered lids. Her long lashes kissed her cheeks and her lips trembled with unfelt emotion.

"You feel at odds and ends. I know that, sweetheart." His arms were around her now. Not as strong as the man from the night before, but definitely richer. "We've been in limbo for so long. Loving each other, working together. I understand. Truly. I think you need something exciting, but permanent, in your life. I think . . ." Giles paused, then waved his hands about in the air like some priss. "Oh, a gesture is worth a thousand words."

Picture, you twit, Bonnie thought as he pushed himself from the floor and hurried toward the closet. She fell back into her chair, wondering how long she could put up with this much adoration. He was back before she was ready for him to return.

"Here, this is just what the doctor ordered," Gile chirped.

"Oh, Giles, I don't want to play . . ." Bonnie began, her eyes opening a bit—then a bit more until she was staring wide eyed at what Giles held up for her to see. "Oh, Giles," she breathed, her anxious little hands reaching for the little, black velvet box.

"Do you like it? I was just waiting for the proper moment. Bonnie, I want you to be my wife. Say you'll marry me."

Bonnie didn't have to think twice. Her mind raced ahead to the years she could make such good use of. She was great as Giles's sidekick. What could she accomplish as his wife? The answer was a hell of a lot, naturally.

Quickly she slipped the ring on her finger and held out her hand, fingers down. Giles, thinking Bonnie was overwhelmed, took her fingertips and kissed them. Bonnie giggled and pulled away. He was so stupid. She needed her hand free to better gauge the weight of the stone. The diamond was three karats if it was one, surrounded by at least a karat of emeralds.

"Do you like it?" He was getting nervous. Bonnie forced herself to speak.

"I love it, darling. It's perfect."

"See how the emeralds sparkle? Just like your exquisite eyes," he gushed.

"You're so thoughtful," Bonnie cooed.

"Then you'll marry me?"

"Oh, Giles, how can you even wonder? Of course I'll marry you! When?"

"Whenever you say. The moment you want to," Giles answered, love filling his middle-aged heart until he thought it would break.

"Saturday," Bonnie said, knowing she answered too quickly. But time was awastin'. Bonnie Barber wouldn't have to wait a second longer to get what she deserved. It had just been handed to her on a silver platter. "Vegas."

"Vegas it is!" Giles danced away from her. "It's going to be so hard to wait!"

"Don't I know it," Bonnie murmured just before she went to Giles and knelt in front of him. She was about to give the greatest performance of her life.

Las Vegas burst on them like a fireball in the middle of the great void. Hundreds of thousands of lights sparkled, twinkled, and glared, creating a whirlpool of brightness that Bonnie felt was a tribute to her triumph.

Though Giles wanted to fly, Bonnie insisted they drive. She wanted to relish every moment of her wedding day; mark it as though the miles were a calendar of her years of struggle chalked off to reach this point where she would finally jump and fly toward her destiny. The highway had melted away too quickly as the Rolls sped through the desert toward their destination. Now the minutes ceased their frantic rush, once again slowing so Bonnie could swell more importantly than they.

As she sat beside Giles the lights softened his look. He didn't appear to be aging any longer. Her twenty-three years were again a match for his forty-eight. Often, without his makeup, when his tan was fading, Bonnie was fully aware that the Hollywood life had not been kind to Giles. Now, though, he looked robust, even excited. She sat by him contentedly, letting him show her the right places as they drove. Bonnie knew they would eventually end up in front of a justice of the peace and that was all that mattered.

"Here we are," Giles quipped. The great car hardly sighed as it responded to his command to turn. "Caesar's Palace. I've always loved this place. Great service. I've reserved the honeymoon suite."

"Giles," Bonnie tittered, "how romantic of you."

"Nothing is too good for you, darling. Can you imagine how our audience is going to react when they find out we're man and wife? Our story is sure to make all the magazines so I want it to be as perfect as possible."

Bonnie laughed, but didn't say anything. Sometimes Giles amazed her. He was just as image conscious as she. They would do all right, and this time the story in *People* would be more flattering than the last.

The black Rolls rolled to a stop. Her door was opened immediately by a handsome man in a silly outfit who offered his hand. She took it and immediately walked to the door of the hotel without a second thought for her luggage. In a car like theirs no one wasted time catering to them.

The huge doors of the hotel were opened also. The manager didn't even ask them to register. Instead, he handed Giles and Bonnie over to a solicitous assistant manager, who almost groveled all the way up to their suite. Bonnie heard him whisper that "everything was in order" as Giles stopped in front of the door. When that one was flung open Bonnie's breath was taken away.

The room was filled with white roses. Hundreds and hundreds of them. The smell was almost overpowering. It was a tasteless gesture, but she loved it.

"Giles, you sweetheart," she cried as she rushed into the room.

"You like it then?"

"Like it?" She twirled about, the hem of her short skirt brushing her long, slim legs. The assist-

188

ant manager forgot to grovel, he was so entranced. "I adore it! I can't imagine what else you have in store."

"Not much. A bit of caviar, dinner if you like, or we can have the ceremony immediately."

"Immediately?"

Bonnie's eyes widened. He was anxious all right. Funny what age did to some people. Television's most eligible bachelor wanted to make an honest woman of her.

"Certainly. And no tacky chapel for you, darling. I've arranged to have a justice of the peace come here. And, as a special treat, Lola Torres is going to stand up for you."

"Oh my God! I had no idea you knew her!"

Finally, Bonnie truly was speechless. Lola Torres was only the most sought after talent in the entertainment business. The things she could do for Bonnie.

Giles flushed. She had never known him to be modest. Now she wondered how he could have kept this association from her. Bonnie would have to be on her best behavior, gauge her impression on Lola Torres so she made the best of this opportunity.

"I thought you might like that," Giles said importantly. "Her show is over at ten, and she has another at midnight, so shall we make it eleven? Will that give you enough time to dress?"

"I'll make it enough time," Bonnie cried happily. "You just see. I'll be the most beautiful bride. Oh, Giles!"

Delightedly, she rushed to him and threw her arms about his neck, pressing her breasts into his

189

chest for good measure. He was going to get the best loving he ever had in his life that night. Bonnie disappeared into the bathroom to ready herself as though she was a blushing, virginal bride.

"Oh, Giles, I'm so nervous. Do you think it will be much longer?"

Bonnie was worried. It was eleven-thirty and if Lola Torres didn't show up soon they'd have to wait until after her midnight show. Giles patted her hand and muttered something, then went off to talk to the justice of the peace.

Bonnie went to the window and looked out. Nothing had changed. The lights still winked, blinked, and twinkled. People still milled about on the street below. But everything had changed, too. Bonnie found that her heart was beating with excitement. She couldn't remember the last time she was excited about anything. Looking out over the city to the black desert beyond, Bonnie thought she might be recapturing something that she had lost long ago or she forgot she ever had. There was a purity in her exhilaration that made her stand in awe.

"I'm here."

Bonnie whirled away from the window. There was no mistaking the voice. In the doorway stood the woman they'd all been waiting for—Lola Torres.

Bonnie knew she paled next to the woman. Lola Torres stood almost six feet tall. Six feet of raw sex appeal. Big breasted, big hipped, her face a chiseled mass of planes and angles that made her look regally sensuous.

Bonnie smoothed her dress. Exquisite though it was, it couldn't compare to Lola Torres's sheath of black silk. Bonnie's lips were dry. She licked them and smiled, trying not to grin. Gracious was the way she would play it; not too grateful, but grateful enough.

Lola looked around the room. She spotted Bonnie and her eyes narrowed into glittering black slits. She seemed to sway. Bonnie stopped. Then Lola smiled — without warmth — and moved toward her. Bonnie held out her hand. Lola did the same. They missed one another by a foot. Bonnie whirled to see where the woman had gone. She had stumbled to the couch. She was drunk as a skunk!

Bonnie felt anger shooting up in sparks from somewhere in the middle of her body. How dare this woman come to her wedding drunk! The black-haired woman might be Lola Torres, but hey, she was Bonnie Barber! Then Giles's hand was on her arm, guiding her toward the star and Bonnie came to her senses. No matter what, Lola Torres was a multimedia star and an influential one at that.

"Lola Torres, my intended, Bonnie Barber, soon to be Mrs. Giles Masters."

Bonnie watched Lola look from her to Giles, as though she were memorizing their names. Weird way for old friends to act, but then she didn't exactly act normally when she was three sheets to the wind, either. This time the two women managed to connect. Bonnie felt the limpness in the other woman and wondered if Lola would be able to stand up during the ceremony, much less perform at a midnight show.

"I think we should get on with this," Lola muttered. "I got a show in fifteen minutes."

"Of course," Giles said heartily.

They took their places. The manager next to Giles and Lola Torres—Lola Torres!—next to Bonnie.

"We have come together in the sight of God," the justice of the peace droned, "to join this man and this woman in the holy bonds of matrimony. It is a holy estate and what God has joined together let no man put asunder. Giles Masters," the minister turned slightly, "do you take this woman to be your lawfully wedded wife, to have and to hold until death do you part?"

"I do," Giles answered solemnly.

"Bonnie Barber." He did another quarter turn. "Do you take this man to be your lawfully wedded husband, to have and to hold until death do you part?"

"I do," Bonnie whispered, punctuating her assent with a flutter of her lovely eyes.

"Then by the power vested in me by the state of Nevada I pronounce you man and wife. You may kiss the bride."

Bonnie turned her face toward Giles. He leaned into her. Their lips met in a chaste kiss. Behind them the manager called his congratulations and Lola Torres headed out the door. Bonnie was the first to see her and the first to go after her.

"Miss Torres," she called brightly, "won't you

stay and have a glass of champagne with us? There are so many things I'd like to talk to you about. I'm an actress, too, though I'm sure Giles told you."

Lola turned regally to face Bonnie. Her eyes fluttered up and down Bonnie's fine body and finally bore right through Bonnie's eyes with a stony stare. She swayed only slightly now, getting herself together for her midnight appearance. Amazing, the power of the mind, Bonnie thought.

"Why in the hell do you think he'd tell me anything about you?" Lola drawled.

Taken aback, Bonnie stuttered, ". . . well, you're such old friends . . . I mean I assumed he had told you . . . I mean . . ."

Lola laughed one hard, long note that sounded more like a chord coming from her talented throat.

"Old friends? Is that what he told you? You got a good one there, honey. So good I wish we were old friends if he's that slick. Hell, I just made a cool five grand for standing up. A grand a minute's the best deal I've ever had. Have a nice life, doll."

Lola, her momentum holding, walked out the door without faltering. Slowly, Bonnie turned toward Giles, who was accepting hearty congratulations from the justice of the peace. She saw an envelope change hands. The man had obviously been well paid, too.

Like a lioness stalking her prey, Bonnie advanced on Giles. He turned toward her, a smile lighting up his face, his arms reaching out to her just before she raised her fist and decked him. The bridegroom

193

fell into a heap at her feet, knocking himself out on the glass and chrome table that held their wedding cake. The wedding cake didn't survive. Giles did — barely.

Bonnie had every vent turned her way and the air-conditioning going full blast as the Rolls sped through the desert pointed directly toward Los Angeles.

In the driver's seat Giles, a lovely lavender bruise on his chin and a bump the size of an egg on his head, had shrunk substantially from his height of six feet. He was so hunched over the wheel he was in danger of becoming one with it.

The rarified atmosphere inside the car was even more unique that day. The chill of the air conditioner was nothing compared to the icy blasts Bonnie gave off now and again. The scent of fear that Giles exuded mingled with the smell of fine leather and expensive perfume.

They had been driving silently for an hour and a half. Not a word had passed between them since Bonnie's "I do." In fact, Giles had found it very difficult to even try to apologize since, by the time he regained his senses, Bonnie had managed to find another room in the huge hotel and was as good as lost to him since she threatened to do the manager in if he so much as breathed a word of her whereabouts.

So Giles had spent his wedding night nursing his lump while feeling queasy from the fall as well as sick to death over the mistake he had made. Bonnie had spent her wedding night pacing in her room, then fleeing to the casino to lose a great deal of her newly acquired community property. Neither of their pastimes had helped to soothe either Giles's guilt or Bonnie's anger.

A rabbit bounded across the freeway in front of the speeding car, taking a nick on the back leg as he was tossed to the side of the road. Giles didn't slow down, but took the opportunity to look at his wife, a sickly smile on his face as he hoped the sight of that poor defenseless creature might soften his darling Bonnie's temper. There was no sign she noticed his conciliatory look; not a flicker of her eyelash, not even a bristling about her extraordinary chest. But she had seen him look, had felt his hope. Bonnie took the opportunity to speak her mind. Now that the ring was on her finger, and they were legal, there was absolutely no reason to pussyfoot about any longer.

"Don't look at me, Giles. Keep your eyes on the road."

Bonnie's voice had taken on an edge akin to that of a drill sergeant. Giles's eyes snapped forward. Bonnie took a deep and labored breath. He slid his eyes right far enough to see her cleavage heave. God, how he loved her.

"I have never been so mortified in my life, Giles. It was horrible. It was despicable. It was so *middle class!* To pay that woman to stand up beside me on my wedding day. How could you, Giles? How could you!"

Giles took a rather deep breath himself, which was difficult given the contorted position of his body. His voice had declined in force in exact proportion to his wife's gaining strength.

"I thought you'd enjoy it, Bonnie. I know how you love celebrity of a different sort than the old tube. I did it for you, baby. I know you so well. It was like my gift to you. My very expensive gift," he reminded her nervously.

"Some gift. That's like saying 'hey, honey, look, I got you a gift certificate to the plastic surgeon.' If I'm not good enough for her to come up on her own, then I sure as hell don't want you to pay to get her there, know what I mean?"

The question was rhetorical, but Bonnie looked at her husband as though she expected an an-answer. Satisfaction spread through her entire being when she saw that he was white as a sheet and sweating like a pig. She had him just where she wanted him. Bonnie leaned closer and saw his white knuckles. She moved in for the kill.

"Giles, from now on, don't think. I am a star in my own right. I've made that stupid show of yours and you know it. People tune in night after night to see me: what I'm wearing, what my hair looks like, how far down I'll let the top of my dress go. Without me you'd be nothing. . . ."

"Bon . . ." Giles gasped.

Her eyes narrowed. He was squirming now. Ah, triumph!

"Don't 'Bonnie' me. From now on I'm going to call the shots. You understand me? You will live and breathe as I say so. Hell, you're going to die if I say so. Is that clear? Is that clear, Giles?"

On cue Giles snapped straight up, his arms pushing at the steering wheel, locked in place. The car careened to the left into the oncoming traffic lane. Luckily, there was no traffic.

"Giles!" Bonnie screamed. "What the hell . . ."

She grabbed at the wheel, attempting to turn it, but his arms were bolted into position. She continued to scream at him. The huge car hit the shoulder of the highway, taking out a yucca tree as it skidded into the sand then back on the highway. Suddenly, Giles went limp, his body slumping against the door. Bonnie saw her advantage and took it. She slid closer to her husband, pushing him aside, wedging him between her and the door. Frantically, she flipped her legs over to the controls and found the brake. Gently, she applied pressure, steering the car to a stop along the side of the highway.

"What are you trying to do?" Bonnie screamed as she scuttled across the seat toward her door. If Giles had lost his mind she'd rather take her chances out in that blazing desert than inside with a madman.

She was breathing hard, her lovely hands raised in a defensive position while she waited for Giles to turn on her. Slowly, she lowered them when she realized that Giles had no intention of coming after her. In fact, she realized, Giles couldn't come after her. Inch by inch she made her way across the beautiful leather seat. Hesitantly, she reached toward him. Turning her head away, she put two fingers on his neck, searching for a pulse point. If Giles had a pulse, she couldn't find it.

"Jesus," she whispered "I didn't literally mean you had to die Giles."

It was a few minutes before she realized she was sitting in the middle of the desert with a corpse. A corpse that had been her husband for a little under ten hours. A corpse who in life had been rich and famous. Not only that, but she was now Mrs. Giles Masters, widow and heir to all he owned . . . all he had become in life.

Her heart stopped pounding in her breast when she comprehended all this and calmly she reached for the car phone. The moment someone on the other end answered, Bonnie's hands flew to her mouth, her voice quavered, tears came to her eyes.

"Hello? I need the police. Please, send the police. My husband is dead. I'm alone. In the middle of the desert. Please. Please help me."

Bonnie wailed beautifully. Meryl Streep had nothing on her.

"We've Only Just Begun" was sung by a young girl in a green dress as mourners filed respectfully past Giles Masters's casket. It had been his favorite song in life; Bonnie appreciated it for its symbolism of her future. But while she thought of the days and months ahead, her posture indicated that she was crippled by grief.

Bonnie wore a lovely, simple black dress set off only by a rope of pearls. Her hair was piled high on her head, a little veiled hat sitting at exactly the right angle over her forehead. She had been light handed with her makeup, causing her face to look a tad more drawn, but gorgeous nonetheless.

Bonnie knelt without moving beside the casket, her head down, buried in her clasped hands. Though she had long forgotten how to pray she thought this the most suitable position for a woman in mourning. Besides, this way she didn't have to look at Giles's face. This close she could see the layers of makeup and the undertone of gray on his skin. It was hard to imagine he was really dead until she saw that, underneath it all, his tan was gone.

A hand touched her shoulder. Bonnie stiffened, then straightened, every move a concentrated effort to get her through this performance. Actually, she was going to miss Giles. They'd been together a long time and, in her own way, she had loved him. But he was well into middle age. It was a blessing he didn't live to get old and really wrinkled.

"Bonnie, I think it's time to leave."

Heroically, Bonnie looked directly at Giles's still form, then over her shoulder at Thomas Matteson. Her hand covered his as he pressed reassuring fingers into her shoulder. He nodded, the way men do who believe it is their destiny to take care of poor and beautiful women without husbands. Bonnie returned the pressure with just the right degree of intimacy. Dear Thomas. Sweet Thomas. Marvelous Executive Producer Thomas.

"Just a moment longer, please?" Her lovely eyes took on the pain of the world as she looked at him through his horned-rimmed glasses. He melted.

"Of course. I'll wait right here. We'll ride to the cemetery together."

"Thank you."

This was said as more of a sigh than words. Thomas moved back exactly one step, ready to stand guard as needed. Bonnie bent her head a second longer, then got up, kissed Giles's cold lips and stumbled back into Thomas's arms. That little bit of drama hadn't actually been planned. But the shock of feeling a dead person really threw her for a loop. Bonnie couldn't even enjoy the thespian quality of her swoon. Thomas helped her out into the cool air and into the waiting car.

". . . So we commend our brother, Giles Masters, to the benevolent hands of God. We trust that even in heaven, Giles Masters will bring to bear his wit and talent and make heaven an even jollier place than it is today and will be for eternity."

Bonnie wanted to stick her finger down her throat. There was nothing worse than a Hollywood minister. They were all looking for a break, too. A flashbulb went off on her right. All the papers had sent reporters to the ceremonies commemorating the death of a truly gamey guy.

Bonnie straightened herself almost imperceptibly. Shoulders were drawn back a bit, chin raised, one of her hands fluttered a lace handkerchief toward her eyes, but didn't cover her face. Now the angle would be just right no matter where the photographers were. She knew it was a super pose since she'd practiced it endlessly the night before instead of really searching through Giles's home to find out what it was she now owned. There would be time enough for that. At least he'd had the good sense to draw up a will. She'd seen to that all right. Seen enough to know that she inherited everything he owned. She only wished she knew how much that was.

Without thinking Bonnie realized she had put out her hand a number of times. Now she focused on what she was doing. Mourners had lined up to pay their respects. Their faces were solemn as they peered at her through the veil. Most were still in shock over the marriage. Then with the death of their colleague they had gone into overdrive. Every man over the age of forty was rethinking his second marriage to the sweet young thing hanging on his arm. If an energetic girl like Bonnie could do in Giles Masters, what did they have to look forward to?

Bonnie murmured her appreciation to a famous talk show host who was there with his fourth, and youngest, wife; to a woman known for being on every pilot since 1968; to a man who was the voice of a famous toon skunk (he offered his condolences in character). On and on they came; those who had loved Giles, those who hated him, and those who wanted to make a fortune off him.

Finally, it was over. Once again Thomas was leading her to the long black car. She was exhausted. Only the reception left to get through; then she could get down to business.

Bonnie composed herself with all the dignity a Hollywood card turner should. She lowered her voice to a cultured level. She even managed to suck in her chest so she wouldn't appear too tartish.

Carefully, on the verge of tears, she guided her guests to a sumptuous buffet, offering them Giles's favorite—caviar and champagne. It was, she told them, as he would have wanted it. She hoped they would always think kindly of him.

They were all finally gone by four. Only Thomas remained, speaking quietly to the caterers as he took command of this sad, sad situation. Eventually he found his way to her, a glass of sherry in each of his hands. She accepted hers, and took a sip as he sat opposite her, patting her silky knee once too often.

"A terrible shame, Bonnie. An aneurism." Thomas sighed heavily as he contemplated his sherry. "I suppose that fall he took in the tub in Vegas just kind of knocked it loose. Caesar's Palace has terrible tubs. Too big. Dangerous." Thomas obviously didn't find what he was looking for in the glass of sherry, so he looked at Bonnie and seemed much happier. "But I'm sure you made his last hours his happiest." Bonnie smiled slightly and took an even larger sip of her sherry. Thomas continued to philosophize. "And that's really what counts, isn't it? That you live life to the fullest, that you get exactly what you want from it. That you live up to your potential."

Thomas let the last word ring out and hover over them like a dove of peace. Bonnie raised her eyes heavenward as though she could see the word potential spelled out in gold letters above her head. Then she looked directly at Thomas, put her hand on his knee and spoke.

"I'm so glad you feel that way, Thomas. Because

202

I think I must carry on where my husband left off. He'd want me to take care of the show. He'd want me to host the show—starting Monday."

Bonnie's long-lashed lids fluttered over green, granite eyes.

Sixteen

Murmurs. Shapes. Light and dark. People moving about. One person forever hovering over her. A bright light, so long ago. So bright. Her parents waiting patiently in the light. So happy. Her mother — smiling gently. Tess climbed toward the light, then was pulled from it again. She was tired.

"Nurse!"

Tess heard the cry as though from an incredible distance, barked by a voice obviously used to being obeyed. Her eyelids caught, struggled to open, then painfully came apart. They felt as heavy as lead. The man's voice spoke again, softly this time. A doctor, she imagined. The light hurt her eyes, though the room was barely illuminated. Concentrating as best she could, Tess tried to focus on the face hovering above hers.

"You're awake. How are you?" the man whispered. His hand was stroking her hair as though she was as delicate as crystal. "It's been a long time."

Tess fought with herself. She could see his eyes, so dark, his lips beautifully formed and tipping in a tender smile.

"Royal?"

Her voice was hoarse, almost nonexistent. The man above her shook his head. He must be a doctor. But she'd never seen a doctor like this, not one who touched as though his patient was precious.

"No," he said. "A friend. When you're stronger we'll . . ."

Suddenly the man was gone, moving too fast for Tess to see him go. She couldn't turn her head. Panic set in as she tried to search the rest of her body with her mind. Could she feel her toes? Would they move? Something cold was placed on her chest, something around her upper arm. She heard air hissing—hissing like the sound just before.

Tess fell off again. The memory was too horrible. It rushed toward her, trying to engulf her. She wouldn't, couldn't, see it again. Not the descent, not the charred people in front of her, not the empty seat beside her. She slept again. And when she woke he was still there, the man with the lovely voice and the hand that brushed across her hair like a silken scarf.

"Hello again," he said. Tess tried to move her head to see him, but it was impossible. He must have known, because she heard him stand, walk closer to the bed. "You look better now. See what a little sleep can do for you?"

Tess tried to smile, but the effort was too great. She only nodded a little, hoping her eyes, now more alert, would tell him she appreciated his kindness. The brightness turned cloudy, though, as she thought of Royal. Her mouth was so dry, her throat parched. It was hard to speak.

"I know what you're thinking," he chatted on. "You're wondering who in the heck is this guy stand-

205

ing by my bed? You probably can't say a word because you haven't had any solid food in over a week. You can't talk because not a drop of liquid has passed your lips. Well, don't worry. I'm here to answer your questions and even offer you a drink. Water?"

He was smiling now, a glorious smile that lit up his face. Strange he should have a face as open and bright as a field of wheat when his looks were dark and could have been construed as sinister. How lovely a contrast.

Tess heard him pour the water into a glass. He came close to her. Frantically, her eyes looked into his, silently asking if it was all right to take what he offered. She didn't really know what happened to her or why she was in this hospital. Fear was now the reality. Fear and immobility and pain.

"I'm going to put this straw to your lips," he told her. "Don't try to move your head. Your neck is in a brace. There was a crack in one of those awful bones that are so delicate. Nothing to worry about, it's mending nicely," he assured her hurriedly. "I just wanted to warn you so that you don't try to do any work just yet. So just put your lips over the straw and sip a little. Not too much now."

Tess did as she was told. The water tasted like ambrosia. He gave her just enough to refresh her, then took the straw away.

"Thank you," she whispered. Now her voice sounded more like her own. She seemed to remember saying something not too long ago and her voice sounded like sandpaper.

"You're very welcome. Now, would you like to hear a few things, or are you tired and want to rest?"

"Hear," she answered.

"Good. I had a feeling you weren't exactly the type to just fall off the face of the earth. The doctors weren't so sure. They thought they were going to lose you there for a while. But I told them you were strong."

"How do you . . ." Tess's voice gave out. It didn't matter. The man in the chair finished her sentence as though it was the most natural thing in the world.

". . . Know? It's simple. I just read what's written all over you," he said quietly. "Now, you're in the Hospital St. Louis. You were in a plane crash at the Paris airport. Do you remember that?"

Tess closed her eyes briefly. "A little."

"That's to be expected. I'll remind you. It's better to face these things head-on. At least that's what I've been told. Your neck, as you already know, is in a brace. Your legs are wrapped because you suffered some burns. Nothing horrible, first degree. Mostly heat burns. There was a fireball that erupted from the cockpit. It was brief, but intense. Your head was down. The people in front of you were the last to catch the brunt of it. The heat seared over the top of the seat and under the bottom, that's why your legs were burned. Luckily, though, you had on cotton slacks. Natural fibers repel fire for a bit. Interesting, don't you think?"

Tess smiled now. He was a funny man to talk about clothing at a time like this. Perhaps it was best, though, that he didn't fawn over her as though she was dying.

"You also had a collapsed lung and some internal bleeding. I'm afraid during a plane crash there aren't many ladies and gentlemen. A couple of people decided stepping *on* you was preferable to stepping *over* you."

"My hands?" Tess questioned suddenly. She remembered not being able to use her hands to undo her seatbelt. Oh, God, not her hands.

"They're fine," he assured her quickly. "Just fine."

"I couldn't undo the belt," she insisted.

"A natural reaction. You felt the heat from the fire, you smelled smoke. It was your mind insisting that your hands had been burned. If it's playing the violin you're worried about, don't."

"Painting." She sighed.

"Ah, an artist."

He was silent for a minute, watching her with a calm that seemed catching. He seemed grateful for this piece of information.

"I should have known that. From the way you picked up your drink on the plane. The way you turned the page of a book."

"You," she said. "You were on the plane. I remember. Behind me."

"Yes. I had the pleasure of being on the same plane with you."

"Pleasure?"

"I'll admit that was a damned hard way to meet a woman." He laughed. "But I have a funny feeling it will be worth it. So don't worry about your hands. Now all you really need is rest. You need to regain your strength. Perhaps the worst of your injuries was shock. You haven't been with us for a week."

Tess watched him as he spoke. Now, almost completely alert, she realized that he, too, was bandaged. It was his hand that had been hurt. What else? she wondered.

"And you?"

"Minor problems. I made the mistake of putting my hand on the seat in front of you while I got you out of that belt. Nothing horrible. In fact, the bandage comes off in two days."

"You saved me?"

"No. I pulled you out with me. I wouldn't ever want you to feel that you owed me anything. Once you were out of that belt we managed a few steps together. You just collapsed before I did. That's all."

Tess knew he was lying, but she accepted his view of the horrible incident. She was too weak to do anything else. Certainly she couldn't deny what he said, her memories were so vague. Except for one.

"Beside me," she whispered, tears coming to her eyes. "The man beside me."

The man shook his head. "I don't know. The plane cracked away very neatly, separating your row and the row beside you all the way down to coach."

"Oh my God," Tess moaned. "Killed? How many killed?"

"Thankfully," he said solemnly, "only ten. But ten is too many." He hesitated then asked, "I'll try to find out about your husband?" Tess shook her head. "I'll try to find out about your friend. What was . . . his name?"

"Royal," she answered, a sob tearing at her throat. "Royal Cudahy."

"You rest. I'll see what I can find out." Tess saw how tall he was when he stood up, how broad of shoulder. A powerful figure of a man possessing a sympathy belied by his physical appearance. At the door he turned. She couldn't see him, but his voice floated toward her, surrounding her with a blanket of safety. "My name is Noel Montgomery, Tess."

He was gone. Tess slept again.

"You have done remarkably well, Miss Canfield," Doctor Albert informed her.

His hands fluttered over her body, removing a dressing just enough to check her injuries, then replacing it. He listened to her lungs for a long while, finally nodding his approval. Carefully, he moved her head, listening for things only a doctor could hear.

"I'm glad," Tess said.

Her long nap had done her a world of good. She felt some strength returning. A nurse had come in to bathe her and change her gown. Unfortunately, the nurse didn't speak English. But Doctor Albert did. She had so many questions.

"When can I leave?"

"Leave?" He laughed lightly. "You are feeling so much better, mademoiselle. I think it would do you good to rest for a month or so before you think of leaving."

"In the hospital?" Tess was horrified.

"No, certainly not. I think I may discharge you in another few days if you are able to get about a little. But I will need to watch you carefully. Your neck is quite a delicate thing. I would hate to see it snap and you not have my services to mend it again. Besides, you won't feel like traveling for quite sometime. Perhaps you would like to talk to our psychologists. It will be difficult for you, perhaps, to fly for a while."

"It has been difficult for me to fly for quite a while," Tess murmured. "But I can't possibly stay here. I have no place to go and not enough money for a hotel for such a long time."

"I wouldn't worry about it, Doctor. I'll see to it that Miss Canfield does exactly what you tell her to do." Noel Montgomery strode into the room and stood where he knew Tess could see him. He beamed at her before directing his attention to the doctor. "What exactly is it she needs?"

Doctor Albert grinned. This, he thought, was a marvelously romantic injury the young woman suffered.

"She needs a great deal of rest and pampering. She needs to regain her strength. I would suggest at least a month, if not more. But the lady says that she cannot. Unless I can release her to relatives who will sign a waiver freeing the hospital and myself from all responsibility."

"Doctor," Tess stopped him, surprised by the vigor of her voice. "I have no relatives. I have no one. But I am also twenty-two and can certainly sign such a waiver on my own behalf."

Doctor Albert raised an eyebrow. "But you are not in a condition to fend for yourself by any means. I'm afraid a smart solicitor would make such a statement useless." He shrugged as though his seeming helplessness would convince Tess.

"I agree. I think you need a great deal more time," Noel said. "I'm no doctor, but I know what it can be like recovering from an injury. Your mind tells you one thing, but believe me, your body will tell you another."

"*Mais oui,*" Doctor Albert agreed quickly. "But I can only advise you. See, Mister Montgomery, if you can convince her."

211

"I'll do my best," Noel assured the doctor, though he was looking at Tess.

She averted her eyes. She wasn't a child to be ordered about. Tess also knew, unfortunately, they were right. But there was someone to care for her. Noel was going to find Royal. Perhaps he had. Or perhaps he had found the worst. Whatever the news, Tess must know it before she came to any decision.

"Royal?" she asked, her mind and body steeling itself for news of his death.

"I'm sorry," he said gently. "He's not here. He was transported back to the States almost immediately. His injuries weren't life threatening, but they were extensive. According to the hospital, he will need quite a bit of therapy to get himself back together. Mostly broken bones. His legs were the worst. He's been gone for almost five days now. I was told a woman came to get him, accompanied by a private doctor."

Tess felt her breath return. Royal was all right. He was alive. The joy she felt was beyond compare. The devastation that caved in on her was beyond belief. Astra had come for him. His wife. But that was to be expected. He was hurt. It was natural she would come for him. Still, if his injuries weren't serious . . .

"Did he leave something for me? He must have left something for me?"

Noel shook his head, "No. I thought you might ask that. There's nothing."

"Then he must have been more seriously hurt than you've let on. He wouldn't have gone without getting a message to me," Tess insisted, more for her peace of mind than Noel's.

Noel couldn't watch her pain. This was worse than

212

the injuries that had racked her beautiful body. The sorrow and denial that now showed in her eyes, her face, was something he couldn't fathom. He knew enough to guess the truth of her situation. Royal Cudahy had been taken home by his wife. This woman certainly wasn't his daughter or even a relative. He wouldn't have left her alone, if she had been. He wouldn't have left her alone if she had meant anything to him at all.

Noel's anger flared. He turned his face away until he could compose himself. Life was so unfair, the heart so cruel in the choices it made.

"Tess," he said, looking at her again. "I don't know why he left the way he did, but I think you should know that he was not so seriously hurt that he couldn't have left a message. He was lucid. That's the way it is. You must accept it. If you don't face that fact the hurt in your heart is going to affect your recovery."

"I won't accept it. I'll use it. I'll use what you've told me to get better because I know there's a reason he left the way he did. Finding out will be the reason I regain my strength. You don't know me. You don't know anything about me. So don't try to tell me that he didn't think of me or left me without a fight. I know he wouldn't do that. I know it."

Tears fell, silently coursing down her face, and Tess cried, using the little strength she had gained. When that had been exhausted she slept. While she slept, Noel Montgomery sat beside her in awe of such infatuation or, perhaps, it was love. Something told him he must find out which it was. For one reason or another Noel believed fate had put him on that plane and a broken Tess Canfield in his arms.

He had never been more sure of anything in his life, and he was not going to let her go until he found out what she was supposed to mean to him.

The nurse who pushed Tess toward the atrium jumped only slightly when Noel put his hands over hers and gently moved her aside. He pursed his lips, playfully requesting her silence. She smiled at him, then looked worriedly at her patient. She hoped Mr. Montgomery's little game might help the poor woman cheer up. Certainly in the last few days nothing else had managed to bring a smile to her lips.

Noel grinned as he pushed the wheelchair past the matron without missing a beat. The woman in white offered the universal sign of thumbs-up, then went in search of another chore.

Noel pushed, glad for a quiet moment with Tess. It was difficult, when he visited her, to hold his tongue. There were so many things he wanted to ask her, so many things to know about her. But Tess was in no shape to handle additional stress, nor did they know each other well enough for her to have any desire to speak with him intimately. He saw it in her eyes, in the very way she watched him, that Tess felt an overwhelming degree of gratitude toward him, but little else.

There had been a moment or two during which she seemed almost curious about him, or his motives for the attention he showed her, or both. At those times her blue eyes had shaded beautifully, growing deeper in color; her lips would part so that he wished he could lower his to hers and kiss away the questions, making himself completely known by that act.

214

But her lips would close and her eyes lighten and the instant would be lost. Now, though, he had arranged everything and the day was coming when his questions would be answered.

Tess still hadn't moved by the time they reached the atrium, a usually sunny, glass-enclosed room spotted with potted palms and trees. The confining brace had been removed, but the way she held her head indicated there was a definite weakness still. Her legs, hidden by her hospital robe, were now left without bandages, but he had seen the bright red skin that was painfully healing and knew that, for a woman as beautiful as Tess, the sight must make her shrivel with disgust.

"Your forest, my lady," Noel said, taking great delight in the way her body shivered slightly at the sound of his voice. He lay a hand on her shoulder. "Don't you dare turn your head, Tess. I'll come 'round to you."

He did just that, relieved to see she was smiling. Not a happy smile yet, but less void than the one she had been offering him for the last few days.

"You look marvelous today," he enthused.

"Thanks," she laughed, "though you're a terrible liar."

"I am not. In fact, I would say you look positively ravishing. What's happened?"

"Other than they've allowed me to wash my hair and actually get into a bath with real soap and water, not much. But I'd say that was a wonderful start. Look, look what's happened to my poor legs. The bath made them worse than before."

Without hesitation Tess pulled at the hem of her hospital robe and leaned over to inspect her legs.

215

They were redder than before. Noel thought they looked as if they were on fire. Tess, lifting her eyes in time to see the look of dismay on Noel's face, quickly put her robe back over them.

"Don't worry. They hardly hurt at all any longer. Doctor Albert says that's just the way new skin looks, all angry and bright like that. Believe me. I would have walked over hot coals for a bath, so a little bit of sensitivity in my legs doesn't bother me a bit. Besides, I'm grateful it wasn't worse. Thanks to you I can still walk. I still have my legs. What would a few scars matter? Because of you I don't think I'll even have that."

"You're amazing," Noel breathed. He looked about, found a chair and settled himself in it. Reaching out for Tess's chair, he wheeled her closer. "I hardly know you, yet I feel I know you very well. I think nothing will surprise me about you, then I'm surprised all over again."

"I can't imagine why you would feel like you don't know me. You know my life story, about my mother and father, the farm, my ambitions. I would say you know me very well. As for being surprised, I don't think there's a thing about me that's surprising. I've never been one to relish things that are out of the ordinary."

"But you're out of the ordinary yourself." Noel laughed. "I'm amazed you can't see it. Any other woman as lovely as you are would be wallowing in self-pity because their legs looked like the leftover coals from a barbecue."

"They do look a mess." Tess shrugged.

"That's exactly what I mean. They do look a mess. Why aren't you wailing over the loss of your lovely

216

skin? Of course, in time, you won't even know that they looked like that. But most people would be so angry. In fact, some people are angry when there's no need to be. No need at all."

Noel fell silent. Tess cocked her head. She had never seen him look that way before, contemplative and worried at the same moment.

"Noel, you've been awfully kind to me. Is there something I could do for you? I know I haven't much to offer, but I am a good listener, if you'd like to tell me what's bothering you."

"Thank you, Tess," he said softly, hanging his head a bit. "I'd love to talk to you sometime about so many things. I suppose I was lost for a second because you reminded me of someone."

"Someone close to you?"

"I had hoped she would be close to me, but I'm not sure it's going to happen."

"I see," Tess said, believing she fully understood his pain. She was in the same sort of misery, not knowing why Royal had left without a word to her; not knowing why he was gone and a stranger stayed.

"No, I'm afraid you don't." Noel's lovely smile was turned on her again. "I'm not talking about my wife or lover. It's my daughter. You and she are about the same age. I never knew I had a daughter until a couple of years ago. She's so unlike you. You have a wisdom that she doesn't possess and I keep hoping she will."

"Maybe she hasn't had the need to grow up quickly like I did after my parents died. That changed my life. The deaths of my parents gave me years I didn't want. Sometimes I feel almost ancient. Some days I think I must have aged a lifetime in the last few years."

"But that's the point. Davina, my daughter, has had to overcome great difficulty. If I had known about the difficulties she and her mother were in, I would have helped. Her mother died. Suicide. Before that Davina had the responsibility for keeping the both of them fed and sheltered. But her experiences have made her bitter, grasping. I don't understand it now that she has everything she wants. I want to, but I can't seem to feel what she's feeling. I've tried everything I know.

"I lavished her with gifts and, I thought, love. I gave her a job and now, as I hear it, she's had to take on a great deal of responsibility in the company quickly because of a horrid accident involving the woman who was training her. I had intended to go back immediately when I heard. Then I thought, perhaps, Davina and I need some space. So I've decided to stay. Those who I trust will keep me informed of what's happening in the business. Maybe I should just let her loose, see if being on her own without the pressures her mother brought to bear will prove that I love and trust her and that she can live without a cloud hanging over her head."

"I think," Tess confided, "that sounds very reasonable. Sometimes the best thing is for someone to be on their own. Then again, sometimes it can be the worst thing in the world. It depends on how you're left in that place. If your aloneness comes from tragedy, it's horrible; if it comes from love and trust, then it can be wonderful. Have you sent word to her? Have you wished her well?"

"No, I haven't. But I will now. That's a marvelous idea," Noel said, grinning. "And now I'll confess the

218

other part of my scheme to you. I thought since it would be best for Davina to be out from under my shadow for a while, I would stay on here. I have an apartment on the Rue de Rivoli. I thought that's where I'd hide out for a month or so. I was hoping, perhaps, you'd agree to convalesce there."

Tess opened her mouth to object, but Noel scooted to the end of his chair and took her fingers in his.

"Before you say no, try to think as reasonably as you have throughout this whole ordeal. You know you're not strong yet. There is no question of that. Doctor Albert wants to keep you as a patient at least three weeks longer. It would be best if he cared for you since he knows the extent of your injuries. You would have me to look out for you and, I venture to say, you've never seen Paris the way an artist should. And finally," his voice grew solemn, "you will want to be well and strong when you see your gentleman friend again. Maybe, just maybe, the time apart would do both of you some good. It is something to consider."

Tess lowered her eyes, thinking about what he had said. Every point had merit, including the necessity for strength when she went back home. Royal might need her to be strong for him. She had no way of knowing what his condition was. Then again, should he be well enough to try and find her, if she left with Noel Montgomery, Royal wouldn't know how to contact her.

"We would tell the hospital to direct any calls or inquiries about you to my apartment," Noel said quietly, as though reading her mind.

Tess bit her lower lip, then squared her shoulders. He was right about everything, and he was kind. She

219

did want to rest, to find herself again and rid herself of the nightmares the crash had triggered; rid herself of the hurt and anger she felt toward Royal because he hadn't sent for her. She knew all those horrible feelings must be gone completely when she saw him again. There was no doubt of her love for him, only a small sadness because that love had been damaged.

"You're a very convincing fellow, Noel Montgomery," Tess finally said. "Thank you. I'd like to stay — for a while. But I won't stay longer than I have to. I have to get home. I have to get back to Royal."

"Today is the day, Tess." Noel grinned as he came into breakfast.

She looked up, giving him a glorious smile. Tess couldn't remember when she felt so good. Her body had healed so well that the only reminder of the accident were the dreams in the night and a few small scars running the length of her left leg. Both were small prices to pay for her life.

And, thanks to Noel, life seemed beautiful again. More so than she ever remembered it. He was right, time healed so many things and, when she got back to Royal, Tess knew she would look at him, love him, as though nothing had happened. Tess knew she would be forever grateful to Noel Montgomery, forever in his debt.

"What day is today?" she asked.

Noel came around behind her chair, putting his hands on the back, unable to look at her for fear what he was feeling would show through too clearly.

Tess was not ready to know that he felt drawn to her as he had never been drawn to any other woman.

Her strength, her acceptance of her situation, her kindness and gentility, her creativity, were qualities he had found only singularly in others. Leaning over her chair, putting his lips close to her ear, breathing in the heady scent of her shampoo, he paused for a moment before speaking.

"You've been lounging around here weeks as though you haven't a care in the world. Today, we are going to see Paris and"—he hesitated, suddenly lost in admiration to her—"we're going to walk. Miles if we have to."

He pulled her chair out gently. Tess laughed, and placed her hands on the table, still needing assistance to stand. If she sat too long her legs cramped, making it difficult to straighten them.

"I'm not sure I'm ready for miles," she answered as she turned. "But I'll do my best. For you, I'd walk to the ends of the earth if I could."

"Really, Tess?" Noel's voice lowered to a whisper, his dark eyes searching her face for the truth.

Tess's heart lurched in her breast. For one moment she walked toward the realization that she had spoken the reality, and the feelings she had for Royal were memory. But the instant was gone almost as quickly as it dawned and she laughed, her eyes twinkling with amusement now rather than glittering with love.

"Well, maybe not the ends of the earth, but I'd come awfully close."

Carefully, she moved away from the table. Noel shifted so she could maneuver more easily. He wanted to reach for her—not to help but to hold—to feel her in his arms. Noel didn't reach; instead, he watched her walk away from him toward the living room. There she sat on the couch, contemplating Paris.

"Come sit with me a minute, will you?" she called, turning her head toward him, inviting him to come to her.

Noel did as she asked, thinking twice, then choosing to sit beside her. It was hard to be so close to her every minute of every day.

"It's a glorious day," he noted. "I can't think of the last time April was so lovely."

"April," Tess mused. "Is it April already?"

" 'Fraid so."

"You know I have to leave soon. I have things I have to do. Royal is waiting and . . ."

"Tess," Noel interrupted, his voice harsh with its natural tone and his frustration. "You've been with me three weeks now. If he was going to contact you don't you think he would have by now?"

Tess hung her head. "Perhaps. Perhaps he can't. We don't know the extent of his injuries."

Noel pushed himself off the couch and went to the window. He leaned his head against his raised arm, his eyes raking the city below. The Seine sat dark and ominous, dirty brown in an otherwise sparkling scene. His heart felt like that river. So many things were hidden under his surface: anger that Meagan Dayler should be suffering so horribly as she fought for her life, concern over his daughter, confusion over their relationship, the pressures of running an empire as far-reaching as *High Life* and, not the least of it, his own exhaustion brought on by a lonely heart.

Now there was Tess. A woman he could so easily love, yet one who belonged to another man; a man

222

who didn't care enough to inquire if she was alive or dead. If Tess belonged to him, only death would have kept him from her side. Tess, in a few short weeks, had become his bright sun. She was enough to drive all the ache of his loneliness away, replacing it with the verve for life he had put aside at some point.

"I won't fight with you about your friend, Tess. I don't know him. I can't make judgments. But I won't have his name mentioned in my home."

Silence filled the room. Noel knew he was wrong to issue a command. Tess was his guest. As far as she was concerned she would never be anything more. Still, the words had been spoken; he could not take them back. He could only wait for her reaction.

Softly, her words came. "I understand, Noel."

"Do you really?" He whirled back to face her, ready to confess his feelings, challenging her to face her feelings for him and for Royal Cudahy.

"I do," Tess assured him. "You're a good man, Noel. You're the most selfless human being I've ever met. To bring me into your home, watch over me in the hospital, provide for me. When I think of the time you took to make sure I had clothes waiting for me, the effort it took for you to straighten out my passport, to go down to the airport facilities and find the few things of mine you could after the crash. Noel, when I think of those things I want to cry from gratitude. There is no reason in the world why you should have cared for me this way. And because of the way you are, you don't understand how someone like Royal could remain silent."

"I'm not that good, Tess," Noel stated.

"You are," she insisted. "But you're also rather

willful. Given what you've accomplished with your life I can understand that. But some people deal with their personal lives differently than they do with their business life.

"I don't like discussing my relationship with Royal, but I think I owe you that much. I don't like discussing it because I'm not terribly proud of it. Royal is married, Noel." Tess allowed a moment to pass, challenging him to react. His face didn't change; only a sadness passed through his eyes. "Obviously, you knew that." Tess hung her head, then with a sigh looked away from him. "I'm not proud of it. I wasn't brought up to sleep with other women's husbands. In fact," she laughed shortly, sadly, "I wasn't brought up to sleep with anyone at all until I was married to them. But time changes people. Time and circumstances. I can't help what I feel for him. He was there for me after my parents died. He was so gentle, so concerned, and he was lonely, too. It was wonderful to be needed."

"Tess, do you hear yourself? You think that you're in love with a man just because he was lonely at the same time you were."

"No," Tess said sharply. "That's not what I meant. There's more to it than that."

"What? Tell me what more there is? You can't, can you, Tess? You've never even given yourself a chance to know what more there is to a relationship. How many men were you with before Royal? How many lies did you have to hear, how many tears did you have to cry, how long did you sit alone and think about the loves you've had? You need to experience more than one man saving you from yourself."

"Oh, Noel, you've got to be kidding. You're talk-

The Publishers of Zebra Books Make This Special Offer to Zebra Romance Readers...

AFTER YOU HAVE READ THIS BOOK WE'D LIKE TO SEND YOU
4 MORE FOR *FREE* AN $18.00 VALUE

NO OBLIGATION!

4 FREE BOOKS

TO GET YOUR 4 FREE BOOKS WORTH $18.00 — MAIL IN THE FREE BOOK CERTIFICATE T O D A Y

Fill in the Free Book Certificate below, and we'll send your FREE BOOKS to you as soon as we receive it.

If the certificate is missing below, write to: Zebra Home Subscription Service, Inc., P.O. Box 5214, 120 Brighton Road, Clifton, New Jersey 07015-5214.

FREE BOOK CERTIFICATE

4 FREE BOOKS

ZEBRA HOME SUBSCRIPTION SERVICE, INC.

YES! Please start my subscription to Zebra Historical Romances and send me my first 4 books absolutely FREE. I understand that each month I may preview four new Zebra Historical Romances free for 10 days. If I'm not satisfied with them, I may return the four books within 10 days and owe nothing. Otherwise, I will pay the low preferred subscriber's price of just $3.75 each; a total of $15.00, *a savings off the publisher's price of $3.00.* I may return any shipment and I may cancel this subscription at any time. There is no obligation to buy any shipment and there are no shipping, handling or other hidden charges. Regardless of what I decide, the four free books are mine to keep.

NAME

ADDRESS _____ APT _____

CITY _____ STATE _____ ZIP _____

( )
TELEPHONE _____

SIGNATURE _____
(if under 18, parent or guardian must sign)

ZB0793

Terms, offer and prices subject to change without notice. Subscription subject to acceptance by Zebra Books. Zebra Books reserves the right to reject any order or cancel any subscription.

GET
FOUR
FREE
BOOKS
(AN $18.00 VALUE)

ZEBRA HOME SUBSCRIPTION
SERVICE, INC.
120 BRIGHTON ROAD
P.O. Box 5214
CLIFTON, NEW JERSEY 07015-5214

ing like I'm a sixteen-year-old."

Tess laughed, though his words had hit their mark. He was right about one thing. There hadn't been anyone before Royal, not really. She had been too intent on reaching her goals, creating her art, to worry about love. When she needed love it wasn't there—until Royal. He had walked in and taken her. Maybe she should have considered what she was giving away before she let herself fall in love with him, but she hadn't.

"Believe me, Tess, if there's one thing I know it's that you're not sixteen," Noel admitted, his face softening as his eyes roamed over her, his lips tipping into a wry smile. "You're a beautiful woman, an intelligent woman, just not an experienced one."

Tess laughed happily now. He was a marvelous man who knew when the waters were getting treacherous.

"Well, I tell you what, Noel, I'll do my best to educate myself when the opportunity comes along if that will satisfy you. Now how did we get to this? I thought we were going to walk through Paris to get the strength back in my legs."

"You're right," Noel said, holding his hands up in amused defeat. "But I take no responsibility for the turn of this conversation. You're the one who requested my presence. You're the one who insisted we sit here for a minute."

"Guilty as charged. So we'll leave it at that."

She held her hands out to him. He reached toward her. Their fingertips met; Noel's hands clasped hers as he pulled her up to him. Tess laughingly swayed away from him. She had been sitting too long, her legs had stiffened. Instinctively, Noel caught her, his

225

strong arm wrapping about her waist protectively. Tess's body responded, fluidly moving back toward him until she lay languidly against him, her laughter now ringing through the cavernous room.

Noel laughed with her until he realized that finally he held her in his arms, held her so closely that he could feel the marvelous tautness of her body, the fine lines of her legs as they pressed against his. Without thinking, unable to stop himself, Noel's lips found hers. Ever so gently he kissed her. Kissed away the laughter and her memories of Royal Cudahy. Kissed her until he felt her respond to him, then pull away. When she did he gathered her into his arms briefly, underscoring his hope.

"Let's not talk of leaving just yet, Tess. Not just yet."

Night had claimed Paris gently while Tess and Noel lost themselves in the wonders of the Louvre. For hours they wandered the labyrinth of corridors coming upon chambers that yielded ever more overwhelming treasures. Tess was lost in the wonder of the world's artistic ability: stylized Egyptian art, Rubens's marvelously rounded women lounging naked by streams and on beds of linen, busts of young Greek men long dead, their beauty living on, *Winged Victory* reigning triumphant atop a staircase of marble worn away by royalty and peasants alike.

They rested when she needed but, more often than not, Tess forged ahead. Her soul insisted on it, driving her forward with an intensity she had forgotten existed in her. All the time she had spent with Royal he had been amused by her efforts to paint or sculpt,

226

always finding something more interesting, by his definition, for her to do. For the first time she realized his interest in her work had been patronizing. Tess realized it only because, beside her, Noel was as intense a patron of the arts as she. His absorption fed hers. His hand felt right in hers, his arm around her waist as their heads came close together in awe of what they were viewing.

When finally he insisted that they rest at the cafe, she was grateful, but also saddened, that such a fine day was coming to an end.

"I can't thank you enough, Noel. I've never felt so in awe. This was wonderful."

"Nothing to thank me for," he replied, his hands cupping his coffee. "It's been a long, long time since I've had a day like this. Sometimes I get running so fast I forget about the things that make the world special. I can't tell you how often I've been through Paris and not taken the time to come to the Louvre or see the *Rodin*. Oh, Tess, there are so many more incredible things to see. Not just museums, but architecture throughout the city that is the highest form of art. Even the cemeteries are incredible. Sculpture on the crypts like you can't imagine. And Paris is only the tip of the iceberg. Rome, Prague, Budapest, Bejing, Athens. Oh, but I forgot, you must have seen some marvelous things when you were in Greece."

"No." Tess shook her head. "Unfortunately, we spent all our time on the yacht Royal's client owns. We didn't get out to see anything." Tess thought back to Dimitri, wondering why she hadn't considered him before. As soon as she could she would contact him. Certainly Dimitri could find out what happened to Royal. Immediately she discarded the idea. She would be home soon enough. She wouldn't bother her new friend. She became more attentive to Noel, knowing that there would be time for Dimitri.

"I'm sorry. You, of all people, would have truly appreciated the temples and sculpture. You have a marvelous eye. I envy you."

"That's funny coming from you. I've seen *High Life* magazine and even one or two of your film productions. I think you have a marvelous eye for what's beautiful."

"Some people call *High Life* a girlie magazine, you know." Noel laughed. "But I always thought of it as more than cheesecake. Certainly the women we highlight are lovely, and sometimes not exactly clad in ways some would consider proper, but the intent is to show beauty in many different ways. We've chosen actresses, singers, models, poets, artists, and novelists as the *High Life* Woman, so I don't feel that we discriminate on the side of physical assets. I think every photo, every article and interview and film we do is tasteful. Unfortunately, I also have to admit that the magazine has taken a more commercial turn in the last ten years. But that's a necessity. One I may not always like, but one I'll accept as long as my staff understands that quality comes first is the key. Always quality."

"I think that's all you can ask," Tess answered, admiring the intensity of his commitment to his work. "Besides, there are enough hit-and-miss operations to satisfy the mundane tastes of the mass. You simply found a market that is both intellectual and appreciative of the physical aspect of the women you profile. I think it's great you've found a niche."

"And you, Tess," Noel said after a moment's silence. "What's yours?"

She shrugged. "Who can say?"

"You can," Noel insisted. "You've probably thought about your future more than any other woman I know. From the moment your parents died and left you alone until your friend found you and promised you a lifetime of ease, you've been thinking about what your life would be like."

"Is that what you think of me, Noel?" Tess asked quickly, her heart breaking at the thought of gaining so little of this man's respect. "Do you truly believe that I took the easy way out with Royal? I'm with him only because of his money or position?"

Noel raised his head, turning to the left as though scanning the crowd, looking for a familiar face. But his lips were set in a hard line; there was something fierce in his eyes. Anger, or disappointment, or even pain, Tess wasn't sure. He looked back at her and she was embarrassed to be blushing, unable to look him in the face.

"No," he said simply.

Tess was surprised to find she had been holding her breath. Now she let it out gently through her rounded lips.

"I'm relieved. Because you must know me well enough by now to know that it isn't comfort I'm looking for. I would never be with Royal just for what he can give me, although he's given me so much. In fact"—her brow furrowed as she thought back to the days just before her trip—"in fact, I must tell you that sometimes I find myself at odds and ends. I can't seem to figure out where I belong. Sometimes it's strange, but I seem to be unable to do

229

anything during the day except wait for Royal to come see me. It's as though he defines my world rather than being a part of it. Have you ever experienced that?"

"Can't say that I have," Noel answered as he tossed a handful of francs on the small table. "And I hate it that you have. Tess, I've never seen your work. I've never seen your home. As you point out, I've known you a very short time. But one thing I do know after watching you struggling for life after the crash, watching you take hold of whatever it is that makes us tick and climb right back out of that misery fighting, I can't stand hearing you talk as though you're half dead most of the time. Because that's what you are if you simply wait for moments and hours to go by until someone else comes and makes you whole. The person you love should make the time away special because of his absence. You should celebrate your life and his in whatever you do. You sound as though you close the door to a cell the moment he leaves you."

"Noel." Tess was on her feet, ignoring the ache in her legs as she reached out for him. "That's not what I was saying at all. It's only sometimes I feel that way. But I do love him. He's so kind, gentle . . ."

She searched for words to describe Royal, to make Noel understand how wonderful he was, yet she found herself lacking. She shook her head slightly, tightening her hold on Noel's arm as though for support. Only she knew it was a desperate plea for memory. Tess couldn't remember the fine points of Royal's face, the way he smiled. When she tried it was Noel's face that came to mind.

She closed her eyes and sat down again. Noel's

230

strong hands were on her shoulders, steadying her. When she opened her eyes she was looking into his. His face was so close that had she moved in the slightest, her lips would have met his. For a moment they simply looked at one another. Tess no longer frantically tried to recall Royal's face. He had faded again. She thought exhaustion had kept the image away. She hoped it was. Royal had been so good to her.

"Gentle and kind," Noel finally whispered, "are wonderful things. But so is freedom, Tess. The freedom to love openly, the freedom to grow together in the bright light of the sun. The freedom to be at someone's side every minute of the day or only when you choose. Those are also wonderful things. If you loved me . . ." Noel's words faded on his lips as his eyes roamed her face, his hands moved slowly up her shoulders, ". . . if you loved me, for instance . . ." He laughed then. "But you don't. You love a man who is thousands of miles away. It's up to this man to take you a mile or two and get you the rest you desperately need. You're pale, Tess. Come, we'll find a taxi."

Mesmerized, Tess put her hand in the one he held out to her. When his arm slid around her waist to support her tired body, she didn't object. Instead, she leaned into him, forgetting everything but the moment. His body molded to hers, so strong and sure that Tess thought of her father, and the way his broad shoulders cut a powerful silhouette against the blazing twilight sun as he surveyed his fields.

Noel Montgomery was like that. A man who could appraise his domain with a sure and forceful eye, then turn and open his arms, letting her fly into them for comfort and love and the promise of all the good things in life, not just the ones money could buy. For the first time in a very long time, Tess felt free to let her thoughts fade and enjoy only what she felt.

At this moment there was no guilt, no fear that Royal would leave and never come back, no shame, not even the tiniest bit. She loved Royal and would go back to him whole and alive. But for now, for this night, she would stand with Noel Montgomery as though they would be together for eternity, for it was he who gave her this strength and purpose.

He handed her into a cab, sitting very close as he gave the address in impeccable French. When he put his arm around her again, she leaned on his shoulder and watched the lighted buildings in silence as they drove toward his apartment.

Inside, neither spoke a word. In the darkened foyer Noel kissed her cheek lightly and brushed back her hair before she turned away and went to her room. There she slipped into the gown of lavender silk Noel had chosen for her and climbed into the huge bed, pulling the down comforter over her.

Through her curtainless window she saw only the sky of France, clear and laced with night clouds. In that room she tried to think of Royal, but thought of Noel instead. Rather, she wasn't thinking of him, simply feeling him. His presence permeated every inch of the apartment and the depth of the night and had touched the places of her heart that, perhaps, she hadn't given away to Royal. So she lay feeling him . . . wanting him though she wasn't aware of that until the night had become very late.

Outside her room Noel Montgomery listened to

the silence from within. His hand was on the knob as it had been ever since Tess Canfield had walked through that door and closed it behind her. Inside himself he warred with his feelings.

She would leave soon, of that he was sure. There was no doubt that Tess was beginning to perceive what was happening. In a few days, a week, she would be unable to deny her feelings for him, just as he was unable to denounce them for her.

Finally, he left her door. Though tired, his mind and heart could not stop the whirling dance that had begun almost from the moment he had spoken to the woman in the bedroom. Flipping on the light over his den couch, Noel poured himself a whiskey, gathered the mail the cleaning woman had put on his desk and sat in the silken glow of that solitary lamp.

Carefully he opened each envelope, hoping to lose himself in the many messages. Only one piqued his interest. Davina was wasting no time in appropriating Meagan's power while the older woman lay helpless in a hospital waiting the first in a long line of plastic surgeries which would hopefully restore her face to something resembling that of the woman she was. In his hand he held a memo outlining her plans for utilizing new production techniques, changing printers, personnel changes. The list went on and on. Noel lay his head back on the couch.

He, too, would have to go back soon. Davina didn't have the experience to handle production for the entire magazine. He wouldn't replace her, though; she had made such wonderful strides. And, in the last year, they had even found an even ground on which they could communicate. The road had been long and hard, but it was paying off. Davina still needed a guiding hand, a powerful one, to keep her on the right track. Though he hoped for the best, Noel couldn't forget the anger Davina harbored when they first met, the ways she had tried to assert herself against him.

He lay his head back on the couch and raised the crystal glass to his lips. The whiskey burned his throat. He set it aside, knowing that a drink was not the answer to what ailed him. Suddenly, he was upright. Davina's letter was folded back into the envelope. Now he knew what must be done. Neither Tess nor he could leave this place until they knew what they felt for one another. Noel Montgomery closed his eyes and prayed silently for a moment; prayed that Tess would realize what had happened between them, too. Then he crossed the living room and went back to the door. This time, when his hand touched the knob, Noel didn't hesitate. He turned it. He went in. In the darkness he could feel her watchfulness.

"Tess," he whispered.

She didn't answer. Instead, in the darkness he saw the silhouette of her arms rising, reaching for him, telling him that all they could do was try.

Noel remained where he was, the only sound in the room was that of their breathing, deep and anticipatory. Slowly, Tess let her arms fall back to the comforter. Noel knew he should speak, ask her whether she was sure, but he was mute, afraid that given the opportunity she might rethink her desire.

Finally he moved, one hand at the throat of his cotton shirt as he slipped the buttons loose. Moving toward her he slipped it from his body, letting it fall between bed and door. Half naked, he stood over her and, from the light of the moon through the windows, saw her as he'd never seen her before. There was no pain in her body any longer—now it was all in her eyes.

He saw everything: her fear, her uncertainty, her wanting, her need, and even her love for him. Whether the love was true or one given from gratitude didn't matter any longer. Noel, the man who had always been so sure of himself, was now confident he could make her love him completely. Together they would explore the depths of that emotion until the end of their days, if only he could have the chance now to convince her the future was for them—not a man committed to someone else.

He saw her blue eyes spark with every stray moonbeam. Her glance never wavered as he shed the rest of his clothes. Softly, he moved in beside her and gathered her to him. He heard her sigh, felt her pull away, then move into him again, her arms winding about his neck as she buried her face in his shoulder.

As though he had done it a thousand times Noel kissed her, his lips meeting her silky hair, traveling down her cheek, her neck, forcing her to turn toward him with his gentle ministrations.

Tess moved and kissed his cheek. Noel grasped her ever more tightly and kissed her again, this time forcing her lips to his. Their bodies pressed together so tightly that Noel felt her as though she was the sand upon which he made his imprint. His heart leapt as her hands began to roam his body, pulling him toward her. He heard her sounds of love, murmurs of desire. His hands had a life of their own as they moved over her body, sliding the silk gown over her, slipping it from her until they were flesh against flesh, generating a heat of passion that Noel had almost forgotten existed.

For him there was no other woman in the world to match this one. She was a sphere of perfection, intellect melting into physical beauty surrounded by the cocoon of her spirit. He called her name as his mouth found one perfectly formed breast. His hands slid down to her hips, his lips followed. Tess's legs parted as her head fell back into the pillows, lost in the pleasure he brought her, so lost that she couldn't find her way back to what had been reality for her before this moment.

Her mind was a swirl of hope and shame, her body aflame with sensation. When Tess could stand it no longer she pulled him up, grasping his face between her hands as her hips rose to take him. He entered her, complete now, sure that this was the way his life would be lived forever. He gave himself to her as she did to him. When they lay in one another's arms, no words were spoken as their hands moved in idle wonderment, until finally Noel slept.

Tess held him for what seemed like an eternity and when finally she released him it was not to seek sleep but rather to seek a place to hide her shame. Shame for her feelings for Noel and for her betrayal of Royal. Tess wanted to hide from the truth and there was only one way she could do just that.

Seventeen

There was a collective gasp as Davina walked into the conference room and stood by the door surveying the group. Department heads seated at the length of the table were looking absolutely shocked, averting their eyes in embarrassment as Davina looked at each one in turn. The ladies and gentlemen at either end of the table were not so thin skinned. These were the executive vice-presidents. Assholes, as far as Davina was concerned, who were all just a bit too big for their britches. They had snubbed her once too often, refusing appointments when she requested them or patting her on the head like a child when they deigned to see her and she told them her ideas.

These were the people who refused to acknowledge that Davina Montgomery would one day be running *High Life* publishing and film. So today, the day of the semiannual corporate meeting, Davina Montgomery invited herself to attend, though the production department had no say in strategic planning.

"Miss Montgomery." Paul Davenport, vice-chairman of the company, took it upon himself to speak since the rest of the people in the room seemed to have been rendered speechless. "Is there some difficulty in production which we can assist you with?"

"No, Paul," Davina replied sarcastically. "Produc-

237

tion, unlike so many departments, is doing just fine."

"Then may I inquire what has brought you to this meeting?"

Davina eyed him closely. He wasn't a bad-looking guy, although he had to be pushing sixty. His gray hair flew in lush wings from his high, clear forehead before dipping into a generous wave. His eyes were green behind his glasses, with still enough life in them to make a head-on battle a challenge.

"I came in place of my father. Since he's out of the country, I want to make sure his interests are represented. After all, this is a . . ." she hesitated, rolling her tongue over her lips as her eyes rolled over the group ". . . a family business. I think it only right that decisions made which affect the family be made in the presence of a family member."

Davina thought she'd been quite eloquent, emphasizing "family" with just the right degree of importance. Those in the room, however, had their own opinion and it was a unified one. Davina Montgomery didn't look in her right mind. Her carefully put together ensemble was spoiled by the fact it looked as though she slept in it. Her makeup sat atop her skin like a filmy mask and her eyes were red rimmed, either from lack of sleep, or as many guessed, an unhealthy interest in pills. She pulled a pencil between her fingers as though trying to break it. The gulf between self-image and public one would never be broached.

Paul Davenport didn't bother to waste his breath with a sigh of disgust. Why Noel Montgomery continued to cater to this creature was beyond him. In some cases blood was not thicker than water. Noel should throw her out on her classless ass as far as he was concerned. If she had been a daughter of his . . . But she wasn't. Davina also wasn't anyone of consequence within the company, so he spoke plainly.

"As usual, Miss Montgomery, your father's interests are being protected. This group of professionals, and I don't use the word lightly, makes policy with or without your father's presence every six months. Every decision we make is duly recorded and your father is informed one way or another. We decide the fate of this publication and our film interests as though we were deciding the fate of our own business. That is because we all feel, Miss Montgomery, that we are part of the *High Life* family. We feel that way because your father has given us reason.

"Now, select department heads are invited to attend this meeting. Others are not. Production is one of those departments that does not have a voice in strategic planning. As you can see, marketing, sales, editorial, and research are the ones most relevant to the discussions we hold here. If this was unclear, we apologize for not being more specific in our memo announcing this meeting. If this was clear to you, then we accept your apology for interrupting us and would now ask you to leave."

Paul moved his shoulders under his well-cut jacket, fingered his beautiful silk tie and cleared his throat, ignoring Davina.

"Okay, where were we? Oh, yes, we were discussing the ramifications of the graying of America."

All eyes turned toward the man at the head of the table. Davina's stomach heaved. Her fingers found her throat. She felt as though she couldn't breathe.

239

A scream was gathering somewhere inside her and would let loose if she wasn't careful. She had to be careful. Very careful. These people were her enemies, yet she needed them a while longer—just until *High Life* was hers and she could hire the kind of employees who would be loyal to her.

But the waiting was wearing on Davina. Noel was too young. He would be around a very long time. Davina had to make them see that she was the one who deserved to be sitting in his chair. She'd tried to make friends—oh, how she had tried! Then she got tough. Everyone respected a tough business woman. Now, though, she was confused. Nothing was working right.

Davina listened while those around the table entered into a spirited discussion as they began to forget her. The meeting was taking on a life of its own. They seemed to come from so far away that it was difficult to focus on them. Then she was moving, listening to her own voice. She was sure she was speaking clearly, effectively.

"Thank you, Paul, I will sit in if you don't mind. Thank you. I think I can contribute quite a bit."

Davina took an empty chair and pulled it out. It toppled slightly. The man sitting next to it put out his hand to steady it. Davina gave him a smile, one she was sure he interpreted to mean the right thing. She wouldn't forget his kindness.

She made a mental note to find out who he was so she could reward him, but forgot it as she sat down. If she was a computer all the signs pointed toward a hard drive crash. She sat in the chair and looked about for a pad of paper. She would take notes. That was the way to look professional.

Heads swiveled from Davina to Paul. He moved his hand slightly. They would ignore her presence and continue. He nodded toward Tracy, vice-president of research. She allowed her eyes to flicker toward Davina once, twice, before she began.

"Yes, hmmm," she began softly, then with greater confidence. "The older population, those aged fifty-five plus, will be growing in the next ten years until they comprise over twenty-five percent of the population. Women will outlive men by a substantial number of years, but the life span of men is extending itself into the late seventies. Despite the reports we hear of the difficulty with social security, we can count on a high percentage of affluent older men and women who will be well able to afford our product since their disposable income will grow through investment. However, our product mix is going to have to change substantially."

"Thank you, Tracy." Paul nodded her way. "George, has editorial been working closely with Tracy on this?"

"Absolutely, Paul."

A middle-aged man with nondescript features now held the floor. Davina's eyes went to him. If she could get him in bed he probably would be forever grateful and do exactly what she said. She almost laughed. There was no "if" about it. He probably had a wife at home who looked more worn out than he did. He would be thrilled to bed someone like her. It was a plan. The vice-president of editorial was a powerful man, even if he looked like a wimp. She made another mental note that hit the same cerebral whirlpool as her last. He was speaking again. Davina bit the end of her pencil, attempting to look attentive.

241

"We've been working quite closely with research. Tracy has all the figures on what we've found, but basically it boils down to the fact that we're going to have to skew our editorial content by at least twenty percent to that particular audience. We're going to have to go after those kinds of articles that appeal to, and look at, their interests. Naturally, we won't give up style just because we might be discussing social security. Sass and brass, as Noel often likes to remind us, is our hallmark and we'll never change that."

Appreciative and tender laughter made its way around the table, skipping Davina as it progressed. She remained tight lipped, her fingers whitening as she gripped the arms of the chair.

"Now, the *High Life* Woman is also going to be taking a turn. We won't be highlighting as many sweet young things as we have in the past. We're going to be focusing on the equally sexy women over forty who may not take off as many clothes, but will offer this older demographic the kind of womanly attitude they find appealing. We'll also focus more on the women who make life worth living—artists, novelists, economists—all of whom hold a great deal of attractiveness for a man of a certain . . ."

"Bullshit."

Davina snorted the word and, when all eyes turned toward her, what they saw was the top of her head, her shiny, black curls bouncing as she shook her head as though to say she couldn't believe what the kids on the playground were talking about.

Slowly she raised her head, her eyes glinting with distaste for these so-called experts. She pierced Paul Davenport with a glare.

"Miss Montgomery!" he began in shock.

"Don't say another word." Davina laughed. "I can't believe what I'm hearing. You don't know shit about what men want. The older they get the more they need sex — or at least the appearance of it."

Davina had risen, pushing herself out of her chair with her hands splayed on the highly polished table. Straightening her body, she cupped her own breasts.

"This is what they want. This and this." Her hands spread down over her hips. "Isn't that right, Paul? When a guy's too old to get it on, he at least wants to look at it — in all its glory. You're talking about showing them the kind of women they sleep with every night. I say bullshit. I say you're going to run this company right . . ."

"That's enough," Paul said quietly. "That's enough."

"It's not," Davina screamed back at him. "I won't sit here and see what my father's worked so hard for be run into the ground. You told me you were looking out for his interests. His interest is in keeping this company young, the magazine young, the films young. He knows where the bucks are."

"As do you, I assume?" Paul asked, raising an eyebrow, challenging her.

"I . . ." Davina's lips parted.

This wasn't right. She'd meant to show them what she was talking about. That was all. Just show them. She had been so sure they would understand. But now they were looking at her like she was a street walker.

Davina blinked, hating the way the younger men's eyes tore into her, without respect or understanding; hating the way the women's lips curled in disgust.

This wasn't what she meant. She only wanted to be strong, to show them they couldn't toy with her. A tremor jerked Davina's neck, her head snapped down. She could see her fingers were shaking; she could feel her whole body trembling.

When Davina looked up again she was almost sure everyone had been laughing when she wasn't looking. Laughing at her, the woman who would get it all.

"Just wait . . ." she whispered before she fled the room. The last sound she heard was silence. She would have almost preferred laughter.

Davina pushed her way past two secretaries in the hall. Anxiously, she waited for the elevator, praying it would come in time. She needed to calm down. Desperately needed something to stop this awful shaking, the headache that seemed never ending. In one instant of clarity, once she was inside the elevator, Davina replayed what had happened in its terrible, embarrassing sequence. She was smart and she knew it, so why did her mind work the way it did? Why did her voice say things she wasn't thinking or turn the thing she was thinking around so it sounded so ludicrous? Why did her body betray her and do things she couldn't control?

The door of the elevator opened and Davina dashed into her office. Rummaging through her purse she found what she wanted. Her glorious pills that calmed her like nothing else could.

Quickly she took three, more than she should, but they worked like a charm. In her chair, behind her own desk, she could feel her body and mind reacting to the medication. It was like a warm wave coming over her in slow motion, easing every nerve in her body, opening up the vessels that brought the blood to her brain.

Sometimes it felt as though those vessels were bracing for an attack, that her brain would simply explode one day when she least expected it. With her little pills, she could actually feel the blood coursing free and warm to her head and back through her body. Now she could think clearly.

Closing her eyes she thought about the conference room and her horrid performance. With the passing of time came the answer. To win she must be cunning, to be cunning she must be calm. Calm, she reminded herself a hundred times. When finally she opened her eyes, they were clear and bright and full of determination. Looking at her watch Davina couldn't believe she had been sitting in the same chair for almost two hours. Two long hours had been just enough time to iron out her plan; now she would put it in motion and still make her meeting. Tonight she would take her first grand step into the world of management decision making. But first she had to see Paul Davenport.

"Paul?" Davina knocked, poking her head into his grand office simultaneously. He looked up, a cloud passing over his brow when he saw who it was. "Do you have a minute?"

"Certainly," he answered warily, putting down his pen and covering the paper he had been working on. "Come in."

"Thank you. I know you have every right to refuse me."

Davina spoke sweetly, yet professionally, as she walked straight toward his desk and sat opposite him. She felt herself smile, concentrating on exactly the right width of lip to make it sincere.

"I do. But I must admit curiosity has the best of me."

"I can imagine," she said softly. "I came here to apologize. I realize I made a fool of myself this morning, and I hope you'll forgive me. If you think it's the right thing to do I'll be happy to apologize to everyone at the meeting, especially George."

"I think an apology to George would be very worthwhile, Miss Montgomery," Paul answered. She could see he was still too reserved, apprehensive of her change of attitude. She would have to do something about that.

"Paul, I realize I'm having some problems fitting in here. You must know that this has been as difficult for me as it has been for everyone. No one likes the boss's kid hanging around or, for that matter, being allowed to take on such a grave responsibility as I have without proving myself. I admit that heading production after such a horrible accident with Meagan was rather frightening. I hope I'm proving myself. But you, and everyone else, must also realize that my life hasn't been easy. It's also been difficult, finding a father I never knew existed and a powerful one at that. Powerful and creative. It's been tough."

"Lots of people have a tough time of it. Many seem to overcome their personal difficulties in private. I would hope that you might see how beneficial that could be."

"Of course." Davina inclined her head deferentially. It almost killed her to do that.

"But how you and your father want to work things out are no concern of mine or anyone else in this corporation. We turn a blind eye until it becomes a matter of concern because it disrupts our work. What you did this morning disrupted our work and made it seem a futile exercise. You made a mockery of everything we were trying to accomplish. Attacking our professional capabilities is a very low blow."

"And one that was unconscionable," Davina admitted, her hair shirt firmly in place.

"I'm glad you see that, Miss Montgomery. Now, if there's nothing else?"

"Only one. Could you possibly call me Davina? I think a little less formality, fewer reminders that I am my father's daughter, will help me along."

"Perhaps we should remind you more often that you *are* your father's daughter. That might be the incentive you need to be more like him," Paul said. Davina began to bristle. Nobody was worth this groveling. Then she relaxed. He hadn't finished. "However, we will start anew, Davina, as of this moment."

He smiled now, in that small way men do when they think they are big. Davina stood, held out her hand, shook his and left feeling quite sure she had won.

Inside his office Paul Davenport pulled a piece of paper toward him and began his note again. The first had been quite detailed. The second was another matter. Putting pen to paper he wrote:

Noel,
Come home quickly. We need to talk.
Paul

He typed and faxed it himself. Davina Montgomery made his blood run cold. She hadn't fooled him and, if she thought she had, Davina was a very unbalanced girl. Only Noel Montgomery could handle a situation like this.

The Sportsman's Lodge was about as far from a celebration of the great outdoors as you could get. Nestled amid the bright lights of Hollywood's La Cienega Boulevard like a frightened rabbit surprised by the glare of headlights, it looked as though it was playing dead, afraid any sign of life might draw deadly attention to it.

The building was long and rectangular, sitting on a piece of property so prime developers actually salivated when they thought of it. The neon sign above the complex of hotel and meeting rooms had been erected in the early fifties and nothing about it ever changed except the light bulbs. The structure itself was rather nondescript, as was the food in the coffee shop and the decor of the rooms.

Still, people flocked to the place, perhaps because its amorphousness translated into memories of tract housing for the baby boomers growing old, or perhaps because it was convenient. Either way, the public kept coming to the Sportsman's lodge and the developers kept trying to wrestle it from the grasp of its owners in order to erect another bright, shiny new high rise that in twenty years' time would show signs of age without any of the character aging should bring.

It was to this place Davina Montgomery drove that night. She was calmer than she had been earlier in the day, full of serenity, firmly believing that she had snowed Paul Davenport with minimal effort.

248

Davina would never consider that her peace of mind was chemical, rather than strategically induced.

So when she pulled into the narrow drive, tossed the valet her keys and entered the lobby in search of the dining room, Davina's mind was unoccupied with worry. This allowed her a great deal of latitude, and she turned up her nose at the obvious mundaneness of the place.

The Sportsman's Lodge was exactly the kind of hotel her mother would have enjoyed. In fact, it was probably very much like the place where Davina had been conceived. She often thought things like this; creating a prelife that was so ordinary as to make her anger at Noel swell all the more.

Tugging at her well-cut jacket, Davina hitched her purse higher on her shoulder as she walked regally to the desk. She spoke even before the nightman acknowledged her presence. When he heard her voice it seemed he had no choice but to leave the people he was helping and deal with the dull-eyed, black-haired woman.

"Madam?" He clasped his hands in front of him as though praying their conversation would be short.

"I'm supposed to meet someone in your dining room. Where is it?"

His prayers had been answered. He smiled. "Down this hall and to your left."

Davina went away without another word, leaving the nightman to thank his lucky stars she was not going to be a guest. He could spot a troublemaker a mile away and she had all the earmarks. Happily, he went back to the couple from Des Moines.

Davina found her way without any trouble. She stood in the middle of the doorway, forcing an elderly couple to swerve from their slow and painful progress toward the lobby. Davina didn't notice them. She was looking about, though she hadn't the faintest idea who she was looking for. When the hostess showed up Davina settled for a little help.

"I'm here to meet Mister Tony DelMarco. My name's Davina Montgomery."

The pretty young girl checked her book and offered Davina a dazzling smile. "He's been here for about ten minutes."

"Tough," Davina answered.

The girl stumbled a bit, regained her stride and hurried toward Mr. DelMarco's table.

"Your party is here, sir," she said and backed away.

"Miss Montgomery. I'm so glad you could meet me. I've been looking forward to having a chance to talk with you."

"Thanks. What you said on the phone sounded very interesting." Davina slid into the blood-colored vinyl upholstered booth and eyed her companion. Instantly, she smiled and he seemed dazzled.

He was a looker, all muscle and bone, his face cut right out of a piece of stone. His nose was a little long, a little crooked, and his eyes, if she looked real close, were set too far apart. But all in all it was a fine figure he cut in his Armani suit with his hair styled just so. A bonus like this absolutely delighted Davina.

"I was hoping you'd say that," Tony said in a voice that was a cross between a cat purring and the sound of its little paws scratching at the kitty litter. "Drink?"

Davina raised one scarlet-clad shoulder, wishing she had worn something more revealing than a business suit. "Why not?" A waitress had magically appeared by Tony's elbow. Davina watched him while she said, "Scotch and soda, heavy on the Scotch."

Tony raised an eyebrow in appreciation.

"Mine's Jack Daniel's straight up with a splash of water."

The waitress disappeared, but not before she slipped two menus the size of Monopoly boards onto the table. Neither Tony nor Davina bothered with them. Each was aware that they were in for a long and involved evening.

"So," he said as soon as they were alone, "what was it about my pitch that got you interested in D&D printing?"

"It wasn't so much what you said," Davina flirted, "as the way you said it. I just knew you were an interesting man the first time I heard your voice coming at me over the wires."

"Okay. You're the kind of lady I can relate to. You know you see so many of these broa . . . women . . ." he corrected himself as he slipped out of his carefully polished salesman role into his natural one, "yeah, so many women today who just don't know how to deal with other professionals. They think they've got to be all business, you know? Nothing wrong with a little friendship in the bargain is there, Miss Montgomery?"

Davina leaned over the table, parting her lips seductively. "Not a thing. In fact, why don't we practice what we preach? I'll be Davina, you be Tony. I think we'll get a lot of business done that way, don't you?"

"No doubt about it."

The waitress was back, sliding their drinks between them, sure that a big tip would be in the offing if she played this table right. All she had to do was decide

251

exactly when to break into the conversation. Of course, the electricity was so sharp at the table she might not even have to serve them. Maybe the slimeball guy would just drop a ten and take the woman to a room. She hurried away, giving them time to decide if they wanted to eat or play.

"Good." Davina picked up her drink, wrapping her long fingers around the glass and holding it toward him. "Then I'd say we're off to a good start. So let's get down to business then maybe we can get down to a few other things."

"Right. Business," Tony muttered into his drink. When he raised his head his lips were wet with liquor and he was concentrating hard.

When Tony told his uncle that he might be able to land the *High Life* magazine account the old man had almost shit a brick right there in the office. Tony'd been screwing up so long that Uncle Vito was just about ready to fire him no matter whose kid he was. So Tony had made up a lie about having an appointment.

It took him three weeks and some heavy promises to convince Davina Montgomery she ought to see him. Now, in the space of five minutes, he knew exactly how to convince her to hand over the printing contract. He started his spiel knowing it would be the least of his tactics to sway her.

"Business," Davina reminded him coyly, worried that she had lost him somewhere between the liquid and the ice cubes.

"Okay, here it is. We can print the magazine cheaper and with just as good quality as you're getting now."

Davina waited. When it was clear he wasn't going

to go on, she laughed. "That's it? That's your whole speech?"

"Yeah," he said, obviously confused. If she wanted more he didn't know what to tell her.

"That's the most to the point pitch I've ever heard. What makes you think you can do it?"

"Hey?" He raised his hands and his shoulders at the same time. "We can. We're a family business. Everybody in on it. We're like clockwork; no screw-ups, know what I mean?"

Davina didn't, he could see, but that was okay. Tony knew what he meant. The printing thing wasn't what the family was interested in anyway. They just needed a couple of big legit customers to make everything else work. It was the best way he'd ever seen to launder the drug and prostitution money the rest of his far-flung family sent their way.

Besides, they weren't bad printers. They did a good job and got stuff out on time. Funny how one thing led to another; drugs led to money, money to a need for a place to clean it up and, in the process, everyone in the L.A. family learns the printing business. Tony got a chuckle out of that every time he stopped to analyze the process, which wasn't often.

"Sounds a little simplistic," Davina noted, not really caring what his explanation was. If the printing contract was hers, Davina would have power over one of the most important steps in publishing *High Life*. From there she could start usurping every supplier and establish her power base.

"I suppose, but what the hey? If it works, why fix it? That's what my uncle always says."

"He sounds like a real brain," Davina drawled. Tony took no offense since that beautiful smile was

253

still firmly fixed to her full, red lips. "Listen, Tony, we've got over two million copies of that magazine going out every month. There's a lot to this. We've got advertisers who won't send in their art and mechanicals until the last minute. We've got five-color runs on some of this stuff, pop-ups that we need done in-house by the printing company and, believe me, we're spending a lot of money to see it's done right. Still say you can come in under what I'm spending?"

"Sure." Tony casually pulled a beautiful oxblood briefcase onto the table. Davina felt a tugging in the general vicinity of her stomach when she heard the latches flick. She liked hard, fast noises. Those latches sounded like a sharp slap across the face. "Here, take a look at this. This is the estimate I drew up based on the last six months issues. Unless you're really going to get screwy and change a bunch of stuff, they should be solid."

"You drew these up?"

Davina almost laughed. This guy didn't know printing from a hole in the wall. He didn't talk the lingo. He was just a salesman, but one she liked.

"Had a little help, but sure, I did it."

Davina took the paper he handed her. Quickly she perused it. The bottom line was excellent. More than excellent, in fact. Her eyes narrowed as she looked from the estimate to her companion. Something wasn't quite right with the bottom line. Nobody could do the job for this amount of money and still stay in business.

"I want this to be a firm estimate. I also want a contract guaranteeing delivery dates to our distributor. I want it signed by the head of your company and you. I'll sign, too. I want the contract in triplicate by

254

tomorrow."

"No problem," Tony said simply.

Davina played his game. Neither indicated that there was anything to worry about. Tony had locked the contract and it didn't matter how he did it. They would deliver and if they didn't, he'd make sure the contract left Davina Montgomery with no way out.

Davina knew that this was the coup of a lifetime if it worked. Her budget would be so far under even Paul Davenport would sit up and take notice of her. Of course, there was always the possibility it wouldn't work. If it didn't *High Life* could sue her. But she doubted her old man would go that far.

"Then let's drink to a new relationship."

"I have a better idea." Tony stood with his briefcase in one hand, his other extended to her. She took it. "Let's seal this deal more privately."

Davina giggled. Tony had her wait a moment while he dug in his pocket and tossed two tens on the table. The waitress watched them go. Drinks had only come to seven bucks. She had won her bet with herself and was ahead in the bargain. Pocketing it she collected the glasses, wiped the wet rings off the table then shivered involuntarily as she thought about going to bed with the guy with the weird eyes. As she strolled to the kitchen with the half-filled glasses she realized what they said was true: there was no accounting for taste.

Eighteen

"Over there, you twits!"

The man with his back toward Bonnie grunted, dropped the end of the sofa he was carrying with a resounding thud and flexed his back muscles so the red Bekins Moving and Storage logo rippled, almost disappearing between his shoulder blades. Slowly he turned his head, snapped his gum and glowered at Bonnie through his beady little eyes. She glared right back.

"Sorry."

His gum popped once more for good measure. After this gig he was definitely never, ever going to have a wet dream over this broad again. He motioned to his partner. They lifted the incredible couch and moved it to the place Bonnie indicated.

"Better. Now a little to the left." They scooted it over with the soles of their shoes leaving little dark tread marks on the white silk. "Okay, if that's the best you can do."

Bonnie turned on the balls of her feet and left the room with her nose in the air. The big man sat his big rear on the delicate arm of the couch and unwrapped another stick of gum. He'd give his eye teeth for a cigarette, but no smoking till they'd left the premises, that was the word.

"You know, Joe," he said to his companion, who joined him for a breather, "television sure can fool ya. I used to think that skirt was the greatest thing since sliced bread. Gave me faith in America again, ya know? Like the peaches 'n cream girl next door still existed. Like virtue could be wrapped in something more than a 32A cup. I thought that kid was the sweetest, nicest, sexiest broad in the universe. Then we get here, we touch all her stuff real reverent like and we get a bunch of lip. Hell, she's a bitch on wheels if ya ask me." Looking over his shoulder to make sure his partner was paying attention, he nodded in a knowing way. "Not that ya asked me."

"Naw, I know what you mean. I used to watch that show, too. But I don't know," his partner said with a shrug. He was a slight man so his shoulders seemed to sort of quiver when he tried to be offhand. "I don't know, there was just something about her. I read faces, you know. I can read 'em, and even before we seen her today I knew she was too good to be true. Yep, told that to my old lady just the other night."

"So, another Hollywood bimbo. Hey, what'd we expect?" The big man laughed like he'd told a really funny joke, but there was a note of sadness in the sound. "Ya think I'd learn. Nothin' but a dream, those kinds of broads. The minute you take 'em off the tube and put 'em in the living room they're just like any other broad."

He sighed and removed himself from the white sofa. It wasn't that comfortable anyway.

"Let's get to it. The way she's got us working we'll

257

be here till midnight. At least the company can stiff her on the bill."

"Yeah, might as well get to it," Joe agreed, shaking his head sadly over the dainty little chair he was about to pick up.

They both felt the shards of their shattered dreams, and that feeling shriveled their hearts. There wasn't much to dream about anymore. Nothin' to do but get up in the morning, work, have a few brews and die. The big man popped his gum and, in a tone his partner had never heard before—something close to a sigh—he said, "Still, she's got a great set of knockers."

They heard a crash in the other room and immediately forgot about Bonnie's chest, knowing they'd get more of her lip if she had broken something important. The two men began to work at a furious pace.

In the bedroom Bonnie stood in the midst of boxes. The mattress and bed frame were propped against the wall. Her suitcases were strewn about and half her clothes were hanging in the mirrored closet. Unfortunately, one half of the mirror no longer existed. Bonnie, in a fit of anger and frustration, had taken Giles's one and only Emmy award and hurled it across the room, effectively obliterating a large portion of the reflective surface.

"Damn you, Giles," Bonnie whispered to her fragmented reflection just before she crossed her legs and sat down on the nearest box.

The top gave slightly, but held. Bonnie propped her elbows on her knees, and her chin on her fists, and thought about what she had come to. It was a far cry from what she had expected.

So much of Giles's life had been a sham. Not the

success of his show, of course, and not his creativity, but certainly his lifestyle. That was a façade with all the trappings of wealth and none of the reserves to back it up. He had borrowed on his life insurance policy, the house in Beverly Hills was heavily mortgaged and the damned Rolls was leased for an exorbitant amount of money each month. His tailor-made clothes were freebies from a men's shop on Sixth. They were paid off with promotional spots at the end of each show.

Of course, it had taken Bonnie a while to figure it all out. Giles's agent didn't want to talk. The executive producer didn't want to talk. Even his lawyer didn't want to talk. Finally, though, after much cajoling and a hell of a lot of screaming, the lawyer caved in. Giles had been a certified lunatic where money was concerned. He loved to spend it and, in lieu of that, he gave it away. Giles was known for writing checks, handing out cash or expensive possessions to just about anyone: his lovers, his crew, any idiot who looked in need on the street and, of course, the track. Giles just couldn't help himself. Boy, had that bit of information been a crusher!

The news had taken all the joy out of Bonnie's widowhood. Not that she wished Giles dead. She had been perfectly willing to live with him as his wife. In fact, she'd been kind of looking forward to it, knowing the marriage wouldn't last forever given the difference in their ages. Still, when he decided to bite the big one in the middle of the desert, there were advantages to that, too.

Bonnie wouldn't have to try to age gracefully with him, and she wouldn't have to share anything he left. Giles had died without relatives, except for a first wife who had long ago found herself another man. So, as Bonnie saw it, she inherited his show and his wealth. Problem was, there wasn't much wealth to be had and that ticked her off.

"Bonnie! Bonnie!"

Bonnie sat up straight as she heard the call. She slumped again when she identified Sy's voice. He came lumbering into the bedroom, his jelly belly proceeding him by a mile. She didn't bother to track his progress.

"There you are, baby." He greeted her jovially, then stopped and whistled low and long. If he'd been wearing a hat he would have tipped it back. "Hey, what happened here? Have you called the real estate agent? If those folks did this before they vacated you've got every right to get 'em right back here and fix this mess."

"Shut up, Sy," Bonnie drawled, casting a peevish sidelong glance his way.

She saw Sy's bushy brows draw together in confusion. Then, as though a light bulb went off over his head, his face cleared and understanding dawned.

"Oh! Oh!" he quipped. "Yes. Well. Hey, you know everybody has their days. They say that moving ranks right up there with the most stressful situations, like getting married and dying. But then what the heck? Bad things always come in threes and you've had 'em all, baby. So, that's the end of that.

"Uncle Sy is here to put an end to your woes. Never let it be said that I've ever let you down or not gone the extra mile. Now, feast your eyes on that. If that isn't one heck of a bit of PR I don't know what is and you've got Uncle Sy to thank for that."

Bonnie was attentive now, taking the magazine he

held out to her. There, on the front cover of *People,* Bonnie admired herself. It was a great shot. She had worn her mourning dress, sans veiled hat. The high neck looked demure and framed her face so that the natural beauty of her features looked almost as if they were too beautiful to be real. It was a waist shot, and she saw that the shadows also accentuated her chest to perfection under the clinging jersey. Yes, a perfect shot accompanied by an even more impeccable headline: BONNIE BARBER-MASTERS: COURAGEOUS WIDOW, WOMAN TO WATCH.

Like a starving woman Bonnie attacked the magazine, ripping through the pages until she found the two-page story. Hungrily her eyes scanned the print, took in the four photos that chronicled her sketchy career.

"Oh, oh, Sy, listen to this. This is perfect. I didn't think they'd buy it, but they did. Listen."

She held the magazine away from her and read.

"Miss Barber-Masters will soon be moving to a new home in the Hollywood Hills. A smaller place than the mansion she and Giles Masters were to share in Beverly Hills but one, she says, suited to the pain she knows she must deal with. 'I couldn't bear to spend one night in the home Giles and I were going to share as man and wife,' Miss Barber said. 'It would be far too painful. I need the intimacy of a smaller place now. One in which I can think and recover from this horrible experience. I don't think there's a woman in the world who can know what I'm feeling now. The suddenness of Giles being taken from me is something I may never get over. Love like that comes once in a lifetime.' Miss Barber went on to say that she hopes to continue with the game show

261

as a tribute to her late husband, but intends to lead a quiet life for the time being until her heart and soul are healed. Bonnie Barber-Masters is truly a woman who understands what heart and soul are all about."

Bonnie closed the magazine, held it to her chest, then opened it for another quick peek at the pictures. She approved of them all.

"Oh, Sy, can you believe those idiots? They bought it hook, line and sinker. They made it sound like I was doing something noble by moving into this little rat trap. God, publicity is wonderful!"

"I thought you'd like it," Sy said, grinning as he lowered his rear end and sat atop a box. It was filled with clothes and gave way promptly. He dusted himself off, looked about and decided Bonnie's dressing table chair was more appropriate for him. "I think they'll be ready to do a follow-up in about six months, so play your cards right and America will love ya."

"I thought I had played my cards right," Bonnie complained, her black mood coming back in full force. "Got anything else for me? I can't keep doing this stupid show forever you know. I want something classy. I've got to move up. Now that Giles isn't here to help I've only got myself, and I don't intend to carry Giles's legacy forever."

"As a matter of fact, I do. Something with real potential. I think it's going to be great. Got a call from Angela over at DDB & O."

"Sy?" Bonnie complained.

"Yeah? What?"

"DDB & O is an advertising agency."

"So?"

"So I don't want to hawk anything. I want some

parts with meat. Get me a feature. Or how about a cameo in some really classy television thing? That's what I want."

"All in good time." He waved his hands in the air. "Right now you've got to take what's offered. Get some new visibility so people don't think of you as card-turning cleavage."

"People don't think of me that way," Bonnie responded icily. "I've been carrying that show for a good while now. You've seen the monologues. You think anybody doesn't see me for what I am now?"

Sy closed his eyes and prayed for something to guide him. Bonnie was one chick who definitely had difficulty with self-perception.

"You've been doing a great job, babe," he said gently. "But doing a monologue isn't exactly being on tap for a feature film. Know what I mean?"

"No, I don't," she groused.

"Well, *I* do. I've been working my butt off to get you something, anything, and now I've got it. DDB & O wants you to be the new spokeswoman for," he cleared his throat, "FortyFine Makeup."

Sy sat back in the chair cautiously, a smile plastered on his small lips. Slowly Bonnie leaned forward, unwinding her body until she was towering over the cowering man. Her face was deathly pale, her hair appearing redder than ever.

In the silence he could almost hear the fury bubbling inside her like the guts of a volcano. The eruption was coming and there was nothing he could do about it. He wanted to put his hands over his ears, but he dare not. He wanted to close his eyes so he couldn't see the red flush that was creeping over her chest toward her face like a deadly lava flow, but his eyes were riveted on her. He was looking into the face of Hell.

"Sy-y-y-y!" she shrieked. "Sy, you *bastard!* Forty-Fine cosmetics are for women over forty. How dare you even suggest something like that? How dare you! I'm only twenty-three. I'll never be forty. Not in a million years. How, how . . ."

Bonnie had lost her breath, her words stuck somewhere in the gooey mass of ire that rested in her throat. Her long, peach-coated nails clawed at her neck as though she could physically release a torrent of outrage. She started breathing faster, faster, then collapsed onto the box again.

Sy jumped up. Bonnie was hyperventilating. He looked around but couldn't find a paper bag. Instead, he dumped the stuff out of a plastic one and crammed it into her face, over her nose and mouth.

"Breathe! Breathe, Bonnie. It's okay. Breathe, baby!" he shouted, his horrible, soft hands stronger than Bonnie would have imagined.

The bag sucked in and out with her breath like a damaged lung. Her big green eyes were saucerlike as they rolled about in her head, her hands covered her agent's, clutching at them.

"It's okay, baby, I've got you. Don't struggle. This is an emergency. I took emergency training at the Y. I've got you covered. Don't struggle . . ." Sy screamed in ecstasy. Finally he was doing something she would appreciate.

Bonnie, realizing there was nothing else to be done, drew up her knee and gave him a solid nudge in the general vicinity of his privates.

Sy doubled over, releasing his grip on the bag. Luckily, the folds of his belly had softened the impact somewhat, but for a man like Sy any physical discomfort was too much to take. He collapsed moaning on the floor while Bonnie caught her breath.

When Sy opened his eyes the first thing he saw was Bonnie's barely clad chest, huge mounds of flesh half covered by day-glo blue spandex. He thought he had died and gone to heaven, those suckers were so close to his mouth. Eyelids fluttering he began to focus, slowly looking past the glorious twin peaks to her stone cold face. Horror replaced desire—hell it killed it. Bonnie was on all fours, kneeling over him.

"Sy," she said as quietly as she could, "never, *never* put a plastic bag over my face again. Paper *breathes,* Sy. *That'*s why you put a paper bag over someone who is hyperventilating. *Not* a plastic bag, Sy."

Her voice was escalating, her eyes narrowing. Sy forgot his injury as she screeched at him.

"Plastic kills, Sy! And I *don't* want to die! And I *don't* want to be forty! And I *won't* do those damned spots even if they pay me a million dollars!"

"But they weren't going to say *you* were forty," Sy whimpered. "You only had to talk about how great this stuff will be when you're forty. I mean, Bonnie," he raised himself on one elbow, pleading with her, "this is class stuff. Along the same lines as L'Oreal, you know. What more could you ask for? There's television and print and outdoor. Your face will be plastered all over the country. It's exposure, baby. Exposure. Lots and lots of exposure."

Their faces were so close now that Bonnie could see Sy had huge pores. She'd never noticed that before. She could also tell he had lox and bagels for breakfast. Controlling herself as best she could,

Bonnie set her face in a mask of opposition.

"I won't do it, Sy. Now get out of my house. I'm in mourning. And next time I see your fat little face it better be smiling because you're bringing me a script. Get out, Sy. Get out now before I really do you bodily harm."

Sy skittered out from under her and scrambled to his feet, his body vibrating with fear. He would save his anger for later. After all, business wasn't good enough that he could let Bonnie Barber go.

"Okay, okay, babe," he stammered. "Just think about it. That's all I ask . . ."

"Sy . . ." Bonnie rumbled.

"I'm out. But don't cut off your nose to spite your face, Bonnie," he warned as he scuttled out the door, bumping into one of the moving men before going around him, still speaking as he flew out the front and to his car. "You may need a gig like this someday. And you never know when that day will come!"

Bonnie listened to the last note of his warning die away. Drained, she picked up the plastic bag, tossed it aside, then opened one of the boxes and began to unpack.

"It'll be a cold day in hell, Sy, before I need a gig like that," she muttered.

Bonnie felt no better the next morning as she headed for the studio. All night she'd dreamed of plastic bags and her fortieth birthday. She blamed Sy, of course, for her misery. The house still looked as though a bomb had hit it, and an idiot neighbor stopped by at ten to bring her a half-eaten cake and ask if she'd possibly speak at her fund-raising luncheon. Bonnie took the cake then left the woman blubbering on the doorstep.

Now, driving to work in the less expensive, but still impressive, leased Mercedes, Bonnie tried to get herself back on track. A firm believer that a good show creates good reality, she was smiling seductively when she entered the office Giles had occupied not so long ago.

Thomas had asked her to come in early for a meeting. The time between getting into the car and arriving at her destination had been spent mulling over the possibilities his request might offer. Thoroughly convinced he was about to offer her an expanded time slot, or better yet, a new show, Bonnie offered him a light kiss and a glorious view of her legs as she sat down and crossed them.

"Thomas, I'll tell you, never try to move. It's just the biggest hassle in the world. I broke a nail last night and the movers were as slow as molasses."

"I'm sorry to hear that," Thomas commiserated.

Bonnie's attention had wavered. She didn't notice that he hadn't heard a word she said. Instead, he was looking at her as though she was a condemned prisoner, as if he felt badly that he was the one who was going to bring down the blade.

"Well, I can manage just about anything, but still, it does wear on one. I hope there's going to be enough time for a massage. That Sylvia is just the best for getting me in the mood to do my thing when we're taping. Now, you wanted to discuss something?"

Her segue wasn't delicate, but Thomas decided it was best to take her up on the offer to get the meeting over with. She was batting her long lashes at him, looking more beautiful than he'd ever seen her. As long as she kept her mouth shut, Bonnie was one in a million. When she opened it every one could read what was written between the lines. Bonnie Barber-Masters simply thought she was better than the rest of the world.

"Yes, Bonnie." He cleared his throat. "I wanted to talk to you about the show and . . ."

"Oh, Thomas, why look so serious?" Bonnie chirped. "I have a feeling I know what you're going to ask so just get right to the point. I'm a strong girl. I can handle anything, including additional time on the air. Now, it may mean rearranging my schedule a bit, but don't you worry about asking me to put in a few more hours . . ."

"Bonnie, it's not that."

Bonnie was immediately silent. She felt a chill run over her bare arms, a harbinger of bad things to come. Beneath her beautifully applied makeup her skin seemed to shrink, hugging her beautiful bones for comfort as she readied herself to hear the worst. It was written all over his face; it was etched in every well-chosen word he spoke. She should have seen it earlier.

"What is it?" she asked quietly.

"Bonnie, this is hard for me. So very hard to tell you right after you've had such grief with Giles's death and all. But it's not working. The overnights are going down every time I look at them. We've done research, Bonnie . . ."

"You did research without telling me?"

She was aghast. They hadn't even given her a chance to try something different. This couldn't be happening. If she'd known she would have done something, anything, to bring those numbers up.

"Bonnie, it's a matter of course. We have ongoing research. We don't like to bother the stars with business."

"But, Thomas, this is my business. I could have done something to turn things around. I could have sat in when you did your research, helped with the questions. That's it!" she exclaimed brightly. "Obviously, your business people didn't ask the right questions. What do they know about how people feel and think when they're watching a television program?"

"They know how to ask the right things," Thomas said, cutting her off. "And what we really care about is what the viewers say. Those people who watch are turning you off night after night, Bon. It's not a trend, it's not a glitch. We know what it is."

"Then tell me, Thomas." Her voice had gone cold now.

She sat stone still watching him. He was so cool, like he'd done this a hundred times; like he'd ruined people's lives every minute of every day and didn't turn a hair.

"Okay, the way it stacks up is it was just fine when you and Giles were partners. But your viewers are mostly women. They didn't react well to your marriage, they reacted horribly to Giles's death and now they've pegged you for a gold digger. They think you did something to Giles so that you could take over."

"Thomas, that's so unfair!" Bonnie was on her feet now, forgetting to use her body to its best advantage.

Thomas was taken aback. He'd never seen her when she wasn't standing straight and tall. In that one instant of forgetfulness he got a glimpse of the future. Bonnie Barber would have tits that hung down to her knees by the time she was forty-five and a stomach to match if she ever had a kid. It wasn't a pretty sight. He turned his head away. She took it as a sign of weakness and used the advantage.

"Thomas," she said calmly, "the audience is reacting to change. These are older women, aren't they?" Thomas nodded. "Well, there you have it. They don't like change. They were probably all in love with Giles and were pissed off when he decided to make our relationship permanent. You know how women can be, fantasizing that they're the one meant for a star. It's natural. I do it all the time."

Thomas closed his eyes. Even Bonnie didn't realize how true her words were. The girl wanted so much and just didn't have the talent to get it. Looks, despite opinions to the contrary, weren't everything.

"Okay, so we agree on that. All it means is that I appeal to a different audience. If you give me enough time I can bring that audience in. Young men who watch game shows . . ."

"Bonnie, Bonnie, young men don't watch game shows. They've got better things to do."

"All right then," she said angrily as she began to pace, her mind whirling to find something that would capture Thomas's imagination and halt this descent into oblivion. "All right, we'll go for older men. I'll have the writers . . . no, you have the writers . . . start working on dialogue that would appeal to them. I can change my delivery. We'll dress me sweeter, no more of that clinging stuff. I'll be everybody's daughter."

He had to laugh then. "The last thing you could *ever* be is everyman's daughter. Bonnie, figures don't lie. Women watch game shows. Women accepted you when you were subservient to Giles. Women don't accept you when you try to tell them how much fun they're going to have. Period. That's it. That's the way it is. I'm sorry."

"Like hell you are, Thomas. You're not sorry at all."

Bonnie's mouth turned down in a bitter line. She walked to the window and looked out over Hollywood. She'd had it in her hand—all of it. The "it" that made her feel alive. She had hosted her own show. She had dressed in beautiful clothes. She'd been on the cover of *People*—twice, for God's sake! Now Thomas was going to take it all away.

"I'm sorry, Bonnie. This is never easy. I hate it. Besides, it's not really my decision. The network simply isn't renewing the contract. Independents will pick up reruns for a while, so you've got those residuals. And we're going to finish out the season. There's plenty of time for you to find something else."

Deliberately, Bonnie turned slowly on her heel. Her body was taut and Thomas realized the aged vision of her had been a moment's dementia. She would never be anything but beautiful. In fact, that was probably all she would be.

"You mean you don't have anything for me?" she asked quietly.

Thomas was taken aback. He'd never been asked that question before. No one had ever been so presumptuous.

"Why . . . no, Bonnie, I don't. I hadn't really thought about you in terms of going on from here with the game-show angle. I always thought you

271

wanted to go back into a series or maybe you'd set your sights higher. Film. Something like that. Bonnie, I'm not an agent. I'm producing a few things now, but you're not right for them. Naturally, if something did come along you'd be the first to know — through Sy, of course."

"Naturally," she answered, running her hand over his beautiful desk. The desk that used to be Giles's. "You know, I never believed this business was heartless, but it is. I always had that golden dream that people in Hollywood wanted to be the best, do the best, wanted to create a fantasy world for the little people. But that's not true. You're just interested in the bottom line. You don't care who you step on or how you do it."

"Bonnie, that's so unfair."

"Is it?" She raised an eyebrow over emerald-green eyes. "I think not. If Giles was here this wouldn't be happening."

"If Giles was here you wouldn't be hosting the show," Thomas reminded her.

He'd had enough of this. As far as he was concerned Bonnie Barber would be waiting for her ship to come in for a long time if he had anything to say about it. Nobody tried to pull his strings. He hadn't come this far by letting bimbos walk all over him.

"A minor point," Bonnie retorted. "The real point is that I was trying to do what Giles wanted. I was keeping the show together. I may have had a lot to learn, but you won't even give me the chance to learn it. I'm telling you, Thomas, the world is going to hear about this and, in the end, you'll be the one begging. Not me."

Counting the moments, Bonnie let her gaze lay on

Thomas like a scratchy blanket, but he turned into it; he didn't slough it off.

Her heart in a panic, Bonnie remembered to play her part. Regally she walked from the room, forcing herself toward the door though she wanted to run back and throw herself at Thomas's feet and beg him to keep her on. Instead, she found herself on the opposite side, the door closed behind her. There was no going back now. In a week Thomas wouldn't remember her name. She knew how the game worked.

There was nothing to do now but call Sy.

Nineteen

The ship approached Los Angeles Harbor like an old woman coming home at dusk from a long walk, her arms tired from carrying her bag of groceries. It moved slowly through the black water, cutting a less than impressive silhouette against a darkening sky. The ship was neither new nor pretty, lacking even the character an old seagoing vessel should have. It was a working ship and, therefore, privileged to wear its scars in the open for all to see, like a laborer who would not apologize for his callouses because they earned him his bread.

It was late May and still California was enveloped by the in-between weather that depressed the millions who had come to the coast for sun and fun. The harbor itself was quiet. Ships, larger and smaller than the *Le Trois,* were moored at the docks, their cargo either dispelled or waiting until the morning for unloading. Various lights burned in various buildings; the lights looked unwelcoming, untended, and the buildings were nothing more than shelters for inanimate objects. There was no warmth to the docks, no intrigue, nothing but the reminder that all beautiful things from afar

274

were first subjected to the offensively apathetic treatment of this place.

On the bow of the *Le Trois*, Tess Canfield crossed her arms over the railing and listened to the voices of the crew calling to one another. There was a muffled quality to the sounds on board, as though the entire ship had been wrapped in wool against the chilly breeze that came off the calm waters. Beneath her two tugs flitted about the hulking bow, nuzzling it like a puppy trying to get the attention of its gigantic master.

Her hair caught the draught, blew up in a golden arc, then playfully swept over her face. She didn't raise a hand to move it away. Tess raised her face, instead, angling it just so and the wind pulled it back again until it flew behind her like a veil. Tugging her sweater closer Tess huddled into herself, trying to find a voice to the emotions that had whispered inside her since the moment she left Noel Montgomery's apartment and faced Paris alone in the hours before sunrise.

She had taken little, carefully opening drawers and closets until she thought he might wake and try to stop her. If he had attempted to keep her with him, Tess wasn't sure what she would have done. Even during the few days she spent in Paris arranging her passage, and the five days she had been on board this ship, Tess had been unable to come to a firm conclusion.

Closing her eyes, she lowered her head and thought of that night of love. This was the first time she admitted that the evening had been more than an aberration. She had tried to tell herself that she brought Noel to her bed out of gratitude, loneliness, need, but those rationalizations had been lies. Tess knew now she had expressed a love born from completeness of emotion. How could she not feel deeply for a man who had not just saved her life, but sat by while she regained her

275

strength, soothed her when she worried about Royal, eased her disappointment when she realized Royal was not going to send for her?

Noel had healed her in so many ways—she would always love him for that. But the rest? That, she was sure, had been a mistake. Now she must erase the memory of that night from her mind since her strength had returned and she was ready to care for Royal if he needed her, ready to love him if he would have her. She owed him much more than Noel. It had been Royal who offered her true love because he understood her pain; her attempt to build a life alone.

Yet, as much as she wanted to move Noel from her memory, she was finding it difficult. His face entered her dreams. In the quietest moments she would suddenly feel his hands on her, touching her with such passion she thought he must be there, and all the rest was a dream.

That was when she reminded herself that night had been wrong, and the memories of him were nothing more than punishment for her transgression. Her guilt would not let her forget. Once she found Royal, once they were together again and he forgave her, Noel Montgomery would be banished forever to a place in her heart. There he would live because of what he had done for her, not because of what he meant to her.

"Mademoiselle?"

Tess turned. Her face felt cold. Her hands covered her cheeks to warm them. She found them wet. Tears? For whom? Herself, Royal or Noel? Quickly, she wiped them away and thanked God it was dark. The first mate waited for her to speak.

"Yes?" It was all she could say. Her mind felt as heavy as her body.

"We will dock in twenty minutes. The captain suggests you gather your things and meet the other passengers in the dining room. We will allow the passengers to disembark immediately upon docking."

"Thank you. I'll see to it."

The man bowed slightly before hurrying away to his duties. Tess walked away from the railing. Home, for some reason, did not feel very welcoming.

In her cabin she packed her one bag, and looked about, making sure she hadn't forgotten anything. Then she chuckled. There was so little to forget in this room.

The walls were bare, the bed serviceable. A sink stood in the corner and there was a closet where the toilet and shower were. Hardly luxury accommodations. Royal had so often spoken of going on a cruise. He told her they would be wined and dined, ensconced in a floating penthouse, as they sailed from island to island in some exotic sea. Somehow the idea seemed less appealing to her now.

The ship, though, had been a godsend. Tess could no more have gotten on an airplane than she could have wished herself to the moon. *Le Trois* was a stroke of luck for more than one reason—it was actually cheaper than flying home.

Sitting on the little bed, Tess opened her purse. Instinctively, her fingers caressed the fine leather. Noel had picked it out for her, bringing it to the hospital with him when he came to take her away.

"No woman should ever go out without her purse," he teased, making light of the situation. Hers had been incinerated in the accident.

It had been two weeks later when she actually opened it. Noel had thought of everything: cosmetics, a brush, a gold compact, and a wallet. The wallet contained money, more than Tess could ever possibly use

277

during her recuperation. When she tried to return it, Noel had insisted she keep it. Now she was glad she had. Without it she would have been lost.

Her first stop after she left Noel had been at the American Express office to replace her card. Then she could send Noel's money back to him. But she was told, in no uncertain terms, that the card had been canceled. Confused, sure that Royal would never do such a thing unless he thought she was dead, Tess did the only thing she could. She used Noel's money, promising herself she would return it as soon as she was able.

Knowing her resources were limited, Tess spent the next few days trying desperately to find a way home without flying and attempting to contact Royal. Every time she reached his office she was told he hadn't yet returned to work. Discouraged, she tried his home number, but the woman who answered told her Royal was not there. Tess had no way of knowing if it was Astra Cudahy who answered or one of the servants. Either way, she couldn't take the chance of revealing herself. She left her number, hoping the message would be relayed to Royal. But the phone never rang and when passage became available Tess sailed for Los Angeles, determined to be with Royal Cudahy in a few weeks' time and start living her life once again.

She snapped her wallet shut. There was enough to get her home, into a hot bath and her own clothes. Then there would be time to figure out the best way to get to Royal.

Tess flexed her shoulders. She hadn't realized that her muscles were tensed, drawn to a painful point. Voices sounded in the corridor as the other passengers moved slowly toward the dining room. Checking her watch, the watch Noel gave her, Tess saw that they were

278

ready to disembark. Quickly, she unsnapped the lovely white gold timepiece and put it in her purse. She wanted no more reminders of what she had done with Noel Montgomery. He must remain in the shadows of her life, the only bright moment in a horrifying experience.

Tess was the last one off the ship. There was no one to see her off, no one who she could thank. The crew members had disappeared, anxious to be off the ship themselves. She stood poised at the top of the gangplank, looking down at its length thinking she was taking a step, not toward happiness, but into the unknown. Gripping her suitcase tighter, Tess held her head high, knowing it was only exhaustion and anticipation that made her feel that way. It was eight o'clock. She found a taxi by eight-fifteen and sank back into the seat. She was going home.

"Thank you so much."

Tess spoke with more life than anytime during the past few weeks. The sight of her little house, looking so cozy under the street lamps, lifted her spirits. All would be well now. Inside was the unfinished painting, her robe, the picture of she and Royal taken at the Santa Monica pier. She was smiling.

"Hey, no problem, lady. It was a slow night. Gotta tell you, though, I was a little worried. When you got in, I thought you might be seasick or something. Wouldn't do to have you sick in the cab. Still, guess worse things could happen. Knew a guy once — oh, that's twenty-five bucks — knew a guy once had a woman have a baby in the back of his cab. That's not for me. I like my fares nice and easy. You tell me where you want to go, I'll take you."

Tess laughed, her blue eyes dazzling the driver.

"Thank you," she said.

"For what? The ride?"

"No. Just for reassuring me that life goes on. I haven't heard that many words in about a week. It's good to be home."

"That's what they all say. Plane or boat or train, everybody's glad to be back." He grinned at her, then eyed the house. "Hey, somebody in there expecting you?"

"No," Tess answered slowly. He seemed nice enough, but you never knew.

"Then I'm going to walk you to the door."

He had the door open and was halfway out when Tess stopped him.

"That's not necessary. I'm just going to go straight in."

"Of course you are. But, listen, I got a daughter your age and I sure would appreciate one of my buddies seeing her into a dark house. Come on, I'll just put your suitcase on the stoop then stand back. I know you gotta be careful these days. I understand, lady."

Tess inclined her head. He was a nice man. She slid out of the cab and stretched her legs as she dug in her purse for her house keys. Her shoulders slumped when she couldn't find them. Of course she couldn't. Nothing was found after the accident. Funny how much of one's life could be lost when a handbag was. The driver was halfway up the walk waiting for her. Nothing to do now but reveal her hiding place.

Tess walked past him with a smile, opened the mailbox and tugged at a little string. She heard the clank of metal on metal and pulled the key toward her.

"Good thing you got an extra," the driver called.

True to his word he hadn't moved but he sure didn't miss a trick. Shaking her head she inserted the key with some difficulty and tried to turn it. It wouldn't budge. There was no click of the tumblers, no welcome opening of the door, no rush of emotion as she laid eyes on all her things, her paintings. Tess stepped back and looked at the key. It was the same. Nothing had changed.

"There a problem?" the driver called.

"I don't know." Tess stepped off the porch, still looking at the key. "My key doesn't seem to work."

"Yeah? Got the right one? Maybe it's for the back door."

Tess shook her head. "No. I've used this key a hundred times. It's for the front."

"It's dark. Maybe you're not doing it right. These old houses, hey, they can be stubborn sometimes. Want me to try?"

"Would you?"

Tess gave him the key, watching his broad back as he worked over the lock. He tipped his hat back when he returned it to her.

"Sorry, honey, it just don't work. Sure you don't want to try it 'round back? That's the only thing I can think of."

"Maybe I will. Do you mind waiting a bit longer?"

"Naw, I was about ready to go off duty, so I'm not looking for another fare. Want me to come with you?"

"No thanks. It'll just take a minute."

Hands shaking, Tess unlatched the gate. The garden was the same. The grass had been newly mowed, the flowers tended. The gardener had been there. There was nothing different about the house itself—there was still the flaking paint around the windows that Tess was going to sand as soon as the weather was nicer, her beach chair still sat by the back door, the little bird feeder she had put out still hung from the lemon tree.

In front of the door Tess took a deep breath and prayed. Then, quickly, she shoved the key in. It wouldn't be inserted. She was sure it was the front door lock. But someone had changed the lock. That was it. Now she knew.

Frantic, she ran to the garage and yanked open the door. It was empty. The car Royal had bought for her was gone. She remembered the day, her protests, his insistence. He had smiled at her, put his arm around her. Told her she'd need all the room of a big car for when they had a family. Kids, he had said, need lots of room.

Suddenly her whole body was shaking, her knees were so weak they were collapsing under her. They folded, bringing Tess down into a heap in front of the empty garage. She sat there stunned for a moment before a wretched cry broke from her throat.

Burying her face in her hands, Tess sat weeping, fearful of what was happening. She was locked out of her home with no car, no clothes save for those in the suitcase and her money was dwindling. Even her canvases were locked inside the place she had lived. Suddenly, she caught sight of something through her tears. Four boxes she hadn't remembered putting in the garage. Shaking, she stood up and went to them. Her name was neatly labeled on the tops as though they had been left for her. Frantically, she tore the first open. Her mother's quilt. Tess felt faint as she fell to her knees, her hands gripping the little grouping of boxes. She knew what was in the rest. What she didn't know was who put them there.

Then there was a hand on her shoulder, a gentle and tentative touch. Tess looked up, her tear-streaked face an exercise in agony.

"Miss?" The cab driver was hunched down beside her. "It don't look like there's much here for you. Is there someplace else I can take you? Free of charge, of course. Any place. A friend? A relative? Any place."

Sadly, Tess shook her head. There was no one. No one at all she could turn to. Awkwardly, the cab driver helped her up. Leaning on him, crying, Tess went back to the cab. He retrieved the boxes, then started the car. For a long while they drove, the only sound that of the motor and Tess's sobs. Finally, she told him to stop. She had to pull herself together. She had to think — alone.

Thanking him, she held out her hand. He shook it. Reluctantly the cab driver left Tess Canfield and her sorry luggage in front of a nondescript hotel in Westwood.

She had been to Royal's home a dozen times. First it was to work on the restoration of this fabulous villa that had been settled, stone by stone, in Pasadena, then it was to see Royal Cudahy, master of the house.

Now, standing at the end of the long drive she tried to remember those first heady days when she realized she was falling in love with him.

How natural it had been. They talked over wine as she worked with her brush. Tess was so pleased when he took her hand and looked at it in wonderment, saying he never knew the human hand could move with such grace.

There had been the quiet kitchen dinners when Astra was out fund raising or traveling by herself, his sons lost in their privileged lives. The gardens where love had finally bloomed, where Royal had spoken of his loneliness; of his desire for a richer life.

Of course she knew he hadn't meant material objects — he could have anything he wanted in the world. The one thing he desired money couldn't buy and that was love. So Tess offered it to him, freely and without guile. Or had she? Perhaps she, too, had been bought and paid for. At the time Tess hadn't really thought about all the things he had given her: the house, the car, furnishings, paints, canvas, a few bits of jewelry, money.

In retrospect, though, it seemed a fortune had been spent on her. Was it to insure her love or loyalty? Or was all that given out of his desire to begin building their life from a simpler point than the one he inhabited?

The answer, Tess was sure, was the latter. Royal would never demean her in such a way. That thought gave her strength and courage. She took her first step up the long, winding drive without stopping until she reached the front door and rang the bell. She hadn't noticed the drapes in the front room sway, part, then sway again as they closed.

Inside the house two women met in the foyer. One was tall and blond with the lean, taut body of a horsewoman. The other was shorter, rounder and older. In many ways she was more appealing than the first.

"I'll get it, Marta," the tall woman said. "But I would appreciate it if you would bring tea into the living room in a few minutes. No more than five, please."

"Yes, Mrs. Cudahy. Would you like scones with that?"

"I think not. This guest won't be staying that long."

"Yes, ma'am."

The older woman disappeared around the curving staircase. When Astra Cudahy was sure the maid was gone she went to the door.

Though mirrors flanked each side of the entry way Astra didn't bother to check her appearance. She had seen the girl and was confident that her perfection would cow her in no uncertain terms. She opened the door slowly, relishing this final face-to-face.

"Good afternoon, Miss Canfield. I'm Astra Cudahy and I've been expecting you."

Tess assumed she might run into Royal's wife and had planned her story down to the finest detail. She would say that Royal had asked her for further advice on one of the rooms, and that she would like to see him. Unfortunately, Astra's entire demeanor told Tess the story was useless. The woman obviously knew who she was though Tess found it difficult to imagine Royal telling her.

Surprised, but also grateful that there would be no further lying either overt or covert, Tess hid her fear. There was no place to go now but forward.

"I see," Tess answered, raising her chin just a bit higher.

She couldn't help comparing herself with Astra Cudahy and find herself wanting. The other woman was the epitome of chic, every hair in place, her clothes cut from the finest cloth. Tess had to remind herself that appearances were not what mattered to Royal, but feelings. The kind of feelings that made him know he was a worthwhile person without his wealth.

"I thought you might. Won't you come in?"

Tess hesitated, then walked through the door. Astra shut it behind her, walked around her and directly into the living room. Assuming Tess would follow, Astra hadn't spoken. Tess followed without a second thought. What was important was finding Royal, not whether she lost face in front of this austerely beautiful woman.

Astra settled herself on a yellow and white floral sofa. Her long legs were crossed at the ankle, her hands were folded in her lap and her eyes appraised Tess lazily as she entered the room.

"Won't you sit, Miss Canfield?"

"No, thank you. I won't take up too much of your time."

"I don't see why you should worry about my time," Astra drawled, "when you've taken so much more that belongs to me."

"I've taken nothing that belongs to you," Tess flared, frightened into defense by the woman's aloofness and the silence in the house. With every fiber of her body Tess could feel its emptiness, its soullessness. Royal wasn't here. She'd know if he was.

"I beg your pardon," Astra corrected. "You have taken everything that is dear to me. My husband has been your lover for quite a long time. You have kept him from my bed, you have kept him from being an integral part of this family. His sons were even aware that something was amiss. Granted, they're young, but they are not stupid. Neither am I."

"I didn't take him from your bed," Tess reminded her quietly.

She had controlled the fury she felt toward this woman and her icy calm because Tess knew it was anger born of fear. Fear that Astra Cudahy had done something to take Royal away when he didn't want to be parted from Tess.

"You gave your husband to me. You gave him to me when you became too busy to make him the kind of home he dreamed of, the kind of home in which he felt welcome. You gave him to me when committees and fund raising became more important than him."

Astra Cudahy laughed without joy.

"Is that what he told you? Well," she said, studying her well-kept nails, "I suppose in a way it's the truth. But you must realize" — she raised her dead gray eyes to Tess — "that has always been Royal's truth. Nothing is ever right in his life. But perhaps you haven't been with him long enough to realize that. Or" — those gray eyes looked Tess up and down, then settled on her face — "perhaps you're simply too young to understand a man's inner character. Oh, Marta, there if you don't mind."

Tess stood still, moving only her head to follow the maid's advance. The older woman didn't even look at her. She simply put a silver tray on the low coffee table and left quietly. The mistress's business was none of hers.

"Please." Astra waved one beringed hand. "Sit."

Tess did as she was told. Not because Astra ordered her to but because she realized she wouldn't get what she wanted unless she played the game.

"There," Astra said as she poured. "That's better. Cream? Sugar? Lemon?"

"Lemon," Tess said quietly.

She took the delicate cup but didn't drink. Her eyes were fastened on Royal's wife. No wonder he had been so unhappy at home. Astra Cudahy was a caricature of sophistication, so highly tuned that the line between reality and studied perfection was blurred into nothingness. She was like a perfectly painted picture, so exact in every detail the artist could have taken a photograph rather than waste his time with paint and brush.

"Now, where was I?" Astra settled back on the couch, obviously more confident, feeling she could relax a little since she had the upper hand. "Oh yes, we were discussing Royal. You see, I think you should know certain things about him so that you will realize how much of your precious little life you've wasted already. Once you know all there is to know, I'm sure you'll simply want to pick up the pieces and go on. After all, for a girl who looks like you, there should be numerous, um, opportunities, shall we say?"

"I have no pieces to pick up, Mrs. Cudahy, and I don't feel that my time with Royal has been wasted. Now, if you'll just tell him I'm here."

Astra wagged a long finger at Tess and chuckled. "Oh, no, no, no, my dear. I've waited a very long time for this, and I will not be disappointed. You see, you're not the first. You're only the first I've had a chance to talk with. I've waited for you for two months now. I haven't been out of this house knowing you'd show up sooner or later, and I will not have you ruin my fun."

Tess knew she should leave then. The woman's voice had hardened to flint, her eyes had narrowed in a face that changed with disturbing swiftness. What Astra said, though, shocked Tess so much that she remained seated, unable to move.

"I see I've surprised you. Oh, my, I didn't think it would be this good. Yes, I'm afraid it's true. Royal has always felt the need for a little extracurricular activity. But I suppose that's natural when you marry very young, marry the boss's daughter so to speak. Royal has always had a bit of the child about him in his personal life. Of course, it's another matter in his professional one. There, in the courtroom, you have never seen a man wield power like Royal. It is something to see, something very special. . . ."

Astra's eyes roamed from Tess, taking on a faraway look of pleasure. Tess knew now that Astra didn't love

288

her husband in the normal sense, but she was drawn obsessively to the power she spoke of. That admiration was written all over her; she seemed to draw strength just from the memory of her husband's performance. Suddenly her attention snapped back to Tess.

"He's a very talented man. He knows how to make and break the best of them. He is wealthy and he often uses that wealth to his advantage. But outside the office or our social circle Royal Cudahy is still a snot-faced wimp trying to get laid. Amazing how many women fall for his act. Without the power, Royal is really nothing, you know."

Obviously finished with her assessment of her husband's strengths and weaknesses, Astra picked up her cup and sipped from it, waiting for Tess's outburst. She was apparently disappointed when Tess spoke quietly and clearly.

"I don't believe you, Mrs. Cudahy. I don't believe he has had other women. And, if he has, I don't believe those relationships meant anything to him. No man could possibly sink that low and, you're forgetting, I know Royal. I know what he is capable of, and what he isn't." Astra shrugged her shoulders as though to say Tess was entitled to her opinion. Tess was not intimidated. "Secondly, I think if anyone has the problem, you do. If you can't accept the whole man, then you don't have a whole marriage. And that is why I know Royal and I belong together. I accept him without question, without reservation. I'm proud he loves me."

"And, my dear, are you proud that you are a kept woman? Or should I say, *were* a kept woman. I'm assuming your visit here has something to do with the fact that you returned from your overseas assignation to find that your home is not accessible to you, your car gone, your money out of reach. Doesn't that change your attitude just a little bit?"

Tess could see the enjoyment Astra was taking from the situation. To her it was a game. To Tess it was a fight for the heart of the man she loved. She would not give up or give in.

"Of course I was surprised. I was hurt in the crash. I was terrified to find I was alone. Then to come back here and discover that life as I knew it had ended without an explanation—I had to come. Even you can understand that."

"I more than understood that. I was counting on it. I must say you, of all of them, have given me a run for my money. You've lasted the longest, kept that idiotic gleam in Royal's eyes for far too long. Between you and me, I was a bit worried. Now I see there was no reason to."

She set aside her cup and leaned forward. Her blouse fell open, revealing a small, tight chest. Tess looked away.

"You've come for an explanation," Astra said quietly. "I'll give you one. You and Royal are finished. I have sold your little love nest. It no longer belongs to Royal. He signs what I tell him to sign these days. Your car was repossessed for lack of payment. Royal, it seems, forgot that he owed on it. It was such a piddling expense. I closed your bank accounts and canceled the credit card. You have been erased from Royal's life with his blessing."

Tess was on her feet, her cup of tea spilling onto the ancient Oriental carpeting.

"I don't believe you," she hissed. "Royal would never allow it. He loves me and nothing would stop him from protecting me. Nothing will stop him from getting away from you."

"Believe it, Miss Canfield. And, if you won't take

290

my word for it, perhaps you'll take his."

Gracefully Astra Cudahy rose and crossed the room. From a small desk she took an envelope. Walking back she handed it to Tess.

"Here."

Tess's eyes clashed with Astra's for an instant. She took the small blue envelope. It was Royal's stationery. They'd had matching note cards made over a year ago. Tess's were silver gray, Royal's a lovely cornflower blue. Tess had designed the letterhead. Her fingers shook as she tried to open the seal. Astra took the envelope from her.

"You seem to be having difficulty. Let me."

Astra ripped open the envelope, withdrew the note and handed it to Tess. Fearfully, Tess looked at it. The words blurred, then came into focus. She read and re-read the message. Her hand dropped to her side and Tess faced Astra Cudahy.

"I will never believe a word of this until I hear it from Royal's lips. Where is he?"

"That, my dear, is for family to know. He is recovering from his injuries in a quiet place. Oh, don't look so horrified. He was hurt badly, but in a few months he will be the same old Royal. The only difference is you won't be around. So go away, Miss Canfield. Go away and leave my husband alone. He doesn't love you. Royal is incapable of deep, true love. It's for the best. Now, I really must ask you to leave. I have so much to do. I'd like to say it's been a pleasure."

Dreamlike, Tess stepped away from the older woman. She faltered and reached for the high-backed chair in which she had sat. Pain-filled eyes sought Astra Cudahy's, but Astra had no sympathy for her. In fact, Astra had one more surprise.

"I almost forgot, Miss Canfield. Royal asked me to

give you something else."

From the pocket of her tailored slacks Astra drew a piece of paper and handed it to Tess. It was a check for five thousand dollars signed by Royal Cudahy. Tess looked at it for the longest time. Minutes ticked away as her blood drained from her face. Then with the greatest determination, Tess raised her head and flung the check at Astra.

"When Royal brings me this, then I'll take it. Not a minute before. Tell him, Mrs. Cudahy. Tell him I won't stop until I hear from him that it is over."

Tess was gone moments later. Astra stood straight and strong in the midst of all her beautiful things. When she heard the front door slam she bent down and picked up the check and the blue note card. Slowly, she read it aloud to herself.

"Tess, I have realized that we were wrong from the start. It's over. I've begun a new life with my family. Royal."

She began to chuckle, knowing she had done an admirable job. The handwriting was almost identical to Royal's. Convincing Royal that the note she had given him from Tess was actually written by the girl had been a much more difficult matter. He had actually seemed crushed when he read it. But now that he was being well cared for, now that Astra was by his side almost constantly, he seemed quite accepting of the whole thing as she knew he would be.

Tearing the note and check into little bits, Astra deposited the pile into a gold leaf receptacle by the little desk. Marta would clean it out later.

That, she thought, was the end of Tess Canfield. Astra Cudahy's little empire was intact once again.

* * *

Outside, Tess ran down the drive and kept running until she could run no more. Her chest heaving, Tess sat on the corner of a wide avenue, oblivious to the gorgeous homes around her. Somewhere she could hear a lawn mower. Other than that the only sounds were the birds singing in the trees.

Over and over again her fisted hand hit her leg.

"I won't believe it. I won't."

Her mind was tugged and pulled and pummeled in so many directions she didn't know which one led to the truth. Royal had written the note, but under what duress? He couldn't have done what Astra said he did. He couldn't have ordered her house sold, her car taken away. He couldn't have left her alone in Paris the way he had.

Tess closed her eyes and, as she controlled her breathing, as sanity returned, she realized he had done none of those things. She had been face-to-face with Astra Cudahy, and she had seen the kind of woman she was.

Royal was helpless against her if his injuries were as she said. It was Astra who had taken it upon herself to wipe Tess out of Royal's life, and she had almost done it. Tess was shamed to think that she had believed her.

Now she didn't know what to do. If only there was some way to find out where Royal was, some way to get a message to him. She thought of Noel. He would know how to find out. But she couldn't contact him. There had been too much between them to make that a possibility. She shook away the thought, hating herself for wanting him with her so much. She had used him enough, pained him enough, then left without a word. No, Noel was not the answer. But there must be someone. Who, she wondered. Who could she turn to?

Then, just as a gardener turned the corner and

293

looked curiously at her, Tess laughed. She knew exactly who she could go to. Soon she would be with Royal. Soon she could ask him herself if he still loved her as she loved him.

Twenty

The only sound in the room was that of heavy breathing. Their entire coupling lasted no longer than three minutes. Tony wasn't big on extending pleasure, Davina's or his own. He let out a yelp. She did the same and they rolled away from each other as though touching was a bad thing.

Tony watched her through lowered lids waiting, as he always did, for her to say something about his performance. Every woman he'd ever been with had a sharp thing or two to say about it. Davina would prove to be the same, he was sure. She was just taking a little while to get around to it. He pulled the sheet around his waist as though that would protect him from her criticism if this was going to be the night. But Davina just lay there, her rounded breasts hardly moving. She was amazing. For her, once it was over it was over. Tony closed his eyes. Davina was thinking.

She had no problem with Tony in bed. Her experience was so limited it never occurred to Davina that she should expect anything more than a quick poke. What they did together satisfied her psychologically, so there was little need to satisfy her physically. As long as she knew Tony found her irresistible, that was enough. Besides, she hated to be touched before or after the act. Tony had been quick, catching on the first time she shoved his hand from between her legs. She liked that. He was okay.

There were too many other things to think about besides how long Tony could keep it up anyway. The first issue of *High Life* since her printing change was due out the next day. She'd seen the blue lines, she'd seen the press proofs and she knew it didn't look good. The four-color stuff would pass muster, but the *High Life* Woman layout with its incredible five-color work looked like shit. That was what she had to worry about, and it was giving her one of her raging headaches.

Davina slid out of bed. Tony remained silent. He knew about the pills and didn't care. Everybody needed something to get them through the night. When she came back to the bedroom Davina carried a towel. She tossed it to him, then sat on the chair next to the standard, round conference table.

Tony cleaned himself up, thinking all the while that she really looked beautiful. Tony appreciated her roundness and enjoyed thinking she would fill out to that comforting chubbiness of Italian women of a certain age in about ten or fifteen years. Tony wasn't in love with her. She was pretty weird sometimes, but she had the kind of look his uncles would appreciate. If she could be counted on to act normal for any length of time he would have taken her home to meet the family. Maybe someday.

"You know the issue doesn't look too good," she said flatly as she twirled a glass ashtray with one finger. It made a scraping sound on the lacquered plas-

296

terboard. When she looked at him the light hanging over the table cast an eerie shadow over her face.

"Yeah, well it takes the pressmen a while to get up to speed. Know what I mean?" Tony gave himself a final flourish with the towel and lay back.

"Not really," she answered quietly, concentrating on the ashtray again. "It doesn't even come close to the samples you showed me, and you promised it would be right up there with the best for a lower price than we were paying."

"Promises," he chuckled, "are meant to be broken."

"Not this one, Tony. I think you ought to be on press tonight and watch the final run. I've got to present it tomorrow at a noon meeting. I want the best copies you've got on my desk by nine."

"Yes, ma'am," Tony drawled, cuddling down in the bed again.

There was nothing like hotel sheets. They felt so comfortable, so well worn, like you were sleeping with a thousand other people. Davina was on top of him before he knew it. He hadn't even heard her move, and there she was digging her nails into his face like he'd just done something really bad to her.

"You bastard," she screamed as her nails raked down his cheek, drawing blood. To Tony's credit, when the situation called for action he rose to it. He flipped her off with little effort, pinning her on her back.

"You little bitch!" he muttered. "What do you think you're doing?"

"I'm showing you how concerned I am about the magazine," she spat back.

"Yeah? Well there's better ways, Davina. Don't screw with me or . . ."

"Or what? What are you going to do?"

Taunting him, she let her tongue slide over her lips. It was too much for Tony. His face crashed down on hers, forcing her mouth open, his knees doing the same with her legs. Grasping both her hands in his, Tony pinned them above her head and let his other hand roam over her body. She struggled, not with the heat of passion but with a disgust he couldn't even imagine. Weird woman! He shoved off her, grabbed his clothes and began to dress.

"I'm not sticking around the presses all night to babysit that job, Davina. No way, no how," he said as he pulled on his underwear, then his pants. "I'll get you your stupid copies in the morning, but I'm not going to worry about it now. Whatever is on that film is on it. We did a good job."

"Good isn't good enough. My father's already pissed off that I signed that contract without him looking at it. I'm on the line here, Tony. Don't you understand? Don't you care?"

When he finally looked over at her he saw she was crumpled on the sheets, her face buried in a pillow. Davina's shoulders heaved and he heard her muffled cries.

Christ, he thought as he moved toward the bed, sitting on it but careful not to touch her.

"Hey, things happen, Davina. I'll do my best. I'll stop in and see how it's going, okay? Okay?"

She nodded her head into the pillow but didn't raise it.

"Okay," he said again, embarrassed to be in the same room with a crying woman. No wonder he wasn't married. Women! They were hardly worth the effort. "Okay, I'm going now and I'll check on it. I'll

298

see you in the morning. Everything will be fine. Okay?"

Tony backed out of the room without another word. When Davina heard the click of the latch she waited a minute, then raised her dry eyes to make sure he was gone. She was mad. She was scared what Noel would say if the job wasn't perfect. But she wasn't an idiot. Nobody and nothing made her cry. Nothing.

It was only one issue anyhow. If they had to do make-goods for some of the advertisers, so what? *High Life* could afford to give away a few pages. To Noel that would be a pocket-money loss. If this didn't work out, she'd just return the contract to the old printers. If it did, then she would have proved her point; that she, Davina Montgomery, was as good as the rest of them. Maybe better.

That's just what she wanted her father to understand. Maybe then he'd treat her like she was worth something. Ever since he'd come home from his trip abroad he'd been more demanding than usual. He spoke little, reacted even less. Her barbs, her gauntlets, were ignored. What fun was it if he wouldn't even feel guilty about her anymore?

Methodically she dressed, taking little pleasure in the feel of her silk lingerie and the fine linen of her dress. It looked like she had slept in the thing, but Davina didn't care. By this time the guy at the front desk of the Sportsman's Lodge must have a good idea of what was going on. Maybe Noel would notice if she got home before he locked himself in his damned study. Maybe he'd ask her where she'd been, demand to know what she'd been doing. Oh, that would be wonderful. Maybe she'd even tell him in all its gruesome detail. That would make him squirm — she hoped.

Slinging her purse over her shoulder Davina left the hotel and headed home. When she got there the lights were on. She sat for a minute thinking what a great place it was. It was just her luck to have a father like Noel. Why couldn't he have been some old fart on his way out, a senile guy she could wrap around her little finger? Just her luck to draw a beefcake like him; a man with a mind like a steel trap.

Knowing she was up to the challenge, Davina parked in the drive and walked through the front door. Benton, thankfully, was nowhere to be seen. She still hadn't figured out how to get rid of him.

She was headed toward the staircase when she heard voices in the study. Quietly, she worked her way to the door and peered through the crack. Paul Davenport was sitting with Noel. He sipped a drink while Noel listened to someone on the phone.

"No sign of her? You checked her residence?" He listened again, nodding his head sadly. "I see. Well," he sighed, "keep on it. Let me know when you have anything."

Noel hung up and swiveled to face Paul. Putting his hands on his desk he pushed himself up, rounded it, retrieved his drink and went to the couch.

"Nothing yet?" Paul asked.

"No. She just disappeared. No sign of her. Her house has been sold. She didn't reapply for a driver's license. They even checked the airport, the trains, the ships. Nothing."

Paul looked about the room, then back at his friend and boss, "Maybe it's for the best, Noel.

What really do you know about this woman? She's no older than Davina. A little young, I would say."

"Not really," Noel said, smiling as he thought of Tess. "There's no comparison. This woman was everything Davina isn't and that's what makes her a woman. Age really has nothing to do with it. I'm not some dottering old fool you know."

"I know," Paul laughed, "but you're getting older, Noel. Hormones can do odd things to a man just the other side of forty, no matter how wonderful he looks or feels."

Now it was Noel's turn to laugh.

"You always were one to point out the downside to things. No, Paul, Tess was unusual. She was a very gentle woman, but not clinging. She honestly didn't want my help. It wasn't a ruse. Even after she found out who I was, it seemed to make little impression on her. She was . . . the only word I can think of is wise. Not worldly, although the situation she was in should have made her so. We spent almost a month together. It was the most glorious month of my life. I need to find her. I need to tell her so many things. Not the least of which is, I understand."

"Anything in particular you understand?"

"That's private."

"I can respect that. I hope you find her if it means that much to you. And, knowing you, I imagine you will sooner or later."

"I certainly hope it's sooner," Noel mused.

Outside the door Davina bit her lip to keep from screaming. How dare he! Comparing her to someone else! Comparing her and giving her the short end of the stick! She pulled in her breath, trying desperately to control her fury.

If this woman Noel was looking for was so special, then what did that make her mother? A tramp? The woman who bore him a child should be the most special woman in his life. It was obvious that Noel hadn't grown at all since he was an eighteen-year-old stud. His lack of feeling galled Davina to no end. It wasn't long before she realized what this little conversation really meant and Davina's heart hurtled toward panic.

If Noel was interested in some other woman he might even do the unthinkable. He might marry her. Then Davina would be out in the cold for sure. A wife would take precedence over a daughter in any estate matter. A young wife would outlive Noel by years and, though Davina was patient, she wasn't that patient.

Quickly she made some decisions. The only way to fight fire was with fire. Goading him hadn't worked, forcing him to face the fact that she was there for the duration hadn't worked, usurping Meagan Dayler's powers as production manager hadn't brought her the respect she wanted. There was only one other thing to try. Gentle, wise, unassuming, is what she'd be. If Noel found this woman she would have to do battle on Davina's already spoken for turf. She made her move.

"Noel," she said in a soft voice as she entered the room. "I didn't know you were still up. It's awfully late. Hello, Paul."

"Davina," both men said. She saw them eye her dress, her hair. She smoothed her skirt.

"It's been a long day at the office. I was at the printer's, too, checking on tomorrow's issue. I should know better than to wear linen on a day like this." She laughed a bit, holding the note that was a little too high, letting it go on a little too long.

"How's it looking?" Noel asked.

"Good. I think we'll all be very pleased," she lied, praying at the same time that Tony would pull off a miracle. "Of course, there are a few glitches, but that's what happens when you've got a new supplier."

"I've never seen that happen," Paul noted coolly. "Usually, a new supplier bends over backward to do things better than right the first time. I'm still a little unsure why we switched."

Paul looked from Davina to Noel. Davina looked at her father, holding her breath as she waited for his answer. Would he back her up?

"Davina found that the price break was just too good to pass up," Noel answered, never taking his eyes from his daughter.

She understood his silent message. He didn't believe the change was worthwhile, either, but she was his daughter. For the first time in their relationship Davina felt a small part of her heart open to him. Unfortunately, it was very small.

"That's right. I have all the paperwork to back it up—the estimates and everything," she said quietly, still looking at Noel, trying to tell him she was grateful but failing miserably. Her eyes still shot daggers into him.

"That reminds me, Davina," Noel said, his gravely voice insistent. "You were going to get a copy of the contract to me. I haven't seen it yet."

"I guess Millie forgot to bring it down to you," Davina answered, using her secretary as an excuse for her own problem. She didn't want Noel to see the contract yet.

"Thanks. I'd appreciate it."

Davina nodded. "Well, good night then."

But Noel stopped her before she left the room.

"Davina, we will reaward the printing contract to Anderson if this new place isn't up to snuff. I won't have my magazine falling one iota short of perfection, is that understood?"

Davina bristled. *His* magazine. Always *his*. She smiled graciously.

"Of course. I wouldn't want anything you owned to go out in public less than perfect."

She was out the door a moment later, leaving the two men sitting in a sorrowful silence.

"How long are you going to let this go on, Noel?"

"I don't know. I have to keep trying."

"At the expense of the magazine? Your baby?"

"She was my baby, too," Noel answered sadly. "I just found out too late to nurture her the way I do two hundred pages every month. I think I can give it a little more time."

"You're a better man than I am, Noel." Paul drained his drink.

"Not better, maybe a little more patient."

"I hope you don't wait so long that you'll find yourself in the eye of the storm instead of just buffeted by strong winds."

"I won't."

Both men rose together and said their good nights. Noel walked Paul to the door and held it open for him.

"Noel," Paul said slowly, "do you really think she was at the presses?"

"No." Noel smiled sorrowfully. "All I can hope is that she chooses her lovers with a little more forethought than she chooses her printers. Good night, Paul."

"Good night, Noel."

The door closed. Noel Montgomery walked back to his study slowly, thinking about Davina, hoping in some way he could find his way to her. Then he thought about Tess Canfield and hoped against hope that she would find her way back to him.

Tony walked in with three copies of the June issue of *High Life* under his arm. Davina watched him, looking for any sign of what to expect. All she could see was the back cover. She could hardly breathe. His face was unreadable. In silence he took the copies and tossed them on her desk. They landed on a pile of invoices. The invoices flew off in all directions. Davina ignored them as she reached for the magazine. The cover looked good. Her hands hovered over the top issue. She could hardly bring herself to open it. Forcing herself, knowing that nothing would change if she hesitated, she picked it up and began flipping the pages.

Faster and faster she went. Pages stuck together, the ink still tacky. She could feel her face lose its color as she turned to the centerfold—to the *High Life* Woman spread—then fell back in her chair. The heat in the office was incredible. Davina loosened the tie of her blouse. Instantly blood rushed up past her face, into her brain where it pounded against her skull. Finally, she looked at Tony, who was lounging in a chair opposite her.

"It's beautiful," she breathed. Then demanded, "Cost?"

"Hey, we got a contract, don't we, babe?" Tony raised his hands heavenward, feeling like the Godfather. Hell, he wasn't that far removed. This sealed it. Davina was his. Now he was going to play a little harder with her no matter how much she said no.

"I don't believe it. I just don't believe it."

"Believe it," Tony answered, trying not to let his body betray his exhaustion.

He had gone to the press. It looked pretty good but he sat on the pressmen, watching them make their minute changes until it was perfect. Why in the hell he had done that he would never know. After all, they did have a contract and like it or not *High Life* was under their thumb with that little "in perpetuity" clause. Still, the long hours were worth it now. Worth it to see Davina actually smile. She was real pretty when she smiled.

"Wait here. I've got a couple of people to see. Wait right here, then we'll grab lunch, okay?"

"You got it." Tony offered her a thumbs-up, but she was out the door before he gave it a final jab toward the ceiling.

Davina walked with a purpose. First stop was Paul Davenport's office. She walked straight past the secretary, ignoring her protests. Paul was on the phone.

"Just a minute," he said, putting his hand over the receiver, primed to read Davina the riot act.

Before he could get another word out Davina lay a copy of the magazine on his desk, smiled a small smile and left the office, her head held high.

Noel was next. Shirley wasn't in the outer office. Her father was seated in his black and gray office. It looked like an extension of him, his black hair, his gray silk Cardin suit. The air was supercharged with his presence. Davina stumbled the moment she entered that room. She always did. This time, though, she clutched the June issue tight as though it might give her strength. It gave her all she needed.

"Davina?" Noel raised a questioning eyebrow.

"Thought you'd like to give me an opinion on the new issue."

"Sit down."

He motioned to a chair, taking the magazine from her. She sat on the edge without realizing it, leaned toward him without perceiving it. Her heart was pounding, waiting for his reaction.

Noel's strong fingers turned each page carefully. Now and again he would linger over one page longer than another. The centerfold should have been the moment he looked at her, his eyes shining bright with admiration. He didn't. He looked at it long and hard, then simply turned the page. All two hundred and twenty-eight pages filtered through his fingers before he finally acknowledged her.

"It looks good, Davina."

That was it. Looks good. Davina blinked, her skin prickled. She waited. For more. There had to be more.

"So what's your call? Retain this new printer?"

"Yes . . . yes," she stammered, knowing she sounded indecisive and weak, but she couldn't help herself. He should have been hugging her, congratulating her. Noel was talking as though they were trying to decide what color to make the logo that month. "I think so. They came in on budget. I think we should keep it up. Put the extra money into, uh"—Davina racked her brain, searching for something that would sound impressive—"uh, photogra-

307

phy. I think we could use a little more creativity on the spread. Maybe add a few pages."

That was it. The best she could do. She felt her body betraying her, melting slightly with her disappointment. Then Noel nodded.

"That might be something to look into. Four more pages, though, might just raise our bulk rate. I'll take it up with circulation and distribution. May I keep this?"

Davina nodded. He was dismissing her. Shakily she got to her feet. Expecting more, wanting more, she was stunned and couldn't even find anger inside her.

"Davina?"

"Yes, Noel." She turned a blank face toward him. He was smiling slightly.

"It was good. You've done a fine job since Meagan's accident."

Davina's lips twitched. It was coming, finally, his approval. That made what she had done to Meagan Dayler more than worthwhile. More than that, it was his confidence that brought a bright bubble of pride to her heart. Now there would be no doubt she could take over his empire one day. Now . . .

"But, Davina, next time pay a little more attention to the reds, they should be truer. You have too much blue. They have to be absolutely correct on those fashion pages."

He bent his head and picked up his work, leaving the June issue on the side of his desk. Davina stood rooted to the spot, her happiness warped by his nitpicking criticism. How dare he!

"Is there anything else?" Noel asked.

Davina so lost in the hatred that was growing inside her she hadn't noticed him looking quizzically at her. Her body trembled under the weight of her ill-will. It was all she could do to speak normally.

"No. Nothing else."

She left him knowing now that her future would have to be apart from Noel Montgomery and the only way to insure a bright future was with money. Davina Montgomery set her mind to devising the best way to get it.

Twenty-one

"Let's try it again, Bonnie."

The frustrated director whined at her from somewhere offstage. She raised a hand and shaded her eyes as she peered toward the direction of his voice. Not that she necessarily wanted to see the little prick, she just wanted to determine how pissed off he was. His wispy little voice always seemed hard-pressed, so it was difficult to know if he was at his wit's end or just in his normal prissy mode.

Squinting, Bonnie identified most of the continually moving mass of bodies. There was the stylist with the big mouth, the account people — all four of them — the client. Oh, there he was. Rick Handly, director. Bonnie wondered how his parents could have given him such a macho label when he looked like an asthmatic kid who never grew more than two inches after his fifth birthday. She saw the top of his head as he conferred with the agency account men — and one woman — but she couldn't see his face.

Turning away, Bonnie put her hands on her hips and looked about. Not one soul was interested in talking to her. Standing alone in her incredible shimmering gown, in the middle of a set made for seduction, made her feel a bit like a bull in the ring just before the matador walked in. Sort of like everybody was watching her, admiring her fine lines but hoping against hope she'd get it in the end.

Fine with her if that was their attitude. She would get it in the end, but not the way they thought. Commercials were just a stopping point, something to pay the bills. Sy called every day saying he was getting closer to cutting a deal with Warner's. He was supposed to be on this set by one o'clock to let her know what was happening.

"Hey!" Bonnie grabbed a woman who was rushing past. "What time is it?"

"Two," the woman said, glancing at her watch. A stack of papers fluttered in her hands; her face was a road map of furrows. She was obviously not pleased with Bonnie's interruption. Bonnie didn't notice.

"Okay."

The woman hurried on her way, shaking her head. Actresses! Thank you wasn't in their vocabulary unless you were someone who could do them some good.

Bonnie started to pace across the silk Persian rug that was part of her make-believe boudoir. Her four-inch-heeled evening sandals bit into her toes. The little one on her left foot was beginning to throb. The throb was beginning to travel up her body, skipping the portions of her anatomy where it would do the most good, and heading directly to her head.

Bonnie raised a hand to her temple and rubbed, then headed to the satin fainting couch that was supposed to be the kind of thing every woman over forty had in her bedroom. Knees bent in her tight sequined dress, Bonnie's tush was just about on the cushion when a bloodcurdling scream scared the shit out of her and she fell helter-skelter over the couch.

Hands were everywhere, pulling her up without

311

ceremony, standing her upright so that she tottered precariously in her shoes, making the strippy leather feel as though it was a surgeon's knife cutting off her toe.

"What? What?" Bonnie asked, confused and afraid what the scream had meant. Was she on fire? Was someone after her? The place seemed as though it was in chaos.

"Don't sit down!"

The stylist and her two assistants were fussing all over her, running their hands up and down the lower extremities of her body. Bonnie was getting dizzy being turned one way, then the other, looking down into angry, frustrated faces.

"Why not, for God's sake? What's happened?" she whimpered.

"This is a Mackie and it's on loan. One wrinkle and we've got to dish out four grand for this dress," the stylist snapped, glaring at Bonnie as she backed up to look at the gown from a better angle. "I think we caught you in time. Just don't do that again."

"But my feet hurt and I haven't had lunch and . . ."

Bonnie hiccupped and sighed and sobbed at the same time. Her hand flew to her mouth. She had never cried in her whole damned life, but she could feel the hot sting of tears behind her lids and her nose was starting to run.

"Oh, for God's sake," the stylist begged, "don't do that. Please, don't do that. You'll ruin your makeup and we'll lose another hour. That'll put us over budget some more. Please, Bonnie, it's okay. We'll get you something to eat. It's okay," the stylist cooed, not caring one twit whether Bonnie was so exhausted she couldn't see straight.

A professional should know better. They couldn't

possibly lose more than half an hour and that was all there was to it. Bonnie nodded her head up and down so fast her helmet-sprayed coif looked as though it wasn't exactly attached to her head.

"What's the problem here?" Rick Handly demanded in his dry-leaf voice as he joined the pack.

"Bonnie, Bonnie," said one of the account men.

"Hey, sweetheart, it's okay," the beautician chimed in.

Bonnie began to cry. Great big tears fell over her arched lashes and coursed down her face until one huge tear fell directly on her cleavaged bosom and started to slalom toward the fabulous gold sequined dress. Someone smashed a Kleenex into Bonnie's chest, obliterating the little bit of moisture.

"Break!" Ricky screamed, losing the fluttery quality of his voice.

"Cricket," the stylist ordered one of her assistants, "get her out of this thing."

"Oh, Jesus," the account people muttered. The word that Bonnie had lost it was passed back like a chain letter through the ranks.

Five minutes later Bonnie was alone in the little back room she had been ushered to with such pomp earlier that morning. She sat shivering in her underwear, the hated sandals still on her feet, her body slumped as she stared into the mirror without really seeing her reflection. She could see herself through the tears that wouldn't stop no matter what she did. Her eyes were now black rimmed like a raccoon's, the pancake had been washed away in rivulets making her look like the east side of Vesuvius after the eruption. She didn't care. She didn't care about anything anymore.

"Bonnie?"

The door opened slowly and a voice hailed her in a

self-conscious whisper. Sy came into the room, un-moved by the sight of her naked body but scared to death by the look on her face.

"Bonnie, Bonnie, what have they done to you?"

He was at her side, kneeling as best he could, his jelly belly pressing into her lovely leg as he took her hand.

"Sweetie, what's happened here? Did someone do something to you? You've got to pull yourself to-gether. Your contract is for a year. You'll make lots of money if you just hang in there. I know you're tired but you've got to try. Talk to me, babe. Tell old Sy what's wrong."

Bonnie blinked, then swung her head toward Sy, as she looked at him with pitiful, lost eyes.

"My feet hurt, Sy," she said with a trembling voice.

"Oh, I can fix that," he answered, leaning down as his fingers fiddled with the tiny strap of her shoe. He couldn't seem to manage the clasp, so he eased it off her swollen foot, knowing he was hurting her. She didn't hit him or scream at him. Things were bad.

"They wouldn't let me sit down. They didn't give me anything to eat. No one talked to me," she wailed piti-fully. "I felt like a piece of meat out there, Sy. I didn't say my lines right and I'm trying. I really am. I don't know what's wrong, Sy. You tell me. What's wrong? I don't cry. I never cry, and now I'm crying. Sy." She grabbed his shoulders in a weak attempt to draw him closer. "Am I going crazy? Things were so good and then suddenly they were all shit. Is it me?"

"No, no, baby, it's not you. It's just this setup. It's different you know," he cajoled. "No audience out there oohing and ahing at you. These people just work different than live TV. What you got to do is think about all those people who are going to be seeing this

314

commercial and looking at your picture in the magazines. You've got to imagine how impressed they're going to be. All the women will want to look like you, all the men will want to have you."

Bonnie's eyes widened. "You really think so?"

"I know so, honey," he soothed, daring to put his hand on her hair and stroke it.

"Don't stop, Sy," Bonnie pleaded. "You're my only friend. You're like a father to me. I can always count on you to be there when I need you. You're so sweet. You understand."

Oh, God, Sy thought, she's cracking up. In all the years he'd handled her he had never heard Bonnie so much as utter a pleasantry, much less give him a compliment. He began to glow under her verbal ministrations. This was his break. He was going to get on top of Bonnie Barber now and keep her under his thumb.

"I've always cared about you, sweetheart, you know that. Nobody else has a future like yours," he said. "You've just got to start listening to me because I know what's happening. Now this gig has really impressed some people at Warner's . . ."

Bonnie's body trembled with an unheard sob. It was worse than Sy thought. Even the mention of Warner's didn't get a rise out of her. At least that's what he thought.

"Really?" she asked.

"Really. They think you'll be perfect for this part in a movie they've got coming. Now," he said hurriedly, "it's not a big part. I won't lie to you, it's a damn small part. But it's a feature. Mel Gibson's going to be in it."

"Mel Gibson?" she asked in a small voice, her eyes flickering toward Sy with some of their usual tartness. "I'll be costarring opposite Mel Gibson?"

"No, not exactly. I mean, you won't be costarring.

You know how it is."

Bonnie sat up a little straighter, her hand covering Sy's wrist. "How is it, Sy?"

"They're going to put you in a highly visible role. Good makeup; nice costumes. You just won't be in for the whole ninety minutes."

"Tell me about the part, Sy," Bonnie whispered. Sy still hadn't acknowledged the razor-sharp edge creeping into her voice, or the insistent pressure on his wrist. He was still under the impression he had her at a disadvantage.

"It's great, baby. You're going to play Emerald Bright, a talk-show hostess who gets murdered, and Gibson is going to solve the murder. Of course you're dead in the first ten minutes, but they've got some great close-ups in this script and you get to kiss Gibson and everything. I mean, if you really do the job, you'll steal the show."

Sy was grinning from ear to ear. A feature, Warner's, he had negotiated a deal that was ten times better than what he thought he could get for Bonnie. But one of the producers wanted to get in her pants and was willing to pay just about anything to get her on that set. He was just about ready to tell her what a great guy the producer was when he experienced a horrible, daggerlike pain in his wrist.

"Ahhhhh!" he shrieked, pulling his hand back. Then he realized Bonnie was holding it tight, digging her razor-sharp nails into the soft skin of his wrist. He almost fainted when he realized she was drawing blood.

"Talk-show hostess, Sy?" she growled at him through clenched teeth. The smeared makeup around her eyes and on her cheeks made her look like Linda Blair from *The Exorcist*. Sy shivered as the image of

316

Bonnie's head doing a three-sixty popped into his mind. *"Talk-show hostess,* Sy?"

"Yeah, talk-show hostess. It's a good part . . . yeow! Cut it out, Bonnie!"

"I'll cut it out when you tell me it isn't true, you blubbering bag of shit. You'd sell me out to play a part like that?"

"Hey, I'm not selling you out to do anything. If the shoe fits, as they say."

Sy made one last stand as a man. He attempted to get to his feet but Bonnie yanked him down, twisting his wrist so that any movement felt as though his arm was on fire.

"You stay right there and listen to me," she snarled. "I will *not* play a talk-show hostess. I will *not* be pigeon-holed for the rest of my life because of that thing I did with Giles. Do you understand me? I want a *feature.* I don't mind a small part; I'm open minded. But it will be a good part. I'm not going to make my feature debut by having to lie still pretending I'm dead with a bullet hole in my head. *I will not.* Nor will I preen about on the silver screen turning cards over and holding my hand above my head to show off the prizes of the week. It's over. That's it. No more. You do it right or you don't do it at all."

Bonnie released Sy so quickly he almost toppled over. Catching himself at the last minute, he was about to make a commanding speech about his standing as her agent and his worth as a human being, but Bonnie flew from her chair, hobbled to the door with one shoe off and one shoe on, yanked it open and hollered at the top of her lungs.

"Let's get this show on the road, now! Makeup! Get the makeup girl in here and let's finish this spot." Bonnie slammed the door, saw Sy and pulled it open again.

"I'll do my job, now you do yours."

Sy ambled past her without looking at her, a tissue held gingerly to his wrist. The door banged behind him. He stepped out of the way as the makeup girl rushed past him into the dressing room. The entire set was pandemonium.

Moments earlier everyone was standing around counting the dollars that would be lost because of a temperamental star. Now they were moving like lightning, Bonnie's piss and vinegar infecting them all. They looked happy. Sy smiled. The FortyFine gig was saved, and it would go well. He walked out of the studio nursing his wrist, grinning from ear to ear.

"The girl's got it after all," he muttered to himself. For the first time he truly believed that Bonnie Barber just might have a future in this business. If only she could learn to wait; if only patience was one of her virtues.

"You were spectacular, Miss Barber."

Bonnie was just buttoning her blouse when Bart Weir walked into the little room that had been vacated only moments before by the stylist and makeup people.

"Thank you," she purred, liking his look immediately. She could smell money and success a mile away. Well, maybe not a mile. She hadn't exactly been on the mark with Giles, now had she?

"You're very welcome. I'm Bart Weir." He moved in a little closer. She batted her now perfectly made-up eyes.

"The name sounds familiar, but I'm afraid I can't place you."

"No reason you should. I'm CEO of DDB & O."

"Really?" Bonnie said, sitting down and slipping on her shoes. She didn't wince, though her feet were still swollen from hours on the set.

"Really," he said, laughing gently, "and I know it really means nothing to you. You don't have to pretend."

"I'm not pretending," she said coolly, knowing someone like him would be impressed with her business knowledge. Actually, she had only overheard one of the account people talking earlier in the day and had remembered some of the things they spoke of. "I find the work your agency does impeccable. I especially like the Chevrolet spots. But you're also very strong on fashion. The Blackglama ads, for instance, have always fascinated me."

"Really? May I sit?" Bart raised an eyebrow in question.

"Be my guest," Bonnie said. "But I was almost finished here."

"No problem. I'll keep you company. I'm curious about your knowledge of the advertising industry. What exactly is it that intrigues you about the Blackglama campaign?"

Bonnie looked in the mirror to see him looking at her. She smiled, knowing full well it wasn't her knowledge of advertising that intrigued him. She improvised.

"I find the simplicity of them interesting." There, that was safe.

"I would have thought you would find the celebrity status of our models interesting."

"Oh, I do. Wouldn't it be wonderful if someday I could fit into the legend campaign?"

"Actually, that would be very nice. Perhaps, we could talk about it. Over drinks? Dinner?"

Bonnie eyed him, her face a mask. She liked what

she saw: the suit, the face, the voice, the diamond ring on his finger. Though Bart would never have guessed it, her mind was running faster than Speedy Gonzales. Commercial success had created celebrities. Look what it had done for Joe Izuzu. It might just be worth her while to follow up on this one.

"I'd like that very much," she murmured.

"Tonight?"

"All right. But I'd like to go home first, change, wash all this stuff out of my hair."

"Naturally. I like to relax a bit from my day, too, before I tackle the night." He rose and smiled at her. "You know, my people were a bit worried today. Thought they might have a prima donna on their hands. It's seldom I'm called into a shoot because of problems. I usually leave that to the vice-presidents. But this is a huge account, one very precious to my agency. I've learned a lot today."

"Really? And what have you learned?" Bonnie asked coyly.

"That account people have a lot to learn and," he paused, his square jaw moving a bit. "I should go back to my roots and attend more shoots. I had no idea how stimulating they could still be."

"Tonight, Bart, you may pick me up at eight."

Bonnie handed him a card.

"Eight."

"It was awful when Giles died so suddenly. It was the day after our wedding."

Bonnie let her silver fork hover over her plate. She knew the pose was a good one. The lighting in Bernard's was perfect, their table simple, but elegantly laid, leaving Bonnie to shine as she always did in such

320

settings. She could feel her face falling into a perfect expression of dreaminess, longing, and sorrow. Why couldn't anyone see how wonderful she would be in films? Perhaps she was too good an actress. Less subtlety might be the key.

"That must have been hard for you. To be a widow so young. It must have been difficult, indeed." Bart paused for the appropriate moments, then brightened. "Do you like your sausage?"

"Absolutely." Bonnie smiled. "Such an unusual delicacy. Seafood sausage. Quite novel."

"I suppose." Bart shrugged. "I don't believe they do it as well here as they do at Taillevent in Paris, but it is definitely acceptable."

Bonnie delicately cut into the sausage arranged so lovingly on her plate and tried to imagine it a burger and onion rings. She'd worked hard that day. This stuff wouldn't keep a snail going.

"And you?" Bonnie asked as she put a bite into her mouth, letting her peach-colored lips slide seductively over the tines.

"Me, what?" Bart laughed.

"Divorced or widowed?"

"Neither."

Bonnie grinned.

"A bachelor at your age, how nice," she said happily, popping another bite into her mouth.

"No," Bart said. "I'm married. Have been for almost thirty-five years. Lovely woman. Does lots of needlepoint."

Bonnie almost broke her teeth on the fine silver as he imparted his news so casually.

"I see."

"Yes, she and I have an arrangement. She's not much interested in the more physical aspects of life.

She understands that men are different from women."

Inside Bonnie was seething. What a worm! What a bastard! But her expression remained pleasant.

"I think that's marvelous. Most women truly don't understand the physical makeup of a man," she said sweetly. "I know that men need to have certain outlets for their energies. That's why so many clubs these days don't want to allow women as members. Men need a place where they can work out properly. Sweat and such. I can't imagine why a woman would want to belong to such a place. Your wife is a very understanding lady."

Bart's face collapsed in direct proportion to Bonnie's words. She had done it. Kidded a kidder, only Bart Weir hadn't been kidding. Screwing around to further her career was one thing, but Bonnie had principles. She would never, ever mess around with a married man on a long-term basis again. The last time with Ben was bad enough. No way, no how and fooling around was exactly what Bart had in mind. Still, it wouldn't do to burn her bridges, either. She'd play along this evening, then decide what to do when, and if, he called the next time.

Bart began a tentative chuckle that turned into a good hearty laugh before it faded away again when he realized Bonnie had a look of confusion on her face.

"Yes," he cleared his throat. "Yes, I can't imagine why a woman would want to join a club. Actually, I don't belong to one myself. I prefer other forms of physical activity."

"How nice. I enjoy a few myself," Bonnie said, leaning forward, her elbow on the table, her face perched just over her hand. "In fact, I was hoping that we might indulge in some this evening, unless you have other plans."

Bart's face brightened considerably.

"That was exactly what I had in mind. I have all evening to devote to you, my dear."

He reached for her but Bonnie was already back to her seafood sausage, eating with relish.

"How marvelous," she mumbled through a mouthful of crab and lobster. "I love to dance and I know just the place. Have you ever been to Coco's?"

Finally, *finally* Bonnie was having fun. She hadn't been dancing for ages and Bart was proving more of a match than she ever could have hoped for. Despite his age, he moved well, throwing himself into the ear-blasting beat with the fervor of a fifteen-year-old. The more she drank, the more she danced, the more attractive he became, and she was considering taking him home with her just for the night, just to discuss the possibility of proving to him that she, too, could be a Blackglama legend.

She had been on the dance floor for twenty minutes already, spinning here and there, reveling in the attention she was given as the rest of the people on the floor moved back from her, giving her room to work. Even Bart had disappeared into the crowd.

Bonnie was on. Bonnie was loving it. Bonnie used her body the way a cowboy uses his whip — gently, then with such force that it stung those who came under its spell.

Her red hair, hanging well past her shoulders, was thick and wavy. It flew behind her, over her face, covering her breasts until she flipped it back again, giving her audience her best profile, her best pout. Bonnie was in seventh heaven, and she was almost drunk.

Suddenly, as she spun around ending in a dip, her

long legs pushed toward the north end of the crowd so that the slit in her dress exposed her thighs almost to her crotch, Bonnie was grabbed around the waist, her hand taken into a man's.

She opened her eyes and looked at them as they stood poised, ready to catch the beat. He was ugly, that was for sure, with his too-wide set eyes and his big nose, his greasy looks, but he was a dancer. She could feel it in the way he held her, in the command of his hand on the small of her back. They began to move, a perfect dancing unit.

The crowd went crazy as he twirled her, caught her, hesitated, allowed her to show off her body. What did she care if he was ugly? He was giving her the spotlight as she deserved.

They danced for what seemed like an eternity. She was lost in the sound of the music, the whirl of admiring faces around her. Then, in front of her eyes, was a face that lacked even the faintest hint of esteem. It was a face that looked familiar, but Bonnie couldn't quite place it. She had an instant sense of déjà vu.

The woman had ripped the greasy-looking guy out of Bonnie's arms and almost thrown him into the crowd. Now she was facing Bonnie. Her hair was a curly black mass, her face pale and her eyes angry as all get out. Slowly, Bonnie came out of her dancing mode, drawing herself up to her full five foot nine inches. She towered over the rounded woman who may have been considered a beauty if she wasn't standing in such close proximity to Bonnie Barber. Bonnie angled her a cold stare, a bitchy smile playing on her lips.

"Stay away from him," the dark-haired woman screeched. "You're a whore taking another woman's man."

The music had stopped. The audience was standing

in a huge circle, hushed, waiting. Bonnie should have walked away. She should have done something neat like apologize, that would have been really sophisticated and made this idiot look bad. A flashbulb popped. The press was there.

Bonnie, a little too much liquor coursing through her fabulous body, grinned wider. She felt full of it.

"I didn't *take* your man. He was looking for a way to get rid of you. He's a slime ball. You can have him."

She turned regally but the dark-haired woman grabbed her arm, scratching her in the process.

"Why you little bitch . . ." Bonnie snapped, shoving the other woman away.

"Nobody calls me a bitch," the dark-haired woman screamed, raising her fist.

But Bonnie was quicker and she'd forgotten what happened to Giles. She couldn't help herself. She drew back her fist and sent it flying toward the dark-haired woman, who fell back just in time. Bonnie's fist only clipped her chin, but she stumbled away. When she was back on her feet she was headed straight for Bonnie, who stood ready to do battle.

All around them the crowd was calling out, taking up sides. Neither woman could understand a single word. They egged the two women on, calling for an all-out fight. Bonnie tensed. The other woman moved forward. Suddenly, Bonnie was spun backward. The black-haired woman had disappeared, too. Her greasy boyfriend had grabbed her about the waist and was pulling her, kicking and screaming, from the dance floor and the club.

A roar of laughter went up. Bonnie pulled away from Bart. He was looking at her with a great deal of amusement and admiration. She liked that. She smiled back.

"Boy, you really know how to pick 'em," he said as the crowd dispersed and the band picked up a slower tune.

Bonnie fell onto Bart, wrapping her arms about his neck. She smelled like Opium and Jack Daniel's. He loved it.

"What do you mean by that?

"I just mean that you picked a doozy to make an enemy of. That was Davina Montgomery."

"Yeah?" Bonnie teased. "She a client of yours?"

"No," Bart answered, tightening his grip on her. "She's Noel Montgomery's daughter. *The* Noel Montgomery," he reminded her. "Owner of *High Life* magazine and *High Life* films and *High Life* everything else. She's a pretty powerful little lady who's going to have one sore jaw thanks to you, and I have a funny feeling she's never going to forget who gave it to her."

Bart twirled Bonnie away from the dance floor, then led her to a table. Bonnie didn't feel like partying anymore. She didn't feel like being with Bart. She felt like killing herself, and that was all there was to it. Davina Montgomery. *High Life* magazine. What Sy couldn't get for her she might have gotten herself if she'd used a little restraint. What rotten luck! She buried her head in her hands and waited for the headache she knew would come. Unfortunately, Bart didn't know it yet. He was still grinning at her, his hand moving further and further down her back.

Everything was ready. Bonnie had spent the entire day going over everything that had happened the evening before. Davina Montgomery was not an ordinary woman who would respond to an ordinary approach. Bonnie remembered just enough to realize that Davina Montgomery was both tough and stupid. Maybe not stupid, exactly, but lost and insecure. Otherwise, why would she have fought like a wildcat for a guy who looked like a toad?

By three Bonnie knew she would have to act quickly or her timing would be off, lessening the chances that her plan would work. Bonnie dressed carefully, changing her hair two or three times before she felt she had just the right look. Bonnie smiled as she patted the tight coil at the nape of her neck. She had pulled her fabulous red hair tightly back from her face, catching it up in pins. Davina Montgomery, she felt, would not appreciate the advances of an overly feminine glamour girl. This chick was not the slumber-party type.

Promptly at four-fifteen Bonnie presented herself at the *High Life* offices, gave her name to the receptionist, waited as she contacted Davina's office and was then politely told that Miss Montgomery could not be disturbed. Bonnie shifted the package she carried to her other arm, asked for pen and paper and wrote a note.

"I wonder if you would mind giving this to her?" Bonnie asked without the hint of a smile. "Now."

The receptionist looked as though a less than gracious remark was about to pass her lips. Luckily, she thought twice about it, took the note and disappeared into the maze of halls. She was back a moment later.

"Miss Montgomery will see you now. Do you know the way?" Bonnie shook her head. The receptionist shifted her weight to her other foot and pointed. "Through the doors to your left, first corridor on your right? Take it. Keep going. You'll see her office on the left."

"Thank you."

Bonnie walked through the double doors feeling almost triumphant. Step one was complete. Step two should work. Step three would take some time, but she could manage it. She found Davina's office without a problem and walked right past the secretary.

Davina sat tapping a pencil against her desk, her eyes trained on the doorway. Her face showed no sign of surprise as Bonnie strolled directly up to the desk and put the box she carried in front of Davina.

Curiosity got the better of Davina. Without a word she leaned forward and opened the top. Inside, nestled in gray tissue paper was the biggest bottle of J & B she'd ever seen. She pulled it out. The glass neck felt cool, the bottle heavy and the amber liquid looked delicious. Davina raised her eyes and stared at Bonnie.

"I didn't think you'd be the kind who'd appreciate flowers when it came to an apology."

"You got that right," Davina answered.

"Friends?"

"We'll see." Davina shrugged. "You really think so?"

"What?" Bonnie's brow furrowed as she was caught off guard.

"Your note," Davina reminded her. She picked it up and read. "That loser wasn't worth the effort. You could do a whole lot better."

Bonnie nodded. "Yeah, I really think so."

Davina indicated a chair with a tip of her head.

"Make yourself comfortable and we'll drink to it."

Bonnie grinned and did as she was told. Two hours later the offices had cleared out for the weekend and Bonnie Barber knew Davina Montgomery was hers as long as Bonnie needed her.

Twenty-two

"Tess! Tess!"

Dimitri Argyroupolis called through cupped hands, his odd voice carrying over the still Hawaiian waters until it finally reached her.

Tess put her head up and tread water, looking toward the yacht. He saw her squint and he raised his long, powerful arm in response, waving it through the air, calling her back. Even from that distance Dimitri could see her smile and it warmed his heart. Such a lovely young woman; such a sad and horrible situation.

It seemed impossible that she had already been with him two months. Hard to believe the reason that had brought her back.

Her message had almost been lost in the maze of assistants and associates who protected him from unwelcome approaches. When she contacted Greece he was on the open seas, already headed toward Hawaii. When she contacted the marine operator her call had been stopped by a well-meaning crew member. Luckily, she had tried until she finally spoke to him.

Through her tears he pieced together her story, insisting that she join him immediately. The crash, Royal's horrible behavior toward her, her inability to reach her lover, losing her possessions had created a tension that even Tess was unable to cope with. He heard it in her voice. He had heard it before in other women — women he cared nothing for. She was on the verge of a breakdown and Dimitri didn't want that for this spunky young woman Royal had brought aboard his ship.

In the blink of an eye all was taken care of. He sent his plane and his private physician. Tess, terrified of flying now, was given a tranquilizer and transported to Hawaii where Dimitri himself met her at the airport. It had all been done so easily, so quietly. He had accompanied her on the skiff, holding her hand as she came out of her sleep, smiling at her, thankful that she had turned to him.

So many years of his life had been spent in pursuit of owning both things and human beings. He loved to own them. Now he found pleasure in simply being needed. It had made Dimitri wonder whether he would have found more satisfaction in his life if he had had children or even a wife he loved enough to care for. Tess had gripped his hand, answering that question. Yes, he had much to give. In that moment, as she looked gratefully and helplessly at him, Dimitri knew he would do anything to help Tess Canfield; anything to protect her.

Now she was no longer helpless. Her body had healed, her mind along with it. The nightmares that began so suddenly, nightmares of fire and abandonment, eased as the days and weeks passed. Even her legs now bore no sign of the burns that had kept her helpless for weeks in Paris. Only her heart had not healed. Though she tried to hide it, Tess Canfield was aching and it wasn't only for Royal, of that Dimitri was sure.

"Let me help you, Tess," he called happily, reaching toward her as she began to climb the sea ladder.

Water poured off her, making her look like a slick little seal. Her hair was smoothed back from her forehead, falling in a long, thick coil. Wet, it appeared darker than usual. Her skin had tanned to a deep gold and her blue eyes sparkled like the sky above them.

"Thank you," she breathed, making the final jump onto the deck of the ship. "The water is wonderful. So warm."

"And you were born to it," Dimitri answered, wrapping a thick white towel around her despite the heat of the day.

"I don't know why you should say that." She laughed. "At home, the only place we went swimming was in the reservoir. Probably not the most hygienic thing to do. Someone had tied a long rope to a tree, and we used to hold it like Tarzan and swing into the water."

"Someday I would like to see Kansas. It's one place I've never been."

"You, I think, would be bored stiff. It's nothing but flat, flat land. Beautiful land though," she said softly now. "There's nothing like seeing miles of wheat swaying in a twilight breeze. There is nothing like the smell of the earth after it's been turned, or piles of grain pouring into a silo looking like the white sands of these beaches."

Tess moved to the railing, letting the towel drop open in front of her as she peered off toward Kauai. There was a sadness in her voice, and a melancholy in her stance. Dimitri moved toward her. She didn't look at him as she continued to speak.

"Perhaps I should have gone home, to Kansas, Dimitri. Gone back to where I came from. Nothing has been the same since I left there. I used to know exactly who I was and where I belonged. I had such a clear vision of where I was going. Everything changed after I left there. I should have gone back."

"To what, dear Tess? You've told me yourself there is no one. Your parents are dead. No relatives. What would you have gone back to?"

"Friends."

"Of your parents or *your* friends?" he pressed.

"You're right. The people I knew there knew me as a little girl, a young woman going off to college. I'm neither of those things anymore. Too much has happened. But I could have gone back to surroundings that were home." She shook her head and chuckled low and soft. "That would have been silly, too. I would stay in a hotel and go out during the day to stand in other people's fields. They would have thought I lost my mind. Dimitri, do you think I've lost my mind?"

"No," he said, patting her hand. "You've only lost your way a little. But if your mind was lost, you wouldn't have known to come to me. I am your friend, Tess. That is important."

"You're Royal's friend."

"I'm *your* friend. Royal has always been an employee. A colleague, in a manner of speaking. You began, and will end for me, in friendship."

Tess leaned over and kissed his hard, aging face.

"Thank you. That means a lot. Have you" — she hesitated, not liking the way Dimitri withdrew from her when she asked the question — "have you heard

332

from Royal? Have you been able to reach him?"

"No."

"Have you tried, Dimitri?" she insisted gently.

He was about to lie, but when he looked into her blue eyes and saw her pain he couldn't.

"No," he admitted.

"Why not?" Tess demanded. "Dimitri, it's been so long. He must be wondering where I am. What I'm doing."

"Tess, Tess," the old man said, taking her by the shoulders. "Don't do this to yourself. You think that woman, his wife, could have sold your home and taken your things without Royal knowing about it? Do you think she could have done all that without his signature on papers?"

Tess's lips pulled together tightly; her eyes blazed.

"Yes, I do, Dimitri. He was hurt in that crash and taken away quickly. I don't know if he went with Astra willingly. I don't know if he was in any shape to understand anything. She could have tricked him in a hundred ways."

"How?" Dimitri insisted, baiting her.

"She could have drugged him or he could have been under medication when she brought him papers." Frustrated, Tess walked away a few steps, then whirled back on Dimitri. "I don't know. I don't think like that. I don't think in devious ways. I can't even guess what she must have done."

"That's the point, Tess," Dimitri told her. "You *don't* think like that so you can't imagine what happened. And because you can't imagine the most devious path you can't imagine the worst scenario either—that Royal consented to everything his wife was doing."

333

"You don't know that. You don't know him like I do. He loves me," Tess cried.

"I don't know him like you do, but I've known him longer than you have, my dear," Dimitri soothed her. "I retained him because he is a wonderful attorney. He has looked after my interests well and good all these years. But you can't work closely with someone and not come away knowing both their strengths and weaknesses. Royal is a creature of comfort. He likes to have his cake and eat it, too. Do you understand? He is not one to take a stand on his own behalf or anyone else's if it means that he will be uncomfortable. He is, first and foremost, an attorney, and attorneys play both sides of the fence; they talk from both sides of their mouth. So many things could have happened. Why torture yourself trying to figure out what actually did? Why not accept this silence and get on with your life?"

"Royal is my life, Dimitri," Tess answered simply.

"Is he?"

Dimitri's wise eyes looked directly into hers, and Tess felt as though he had lanced her heart, piercing it to let out a benevolent demon. Noel Montgomery's visage flew into her mind's eye, only to be banished by her.

"Yes." Dimitri felt, rather than heard, the hesitation in her voice. It was all he needed to know. "Will you find him for me?"

"I will do my best."

This time Dimitri lied easily, knowing Tess wasn't even sure if she wanted such a reunion. He felt that in his old bones as he now felt all the aches and pains of age. He would do nothing for a while.

"Thank you. Thank you, dear friend."

Tess rushed to him and threw her arms about his broad shoulders. He held her gently, burying his face in her damp hair, wondering if, when he reached heaven, would there be such a delightful feeling as this. Just as quickly she held him away, her smile dazzling.

"Now, why did you call me in from my swim?"

"Because lunch is ready and has been for some time. I'm afraid the chef will have our heads. We've been chatting out here like magpies."

"I'll handle him. Henri and I are old friends now." She pulled back the towel and patted her bare stomach just above the white bikini. "Look what he's done to me. I've never had a tummy in my life. I . . . ."

Tess still spoke as she turned happily away, linking her arm through Dimitri's as she stepped toward the cabin. When she stopped, Dimitri imagined something on shore had caught her eye. Her lips were still parted as though to speak, but her eyes had gone blank, her face lost its golden sparkle. He felt her arm stiffen against him and then she was falling . . . falling . . . falling . . . so slowly. At first Dimitri thought she was slowing her pace for him. Then, as she crumpled, his arm finally clutched her around her waist, stopping her downward spiral just before she hit the deck. Gently, he laid her on the warm wood, brushing at her hair as he did so. Instantly, he raised his head, bellowing toward the front of the ship.

"Captain! Doctor! Come quickly!" Then, more gently, he leaned close to Tess, his hands hardly daring to touch her face. "Please, Tess, wake up. Please."

"You're awake," Dimitri said with a geniality that

335

belied his concern. "You had me worried, my dear. I've never had a woman faint just because I called her into lunch. If you didn't want to eat, all you had to do was say so."

Tess smiled weakly as she began to struggle to sit up. Dimitri pushed her gently back against the pillows.

"You have to rest now."

"I'll do no such thing. This is silly," she answered feebly. "I'm perfectly fine. Just too much sun." She smiled, but Dimitri's face had changed, drawing into itself. "I *am* fine, aren't I, Dimitri? It's nothing serious? Nothing from the crash, I mean?"

Dimitri stood up and walked the length of her stateroom. His silence unnerved her. Tess steeled herself for the worst, running over her injuries as best she could. There had been some internal bleeding, but the doctors in Paris had told her everything was fine. She would have a few aches and pains and her system would take some time to get back to normal. Perhaps that was it. Difficulty with the flow of blood. Dimitri turned back to her without reassuring her.

"Tess," he said quietly, "you never really told me what happened in Paris."

"Dimitri, I don't want to talk about it," Tess answered. "The crash . . . it was horrible. I don't want to relive that. Please. If it is something to do with my injuries, just tell me. Don't make me relive . . ."

"That isn't what I mean, Tess," he said. "I meant you never told me what happened after Royal was taken away. What happened in the hospital? How did you live when you were recuperating?"

Tess turned her head to the wall. "It isn't something I like to talk about."

"I think you should. I think it would do you good. It would answer some questions."

"What questions?" she mumbled. "I've already told the doctor everything I know about my injuries."

"What is wrong with you isn't an injury, Tess."

She turned back to him, this time managing to sit up. Her face was a mask of terror. The unknown was always frightening. Dimitri knew the reality would frighten her even more.

"You're pregnant, my dear," he said gently. "You're going to have a baby."

Tess's eyes widened in disbelief just before she buried her face in her hands and sat in silent anguish.

Dimitri stood when she came into the dining room. She had changed into a beautiful caftan of sky blue and gold. A present to her from him. His face was grim; Tess's was composed. He had left her alone, inviting her to come to him when she felt like talking. That had been almost four hours ago. She sat on one of the damask-covered chairs as Dimitri fetched her some tea and waited.

"I owe you a great deal, Dimitri. So much that I will never be able to repay you. The only thing I can offer is my honesty. I suppose I didn't tell you about Paris because I was ashamed. Now, I will carry the reminder of what happened there for everyone to see. I want you to know, though, I am not ashamed of this child or the child's father, only of the situation in which I, myself, created. I thought I had run from it. I should know better. My father always told me to be careful of what you do, for sooner or later everyone will know."

She raised her eyes to him as though to underscore her intent to take full responsibility for her actions. Dimitri nodded, silently urging her on.

"A man rescued me from the plane. Royal's seat had been torn away. There was a gaping hole next to me. I could see the runway, the scruff beyond the pavement. I remember the day was not a beautiful one. The colors were off. Not quite stormy, definitely not sunny. I felt the fire. I couldn't get my seatbelt off. The latch was so hot. My fingers weren't burned, but I was disoriented. People had panicked. They were climbing over me trying to get out. That's how I received my internal injuries. Then someone had undone the seatbelt and taken me from the plane. That was the last I remembered.

"When I woke up many days later a man was sitting beside me. I remember thinking two things, that he was a handsome doctor and that he wasn't Royal. It was days after that when I found out he wasn't a doctor. He was the man who had pulled me from the wreckage. He had stayed with me the entire time, watching over me, caring for me without a thought for his own life going on without him. As I found out later, he's a very powerful and successful man in the United States, yet he put everything on hold to care for me.

"He was the one who told me Royal had been taken away. He was the one who attempted to find out about Royal's injuries. To make a long story short, the doctors were willing to release me, but I had to go back to the hospital for therapy and observation. This man convinced me that I should go with him. He took me to his apartment, and I stayed there for three weeks. I gained my strength and a friend. He was more than kind. He was . . ."

Tess's eyes wandered about the room as though trying to capture an elusive memory. Only she knew the memory was not elusive, but crystal clear. Her hands covered her stomach beneath the beautiful caftan and she closed her eyes, though only for a moment.

"Dimitri, he was so kind and understanding. A quiet man with a sort of rough voice. There were so many things we discovered we shared a love for — art, attempting perfection — stupid things that mean nothing in real life. He knew about Royal, though I never told him in so many words what our relationship was initially.

"At times I felt something from this man. No, that's wrong. Many times I felt something growing between us, and I ignored it, I told myself it was gratitude for all he'd done for me. It was more than that and I did nothing to stop it. He felt like a kindred spirit. But kindred spirits are dangerous. They're so much like yourself that it's frightening.

"So, we lived that way, platonically, for three weeks, despite the closeness we felt. Then, one night, after we had been to the Louvre that day, he brought me home. I was very tired, yet I was restless. Something in me didn't want him to go away, but he did. He's a very good man. During the night, as I was lying awake, I think I willed him back to me. I was so lonely, so scared to be alone, scared for Royal, and also full of a certain kind of love for this man. I willed him back and he came and I held him. I thought that was all it would be, but it wasn't. We made love. I was so ashamed and confused that I left that night. I never said goodbye. I never said thank you. Now, I'm carrying his child."

Tess fell silent. Dimitri allowed her to relive her memories for a bit.

"I think you and this man had something quite special, Tess. Perhaps you loved him more than you know."

"Perhaps," she sighed, "in a special way, as you say. But it is Royal I loved first, and Royal I've betrayed."

"You mustn't think like that. People are people. Sometimes their hearts and bodies think for them before their minds do. If Royal loves you truly, he will understand."

"Do you really think so?"

"I do. The question is, do you think he loves you with that much depth and commitment?" Dimitri raised an eyebrow. Tess didn't answer right away.

"He did. Whether he does now, I don't know. Astra has confused me. What if the note was real? What if he really did write it, pushing me from his life?"

"Then it's over and you go on."

"And if he didn't write it? If he still loves me?"

"Then he loves you." Dimitri raised his hand skyward.

"You make it sound so simple."

"It is, Tess. What isn't simple is what you intend to do about this child."

"If Royal will have us, then we'll belong to him. If he won't, then I will love and care for this baby as long as I live."

"And the other man? The man of kindness with his understanding ways? What of him?"

Tess started. She had been so single-minded, desperate to reunite with Royal, that she hadn't thought of anything else.

"I don't know."

"You don't think he has the right to know you're carrying his child?"

"No," Tess said adamantly, then more softly. "Yes. Oh, Dimitri, I don't know. *I don't know!* I have no one but you to guide me."

"That's not true. You have yourself. You're not a silly girl, Tess Canfield. You're a woman with the responsibilities of a woman. First with the love you have given one man freely, then the love you harbor inside you for another and finally for the baby. You must guide yourself. Take time to do so. The doctor says the baby will be born at Christmas. Think about what you will do. Rest. Care for yourself and listen to your heart. You're the only one who can make that decision."

Dimitri started to leave the table but Tess put out her hand, stopping him.

"If it were your child, would you want to know?"

"If it were my child, dear," Dimitri answered, "I would move heaven and earth for it."

"You'll try to contact Royal?"

"Yes."

"I'll make my decision after I hear what he has to say."

Dimitri nodded and left the room. Tess sat for a very long while. Her tea became cold but her despair left her, warming her heart. No matter what happened she would have her child. A child by a man who had eyes the color of coal and a heart that burned steadily. She would love her baby; she just wasn't sure if she would love it alone. Tess closed her eyes and, for the first time in a very long while, she prayed.

* * *

Tess knocked gently at the door of Dimitri's office. She waited a moment, then heard him call to her to enter. He looked up, taking the glasses from his eyes as she came toward him.

"Tess, just what I needed. A visit from you to save me from the horrors of my work. Don't ever let anyone tell you that wealth is the great healer. There are more headaches with each dollar one acquires."

"I'll never believe anyone who says differently, and I doubt I'll ever have to worry about it myself. I have enough headaches to deal with as it is." She laughed.

"Are you not feeling well?"

"No, nothing like that. I feel surprisingly well. In fact, my body, it seems, was made for pregnancy. I'm eating enough for four, I'm lazy as a cat and my tummy has definitely decided now is the time to start announcing my condition to the world. See?"

She turned sideways. The gauzy white pants and top she wore were filmy enough that Dimitri could just see the outline of her skin. She was so beautiful. Inside and out. God, what a child she was going to bear! He smiled.

"Do you feel it yet?"

"Yes. Last night for the first time. A little fluttering. A marvelous feeling."

"And have you decided?"

"That's what I wanted to speak to you about. May I?"

Dimitri nodded. Tess drew a chair alongside his, and reached for his hands. She studied them while she collected her thoughts.

"You have wonderful hands. I would like to paint them sometime. I would like to hold a brush again."

342

"You should have told me . . ."

"No. That's not what I meant. I couldn't paint now. Not when there are so many other things to think of. And that's exactly what I have been doing: thinking, praying, trying to plan."

"And what has God told you to do?" Dimitri asked gently.

"Unfortunately," she answered wryly, "I don't think we're on speaking terms. He's leaving me on my own on this one."

"As well it should be," Dimitri assuaged her. "After all, he made your heart, so what it tells you is the right thing."

"You're a wise man," Tess answered with a gentle smile.

"I try. So?"

"So, I know a few things now. Or I think I do." Tess sat back in her chair, laying her arms gracefully over the arms. "I know that I cannot go back to Royal like this. I would like to have the baby and then tell him about it. I think it would be too difficult now. And, there is the very real problem of his continued silence. He hasn't answered your wires. He hasn't answered your calls."

"But I told you. He continues to convalesce away from home. He's taken a leave from his office and another attorney handles my business."

"Still, that doesn't sound like Royal. He thought the world of you. He should have at least answered your calls."

"If he heard about them," Dimitri pointed out.

"Yes." Tess agreed. "Therefore, I'm assuming Astra has not allowed him to take your messages for some reason. A rather dangerous ploy considering her love

343

of power. Whatever is happening there it's impossible for us to know. By the time the baby is born either Royal will be recovered and will see me or, if the excuse continues to be his injuries, I will know that he wants nothing more to do with me."

"In the meantime?"

"I thought of staying here, but I won't. You've been very kind. I'll go see the baby's father. I think you're right. He should know. If he doesn't want anything to do with us that's fine."

"You know that won't be the case, don't you?" Dimitri asked.

Tess nodded. "Yes, I know. I believe he'll try to keep me with him."

"Will you stay?"

"Until the baby is born. I owe him that much and more. After that I'll have to speak with Royal. I'll make it very clear that I still love Royal very much. If this man accepts that, then I shall be more than happy to have him with me when this baby is born. But the baby will be mine to care for when I go back to Royal."

"I see."

Dimitri tented his fingers and tapped them against his lips. He knew she would do the right thing. There was only one problem. Tess's mind sometimes overruled a heart that knew better. Though Dimitri did not know this man, the father of her baby, he felt something about him. He felt there was a strength in him that Royal did not possess. It had been in the way Tess spoke about him. Dimitri felt in his gut that this man meant more to her than she would admit.

"Tess, if I may say one thing. As you go through the next months of your life don't forget to open both your mind and your heart to whatever may happen. Enjoy this time, share it with this man. Do not put him away from you because of a dream you have. Do not confuse love with loyalty."

"I may feel gratitude toward him, Dimitri, but I don't feel loyal to him. I'll make sure he understands that."

"I wasn't considering the situation in quite that way, my dear. I don't want you to confuse your feelings for Royal. I want you to ask yourself if it is loyalty you feel toward him."

Tess couldn't answer. The thought had never occurred to her and now that the seed was planted she refused to let it grow. Noel Montgomery deserved to know he was the father of her baby. She admired him, respected him. But she loved Royal. Loyalty had nothing to do with her feelings.

"Thank you for your advice, dear friend. I'll ask you only a few more favors. Could you get me back to Los Angeles? And could you be there for me in case this man doesn't want us?"

"I'm at your service, Tess. And, I shall expect to be the first to hold this love child after its mother and father can bear to let it out of their arms."

"It is a love child, Dimitri. A child who will be loved by both its parents, I'm sure, even if those parents cannot love each other in the way a man and woman should."

Dimitri let her have the last word. He let her leave the room and the yacht with her determination to be with Royal intact. And when the time came for her to board the plane he held her close, giving her his strength, for he knew what fears she had—both of the plane and of the place she was going to. Tess kissed his hand and disappeared into the gleaming silver jet. Dimitri watched her go until the plane was no more than a speck in the sky. Then he returned to the yacht, which now felt like an island. He was so alone.

August in Los Angeles was hot and dry. Tess felt heavy and fearful. Without Dimitri there to offer his quiet support she found it almost impossible to do what she had come to do. Thousands of questions flew through her mind, not the least of which was what Noel would do when he found her on his doorstep. Had she dreamed him? Had she given him qualities he didn't possess? Would he discard her? Call her a liar? Accuse her of using his kindness for her own gain?

On and on she thought of what may happen, until one morning a week after she had reached Los Angeles she rose without thinking. If she did she knew she would lose her nerve. Dressing carefully in one of the few things that allowed for her quickly expanding stomach, Tess took a bus to downtown Los Angeles and the *High Life* building.

Now her courage was waning. There were so many people milling about. She had wanted so much to have a quiet meeting, tell him calmly about the baby, but she hadn't been able to locate his telephone number at home or his home address.

"Can I help you, miss?"

Startled, Tess faced the receptionist.

"Yes. I'd like to see Mister Noel Montgomery, please." Tess's voice shook as she said his name.

"Do you have an appointment?"

"No, I'm sorry, I don't. But please, could you tell

him that Tess Canfield is here. I think he'll see me."

"I'll try. Just a moment."

The woman pushed a few buttons and waited.

"Shirley, it's Rita. I have a woman here by the name of Tess Canfield asking to see Mister Montgomery. Could you let him . . ." The receptionist stopped talking. Tess felt the girl's eyes flick over her. ". . . um — hmm. Um-hmm. Sure. Okay."

"Is he in?" Tess asked the moment the receptionist replaced the receiver.

"Yes, he is. His secretary wondered if you'd be kind enough to . . ."

She never finished her sentence. Instead, the doors behind her burst open. Noel Montgomery held them back as he stood framed by them. His face was a montage of relief and wonder and happiness. Tess began to smile, but before she could say a word he had her in his arms, crushing her to him as though he would never let her go.

Part Five
Coming Together

Twenty-three

"I'm out for the rest of the day, Rita," Noel told the receptionist without taking his eyes off Tess. "If anyone needs me tell them I've died and gone to heaven."

Tess blushed. Over Noel's shoulder she could see Rita was floored by the great Noel Montgomery's enthusiasm for his visitor. Obviously, the rumor mill would be working overtime that day. Tess smiled slightly and averted her eyes.

Nothing had changed. His voice was still deep with that stony undertone. His eyes were still black, sparkling with life. Even here, in the heart of his empire that one time seemed a lifeless thing to Tess, Noel was not the great leader—he was simply Noel.

"But Mister Montgomery . . ." Rita sputtered.

"No buts, Rita. Call Shirley this instant."

With that Noel whisked Tess out of the lobby toward a bank of elevators. There he twirled her against the wall gently, imprisoning her as he lay his hands against the wallpaper on either side of her head, leaning close to her while they waited.

"Do you know," he whispered, chastising her gently, "how many people I've had looking for you?"

"You shouldn't have," she answered, staring into the

351

silk of his suit, unable to look into his intense black eyes.

Every memory flooded back to her, stinging her senses. She was looking at his arm and suddenly remembered how good it felt wound around her naked waist. She turned to look into his eyes and remembered how the shadows of a Paris night caressed him. She closed her eyes and breathed in to steady her beating heart, finding instead that she remembered the aftershave he wore as though it was an integral part of her senses.

"Of course I should have. How could you have done that? Left me that way? I never meant to frighten you or hurt you . . ."

A small bell sounded above them. Tess looked up. Noel looked at her.

"Saved by the bell," she whispered.

"Only just," he answered, reluctantly letting her go only to take her arm as he guided her into the mirrored metal box.

They rode down in silence. Everywhere Tess looked she saw the two of them reflected. Her heart broke each time she dared meet his eyes in the mirror. What she saw there was too devastating for words. Noel was thrilled to see her. The baby would make no difference to him unless it was to heighten his excitement.

To her dismay, Tess realized how much he loved her. She lowered her head, trying desperately to listen to her heart as Dimitri had counseled, but she couldn't. Noel's emotions were running too high, surrounding her until she felt she could hardly breathe.

When the door opened Tess stepped gratefully into the cool underground garage and breathed deeply. Alone now, Noel pulled her to him again, his lips searching and finding hers. He kissed her as though she was a long, cool drink of water and he a very thirsty man.

"Tess, I needed to find you so badly . . ."

"There's so much we have to talk about . . ." she insisted, hands against his chest, though she didn't push him away.

"I know there is . . ."

"No, you don't . . ."

"But I do. Your coming back proves what I've known all along. You need . . ."

"Noel," she insisted. Now she did push him away, averting her gaze from the pain that flashed over his face. "You don't know what we have to talk about. You don't know what brought me back."

"Then tell me, Tess. Tell me what it is."

Looking over her shoulder at the man she so respected, Tess said, "I'm pregnant with your child."

"Tess," he breathed.

She watched him closely, waiting to see the flicker of disgust, the sign that would tell her he honestly didn't feel a deep commitment to her. She was disappointed. His entire face softened into a gentle look of love. His eyes wandered to her body. Now that he took the time to really look at her, Noel was aware of her condition. He smiled, coming toward her and gathered her hands into his. Raising those hands, he kissed her fingertips.

"We do have a lot to talk about, don't we? I should have known. Flowing garments weren't your style in Paris. I thought I had a better eye for women than that. Just shows you, you can teach an old dog new tricks, and this particular old dog intends to learn quite a few."

"Is there someplace quiet we can talk?"

"Let's go home."

"*Your* home, Noel. It's your home. Please don't forget that," Tess pleaded.

"I'll try not to. It will be difficult. The car's just over there." Noel nodded to the limousine. Tess made a move but he pulled her back. "Are you all right?"

"Yes. Both of us are just fine," she answered, smiling happily for the first time since she'd seen him.

"Then I will be, too. I promise. Everything will be fine. Come."

Noel walked her to the car, settling her gently in the back. He was around the other side in an instant, giving the driver his order before sealing them into the back as a glass partition rose automatically.

Tess showed that she was neither embarrassed nor overly impressed by his wealth. Noel shook his head, realizing she had not been a dream. As much as he needed to, Noel didn't touch her on the long ride home. Nor did he press for the answers he wanted. In good time she would tell him everything, so Noel settled for the small talk she insisted on making, settled for a sidelong glance, a nervous laugh. They had been apart too long and known each other too little. He would rectify that problem in the months to come.

Soon the car was in the drive; Noel and Tess were comfortable in the blue and gray living room. A maid brought iced tea, but Tess refused it. She felt more comfortable walking the room than sitting across from Noel. He watched her every move, seeing now how her slender body was fuller, more rounded, admiring it as she moved. Noel watched her marvel at his art collection, delighting in each for the sake of the work, not the fact that he owned them.

He had forgotten how exquisitely she moved. Not forgotten really, but he had been unable to conjure up the exact way she tilted her head when thinking; the manner in which she used her hands. Tess felt him watching her so intently she was forced to begin the journey that would end for them at Christmas.

"Noel," Tess began, her back to the huge white marble fireplace, "I want you to know right now that I didn't come here expecting anything of you. I came because I felt it was your right to know that I'm carrying your baby. I won't presume on your nature or your wealth. When the baby comes you're free to be part of his or her life. I could think of nothing more wonderful. But I still have" — she paused looking for the right word — "commitments that make it impossible for me to consider being a part of your life. The baby, yes, but me, no."

She stopped speaking, realizing how cold her speech sounded and, indeed, how presumptuous. Noel hadn't said anything about wanting a relationship with her, really. He'd had people look for her, he seemed thrilled to see her. She prayed that he only wanted to tie up the loose ends she had left him with and nothing more. But that wasn't to be.

"Tess, please, talk to me," Noel pleaded quietly, leaning forward as he offered his hand.

"I can't touch you."

"Am I so repulsive? Are you so angry with me because you're pregnant?"

"No!" she protested, the very thought that she might be angry with him paining her. "Oh, Noel, never think that. It's just that you confuse me. I've thought about you so much. When I would see a painting we had discussed; when I saw a street fresh from the rain; when my legs ached and I remembered how you massaged them to make them feel better. You were with me so often."

"But there wasn't enough of me in your heart to make you want to keep me with you," he said, unable to keep the sadness from his voice. "Is that it? Is that why you ran away?"

"I ran away because I realized what I had done was wrong. Not loving you the way I did, not making love, I should say. But I did that for the wrong reasons. I took you to my bed because of your kindness, because of our friendship, because I was lonely and aching and scared. . . ."

". . . And I helped you through the night. There isn't anything wrong with that, Tess. Nothing. Many relationships are built on much less than the things you describe. They aren't emotions and reasons to be ashamed of, but rather to be built on. I think we shared the indefinable quality of love. No"—he waved his hand through the air—"I know we did. Can't you see that?"

Noel came toward her. Something in her eyes warned him away. She was like a kitten unsure of its new playmate. Her blue eyes clouded, pleaded. He stopped where he was, then turned away from her, putting his hands deep into his pockets as he thought.

"Tess," he said slowly, "I realized long before you left that my feelings for you were not frivolous by any stretch of the imagination. I felt something for you I've never felt for any woman in my entire life." He stopped, twirled toward her and planted his feet as though he had dug in for the duration. "I love you.

"How awful those words sound when you're afraid to say them with the emotion they deserve. I love you because of all the things you told me. I felt you were a kindred spirit. Do you know how often one of us would begin speaking and the other would finish a sentence when we were together? Did you realize that when we walked instinctively we would turn the same way or stop at the same moment?

356

"Well, I didn't realize it then, either, but after you left I thought of all those things in such detail, and I felt lessened when you weren't by my side any longer.

"It wasn't just that our interests were the same, that our temperaments were so closely attuned, but that we thought alike in so many ways. And part of the allure of us as a couple is that we don't think alike in so many ways. You aspire to the stars with your art; I'm satisfied with doing the best job one can do in the commercial field. I adore the trappings of wealth — I don't live for them, but I like them — yet you are satisfied with the simplest of things.

"Tess." His voice was deepening and growing with emotion; his eyes swam with tears of desire. "We're going to create a child who will have each of our best qualities and some of our worst. We have a chance here not only to build a beautiful life together, but to mold an equally beautiful and promising life for this baby. Together we can do that. Apart we can only create confusion for a child. I know there is love for me in you. I see it in your eyes; I felt it in your touch that one time we were together. I still see it in you."

He moved closer until he could reach out and take her hand. He raised it up, pulling her ever so tenderly toward him. Tess hesitated. She stepped forward, wanting to go to him. He smiled.

"Marry me, Tess Canfield. Marry me tomorrow."

Tess snatched her hand away. She had heard those words from another man. A man who wasn't free, but one who loved her as deeply as Noel Montgomery did. Still she believed that. Royal was not dead — he was only thwarted in his desire to be with her by the accident and his wife. He couldn't reach her.

"I love Royal. I can't . . ."

"Royal!" Noel bellowed, throwing himself back

357

away from her, one hand running through his raven hair in frustration. "I don't want to hear about him. I haven't asked. I assumed since you're here, since I couldn't find you anywhere I looked, that you were not with him. He's been in a hospital in Pasadena. He's now recuperating somewhere else. I have no idea where. I don't really care. But if he's been in those places and his wife has been by his side, then you haven't been."

"Noel, you know where he is?" Tess had run to him without thinking, grabbing his arm as she asked her question. "Where? Where's Royal? Is he all right? How do you know his wife was with him? Please, please, Noel."

Tess begged him, but his back remained to her. Noel Montgomery was shot through with a pain so intense he thought he couldn't stand to look at her face an instant longer. When finally he did turn, he saw the thing that he most wished not to see—hope.

"Yes, I know where he is," Noel answered quietly, defeated only for the moment. "Do you want to go to him?"

Tess stepped back. So simple. Noel was making it all so simple. How could he when Dimitri could not? She shook her head and walked away.

"No, not until we've settled things. Not until the baby is born. I think that is the most important consideration now. If you still believe it is, then we should make some plans."

"I see," Noel said sarcastically. "Yes, I can see how awkward it would be for you right now."

"Noel." Tess's voice reprimanded him. "You know it's not like that. I care so much for you. I owe you so much. This baby should know what a wonderful man his father is. Please, let's decide what to do, but let's do as friends. Deep friends who have no anger between them. Let's bring him into this world with all the hope you just spoke of. So much can happen in the next few months. Let's experience it together."

Noel began to protest, catching himself before he spoke. He knew as long as he lived he could never deny his woman anything. Hadn't he been denied himself, once before, of the joy of watching a child grow up? He thought instantly of Davina and how sorry her life was. He would not make the same mistake twice. Noel smiled, raising his head high. She was right. In the next few months so much could happen. He could even make Tess forget Royal Cudahy. He was sure of it. Carefully, he controlled his anger and frustration.

"I can't think of anything I'd like more than to have the next few months with you, and be there when our baby is born. We'll talk of nothing else in that time. I promise. And, when you're able, when you're ready, I'll get you to Royal. Just promise me one thing. Don't make any decisions about your life until then. Wait and talk to him. Don't count on what you feel now."

"I promise," Tess said quietly.

"Wonderful." He came toward her and placed his hands on her shoulders. "You'll stay here, won't you? I don't want to miss a minute of this."

"Only if you let me pull my weight. Only if you'll allow me to work for my keep."

"I think that can be arranged."

Noel bent to kiss her. This time Tess offered her lips willingly, sure that she would feel the difference in her now that things were settled, positive that she wouldn't feel the electricity that coursed through her the moment he came through those office doors and swept her into his arms. How wrong she had been. Her desire tugged at her until she thought nothing would hold it at bay.

"Well, I didn't know you were entertaining."

Noel whirled toward the door. Tess looked past him to the dark-haired woman standing in the doorway. The look on her face chilled Tess to the core. Slowly, the woman came into the room as though she were stalking prey. Her jacket was slung over one shoulder and her face was pinched in an expression that Tess supposed was a smile.

"Davina, I'm glad you're here," Noel said happily, winding his arm protectively about Tess.

"I'll bet you are, Noel." She gave him an ugly wink. He ignored it and brought Tess forward.

"Davina, this is Tess Canfield. Tess, this is my daughter, Davina."

"How do you do," Tess said.

"Fine, thanks." Davina ignored her. "I'm going out tonight, but I wanted you to know that we put the first half of the September issue to bed."

"That's fine. I'm glad to hear it. Tess, would you mind if I had my man Benton show you upstairs? I'd like to talk to Davina alone."

"Of course. Actually, I need to collect some things. Would it be all right if I used the car?"

"Certainly. John's still in the drive."

They moved toward the door, and as they came abreast of Davina, she turned her head.

"Staying awhile, are we?"

Tess glanced at Noel; his face was white with fury so instantaneous it frightened her. Realizing Tess was watching, Noel answered his daughter quietly.

"Tess is going to be our houseguest for a long while. I expect you to treat her with the respect she deserves."

"I see," Davina drawled before going to the bar. She

poured a drink as though feeding a log to the fire. She was lounging on the couch when Noel returned.

"Don't you ever speak to her like that again," he growled. "There are going to be some changes around here and if you don't like them you can make your own living arrangements."

Blood drained from Davina's face. This was serious. How stupid she had been not to pick up on it. Suddenly she remembered the conversation she had overheard. This must be the woman Noel had been looking for way back when. Davina castigated herself. She was slipping badly and this was only the beginning of the war.

Bonnie continued filing her nails placidly while Davina moved around the living room like a caged animal. If she listened closely, Bonnie was almost sure she could hear Davina snarl.

"Can you believe it? The bitch is pregnant after a one-night stand, and Noel welcomes her with open arms. I mean, he's got her up on the second floor in the best bedroom like she was a queen or something. Where was he when my mother was pregnant? Where was his money then, huh?"

"I think you said he was in Vietnam. Kind of hard for him to coddle your mother when he was thousands of miles away in some jungle," Bonnie drawled."

"So, you're on his side, is that it? And I thought you were my friend. You're more of a slut than she is if that's the way you feel about things," Davina snapped.

"Now wait just a minute," Bonnie said, sitting up so fast her breasts jiggled under her leotard. "I resent that. Nobody calls me names and gets away with it."

Davina backed off, sorry she'd let her mouth run on

like that. Bonnie was the first true friend she'd ever had. She let her come to her place like it was the most normal thing in the world. She drank with her, danced with her, schemed with her. Bonnie was okay, and if Davina didn't have her she wouldn't have anyone — except Tony. That thought made her shiver. A man was never as good as a woman.

"I'm sorry, Bonnie. I just . . . I'm upset. How would you feel? This blond bimbo comes out of nowhere and says she's pregnant so the wonderful Noel Montgomery falls all over himself. What's he owe her that he doesn't owe me? I'm first in line. I've been waiting a long time to get what's coming to me and he's going to hand it to her on a silver platter."

Bonnie settled back, attacking her nails with a new fervor. Davina was whining and nobody could whine better than Davina. Bonnie settled in for the long haul.

"Life's hard all around, Davina. Sometimes you just got to cut your losses, know what I mean?" Bonnie gave her thumb nail an extra flourish, then reached for the bottle of undercoat. The smell of it permeated the room. Davina looked on in disgust. That stuff made Bonnie's living room smell like a hospital. Like all those rooms her mother would be in when she got too violent to be kept at home.

"Do you have to do that?" Davina demanded.

"Yes," Bonnie answered with such pained patience even Davina got the message.

"So what am I going to do?" Davina crumpled onto the couch, her hands hanging between her legs. She looked far from devastated, though. There was a tautness in her body, like a spring pulling too tight. Davina was ready to snap.

"I don't know. Want to wash your hair or something?"

"I mean what am I going to do about Tess Can-field?" Davina shrieked.

With the utmost composure Bonnie set aside the tools of her trade and motioned Davina over to the low black couch on which she sat. Davina came and sat heavily, supporting her elbows on her knees and her chin on the palms of her hand.

"Look, I know you've got a problem, and I'm going to help you solve it. I've been around the block a few times and, if there's one thing I know, it's all the ways there are to skin a cat. Now, the trick is to just go after what you want. But before you do that, you've got to decide what you want."

"Everything," Davina muttered, closing her eyes against the headache that was sneaking up on her.

"That's not the way to do it. You have to be very specific."

"Okay, I want that woman out of my father's house and out of his life."

"Now you have to be realistic," Bonnie warned. "In the event that you can't get this person out of your life what are you prepared to do?"

"I guess I'd have to leave. I told Noel that that's what I'd do and he said fine, so I guess if I back down I'll look like an idiot."

"Is that what you want to do?"

"It'd be better than living under the same roof with them. You should have been him. He was all over her."

"There, you've solved it. Move."

"With what?"

"Jesus, Davina, you're working. You've got a salary."

"Yeah, but it's not enough," Davina complained.

"Then get more," Bonnie said offhandedly. "Your dad owns the company. Have him give you a raise. And

363

if you can't get it from him, think about where else you could get money.

"Maybe you could go to a competitor and they'd pay you a whole bunch of money for all the inside secrets, or talk to the tabloids and sell the story of your father and this blonde . . ."

Bonnie disappeared into the kitchen, her voice rising so it carried to the living room.

". . . But whatever you do, *don't* burn any bridges. Remember, you promised that you'd get me in the running for the *High Life* Woman." Bonnie's heels clicked on the kitchen floor as she came back to the living room. "Wasn't that supposed to be set up by now . . . ?"

Bonnie stopped in her tracks. She was talking to an empty living room. Damn it all to hell. Davina was just the weirdest bird Bonnie had ever run into. She shrugged and went back to the refrigerator.

It didn't really matter what Davina did. If it appeared that Davina couldn't get her a spot in *High Life* Bonnie would drop her in a minute. She'd give her another month or so, then take matters into her own hands.

Grabbing a piece of pizza, she ate it cold. Sitting on the sofa she picked up the papers the ad agency had given her listing what time the FortyFine spots were going to air. Happily, she realized she could spend the next hour and a half with her remote control and do nothing but watch herself. She hoped Davina had half that much fun whatever she had gone off to do.

Tony was doing the usual — Atlas exercises in the nude — when Davina came knocking on the door. He peeked through the spy hole, saw who it was, then flung the door open, exposing himself to her in all his glory.

"Davina, baby," he cried in delight.

She pushed past him, using her elbow to move him out of the way instead of her hands. "Get dressed, Tony."

"Hey, you can't come bargin' in here like that. This is my place, remember?"

"How could I forget? Get dressed anyway."

"Okay, what you got planned?" he asked on his way to the bedroom.

"A little business talk," Davina answered.

"Sounds serious," Tony said as he ambled into the bedroom.

He returned dressed in a pair of jeans and a polo shirt.

"There a problem with the job, Davina? We've been going along pretty good here for a month or two and you should be happy."

"Yeah, the job looks real good, Tony. Nothing wrong with the printing. But I've been thinking. You know I just handed you the account of a lifetime. You didn't have to work for it at all. You came in, gave me your spiel, and walked out with the order. Now, I call that a pretty easy take, don't you?"

"Yeah," Tony said warily, not liking the way her voice sounded.

"I thought you'd agree. And I suppose you also know that kickbacks aren't anything new in a business like this. Everybody takes them. Art directors take them from photographers, production managers take them from typesetters. You know how it goes."

"I've heard about it," Tony acknowledged. He was starting to sweat. He didn't like it.

"Then you won't be surprised when I tell you that

365

now's the time to pay the piper. I want you to up your bill by twenty grand every month. I'll put the billing through, and when your accounting department gets the check I want you to send that twenty right back to me the next day. I don't want to argue about it. Twenty grand's a drop in the bucket, to your company and mine. In fact," she mused, contemplating the situation, "we'll still be under the old budget if I have you up it by thirty, so let's make it thirty. Now, do you want to go to bed?"

Tony shook his head furiously. Bed! Jesus, that was the last thing he wanted to do. He was feeling himself shrivel away with every minute that passed. He'd have to talk to his uncle, but he didn't tell Davina that. What in the heck would they do to her? Certainly not pay her. This was a shakedown, pure and simple.

"No? Okay. I have things to do anyway. I'll talk to you in a few weeks. The billing should go through by the twentieth at the latest. I'll expect you to deliver the check no later than the twenty-fifth. Bye, Tony. Call me when you want to go dancing."

Davina left Tony sitting with his mouth open.

The house was quiet when Davina got home. Everyone was asleep and she felt so much better. Thank God for Bonnie. Her advice had been absolutely on target. Tony couldn't have been more amenable. Davina was actually grinning as she went up the stairs.

Over the next six months, according to her calculations, she would take back one hundred and eighty thousand dollars, plus her salary. It didn't matter what her father's "guest" did now. Davina would be able to take care of herself if she was squeezed out of the picture by the new baby, maybe a new wife. She'd keep it up as long as possible. If she was found out she'd take off. If she wasn't, she'd keep going. Either way, she was going to be rich and she had Bonnie to thank for pointing her in the right direction. Soon she'd return the favor. When she had a minute and she could talk to Noel without wanting to scratch his eyes out, she'd mention Bonnie for the spot as *High Life* Woman.

Twenty-four

"Where's Tess this morning?"

Davina snapped her napkin open and laid it over her lap, then reached for the coffeepot. Noel watched her, a playful grin on his face. Davina was a new woman and he adored the change in her.

Finally his daughter was exhibiting signs of growing up. Gone were the attacks on his character, the attempts to wheedle her way into every decision made at the magazine, the seesawing between subservience and anger. There had been fewer complaints at work and less confrontation at home. Not that he really saw her that often; her nightlife continued to be active though Noel had little idea where she went or with whom.

"Sleeping late, I imagine. I suppose when women get to the last trimester they need more of it."

"I suppose," Davina answered, burying her nose in her coffee cup.

A sharp retort had been on the tip of her tongue; the desire to wound Noel with reminders of his failure as a father. There would come a time when she would be gloating about her victory over, not only Noel, but that pregnant idiot he had taken in. She would simply bide her time and play the game. Wouldn't they be surprised when she finally walked with enough money to start her own magazine? Her little arrangement with Tony was going so well Davina was thinking of upping the ante that night. After all, thirty thousand wasn't much. Three months ago it seemed like a fortune, now it appeared to be a drop in the bucket since she'd devised her master plan to go head to head with her father.

Davina set the cup down while simultaneously reaching for a piece of toast. Whoever said you could catch more flies with honey was absolutely correct. She had Noel right where she wanted him. He truly believed she had changed, and he was trusting her with more responsibility every day. Grudgingly, she had to admit that Tess Canfield's appearance on the scene had helped the act immensely. Noel was so abhorrently smitten with the woman his defenses were down. Funny thing, though, they still had separate rooms. Davina was dying to know why. That little arrangement gave Davina hope that both Tess and the baby would disappear soon after the stork arrived.

"Noel," Davina said cautiously, "I was thinking about the *High Life* Woman."

"Yes?" Noel folded his paper, his full attention on his daughter.

"Well, I know that we're starting to make the transition to an older type . . ."

"And you still don't agree?"

"Whether I agree or not is of no consequence, is it?" She couldn't keep the acid tone from her voice. Either Noel didn't notice or he ignored it.

"Of course it's of consequence," Noel answered patiently. "What *is* wrong is the way you disagree. But that little display in the planning meeting is water under the bridge. What were you thinking about the *High Life* Woman?"

Barely controlling herself, Davina forced a look of utter concern and professional musing.

"It's the speed with which we're doing it. I think our readers will be shocked if they're suddenly confronted with women over forty in the next six issues. Don't you think it might be better to ease them into the change by interspersing a more traditional *High Life* Woman in a few of the issues. Say the Christmas issue?"

Noel picked up his orange juice. Davina held her breath, waiting for his answer. Now she could honestly tell Bonnie she had given it her best shot and broached the subject of making her the new *High Life* Woman. Bonnie had gotten so bitchy about the whole thing that it would be a relief to have her off her back. And, if Noel agreed, it would be another chink in his armor. Davina would have gained just that much more control.

"It's something to consider," he said. "We may have been moving a little quickly. Unfortunately, all the layouts are done for the next six issues. We've shot and it would take too long to do another casting. It takes time to find exactly the right woman. No, Davina," he decided, "I don't think there's time, but I do believe you're headed in the right direction. We're going to be casting for the next year in a month. Maybe then we'll do a celebration issue of a full range of women, all ages and occupations."

"What if I could deliver the perfect woman? What if I told you she was waiting in the wings, and that I already talked to the art department, and they assured me they could shoot within a week?" Davina leaned over the table, encouraged by his agreement of the concept. "I could easily make the necessary adjustments in production if I worked closely with the art department and chose colors that wouldn't demand fancy press work. What then?"

"You really believe in this, don't you?" Noel laughed.

"Yes," Davina said, serious now that she could see a triumphant end to this discussion. She could hardly contain her excitement. If she managed to secure his blessing, she would have full control over the Christmas issue. She would be calling the shots. It would be a big step in her master plan.

"Who is she?"

"She's well known. An actress," Davina answered, not wanting to tip her hand. "She'd be perfect."

"Don't I get a name?"

"No, I'd like it to be a surprise."

"Sorry," Noel said, shaking his head. "That's where I draw the line. I've always had the final word on casting for that spread. Now tell me who she is, or this discussion is over."

"I'll go one better. I'll bring her in. You'll see her in the flesh. You'll see that she's perfect. She's beautiful. I can already see her in the layout. Cool greens behind her . . ."

"Davina, beauty isn't the only prerequisite. We're also looking for a woman of taste and accomplishment. Still want to surprise me?"

"Yes. How about tomorrow?"

"How about today?"

"You mean it?"

"I wouldn't say it if I didn't. Call Shirley, she'll set up a time. Now, I think you'd better be off. Don't you have a thousand galleys to check today?"

"Sure, Noel. I'm out of here. I'll call this woman and have her in your office any time Shirley says. You won't be sorry."

Davina stood to leave just as Tess came into the dining room.

"Good morning," she said brightly.

Davina turned and tried to smile. It was getting more difficult as the days went on and Tess's pregnancy became so evident. Today she was dressed in a simple outfit, a navy blue jersey that fell to her knees, outlining the beautiful swell of her stomach and white pants that clung to her shapely legs.

Davina tossed her napkin on the table, eyeing Tess's exquisite simplicity.

"Morning," Davina said. "How are you feeling?"

"Wonderful, thanks, Davina," Tess answered cautiously. Tess was still not convinced Davina's change of heart was sincere.

Noel sat in his chair, quietly watching the exchange. His daughter and Tess were the same age, yet eons apart. Tess, with her hair pulled sleekly back from her face, looked as composed as a woman who had lived three lifetimes. Her voice was lovely and low without the frantic cadences Davina was given to. Tess was bursting with emotion; Davina was gripped by hers. How could they be so different? Then he realized Tess was giving him her glorious morning smile. But Davina wasn't finished with her morning routine.

"I thought you might have been sick. It's so late. You must have slept like a log," Davina drawled. There were certain times she drew the line on her new personality.

"I did sleep well . . ."

"That's good. I thought you'd been looking a little green lately. You know, a little puffy around the face."

Tess's eyebrows rose just slightly. Though there had been a marked change in Davina's attitude toward her in the last few months, Tess knew the storm lay just under the surface of Davina's attempted charm. She could feel it every time she walked into a room — her resentment was boiling just under the surface.

Tess shrugged. "I guess that happens."

"Guess it does. Well, I'm late. Must be nice to sit around all day, Tess. Some of us have to work. Bye."

Davina was gone, the door slamming behind her. Noel and Tess looked at one another. Both laughed at the same time. Tess slid, as best she could, onto one of the chairs halfway down the long table. She couldn't bring herself to sit next to Noel. Every day that passed he became more and more important to her. He never asked a thing of her other than that she be with him and healthy and happy. How odd that a man should be so complicated in some ways and so simplistic in others? Royal would never have been happy with a relationship like this. Giving things to her was as much a part of him as giving his time and attention.

"I think it's chemistry, Noel. Davina and I simply have elements that are explosive. I feel so badly for her. I suppose I would have felt the same way if my father brought a pregnant woman into the house and put her in the guest room."

"There's a difference. Your father would never have done anything like this with your mother around. Sounds to me as though she was pretty formidable."

"You've got that right. Times change, I guess, but certain things never do. A daughter will always think it's her duty to protect her father. I can't blame Davina."

"You know, I can't, either, lately. She does have a right to her anger. After all, as far as she and I are concerned she's only a few years old. I wasn't there in the beginning. I think she's got to resent this baby very much because she knows it will have certain things she never will get."

"Hopefully those things are love and attention."

"You have any doubt?"

"No." She smiled. "I don't. If there's one thing I'm sure of, this baby is not going to lack those things from either of us."

"Good. I'm happy to hear that you're sure of one thing at. least. I just wish you were sure of another."

"What might that be?" Tess laughed.

"Me," Noel answered seriously. "And my love for you. Tess, I've been so patient. I haven't said a word about your feelings. I haven't asked, and you haven't given me any verbal indication that they've changed. But I see it in you, Tess. I see your feelings for me growing."

"Of course they are, Noel," Tess interjected. "How can they not be growing? You've given me so much and I'll always love you for it. You've honored the bargain we've made. My feelings for you will never end because I'll see the result of our affection for each other every day of my life in this child. But the other hasn't changed, either. Royal is out there. He's been sick, but I know he's getting better.

"You can't expect me to throw him away and everything we meant to each other. That's what love is all about. Constancy. Caring, no matter how close or far away people are. If Astra understood that, then Royal wouldn't have needed my love. But that's the difference between that woman and myself. The difference is that I understand this commitment."

"Are you sure he does?" Noel countered.

"I'm sure he loved me, therefore I have to assume his commitment is the same."

"There are many different forms of love," Noel suggested.

"Yes. So I've heard." Tess averted her eyes. He was so handsome in the mornings, fresh from his bed, rested and ready to tackle the world. She felt a twinge of regret that she hadn't allowed herself the pleasure of seeing him wake that morning in Paris. It would have been nice, just once.

"Well, this is getting us nowhere, but you can't blame me for trying," Noel said jovially, though he was beginning to feel that his hopes for gaining her love were foundering. He pushed his chair back and in a great show of good feelings grinned as he came toward her. "So, since I can't convince you that you and I are meant to be together, maybe I can convince our little friend here to put in his two cents."

Noel knelt by Tess's chair and lay his hand on her stomach. She laughed, covering his hand with hers.

"Listen in there, if you think your mother ought to marry me and forget everything else that ever happened in her life, kick once. If you want to go away after you're born, kick twice."

Noel waited. Suddenly Tess's stomach began to move under his hand, rolling gently as he felt the child moving inside her. His breath caught. He had never touched her, not once since she had made her feelings clear. Now, in a moment of levity and togetherness he had unthinkingly touched the core of his love for her. They were meant to be three. In her was a living being made by them, longing to be held by them, not on alternate weekends, but every day of its life.

Noel's eyes flickered to Tess. Her face was a vision of calm and her eyes shone with love she had not yet acknowledged. Over his hand he felt her fingers instinctively press against his. She smiled so gently the entire world seemed to calm itself.

She whispered, "I think that means he's hungry. You'll have to wait for your kicks another time."

Noel opened his mouth to speak, then looked back at Tess's stomach. The baby was quiet now, but Noel was still feeling the incredible movement in his hand, in his mind, and his heart. He let his hand slide from under hers.

Without another word he rose. Tess's eyes followed him. Slowly, he lowered his face and kissed her hair. Gently, he lay a hand on her shoulder and let it slide over her back as he left the room. Noel Montgomery had been moved. Incredibly so. In his soul he mourned for Davina's first moments of life, wishing he could bring them back and he rejoiced for the first moments of this baby's new life. Inside him, too, was the terror that Tess might not be his some day. Noel Montgomery's confidence was as sorely shaken as his joy was increased that morning.

Bonnie moved well. She knew it. Her hips had just the right sway. She could move her torso without disturbing the rest of her body, she could push out her breasts and dip her shoulders so that her cleavage swelled threefold. Bonnie was hot and she'd been convincing herself of it all morning, ever since Davina had called.

Finally, Davina had come through for her. Just when Bonnie had been about to give up and look for another avenue to fame, Davina did it. Her interview with Noel Montgomery was scheduled for four o'clock, and all Bonnie had to do was show up in the right frame of mind, so to speak.

Davina had warned her that Noel was looking for a

class act and Bonnie had listened to what she said very carefully. All morning was spent going through her wardrobe, pulling out this and discarding that, unable to decide. So, as Bonnie thought about her outfit, she rehearsed what she would say, trying on voices until she found what she considered just the right one — not too tinny, but not too seductive. Then there had been the moves. The moves had been practiced repeatedly until she felt like a virtuoso ready for her debut at Carnegie Hall.

Now she had the moves and the voice, but the outfit was still a big question mark and time was flying. Sitting cross-legged on her bed, Bonnie considered every possible combination to come up with just the right look. Finally, she decided.

Davina had said class but Noel Montgomery was a man — and a very nice-looking one at that. Every picture she'd ever seen of the guy had been a knockout. He was young (anyone younger than Giles was young), handsome, and available.

Bonnie decided. She reached for a suit. A suit would be just the thing. Especially this one. Happily, she trotted off to the bathroom, stepped into the shower and sang "I'm Just a Girl Who Can't say No" at the top of her lungs. She had always liked that song from *Oklahoma*.

Davina checked her watch. It was almost four and still no Bonnie. Angrily she picked up the phone and dialed. The machine came on and Bonnie's idiotic message began to play. Davina cut it off, slamming the phone onto the hook. She picked up a piece of paper, trying to concentrate on the budget numbers, but it was useless. Bonnie was going to blow the whole thing if she didn't move her ass.

Davina swung herself into her chair and lay her head back. She could feel the beginnings of a headache. She rubbed her temples. It had been so long since she'd had a really raging one that the onset surprised her. She thought of something happy. She thought of Tony.

Soon she was giggling, remembering the shocked silence that greeted her new demand. Fifty thousand a month kickback. It had been a breeze. He hadn't said a word, but she'd heard a gurgle that sounded like an okay before she hung up. She liked this kind of power. Tony, of course, would have to do all the dancing with his uncle, but Davina only had to sit back and wait for the check to arrive. God, she had so many plans, so many contingencies. Davina knew she had covered every avenue. No matter what Noel Montgomery did, no matter if he lived or died or if he married Tess or not, Davina was going to be a winner one way or the other.

By the time the door to her office opened, her headache was gone and she was smiling.

"I'm here, I'm ready!"

Bonnie Barber stood in the doorway, her arms thrown wide as she displayed herself in all her perfection. Davina's mouth dropped.

"Oh my God!" Davina breathed.

"What? What?" Bonnie rushed to Davina as best she could on her very high heels. Davina's face was pale, her eyes glittering points in her rounded face.

"How could you do this to me?" Davina asked, her voice escalating until it was a strangled scream. "You look like a hooker."

"I beg your pardon," Bonnie sputtered, stepping back from the desk, craning her neck as she looked down to survey her body.

"Look at this. I said class, Bonnie, not brass."

"I wore a suit," Bonnie insisted.

"Yeah, and nothing else! That skirt comes up to your crotch. And what's this thing?" Davina had rounded the desk. She reached out toward Bonnie's chest. Bonnie turned away clutching, her arms protectively over her best assets.

"It's a bustier, thank you," Bonnie said coldly.

"A black satin bustier with a cherry red suit that has a miniskirt that barely covers your . . ." Davina could say no more. Frustrated, she turned away and beat her fists on her desk in little staccato motions.

"Hey, who are you to come down on me like this? I know men and your father is a man, right?"

"Who am I?" Davina asked in amazement, rolling her body toward Bonnie. Bonnie stepped back. She'd never seen Davina so crazy. "I am the one who calls the shots around here. I'm the one who knows the ins and outs, and if you want to play, then you do what I say. Now, get out your brush and lower that hair by about two inches. I'll be back in a minute. We're due up in his office now, so we've got maybe five minutes before he decides we're a no-show. Get to it!"

Davina disappeared through the door. When she came back Bonnie's hair had been combed into a sleek, side parted do. She had even taken the initiative to redo her makeup. Her lips were now about half their size and colored with a haze of peach instead of a striking apricot.

"Better," Davina muttered. "Stand up."

Bonnie did as she was told, controlling herself as best she could. This was her shot. A chance not only to be the *High Life* Woman but to get into *High Life* films. She had to play it Davina's way if she wanted to get past Noel Montgomery's office door.

Efficiently Davina draped a long scarf around Bonnie's neck, crisscrossed it and tucked it into her now buttoned jacket. Davina stepped back.

"Better. Nothing we can do about your skirt so you're going to have to dazzle him with your conversation. Now come on. He's waiting."

Davina charged out the door. Bonnie followed, then remembered people might be in the hall who would look after her. She minced her steps, putting her hips into perfect sway all the way to Noel's office.

"Shirley, Noel's four o'clock is here," Davina said like royalty as she breezed past the secretary.

Bonnie, hot on her heels, looked down her perfect, slender nose and gave the secretary a smile. Shirley's mouth fell open. She never thought she'd see the day when a game-show hostess was on the docket for *High Life* Woman.

Bonnie grinned wider, interpreting Shirley's wide-eyed look as one of complete adoration, as she swept after Davina. The door opened and closed quickly. Shirley went back to her typing, all the while wishing she could be a fly on the wall. She chuckled, imagining Mr. Montgomery's look when he was presented with that redheaded bombshell. Yet Shirley hadn't worked long enough for Noel Montgomery to know that his reaction would be the same whether he was faced with Katharine Hepburn or Bonnie Barber.

He rose as the ladies came into his office, rounded the desk and greeted them graciously. Davina did the honors.

"Noel, this is Bonnie Barber. Bonnie, Noel Montgomery."

"How do you do?" Bonnie said in the low voice she had conjured up only that morning.

"How do you do, Ms. Barber?" Noel greeted her cordially, holding her hand until he seated her on the couch.

"Clear your throat," Davina whispered as she sat next to her friend. Bonnie glared at her. Davina was already leaning toward her father.

"Bonnie is the woman I told you about this morning when we discussed possibly interspersing our traditionally younger, beautiful woman with the new look."

"Davina sang your praises this morning, Ms. Barber," Noel said, directing his words to Bonnie.

She almost died under the simmer of his incredible black eyes. He was so fabulous. There might be more here for her than met the eye. If Davina could get rid of the pregnant blonde, Bonnie would love to move on him. She shook her head slightly, her long red hair bouncing about her shoulders. She had to pay attention to the here and now. Tomorrow always came, and with it opportunity.

"I beg your pardon?" Her voice an octave higher now.

"I was only confirming what my daughter already told me. You are indeed an extremely beautiful woman. I have a feeling I've seen you somewhere before. Unfortunately, I can't quite place it."

Noel smiled, but Bonnie forgot to admire how nicely his lips spread across his face, how his eyes matched that smile with a glow.

Seen her somewhere before! Seen her! How dare he! Her blood was boiling deep in the pit of her stomach, begging for an eruption. She ought to get right off his really expensive couch that instant and walk out his very expensive door. That would show him. That would . . .

Bonnie bit the inside of her cheek. That wouldn't do anything to him. He'd think she was a nut, and she'd never have another crack at being the *High Life*

381

Woman. Bonnie swallowed hard and smiled with her lips together, trying to open her teeth while she spoke.

"I'm sure you have. My face is plastered all over town."

"Plastered?" Noel almost laughed.

Noel knew the moment Bonnie Barber walked in she was not the kind of woman he wanted to celebrate on the pages of *High Life*. He heard nothing to convince him otherwise.

"Daddy, Bonnie is the FortyFine woman. There are billboards and television spots and ads for her all over the place."

"Oh, forgive me, of course," Noel apologized. "How could I have been so stupid? I'm afraid I pay more attention to those advertisers who grace the pages of *High Life* and, since we attract mostly a male audience, we've never carried women's cosmetics ads."

Bonnie gave her head a little twist as though to tell him he was forgiven, but just.

"I can understand that. Men don't often look at women's ads. But, of course, that isn't really what I do for a living—model, that is. I'm an actress."

"I see," Noel commented.

"Yes, I was the assistant on *Table Top*—the game show—then I was the hostess after my husband Giles Masters died. You probably heard about his death."

"Actually I did," Noel said, his brow furrowing. This was a new twist. A young, beautiful woman widowed so soon after her wedding, then carrying on her husband's business. That might be an angle to follow. Bonnie deserved a little more time. "I was sorry to hear about his death. He'd been in the business a very long time. I understand he was well respected in the television industry. I didn't know him. *High Life* deals only

382

with feature films so I tend to be more attentive to that medium."

"Thank you. It was tragic."

Bonnie allowed her face to fall, her body to go limp for an instant as she relived her tragedy. She rotated her shoulders delicately. Her bustier had slipped and the stupid scarf Davina had wound around her neck was coming loose. This whole thing was ridiculous. Bonnie could tell Noel found her attractive. Davina could take a flying leap for all she cared. Bonnie was sure her original tact was the right one. She began to fiddle with the scarf.

"*High Life*, as you may know, is a magazine dedicated to many things, but especially to the celebration of beauty, intelligence, and strength. I imagine you must have a very interesting story to tell regarding the death of your husband and how you handled things once you found yourself widowed."

"Oh, you better believe it. It was just awful after Giles died. So many things happened. After the funeral I did the only thing I could think to do. I took his place on the show as a tribute to what he had created. I didn't miss one show. We weren't off the air for a minute. I think Giles would have liked that. It was difficult, touching the things he touched, clipping his microphone on me, standing behind that huge table and handling the props he handled."

Bonnie allowed one, small tremulous sigh to escape for the great expanse of chest. As naturally as possible she tugged on the scarf, loosening one end and using it to dab at her eyes. Her other hand snuck upward and tugged at the other end of the scarf. It fell open slightly, but not enough.

"It's so warm in here," she breathed, undoing her jacket button at the same time. The jacket fell open, taking the scarf with it and Bonnie was bared, finally feeling comfortable as she watched Noel watching her chest. She wiggled in the bustier, trying to get it straight.

"Would you like something to drink, Ms. Barber?" Noel asked, looking again at her green eyes. Bonnie shrugged mentally. His gaze hadn't lingered on her breasts; maybe he was a leg man. She crossed her legs.

"No, thank you. I don't want to take up too much of your time. But you were asking about the tribulations of widowhood. Well, despite the fact that I had taken over the show so professionally, the producers canned it not long after. Then, of course, there were the other problems. Giles hadn't been a very good money manager.

"I had to get rid of *everything!* The home in Beverly Hills, even the Rolls-Royce. It was so *difficult!* Have you ever tried to move a big house of furniture into a small one? Very difficult. Not to mention the lonely nights. Thank goodness I met Davina at Coco's. I had been so lonesome for companionship and there she was, appearing out of nowhere to take me by the hand. You're very lucky to have a daughter like her."

Bonnie beat her lashes in Davina's direction. Davina sat stoically, buried in the corner of the couch. Her eyes stared straight ahead. There was no need to look at her father for an opinion. She had ears. She could hear what Bonnie sounded like. The minute Bonnie loosened her jacket Davina knew what Noel's decision would be. Bonnie didn't cut it. Period. *Finis.* It was over and Noel would never let her have a hand in picking the *High Life* Woman as long as he was still breathing.

So Bonnie kept on grinning, Noel kept on looking at her and Davina kept on letting the cloud over her head grow to storm proportions. The whole thing was over less than ten minutes later and Davina found out that Bonnie didn't take rejection very well.

"You bitch," Bonnie jeered the minute the door of Noel's office closed. "You sabotaged me! You never wanted me to be the *High Life* Woman. You never wanted me to succeed!"

"You're right, Bonnie, you're absolutely right," Davina spat back in frustration. "I took you into my father's office, and told him that you were my choice for the *High Life* Woman because I wanted him to think I was a dyed-in-the-wool idiot. I've been thinking about this for weeks. I've been dreaming of the moment he would look at me like I lost my mind because I brought a half-dressed bimbo into his office and tried to convince him that you had an ounce of class. Jesus Christ, you're dumb!"

With that Davina put out her hand and straight-armed Bonnie, pushing the redhead out of the way as she stormed past Noel's shocked secretary. Before she reached the outer office door, though, Bonnie was on her. Davina's head jerked back as Bonnie wound her long-nailed fingers through Davina's black curls.

"Ow!" Davina yelped, her hands flying to her hair just as Bonnie yanked her around, then let her go so that she stumbled back toward the open doorway.

"Half-dressed bimbo! Dumb! How dare you . . ." Bonnie sputtered, whipping the scarf off her neck and holding it as though she would strangle Davina.

"Shut up. *Shut up!* Noel is right behind that door," Davina warned, glancing over Bonnie's shoulder in time to see Noel's secretary reach for the phone. Davina cringed. If that woman called security Davina knew her time at *High Life* was over. Noel would never allow her to stay if security had to break up a cat fight.

385

"Do you think I care if Mister High-and-Mighty-Montgomery hears a damned thing I say now?" Bonnie asked incredulously.

"You may not," Davina growled. "But I do."

Grabbing Bonnie's arm, Davina steered her out of Noel's office and rushed her down the hall to her own. Bonnie protested the entire way.

"Let me go, you bitch! I thought you were my friend. I thought you'd fixed everything with your *daddy*." Bonnie drew out the last word, mocking Davina. The black-haired woman dug her nails deeper into Bonnie's arm without speaking. "Ouch! Do that again and I'll own this place, I swear. I'll sue you and your father and this fucking magazine for defamation of character! Slander! I'll . . ."

"You'll do nothing," Davina ordered, finally dragging Bonnie into her office and closing the door. "Look at yourself. Just look, and then tell me Noel had one reason in the world to hire you as the *High Life* Woman?"

Bonnie looked down at herself. Her bustier was awry and barely covered her ample breasts. She put her hand to her hair, feeling that her exquisite coif had not lasted as it should have. Her skirt was half turned and there was a run in her stocking.

"You look like a slut, Bonnie," Davina noted quietly.

Slowly, Bonnie lifted her head and glared at Davina Montgomery. In that instant she hated the other woman. Hated her beyond reason even though she also knew Davina was the best friend she'd ever had. Bonnie could feel her eyes grow hard and cold as she parted her lips to speak, not knowing if she would speak to her enemy or her friend until the words lay between them.

"It's better than *being* a slut, Davina," Bonnie said calmly, obviously choosing to confront her enemy.

She stood without moving, her anger spent, crystallized into a hard ball of hatred somewhere near her heart. She was too tired to fight and too proud to cry. She didn't care what happened anymore, and her observation about Davina would probably cost her the only female friend she'd ever had.

Davina, too, was statue-still, her black eyes blazing at Bonnie one moment and flat-lined the next. It was an eon before Davina broke the silence and when she did Bonnie felt a wave of relief.

"You're right. It is better to look like a slut. So, since you look like one and the general consensus is that I am one, you want to go have a drink?"

Bonnie smiled. Things weren't so bad after all.

Tess looked at the clock at five-thirty. She'd been working over her paste-up board for more than three hours and her back was stiff. The baby kicked, happy to be released from such a confirming position. Tess sat back in her chair and surveyed her handiwork.

True to his word, Noel was letting her pay her way. She had refused paints and canvas and instead opted to work as a paste-up artist from Noel's home. Carefully she patched editorial pages together for him to take to the office. She couldn't believe how much she enjoyed the work. The meticulousness of it kept her mind occupied, and away from the continuous thoughts of Noel and Royal that jumbled in her mind.

She found it strange that the last months had gone so easily. For some reason Tess had expected her pregnancy to be a time filled with grief and tears. She had seen herself wishing away the days and weeks so that, after the baby was born, she could immediately find Royal and force her way, if necessary, into his home to see him.

Instead, she found her days passing at a beautifully leisurely pace as she did her work, napped, ate and was waited on by Benton, who she found to be very dear. Evenings were like sand sifting through her hands. Noel appeared every night at six. They dined together, walked the garden, sometimes they strolled through the neighborhood arm in arm. He would tell her about the office, she would talk about her plans for the baby, they considered names, discarding almost every one. Life would have been perfect, except for Davina.

Davina, no matter how hard Tess tried to convince her, would not believe that Tess's stay was temporary. Tess told her over and over again those first few weeks that she was in love with another man, though circumstances kept her from him. Davina's mean and ugly accusations turned Tess's head around. In some ways Noel's daughter was right. It did appear that Tess was using Noel. But, as long as he knew Tess was only doing what was right, that was all that counted. Then Davina changed. She wasn't exactly friendly, but at least she was civil. So they settled into a less than normal routine and made the best of it.

Glancing outside, Tess saw that the evening was fair and already darkening. She looked over the treetops and to the street, admiring the architecture of the house across the way. Suddenly she sat straighter. There it was again. The same car she had seen cruising in front of the house earlier in the day. Now it was stopped on the other side of the avenue. She could see a man's arm leaning on the open window.

Slowly, Tess got out of her chair, her eye still on the car. She couldn't see who was inside but in her heart she felt the growing seed of hope. Perhaps Royal had found her. Perhaps Dimitri had finally managed to get a message through to him, telling Royal where she was. The car was a Mercedes, just like the one Royal drove. But it was dark blue, not black. Through Tess's hopeful eyes, though, the color didn't matter. Sure that it was him, she flew down the stairs, holding her stomach as it fluttered with anticipation.

"Miss Tess, be careful," Benton called as she dashed past him.

"Don't worry, Benton. Everything is fine," she called happily behind her.

Onto the porch, down the drive Tess went, walking quickly. Hope had turned into certainty. She knew it was Royal. He forgave her her trespasses with Noel, she could feel it. She wanted that so badly. Yet, when she finally passed the gates and headed toward the car, the man inside quickly started the ignition and tore away, his tires squealing as he sped down the street and disappeared.

"Tess?"

Noel came cautiously into the room. Tess pushed herself up onto her elbows.

"You're resting. I'll come back," he whispered.

"No, it's all right. Come in. I've finished all the mechanicals. They're over there."

"I didn't come to find out if you'd finished your work." He chuckled. "Do you mind?" He indicated the side of the bed. She shook her head and he sat down. "I just wanted to make sure you were all right. Benton said he saw you dashing down the stairs like the devil was after you this evening. Did something happen?"

Tess shook her head. "Not really."

389

"Tess, I want to know. Usually you greet me with one of your great big smiles when I come home. I find you lying up here in the dark tonight. That means something's wrong."

"I saw a car this afternoon," Tess said quietly. "It kept driving past the house, then it stopped across the way. A man was inside. I only saw his arm. But I thought . . ." Her voice trailed off.

"You thought it was Royal," Noel finished for her. His hands lay quietly on his lap, but Tess sensed he was clasping them hard.

"Yes," she admitted.

"I'm sorry you were disappointed. But I'm not sorry it wasn't him. Tess, I don't want him to come for you."

"I know that. But I'm going to him."

"And I know that. But unless you've changed your mind and want to see him now, we still have a few months to go before you leave."

"I haven't changed my mind. I couldn't see him now. It's so close to the baby. Just a few more months. It's already October—almost November."

"Six more weeks," Noel mused. "I thought it was longer."

"Six more weeks and you'll be a father," Tess said brightly, forcing herself to good humor.

Noel didn't deserve depression nor did she want to wallow in it. Surprisingly, just having him walk into her room made it fly slowly away like a crane taking wing. It seemed heavy and oppressive until it was gone. Then she couldn't remember the way her sadness felt.

"I can't wait. Tess, I'm so excited. Sometimes I sit in my office and think the phone's going to ring and it will be Benton telling me he's taking you to the hospital." Noel chuckled at this piece of sentimentality. "You know what I'm going to do? I'm going to take off the week before the baby is due. I'll take you to the hospital. In fact, I'm going to be the one holding your hand in that delivery room, and I'm going to be the one to hold the baby when it's born."

"We'd both like that. I have a feeling I'm going to need a lot of hand-holding." Tess giggled.

"You? Never. You'll be a trouper." Noel reached out and smoothed her silky hair. Instinctively, Tess moved her head into the touch. But Noel moved his hand away as she did. He knew they were too close. Far too close. He got up quickly and stood away from the bed, stuffing his hands into his pockets. "You know what else I'm going to do?"

"What?"

"I'm going to cheer you up. I've kept you to myself far too long. Get dressed, madam, for tonight I'm taking you for a celebration. You haven't been out of this house since you arrived. We'll do anything you like. We'll dress up and paint the town red or we'll go down to Apple Pan and have a burger while we perch on those horrible stools. You name it. The evening is yours."

"Oh, Noel, that sounds wonderful. I vote for the burger," Tess said, swinging her legs awkwardly over the bed so she could sit up. She switched on the bedside lamp, illuminating only herself in the soft golden light.

Noel's heart caught as he looked at her. She had taken her hair out of the rubber band so it flowed over her shoulders and down her back. Her skin was the color of pink pearls, and she had gained just enough weight to make her look ultimately touchable. She smiled at him.

"Burgers it is and a drive down Highway One. I've always thought the ocean was beautiful this time of the year."

"Ten minutes?"

"Ten minutes."

"Oh," Tess said. "What about Davina?"

"I think Davina will manage just fine by herself. Besides, when was the last time she wanted to join us for dinner?"

"With our luck it will be tonight."

"Then let's make it five minutes. I want the three of us to be together tonight."

Tess's hand went to her stomach. "Sounds good to us."

Noel left, his heart as light as a feather. This was going to be an evening to remember.

Noel had finally called it quits when Tess ordered a second piece of apple pie. Reluctantly, she admitted she and the baby had probably had enough to last them through the next six weeks.

Arm in arm they strolled down Pico, trying to ignore the marvelous feeling of simply being together like an old married couple. They stopped to window-shop at Nordstrom. Noel bought Tess a gown of peach silk for the hospital, despite her objections, then smiled when he saw how closely she held the package as they made their way back to the car.

Now they were driving toward Malibu in silence. The windows were open and Tess's hair whipped about her face like traces of starlight. Her head was back, her eyes closed. Every nerve in her body was reaching up and engulfing the fabulous feeling that permeated the car. It was quiet. She could hear the pounding of the surf below. It was dark. She could feel the restfulness it brought. And Noel was beside her. She could feel the security he offered her. She let her mind wander, thinking of nothing and everything all at the same time.

"Oh my God," Noel muttered beside her and the car lurched forward.

Tess was up in a flash looking forward on the two-lane highway. She couldn't see a thing. Ahead of them the lanes were clear.

"What? What is it?"

"Behind us," Noel said, gritting his teeth and gripping the steering wheel. "Some idiot is coming up on us doing about eighty. Hold on, I'm going to hug the side of the mountain and hope he isn't drunk. Pray that he has enough smarts to either slow down or pass."

But Tess hadn't time to pray. Everything happened so quickly. The moment she turned her head to look for the car it was on them. The driver had not slowed nor had he veered from his course. Ahead of them there were headlights. Someone was coming from the other direction now. Noel saw it, too. He couldn't turn into the other lane and hope the driver behind them would pass on the right. If he turned to the right he'd hit the mountain.

Then in a split second, she saw the turnout. Noel was already making his move toward it when the car behind them smashed the rear of theirs. Noel had been doing sixty. The car behind them eighty. Noel's car flew ahead, the right fender smashing into the side of the cliff before falling heavily down to earth into the sand of the turnout. Then everything stopped. Only the hissing sound that came from the engine.

Tess lay crumpled in her seatbelt, a trail of blood coursing down the left side of her face. Noel was about to lose consciousness when he heard footsteps slowly crunching the broken glass on the ground. He knew this wasn't help coming. He knew in that moment this hadn't been an accident. Desperately, he tried to focus. His hand shook as he reached for Tess, but he hadn't the strength to grasp her hand when he finally found it. A shadowy face leaned down and peered at him.

"Who . . . why . . ." he asked weakly.

"Tell your daughter that she's asked too much. Tell her there isn't any more. Tell her Tony won't be handlin' the account no more."

As the man righted himself and the sound of his footsteps faded, Noel Montgomery lost consciousness.

"Is she all right?"

"Absolutely, Noel. You were lucky you were in the Volvo. Good car, those. Probably saved your life. That and the fact you were wearing your seatbelts."

"Can I see Tess?" Noel asked, sitting up on the hard table where he had reclined for his examination.

"No, well, you could look in on her. But she's sleeping. She had quite a scare. We've monitored the baby and he's just fine . . ."

"He?" Noel said.

"Oh, oh," the doctor muttered. "I didn't know you guys were waiting to find out. We had to do a sonogram to check on him. He's in superb condition."

"He," Noel mumbled as he closed his eyes. His head was splitting. Both he and Tess had taken a good whack, but thankfully they were both all right.

"That's right. So anyway, if you want to peek in that's fine, but my suggestion would be that you check yourself into this hospital and get a good night's rest like your wife."

"No," Noel said quickly. "I'd like Tess to stay overnight or longer if you think it's necessary, but I have a few things I need to do."

"Put them off," the doctor ordered, "and go home and lie down. That's the only thing you can do now. Here are some pills to help you sleep and some pain-killers. You'll be surprised in the morning. Every bone in your body is going to ache."

Noel pocketed the pills. "Thanks, Doctor. I promise I'll rest. I'll be back in the morning to check on Tess."

"Fine. Now, if you're sure you're up to it, you can leave. But I want someone to come get you."

"My friend is right outside. He brought the other car."

"Good. Let me help you."

The doctor grasped Noel under the arm and steadied him as he stood up. Noel knew he was in no shape for a confrontation, but he intended to be soon. Benton was waiting for him when he came out of the emergency room.

"Miss Tess?" Benton asked. "And the baby?"

"They're fine, Benton."

"Thank God."

"I agree. Now get me home."

"Of course, Mister Montgomery. You need to get into bed."

"No, just get me home. I want to see Davina."

"I can't believe he turned me down," Bonnie moaned. "He hated me."

"It's your own fault," Davina said flatly, raising her hand to order two more drinks.

"Almost closing time, ladies," the bartender informed them as he took their glasses away.

"Sure." Davina glanced at her watch. She and Bonnie had been in this dive for over six hours. Unfortunately, neither of them was drunk. That's what happened when you were mad and drank. The anger overcame the liquor and you were more angry than you were in the beginning.

"It wasn't my fault. If you hadn't been there I would have had him eating out the palm of my hand. Did you see his face when I finally took that stupid scarf off?"

"Yeah, I saw it. Noel's like any other man. He can admire the fine lines of a car, but if he gets in and the seats are vinyl he won't buy it."

"You think I'm vinyl?"

"Well, you aren't leather!" Davina snapped.

"Thanks a hell of a lot," Bonnie hissed. "And I thought you were my friend."

"There are no friends, Bonnie. Only acquaintances. You helped me when I needed it, and I tried to help you and *that* is *that!*"

"So we're just going to call it quits? That's it? After all I did for you?"

"All *what?* You gave me *one* lousy idea. You think I owe you something for having a drink with me once in a while?"

"I did more than that," Bonnie objected, jutting her chest out adamantly. "My door was always open to you. How many nights have you sat in my living room drinking my booze and crying on my shoulder? Well, if that's all we mean to each other, then I'm out of here as of now. I'll take a cab. And listen, next time you need someone to tell your troubles to, why don't you try that loser I found you with?"

Bonnie twirled out of the club and was gone. Davina watched her go.

"Your friend's not drinking?" The bartender was back.

"No friend of mine," Davina answered, dragging both glasses toward her. "Don't worry. I never waste a good thing."

"Ten minutes," the guy warned. "I want to get home."

"Got someone special?" Davina asked, liking the looks of his slim body, his blond hair.

"Yeah, and he doesn't like me to be late."

"Shit," Davina moaned and downed the two drinks.

She left five minutes later feeling as though her life was now well ordered. She'd done what she could for Bonnie, but Noel had been right. She wasn't a class act. Davina needed better people than Bonnie to hang with. She was still chuckling, as she realized she and Noel agreed on something, when she let herself into the house. He was standing by the door and grabbed her the minute it opened, throwing her up against the wall.

"What have you done, Davina? What was it that almost got Tess and I killed tonight?"

Noel's hand was around her throat, his face was close to hers. For the first time in her life Davina felt something other than hatred and anger toward her father — she felt icy cold fingers of fear stabbing at her. She was light-headed, her breath coming in shallow gasps. Her fingers clawed at her father's, but he didn't seem to notice how desperately she needed air. He just kept staring at her, his hand tightening until finally, she saw the light of realization in his eyes. Noel stepped back, still quivering with rage.

Davina coughed, doubling over. Her purse had dropped near the door, her ears were ringing from the blow against the wall. When she stood upright it was cautiously. She hugged the wall, looking from her father to the door, gauging her escape.

"I don't know what you're talking about," she said quietly, knowing that calm was needed if she was going to talk her way out of whatever had made him so angry.

"You know and you're going to tell me so I'll know. Because, Davina, I want to know everything. For over two years now I've put up with you. I've tried to help you find your way out of the hatred you've wallowed in all your life. I've had to soothe over ruffled feathers at the office, I've taken every conceivable insult you could throw at me; I've given you money, a job and a home and you repay me with more misery. Now that it's come to violence, I draw the line."

"What violence?" Davina shouted. Noel reared up and Davina clutched tighter to the wall. His fists were clenched but he lowered them without striking.

"Tonight, Tess and I were driving on the Coast Highway. A car came up fast on us. I thought it was a drunk driver. He hit us, threw the car into one of the cliffs."

"Tess, the baby . . ." Davina asked, her heart actually aching for Noel if he'd lost those two.

"No, much as you'd like it, they aren't dead. We were all lucky."

Noel's sarcasm was like a slap in the face, a kick in the gut. Davina hadn't meant that. She didn't want them dead, only gone. He always thought the worst of her, always. Well, maybe she'd just give it to him then.

"Then what?" she said sarcastically. "You're going to hold me responsible because you had an accident?"

"No, Davina, not because I had an accident." Noel came toward her and put one hand on the wall just above her shoulder. His face was close to hers, his breath hot. "I'm blaming you because you caused it. A man came to the car while Tess and I were stunned. He leaned down. It was dark. I couldn't see his face. He

398

said to give you a message. That they'd had enough. That Tony wouldn't handle your account anymore. Do you think, Davina, that this man assumed you were in the car with me? Do you think they were trying to hurt you and got us instead?"

Davina's mind flew in a thousand directions. She knew what it meant. She'd gone too far with Tony. His uncle had accepted the proposition at first; now he was mad. But who would have thought a printer would do something like that? And the answer came as quickly as the question. Tony and his talk of uncles and family. Jesus, were they mob? She dared a look at her father. What should she do? Confess? He'd like that. Noel and his principles.

"You said you were stunned. You dreamed it. Maybe it didn't happen like that," she said quickly, taking the only shot she could think of. Noel raised back, his hand leaving the wall and swiftly coming down, catching her across the cheek.

"Don't lie to me! For once tell me the truth!"

His sandy voice had taken on a murderous quality. Davina knew that there was no other way out than the truth. She began to speak and when she had finished Noel was standing, leaning against the staircase.

"You used *High Life* for your own gain? You used my company, me, just so you could take a kickback?"

"I had to do it," Davina insisted, tears of fear coming to her eyes. He was going to throw her out now, and she wasn't ready. She'd be alone, poor again. Davina conveniently forgot the thousands of dollars she already had in the bank. "Don't you see? You have Tess now, and a baby coming. You wouldn't want me. It was only a matter of time. Don't you see?"

Noel's head swiveled her way. It was dark in the hall and Davina couldn't see him well. He seemed tired.

"I see, Davina. I see that no matter what I do it will never be good enough. I see that I've brought this upon myself, and that I've let you get away with too much. We've got to start again, Davina. We'll try one more time, but not here. Not in this house. I want you out of here tonight. I don't care where you go. You've got money, find a hotel. But I won't have you here until we figure out how we can live with each other."

"My job?"

"You can keep working. You'll have to be on time. I'll check your work. I expect it to be perfect. Things are going to change, or you won't be around any longer. I want the name of the printer and your contact on my desk in the morning. You will immediately award the contract to Anderson, and they will begin printing as of the next issue."

"But Tony, his family, they won't like it."

"You let me worry about that," Noel roared.

His head hurt. His body hurt. His soul was tortured. First by the memory of Tess laying so still next to him in the battered car, then by the realization that Davina needed the kind of help he couldn't give her. There was so much to do now. He felt weak with the thought of it.

"I have to go upstairs and lie down," Noel mumbled. "Call Benton and let him know where you are. Be at work in the morning, and make sure you get me the information I want. Then I want to see you in my office at two tomorrow."

Noel walked painfully up the stairs. So much was wrong. If only he was climbing the stairs to his bedroom and Tess's arms. But even that dream was gone now. He felt so defeated.

Downstairs, Davina didn't even stop to collect her things. Shaking, she grabbed her purse and hopped in her car. Thirty minutes later she was at the only place

400

she knew to go.

Bonnie opened the door sleepily, her hair a mess, her lips an angry snarl.

"What do you want?"

"I need a place to stay. Please? I'll make it up to you. Please?"

Bonnie eyed Davina. The little princess had come down a peg or two. She looked young and frightened. Bonnie was no slouch. She knew what it was like when the chips were down. Hey, it had happened to her a number of times. Sighing, she opened the door and pointed to the couch.

"Welcome," was all she said before hitting the sack again.

Part Six

Coming Apart

Twenty-five

"Davina, get out of the shower! Davina!"

Bonnie banged on the door again. Davina had been running the water for an hour. She seemed to think Bonnie was made of money. Sure, Bonnie had the residuals from the commercials, but Sy hadn't come up with anything new in months. It was almost Christmas and there wasn't even a good wealthy man in sight. The latter, more than anything else, put Bonnie in a rotten mood.

"Davina!" she hollered again, gratified when the water finally stopped.

"What?" Davina stuck her head out the door. Her eyes were red. She'd been doing pills again, and it wasn't even six o'clock Saturday night.

"May I get into my own bathroom?"

"Certainly," Davina opened the door, waving her arm cynically, ushering Bonnie into the small bathroom.

"I meant alone. Get your clothes on," Bonnie griped.

"The sight of the female body make you uncomfortable?" Davina drawled. "I wouldn't think so; you like to look at your own so much, I figured it was a real turn-on."

"It is, but only because it's mine. If I didn't know better, I'd think you were a lesbo, Davina. Now get out and let me have a turn."

"Got a hot date?"

"No, I've got to go to the john, do you mind?"

"Okay, okay. It's all yours."

Davina grabbed her robe and stomped into the living room. Just as Bonnie was about to close the door she heard Davina heading to the kitchen, then the refrigerator door opened.

"Eat it only if you pay for it."

Bonnie slammed the door hard. Life was not much fun anymore. She hated having a roommate, but couldn't seem to shake Davina. Every time she tried to kick her out the dark-haired woman fell apart. It was like living with two people, one who was as tough as nails, the other who was no better than a two-year-old. That chick needed help, in Bonnie's opinion, and she had no desire to give it.

Bonnie flushed the toilet, leaned close to the mirror and checked her eyelashes before heading to the living room, ready to send Davina packing.

"Listen, Bonnie, I really appreciate you having me here all this time. Really, I do."

Shit, Davina had done it again. She was as docile as a lamb. Bonnie clicked her tongue and went to get herself a diet Pepsi. When she came back Bonnie didn't have the heart to be cruel. Sitting cross-legged on the floor she looked at Davina. She would use psychology. The understanding friend hype.

"Hey, I know it's been rough on you, Davina. But it's got to stop. All this being mad just isn't any good for

406

either you or your dad. Why don't you go on home and try to patch things up?"

"I can't."

"Why not?"

"He's home all day now. He's been waiting for Tess to have her baby. Can't you just imagine what it's like around there? Him making all the right noises, and her looking so gorgeous even though she's as big as a tank. I need him to ask me to come home, see? Besides, I don't think he's gotten over that printing thing."

"I can see it," Bonnie said before taking a sip of her soda. "If I had to pay half a mil to get out of a contract I'd be pissed, too. Then again, if I had that kind of money to spend on getting out of it, I would have made a whole lot while I was in it."

Davina looked at the redhead. Bonnie's face was all screwed up as she tried to figure out the logic of what she just said. Davina sighed. Bonnie continued with the Freud approach.

"Okay, so he's mad at you and you can't go home and play kissy face. So, like my dad used to say, don't get mad, get even. Do something that will make you feel better. Get a better job and really do a number. Or start your own thing or . . ." Bonnie wanted to say "just get the hell out of my life," but she had to take another breath and Davina was quicker than she. It was that thoughtful look behind Davina's red, red eyes that did it.

"Or sabotage what he's got," Davina said slowly.

"You going to do something to Tess?" Bonnie asked in amazement.

"No, don't be silly. She's never really done anything to me. She's kind of like me in a way—you know, he's used her. I used to think it was the other way around,

407

but now I don't think so. He'll toss her soon enough. It's him. He's the one who's got to be taught a lesson. He's the one who has to see he isn't infallible. If I could pull something off right under his nose. Something spectacular, you understand, then he'd have to admit I'm at least smarter than he is."

"Sure, why not?"

Bonnie leaned back, bracing herself on one hand as she drank her diet soda. The place was a pigsty. She needed money, but more than that she needed exposure. Sy wasn't getting it for her. Davina couldn't get it for her. Noel Montgomery wouldn't give it to her. While Davina thought of revenge, Bonnie thought of her future.

"Bonnie," Davina said slyly, "how would you like to appear in the March issue as the *High Life* Woman?"

Bonnie sat up slowly. "But Noel already nixed me."

"Yeah, but Noel doesn't do the grunt work. I do. And I say I can get you in. Are you in or out?"

"In," Bonnie breathed.

The two women sat in the middle of the clothes-cluttered living room and grinned at each other for a long, long time. Then they got down to business. They started to plan. They would to have to work fast if Davina's scheme was going to work.

By week's end they had everything done. Davina had taken a good hunk of her money and arranged for a session with a trusted photographer. The negatives had arrived earlier that morning. She had also written the copy herself; copy that extolled Bonnie's assets, her mind, her ambition. It was a great spread. When the actual mechanicals for the March issue came through her office Davina worked at night, repatching stats as best she could, positioning the copy until it looked almost perfect.

Davina's was the final signature needed to send the whole package to the printer. Everyone at *High Life* had worked on a layout featuring Caroline Thomas, the author. Only Bonnie knew that, at the last minute, the mechanicals of Bonnie Barber would be substituted.

Now she needed only one thing. She needed Tess to have that baby so Noel would be completely out of the way. Once the mechanicals were in the hands of the printer and on the press, the only thing Noel could do would be to stop distribution of that issue completely. March would come and go without an issue of *High Life*. Davina knew Noel would never do that.

The spread was marvelous. Bonnie, the photographer, and Davina had worked hard and it was better than anything Noel's staff had ever put together. Of that Davina was sure. When Noel saw it he would be angry, then he would realize that the planning had been sheer genius. Davina would finally prove herself to be his daughter to the core. Her mind conjured up scenes of his heartfelt apologies, meetings with lawyers as Noel turned over the vice-chairmanship of *High Life* to her, Davina, his daughter.

The waiting would be the hard part. Four days later Davina didn't have to wait any longer. She packaged the mechanicals for the March issue, carefully substituting Bonnie's layout for that of Caroline Thomas. The package was ready to go first thing in the morning when the printer's messenger came for them. Everything was set.

Harvey Noel Montgomery was born at midnight

December 23rd. Tess thought the name a big one for such a little creature, but she had wanted the baby to be named for her father and his father and there was nothing to be done except christen him Harvey Noel.

Noel had stayed with her through every pain, whispering to her—her name, his love, encouragement. While Tess labored, she gratefully accepted every murmur from him. This was their time together. They were bringing a baby into the world that they had made. Royal didn't belong with them at that moment, and Tess pushed him from her mind more easily than she thought possible. Noel was the only one she thought of; Noel was the one she clung to.

Noel left her at one in the morning, sure that she was sleeping. He kissed her sweetly, went to the nursery to look once more at his robust son, then left the hospital. But he was restless. Sleep, he knew, could never overcome the awe he had felt that night, the love he experienced both for Tess and the little boy with the shock of black hair.

When he left the hospital Noel turned his car toward downtown. Work was the only thing to soothe him. He had been away from it for over a week, concentrating all his effort on Tess as they waited for the pains to begin.

He nodded to the night guard as he signed in, exchanged pleasantries and went up to his office. But he didn't want paperwork; he wanted to feel work in progress. Reveling in the silence of the office he went toward production. There he found just what he was looking for. He unwrapped the carefully tied bundle of mechanicals and began to sift through the March issue that was due to be printed within the week.

He was still sitting at Davina's desk when she

strolled in the next morning. He didn't tell her about the baby. He had only one thing to say to her.

Noel slid the Bonnie Barber mechanicals toward his daughter.

"Get out now. Out of this office. Out of my home. Get out and don't come back."

Davina turned on her heel and left without a word. How dare he judge her. Hadn't he risen because of the risk he took and wasn't she the daughter of Noel Montgomery? To be turned away without . . . He thought it was the end, but he was wrong. So very, very wrong.

As she walked away from the *High Life* building, Davina thought of her mother for the first time in a very long while. The images were jumbled. Flashes of life moments coursed through Davina's mind. Her mother, young and beautiful; her mother enraged and dangerous; her mother helpless; her mother dead. And it was thoughts of her mother that kept her moving toward the one place she knew she would be welcome.

Bonnie paced the living room, counting her steps, trying to figure out what to do.

Davina had appeared on her doorstep two hours earlier and Bonnie, for the first time in her life, had actually been apprehensive. There was something different about Davina, something that definitely wasn't right. Sure, she was upset about being thrown out of the house, about Noel discovering the little subterfuge with the March issue, yet Bonnie sensed some deeper disturbance in Davina.

There was the way Davina moved — twitching sud-

411

denly—as she drank on the sofa and Bonnie brainstormed ways to get her back into Noel's good graces and out of her house. Bonnie thought she was doing a great job, coming up with some of the most creative ideas she'd had in ages. Davina's eyes were on her, hopeful, as she listened carefully. Then, suddenly, Davina jumped. Not really jumped, because her face never changed expressions. It was as though Davina wasn't aware what her body was doing. Her legs jerked out and up, she seemed to be cold, her entire body shivered and shuddered. Then she'd ask a question as though nothing had happened. It gave Bonnie the creeps.

Finally, Davina asked for something to help her with the headache that had blasted through her skull with the speed of lightning. One minute she didn't have it, the next she was in excruciating pain. Bonnie sent her to the bathroom, inviting her to take whatever it was she could find that would help her. Luckily, there wasn't much. Bonnie didn't especially care for pills. A good stiff drink or a good stiff man usually did the trick when she felt a bit under the weather.

She checked her watch. Davina had been in the bathroom twenty minutes. That was okay with Bonnie, at first. She figured Davina was sort of getting her act together: a cold splash of water on the face, a few minutes on the pot, that kind of thing. Then it dawned on Bonnie. She hadn't heard a sound from there in the longest time. In fact, the only thing she had heard was Davina opening the medicine cabinet. The hinges squeaked. But there had been no rifling of bottles, no running of water. Nothing.

Bonnie took another measured step toward the window, then deciding without really thinking about it,

412

she twirled around and strode to the bathroom. She would never know what prompted her to simply fling the door open rather than knocking. She was eternally grateful she did.

"Davina, you idiot!" Bonnie screamed when she saw what was happening.

Bonnie lunged toward the toilet. Davina was sitting slump-shouldered on the lowered lid, her legs splayed on either side of her. Her left wrist lay limply in her lap. Her right hand held a razor blade. The edge rested against the pulsing vein of the opposite wrist. It just was there, not cutting, but not shaking, either, as though Davina didn't have the strength to cut.

Bonnie's hand slashed at Davina's. There was no resistance. The razor blade flew across the small bathroom, tinkling as it hit tiled wall and floor before skidding toward the door and stopping against the hall carpet.

Davina didn't even look up. Her right hand had snapped back into position as though nothing had happened. Perspiration dotted her forehead, a rivulet ran down her cheek.

Bonnie collapsed onto the tile floor, trying not to imagine what would have happened if Davina had completed her grisly task. Noel Montgomery's daughter commits suicide in Bonnie Barber's bathroom. That kind of publicity she didn't need.

The only sound in the ceramic-cold room was Bonnie's heavy breathing as she tried to pull herself together. She'd never moved that fast in her life. Watching Davina now, she wondered why she actually had allowed Davina back into her home. The other woman actually looked like she wanted to die. Not with the crazy, wild-eyed look they show on television, but with a calm and sadness that ran so deep Bonnie seemed to finally understand Davina's pain was real and had been with her all her life. Pulling herself to her hands and knees, Bonnie crawled toward Davina, taking the other woman's hands in hers.

"He isn't worth it, Davina," Bonnie whispered, her voice quaking with relief. "Don't you see? Hurting yourself won't hurt him? He won't even feel it. If you want to hurt someone, then let it be him. Do something that would really hurt him. Get it out of your system, then get on with your life. But don't do this. The only thing it would prove is that you can die just like everyone else."

Davina didn't move for the space of time it took Bonnie to take two tremulous breaths. Then, slowly, Davina moved her head until she was looking directly at Bonnie. Their faces were so close they could feel one another's breaths. Bonnie's was warm and deep with life; Davina's shallow with a despair and sickness only she could define.

"Really?" she asked quietly.

"Really," Bonnie answered cautiously. "What good is being dead? You've had nothing all your life; you'd die with nothing. Why should you be dead and him alive to enjoy all that money and stuff? See?"

"Yes," Davina answered.

Bonnie sank back, balancing herself on her heels as she released Davina's hands. Finally, Davina appeared to reenter the land of the sane and living. Now she seemed to understand that revenge was sweet only if you were around to enjoy it. She smiled. Bonnie did the same—tentatively. In a daze, Davina rose and looked down on Bonnie. Davina's left shoulder twitched ever so slightly.

"You're right. I'll think about it. I'll think of some other way."

"Good. Good," Bonnie said, encouraging her. Anything to keep her mind off suicide.

"He's really not a very nice man, is he, Bonnie? I shouldn't always be the one to pay for his mistakes, should I? There's got to be another way and all I have to do is think really, really hard. Right, Bonnie?" Davina asked dreamily.

Bonnie shook her head wearily, knowing it really wouldn't matter how Davina tried to extract her revenge. The girl was doomed to failure from day one and would continue to be. Her mind couldn't figure out a foolproof plan if her life depended on it. Bonnie relaxed. In the morning she'd probably have forgotten everything. That was the weird way Davina's mind seemed to work sometimes. She'd be happy one minute, down in the dumps the next, only to climb back out of her depression and head for the highs again.

"Yes, it will be good," Davina said softly, "when I figure it out. Thank you, Bonnie."

"Hey." Bonnie shrugged one alabaster shoulder before pushing herself off the floor. "No problem. Let me know how it goes. Okay? Just give me a ring."

"Oh, I'll tell you in the morning . . ."

Davina headed to the door. Bonnie put a hand on the other woman's arm. Davina turned slowly around.

"What do you mean in the morning?" Bonnie demanded, forgetting the delicate position she had found Davina in only a few moments ago.

"In the morning," Davina answered firmly. "I'll tell you at breakfast."

"Hey, Davina." Bonnie laughed nervously. "I think we've just about reached the end of our rope, so to speak. You know it's been a kick and all, but a girl needs her privacy. Know what I mean? You've got a bunch of money left. Why not take a hotel room for a while? Pamper yourself. Room service and all that. Hey, you deserve it."

Bonnie's fist playfully tapped Davina on the shoulder. The dark-haired woman swayed like a sapling. Her face never changed. Those black eyes of hers bored through Bonnie as though the redhead wasn't there. Bonnie was starting to sweat.

"I'll tell you in the morning," Davina reiterated as though she hadn't heard a word Bonnie said.

With that she left the bathroom. A minute later Bonnie heard the door of the second bedroom close and lock. She sank onto the top of the john and buried her head in her hands and wished Giles were alive again or Sy would find her a starring role so she had enough money to hire bodyguards and keep Davina Montgomery out of her life.

In Bonnie's guest bedroom Davina lay fully dressed and completely awake until well after two A.M. She'd been thinking very hard, all her energy focused on what needed to be done. Hurting Noel, proving that she was worth more attention than he gave her, that was a puzzle of extreme proportions. He was a man who valued only truth and loyalty. You couldn't hurt him by taking his money or his reputation. Finally, just before the digital registered three in the morning, a plan formed in Davina's mind. A plan that would require the most unique planning. For a moment only Davina questioned whether or not she was up to it. But the moment passed and with it any doubt that she was on the right road.

Rolling over, Davina picked up the telephone and di-aled.

"Tony?" she whispered when it was answered. "It's Davina. I need someone to do a job for me. Someone with a very special talent . . ."

Twenty-six

"He's marvelous, isn't he?"

Noel was bending over the cradle that had been put in the living room so Tess wouldn't always have to be rushing up and down the stairs to attend to him. At least that was the reason he gave when he brought the antique cradle home as a present. Tess sensed that it was only Noel's way of keeping the baby close.

Now that Harv was two weeks old Tess had seen a change in Noel. His brightness became almost excessive. He showered them both with presents so that Tess finally had to put a stop to it. When he was home, supposedly to find some peace and quiet where he could work, Tess would come upon him sitting by the cradle, his strong finger clasped in the baby's hand.

At those moments she would turn away, not because she respected the privacy of those instances he spent with his son, but because she feared the feelings that welled inside her when she looked at Noel in repose.

Tess knew why he was home, why he brought the gifts, why he smiled broader and laughed too often: Noel Montgomery was afraid. In his home was everything he wanted — the baby and Tess. Yet, though they

418

never spoke of it, there was also the specter of Royal and Noel was trying to banish him any way he could. Now Tess smiled softly, her eyes first trailing over Noel, then seeking the baby.

"Marvelous seems too small a word for him. Funny, but I don't really think I thought the baby was real until I held him that first time."

"I knew he was real. I knew exactly what he'd look like. My hair, your eyes. He's us, together. He's us, Tess."

Noel picked the baby up and held him against his broad chest as though protecting him. Ever so gently he tucked the soft white blanket under Harvey's chin. The baby yawned and turned its face into him, tiny lips moving in sleep. Tears stung Tess's eyes. If only this time hadn't come; if only she'd had no life before Paris to pull her away from this man. But the pull was strong, the memories of Royal etched in her heart.

"This child, Tess, was made because of a night of love. Not one simply of passion or need, but of love. I felt it from you, and I gave it to you. He deserves to grow up in a house of love."

"He will, Noel, I promise you," Tess answered softly, knowing in her heart it was true.

Noel shook his head.

"No. He won't have the most the world can give him because you and I will be apart. Do you think all these months that nothing has happened to us while we lived in the same house, sat across from one another at breakfast, talked into the night when neither of us could sleep? Don't you see what's happened? We've solidified our love for each other. We think alike, we feel alike. There's so much about us being together that can't even be put into words. Don't you see?"

For a moment the only sound in the room was the baby softly breathing. Then the sofa sighed as Tess went to Noel. Gently, she put her hand on the baby's head. She had never seen anything so lovely as her child nestled in the arms of his father. Noel was such a wonderful man she found it hard to believe that she actually would leave him someday. She wondered when that day came if she actually could find the strength to go. Knowing she must think only of what she was going to do now, Tess raised her hand and held Noel's cheek. She would worry about leaving when it happened.

"I see, Noel. I see so many things. You've always known, though, that there was a prior commitment," she said.

"Tess," he begged, his head shaking in frustration. "Listen to what you're saying. Commitment? That sounds like a business transaction."

"It's what I want," Tess countered, keeping her voice low. "It's what was always meant to be. I've been kept from Royal too long: by his wife, by you, by Dimitri, by my own sense of what is right. I won't have it anymore. Yes, I agree a lot has happened since I've come to this house. I never would have believed that I could love someone the way I love you."

"Tess . . ." Noel whispered.

"But it's wrong. Wrong because you and I found each other at a time we shouldn't have. It was fate that put you in my path. Maybe to test me, I don't know. But I've struggled and worked and waited, and now I am going to Royal because it's the right thing to do. He was my first love, he'll be my last if he'll have me."

"And do you think he will?" Noel challenged.

Tess hesitated and turned away. Her voice was quiet

when she answered, quiet without the conviction she had meant to use.

"Yes."

"When are you going?"

"In a moment." Tess's back was to Noel. She couldn't look at him. She heard Noel's sigh flutter toward her. "Dimitri called and told me Royal was back at work a week ago. I've checked with his office, and his last appointment is at six. I'll wait for him at the office. I don't want anyone to stop me this time."

"Not even me, Tess?"

She looked over her shoulder. He still clutched the baby to him. He looked taller to her now, like a pillar of strength. How badly she needed his strength!

"Not even you, Noel," she said simply. "You'll watch the baby until I get back?"

"Yes."

"Thank you, Noel."

She began to leave the room, but Noel stopped her.

"Tess?"

"Yes?"

"You will be back, won't you?"

"Of course. There'll be time."

She left him with the baby, unsure of what she had meant. Time for what? Tears? For a leaving that was painful? For goodbyes that were said without a touch or a kiss? Hand on the balustrade, Tess rested her foot on the first step and waited. For one crazy minute she almost thought she was going to turn around and go to Noel. Forcing herself, she went up the stairs and began to dress. It was time to find Royal.

"Do you know what to do?"

Davina hovered over Bonnie as the redhead put the final touches on her makeup. Bonnie glanced at her peevishly, then drew her eyeliner in a perfect line over her left eye. She sat back on the small stool.

"I know what to do," Bonnie snapped, "but I still can't figure out how you talked me into this. This is the stupidest thing I've ever heard of."

"Don't tell me it's stupid. It took two weeks to plan this and get it right. It'll be great," Davina growled.

There was no delight in her voice, no fun. If Bonnie had been out to get revenge she sure as hell would've had a good time of it. But not Davina. Davina had a black hole where her humor button was supposed to be.

"I know it took that long. You didn't come out of that bedroom the whole time. That room is a disaster now." Bonnie was grumbling, frantically stabbing at her lower lashes with her mascara. "Don't forget our deal, though. I help you out and you find another place to live after tonight, right?"

Davina giggled, an extremely irritating sound. "Sure. After tonight, I don't think I'll have a problem with that."

Bonnie shot her a suspicious look, then regained her mascara momentum. It was no skin off her nose whatever Davina did after tonight. A few minutes' work with Noel Montgomery, and Bonnie was off the hook for good. Hopefully.

"Okay, so tell me about it again," Davina ordered. "Tell me what you're supposed to do."

Bonnie sighed, put down her makeup and pulled the towel tighter around her chest. Like a child called on in school, she rolled her eyes and recited.

"I go to the house and ask to see your father alone. I

et him into the dining room right in front of the rench doors, and you're going to have someone out- de to shoot him after I get him in a compromising osition."

"You got it. And I want it to be really compromis- ig. The great Noel Montgomery shot with his pants own. That will be something to see."

"Yeah, I guess," Bonnie shrugged, "but I still don't ee what it'll matter to your father. Even if the tabloids rint a couple of pictures of him screwing around with 1e, what does he care? He isn't married. He's got all he money in the world. He'll just sit there and laugh vhen he sees it, so what good is it going to do to shoot 1im?"

Bonnie leaned close to the mirror as she spoke, in- pecting her lashes like the professional she was. Be- 1ind her Davina's mouth fell open, a look of surprise ame over her face.

"Tabloids? Pictures?" she stuttered.

Then suddenly Davina started to laugh. She laughed o hard tears rolled down her cheeks. She was holding 1er sides when Bonnie angrily turned to glare at her.

"What in the hell is so funny?" Bonnie demanded.

But all Davina could do was laugh.

With the excitement over Harvey's birth, Tess had almost forgotten it was Christmas. On December twenty-fifth, when she was still in the hospital at No- el's insistence, Tess nursed the baby and lamented the fact that she hadn't shopped for a present for Noel. He had only shaken his head in wonder, sat upon her bed and kissed her forehead.

"Could you have given me anything more wonderful

than the present you hold in your arms?"

Tess had blushed, knowing he was right. There wa
no need for elaborate ceremonies or gifts; only the cel
ebration of life. And for that particular party Tess an
Noel needed to make no arrangements.

Both of them shone with joy as they passed the firs
days of Harvey's life in each other's company. Even th
servants seemed to join in the peaceful feast. The onl
sadness was in Davina's absence.

Tess was well aware that with the birth of his son, th
loss of his daughter was even more devastating to Noe
Montgomery. He regretted his actions but not his an
ger. He realized now that Davina needed professiona
help. It was as though his daughter was on a course t
self-destruction. With every word, every scheme, ever
action, Davina made him realize how much she needed
help. Unfortunately, she hadn't been home since tha
horrible night, nor had she been at the office. Bu
Noel remained hopeful that the new year would bring
a new chance for Davina and him or at least peace o
mind for his daughter.

Tess had the same hopes for her life. Standing in the
lobby of a huge glass skyscraper in Century City, Tess
tingled with anticipation as she watched people pour
from the elevators. It was six-thirty. Half an hour later
she checked her watch. The time seemed alternately
flying and crawling. Still, she hadn't see Royal, and she
began to worry. So much could go wrong. Perhaps he
had left early, been called to court, perhaps his appointment had requested they meet outside the building and even now were dining or drinking in a place
Tess would never find.

Anxiously, Tess called for an elevator and took it to
the twenty-sixth floor. The year fell away from her like

petals from a flower as the elevator brought her closer to her destination. To Tess the year seemed forever. So much had happened: so much pain and happiness and sorrow and regret. Would Royal have felt it, too? Would he have spent the last year wondering about her, longing for her, calling for her in his dreams?

Tess shook her head, not wanting to consider that the answer would be anything other than yes. The doors opened. She stepped onto the lush carpeting in the lobby of Royal's firm. Everything was quiet, the lights were low. To her left was a walnut desk, a discreet telephone console sitting to one side. The receptionist was gone as, it appeared, was everyone else. Tess looked right. A bank of doors waited for her. She walked to one and tried it. Locked. She knocked. No one came.

Bravely now, pushed on by her need to get to Royal, Tess went to the glass doors behind the receptionist's desk. They were unlocked. The interior office halls were quiet. Tess looked one way, then the other. It had been so long since she'd been here. Even when she and Royal were together she'd only visited the place once or twice and that was after hours. Now she searched her memory, trying to call up the location of Royal's office, as she moved slowly down the hall.

Her skin felt cold. This place was so somber, not at all as she remembered. Every office was paneled with dark wood. Desks of the same shape and size sat squarely in front of the bank of glass. Each office had two chairs, two filing cabinets, and a phone. Only an occasional family photograph distinguished one office from another. It was as though the principal had admonished the students to clean up at day's end. Tess's brow was a furrow. This wasn't how she remembered things. Did Royal really expect people to work in such an antiseptic environment?

A sound caught her ear. She stopped and listened. Someone was speaking at the far end of the hall. The corner office. She moved ahead, the voice becoming clearer with every step she took. Royal, it was Royal, and he was alone. He spoke to someone, but there was no answer. He was on the phone. Quickly now, she half ran down the hall, stopping just outside the door to listen to the resonant sound of his voice. She leaned back against the wall, her heart pounding, her emotions in turmoil.

Closing her eyes, Tess thought back to those days and nights so long ago when Royal had held her in his arms, loved her, cared for her. Again, she relived their trip to Greece. Royal diving in the warm ocean water to pull her out after her boating accident; Royal holding her hand when she balked at getting on the airplane; Royal whispering his undying love in the middle of the night.

As Tess's head rolled against the wall, a smile came to her lips. He loved her so. Everything else wouldn't matter now. He would love Harvey, too, and forgive her for Noel. He and Noel would respect, perhaps even like one another, because Tess was their bond. It would all work out fine. Almost in a trance, Tess listened to his voice and let it bring back the memories — until she heard what he was saying.

"I'm leaving right now. I promise. I can hardly wait to get there." He listened, then chuckled. "You know there won't be time for anything like that if we're going to get to the Jacksons on time." Silence again. "All right. I'll hurry. We might just have time for it, so why don't you turn down the sheets while I try to break through the traffic? In fact, promising me things like that will make me fly over the traffic instead of trying to drive through it. See you soon . . . oh, Astra, I love you."

Tess gripped the wall as she heard the last. Her mind had tried to save her, making up all sorts of reasons why he was talking about business and not pleasure. With Royal's last words, though, her world was shattered. All the waiting, the hoping, all the times she guarded her heart against Noel, was for nothing. Nothing.

Pushing herself away from the wall, Tess turned to go, then paused before she had taken the first step. Suddenly, she found herself standing in the doorway to Royal's huge office, shadowed by the dim light. She had a moment to look at him as he bent over a final piece of work.

His hair still shimmered like gold, his face was a perfect vision: soft, but not without character. His long lashes lay against his cheeks. She had marveled at the beauty of those lashes so often while she watched him sleep. His shoulders were broad, clothed in a suit of the finest wool. Sensing her presence, Royal looked up slowly, without astonishment. His eyes sparkled without depth as he looked her way.

"May I help you?" he asked quietly. Tess remained silent, rooted to her spot, a fairy in a shadowy forest. She saw Royal's smile fade into a look of surprise and disbelief. Slowly, she moved out of the shadows, fighting the trembling inside her.

"Tess," he whispered. "Oh, Tess."

Still, she couldn't speak. Still she watched him, waiting for his reaction. She wanted him to fly to her and wrap her in his arms, making everything all right.

427

The other—the conversation with Astra—had only been something of the moment, she was sure. He had to say those things to his wife until he knew where Tess was. But then Dimitri would have told him, wouldn't he? Dimitri had been in constant contact with Tess, and he would have been the one to tell Royal how to find her. Finally, she realized that if Royal wanted to find her he could have—and he had not.

"Tess, you look so well." Royal was in front of her, taking her hands and holding them out so he could look at her. She shivered as his eyes traveled over her full, full breasts and her now more voluptuous figure. "How are you? You must tell me. Though I'll admit I should be angry with you."

"Angry? With me?" Tess let herself be led on. He seated her in a chair near his desk. He half sat on the edge of the desk, one leg dangling jauntily over the side.

"Why, of course! I was quite distressed when I read your note. I mean, I was in no shape to be thrown away like that. After that dreadful accident and all. Of course, I was so happy to hear that you were all right."

"Who told you I was all right?"

"Well, Astra told me she'd checked into it. Of course, I had to tell her why I was asking. There was quite a row, but she got over it. She always does with things like that," Royal said offhandedly. Tess's heart skipped a beat. Astra had not been lying. There had been others. She turned her face from him. Royal didn't notice.

"But she checked and told me you were fine. Of course, I was away at our house in Florida recuperating. I was damned lucky, physically, but the shock of that accident really threw me for a loop. I took months

428

and months off. My psychiatrist finally decided I was ready to come back to work only two months ago. Funny that you should choose now to come and see me. I must say though, I'm not sure I'm over you. To see you now, you look different somehow. More lovely than I remembered."

"Royal, Astra never checked on me. You left the hospital without leaving me a note. I was alone in Paris. Alone and hurt and afraid." Tess spoke softly, giving him every opportunity to explain himself properly.

"Oh, Tess, I had no idea. I'm so sorry." His brow pulled together. He looked truly pained, but Tess could see he felt none of the pain.

"I was burned, internal injuries. I asked for you the moment I woke up but you weren't there."

"Oh, my baby, how frightened you must have been. I'm so sorry."

Royal had slid off the desk and knelt in front of her, gathering her in his arms. He lay his head on her shoulder as though he was the one in need of comfort. Tess's jaw clenched. He seemed not to notice her stiffness. He leaned back from her, his hands smoothing back her exquisite hair.

"Royal, didn't you wonder what had happened to me? Didn't you even try to contact me just once?"

"Well," he said, confused now by her attitude, "after I received your note I assumed you wouldn't want me to come after you. I had to deal with that harrowing experience and your change of heart all at the same time."

"What note, Royal?" Tess insisted.

"The note saying that we would be better off without one another," Royal answered.

"I didn't write a note to you. I couldn't. I was sick for such a long time."

"Of course you did. I have it right here. Kind of a keepsake. When I get lonely for you, I take it out to remind myself that you didn't want me any longer. Here, I'll show you, though I can't believe you've forgotten."

Royal was up in a moment, rifling through his desk. Tess almost laughed. If he referred to it so often, why couldn't he put his hands on it?

"Here it is!" he said triumphantly, handing it to her.

Tess found it difficult to tear her eyes from him. Reluctantly, she did so as she glanced at the note.

"Royal," she said quietly, "this note is typed. You believed I did this?"

"I saw no reason not to."

"Who gave it to you? Who delivered it?"

"I don't know. I suppose Astra. She opens all the mail."

"Including yours?" Tess asked incredulously.

"Of course, at home," Royal answered, perturbed by her attitude. He had welcomed her with open arms and now she was cross-examining him as though he had been in the wrong.

"Royal, I didn't write this. Astra did. Astra locked me out of the house, she had my car repossessed. When I went to see you, she wouldn't even tell me where you were."

"No," Royal insisted. "Astra wouldn't have done anything like that. She may have been angry when she found out about us, but she never would have made decisions like that for me. It's beyond her. She has no guile."

Now Tess did laugh, sadly. "Royal, your wife has

nothing *but* guile. She managed for us to be apart so long. Royal, I don't even own a typewriter. Didn't you even think of that?"

"No," he answered, defending himself coldly. "It didn't cross my mind. I was in quite a state and taking inventory of your belongings was not a priority. I had to be cared for. Astra was the one doing just that. She made sure that nothing disturbed me. She arranged my business affairs, kept the house running, took care of the children. I owed her so very much and when I knew you weren't coming back to me I felt I owed her my love, too, as best I could give it while I mourned for you."

"And what," Tess asked quietly, "did you owe me? Did you owe me the chance to defend myself? Did you owe me the opportunity to speak to you?"

Tess rose from her chair and went to the windows. Below her Los Angeles glittered in the night. Thousands of lights burning bright in thousands of offices and homes where people just like she and Royal were arguing, loving, talking, crying. She and Royal were only two people trying to put their lives together in an ever-changing puzzle. They probably didn't mean much in the grand scheme of things. But in Tess's heart the two of them were the only ones left in the world.

"I didn't think I really owed you much of anything, Tess," Royal said behind her. "I gave so much during the time we were together."

"I suppose you had, Royal. The funny thing is, though, I was cherishing the things I thought you had given me rather than the things you actually did. I cherished the love you gave me, the respect, the emotion—not the house or car. But for you there is no difference between emotional support and things, is

431

there? I must have been very lonely then or too young for my age to think that we meant the world to one another." Tess turned from the window and looked at him sadly. "You were never going to marry me, were you, Royal? Your love for me could only reach a certain point and then it ran right into a brick wall of contentment and ease. Those are the things Astra gives you. She asks only that you retain your wealth and power and provide her with her proper place in the world. I suppose that isn't much to ask compared to what I was demanding of you. It's hard, isn't it, to put someone before yourself, to be entrusted with their feelings and hopes, with their life?"

Tess turned back to Royal. Looking closely at him she realized that her inability to judge him properly sprung from her lack of a model to hold him up to. Farmers, she understood. Slick men in suits were another matter. Now, though, she had someone to compare Royal to — now there was Noel.

"Tess, you're being so unfair. I don't remember you being a person to judge so harshly."

"And I don't remember you being a person who didn't know how to give what was really important, Royal. So," she sighed, "we're even."

Tess took a few steps to the door. Royal's hand shot out, clutching her arm. Through the fabric of her dress Tess felt the strength of his fingers, but she knew it was only a physical strength he possessed. Royal was a shell of a man, a recording with all the right words on it. Tess knew, now, she would let Astra listen to that recording for the rest of her life. Tess didn't want to hear it any longer.

"Goodbye Royal. I have to leave now. I have to go home."

"Ms. Barber to see you, sir."

Noel turned his head. Benton was standing in the doorway. He glanced again at the baby in his arms, checked the bottle, then addressed the man.

"I don't want to see her. Tell her I'm busy, will you, Benton?"

"I've already tried that, Mister Montgomery. The woman is quite insistent. She walked right past me into the dining room and said she wouldn't leave without seeing you."

Benton's shoulder's raised slightly in what passed for a shrug of contrition. He had actually done his best. Noel sighed.

"All right. I'll see what she wants. Actually, she might know something about Davina. Here."

Noel passed Harvey over to Benton. The other man accepted the bundle stiff-armed.

"Relax, Benton. He doesn't bite. He doesn't even have teeth yet." Noel chuckled. "See that he takes every last ounce of that bottle."

"I think he's asleep, sir," Benton noted. Certainly the baby's eyes were closed, even if its tiny mouth kept working.

"Just put the bottle in and he'll do the rest." Noel paused for a moment. "Take this."

"What is it, sir?"

"A burp cloth, Benton. You'll get used to it."

"I hope not," Benton murmured as Noel left the room.

Bonnie was exactly where Benton said she would be. Noel found her fingering a revolutionary period piece of silver. She smiled winningly when he came in.

"This is nice," she cooed.

"I think so. I've had it a very long time," Noel answered, striding forward, taking it from her and replacing it on the sideboard. She moved away toward the bank of French doors and looked out.

"Is there something wrong, Ms. Barber?"

"Uh? What?"

Noel nodded, indicating the gardens beyond the door.

"Is something wrong out there?"

"Oh," she giggled. "No, just checking my makeup."

Noel sighed. "I see. Benton said you needed to see me. I gather you're here about Davina? Do you know where she is?"

"Well, yeah, I'm here about Davina," Bonnie said cautiously.

Noel Montgomery was still not close enough to the window. Davina had been very specific with her instructions. Noel was to be standing as close to the window as possible.

"Well?" Noel was becoming impatient. Bonnie knew she better get her rear in gear. She feigned a swoon.

"Oh, Mister Montgomery, it's just too awful for words."

Hand to her brow, Bonnie let her eyes roll back and her head nod toward the French doors. Unfortunately, she miscalculated and banged her head into the glass. Noel was beside her instantly.

"Ms. Barber, what is it? What's happened?" Noel asked, frantically taking her by the shoulders, pulling her up, fearing that she would faint before telling him what she'd come for. Bonnie leaned into him.

Bonnie's head was back, her luscious hair falling down her back. She had chosen to wear a silk blouse

434

with just enough buttons open to entice Noel Montgomery. Her eyelids flickered, her chest heaved. Another button popped open. She looked at him through lowered lashes. The idiot hadn't even noticed she was trying to expose herself. Bonnie let her lashes flutter once more before opening her eyes. For a minute she almost did swoon. God, he was a hunk!

"Oh, Mister Montgomery," she wailed, throwing her arms around his neck. "Hold me. I've been so frightened. Davina is out of her mind. She tried to kill herself. I've been alone with her for weeks. I need help. I need comfort. Oh, oh, oh, Mister Montgomery!"

Bonnie threw herself against Noel, her right leg rising as she wound it about his waist. She parted her lips, turning her torso just enough so the photographer on the other side would get a good shot of her breasts. She clutched at his shirt, tearing a few buttons off in the process. Noel, losing his balance, grasped her about the waist.

"I don't know what you're game is, Ms. Barber," Noel snapped, "but I'm not playing."

Just as Noel was about to push her away, just as Bonnie was about to use all her strength to keep him close to her, she caught sight of the man in the gardens. Her eyes widened. Her mouth dropped open in surprise. Her heart stopped beating in her fabulous chest.

Outside the window, in the dim landscape lighting, Bonnie Barber was not staring into the lens of a camera, but into the barrel of a gun.

Noel, realizing that she was no longer paying attention to him, followed her eyes. He saw the gun too late. He was standing right in the line of fire.

Bonnie, having the advantage of a split second of realization, dove past Noel Montgomery in an attempt

435

to save herself. She felt a weight at her midsection just as her feet left the ground in a lifesaving dive. It was only later she realized that Noel Montgomery's watch had caught on the belt of her skirt. He came tumbling after her just as a gunshot broke through the glass, ripping its way through all the flesh that stood in its way.

Tess was at the door when she heard the sound of gunfire. She was frozen on the doorstep for only a moment. Then she burst into the house.

"Noel! Benton, the baby!" she screamed.

Benton was rushing through the foyer as she came in. He grabbed her, pulling her away, throwing her down outside the doors of the dining-room door until he could assess the situation.

"The baby is fine, miss. Mister Montgomery, though . . ."

"Where?"

Benton nodded toward the dining room. Without hesitation, Tess bolted from her squatting position and rushed through the door. Benton called for her to stop and, when she didn't, rushed in after her.

Tess was the first one to kneel beside Noel. Gingerly she turned him. Blood poured from a wound. She couldn't tell where the bullet had hit. Noel's eyes were closed. His skin was deathly pale.

"Noel, it's Tess. Don't die. You have too much to live for. We need you, Noel. We need you."

Tess began to cry just as Bonnie let out a bone-rattling moan, raised her head, saw the blood and fainted, sure that the only way she'd ever see a star on Hollywood boulevard now was from heaven.

Outside someone laughed and laughed and

laughed. Tess looked toward the shattered window. Davina Montgomery lay against the glass, her hands gripping the door frame as she surveyed the scene.

Twenty-seven

"Bonnie, Bonnie, Bonnie," Sy chirped when she let him into the house. "How does it feel to be a heroine?"

"Oh, Sy, you old flatterer," Bonnie cooed. "You're making too much of this."

"Not me, baby, the world is making it a big deal. Check out *Variety*." Sy handed her a copy of the paper.

Bonnie took it with her good hand. Her arm was still in a cast, the shoulder bone nicked by the bullet. She had tied a spandex sling around her neck. It was silver and sparkled just like her green eyes as she read.

"Bonnie Barber, television star, saved Noel Montgomery, publishing and film magnet, from certain death last night when she heroically pushed him out of the way of an assassin's bullet . . ."

"And the *Times*"—Sy handed her that paper—"the *Press Telegram, The Daily Breeze*."

Sy threw the papers in the air, his stomach jiggling with the effort.

"Oh, they've just been too kind," Bonnie murmured. "I only did what any other person would. It's too awful to even think about, isn't it ,Sy? I mean, I had that woman in my house. I *befriended* her!"

"Well," Sy said jovially, "I hope it's not impossible to think about, because I've got some more news for you. Sit down, sweetheart!"

Bonnie did, gingerly piling pillows under her bad arm. It hurt like hell, a bullet wound, but it certainly was the way to get exposure. She'd have to remember this for future reference. Gamely, she turned her big green eyes on her agent. His cheeks were actually flushed. All three of his chins were quivering with excitement.

"What, Sy? Something good, I hope?"

"Better than good. I've got an offer from De Laurentiis. He wants to make a movie out of your heroic experience. He wants you to relive it on the screen."

"De Laurentiis!" Bonnie hopped up so fast she almost fainted from the shot of pain that coursed through her arm or was it the offer that made her feel like this? She sank back onto the couch.

"That's not all," Sy continued. "We've got Random House looking to buy rights on the book. We've got the governor asking you to host the ball at the Academy Awards. Bonnie, you've got it all."

For the first time in her life Bonnie Barber was speechless. She had worked so hard, tried too long to get this kind of attention. Now, because of a watch and belt she was going to be a star. For an instant, she thought how wrong it all was. She had been trying to save herself, not Noel Montgomery. She hadn't really done anything. Not really . . .

Finally, she looked directly at Sy. Her lips parted. She smiled. What the heck. She'd waited long enough.

"You're right, Sy. I'm going to be a star. I'll just

have to do my best to deserve such an honor."

Sy giggled. Bonnie smiled. Damn straight, she deserved the honor.

"So you see, I had no choice. It was the only thing I could possibly do. Tony arranged for a man to come to the house. I couldn't do it myself, after all. He's my father. That counts for something. So I had to hire someone else to do it while I watched to make sure he was dead. That way they would be safe—that woman, Tess, and her baby.

"Doctor, I knew what he would do to both of them if I didn't step in. He'd done it to me already—tortured me and my mother. He never gave us one moment's rest, even though I tried my best to please him. It was never enough, the things I did . . ."

Davina's voice caught. She shoved her cigarette into her mouth and looked away from the doctor who watched her carefully. There were tears in her eyes. Whether she saw things as they really were and sorrowed for the pain she brought or saw things as she believed they happened, the man in the white coat didn't know. The only thing he did know, one way or the other, was that Davina Montgomery would never leave the sanitarium. More than likely she would be retelling her story to the next staff psychiatrist and the next one after that.

But today and for a few years, perhaps, she was his responsibility. He shook himself out of his reverie. Her black eyes were on him again. Actually, they would have been quite lovely save for the lack of depth. He sighed and tapped his tented fingers against his lips thoughtfully before he spoke.

440